Dr. Phineas Fairfax

Dr. Phineas  Fairfax

Andrew Shaffer

Calapooia Press
Portland, Oregon

To Toni Christensen,
My One-Woman Marketing Department

CONTENTS

VERY DRAMATIS PERSONAE

Bobby Lumbar, a newbie scientist at MAXIFAX Laboratories (somewhere in the American Southwest)

Bella Freestone, Baba Savarin, & Martie Turkscap, three "older models" finding themselves facing a trip to the parts department

Dr. Phineas Fairfax, formerly of MAXIFAX Laboratories, now master of the Orphis New Life Exit-Counseling Clinic

Dr. Sheena Lypotrope, currently of MAXIFAX Laboratories

Zoe, a sensitive maiden who hosts funerals for birds

Mother Deborah, abbess of a Ruthenian convent

Mother Johanna, a hermit living in a water tower

The Bag Ladies, including *Frannie* and *Angela,* out for what they can get, no matter who gets broken into pieces

Belleweatherians and their athletic subspecies, *the Happy Hags*

Several Ruthenian nuns, dwelling in holy anonymity, but armed with butterfly nets and mounted on ATVs

Jeremy, Ian, Kevin Chang, & Noah, junior scientists on the MAXIFAX payroll

Dr. Guagamal, Dr. Helsingfors, & Rachael, functionaries at MAXIFAX Laboratories

Evan, a strapping graduate of the Orphis New Life Exit-Counseling Clinic

Madison, Greta, Steffany, & Russell, staff and/or inmates at Orphis

Edna & Connie, regulars at Lovelies Salon

Sheriff Bob, the local constabulary

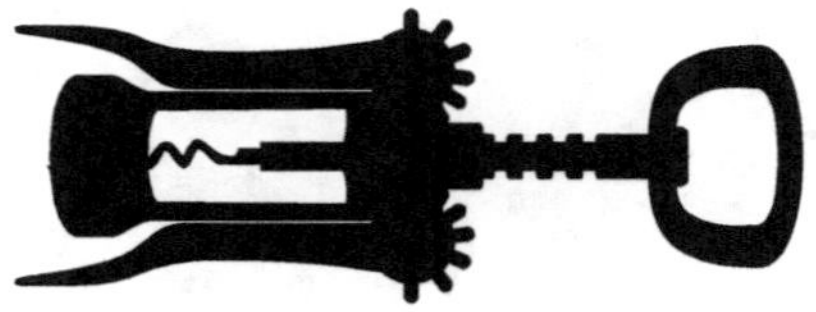

PROLOGUE
CALL OF THE WILD, OR THEY HEARD IT
THROUGH THE GRAPEVINE

During these last twenty years, our fair town of Merryweather lost any claim to talking about "the outskirts of town." This change in label for the fringes of our former fruit-farm community came about pretty predictably, since it happens anyplace with a little natural beauty, temperate weather, and a charming downtown district. That is to say: over a nice Pinot picked up on her last winery-tour weekend, some chatterbox with plenty of money ends up rhapsodizing to her friends from the swirl-swish-and-swallow crowd about getting away from the rat race through blissful self-exile to "the country." En masse, her nip-and-tuck friends end up convincing their mates that a migration to pastures new (or at least to property taxes lower) is a Good Idea.

Thus, our Merryweather fell victim to the gentrifying invasion of the chatterbox and her friends. In their fresh-off-the-lot, jacked-up SUVs, these grandmotherly barbarians charged into town like archers atop war elephants, armed with *Sunset, Southern Living, Country Living, Country Home, French Country Style, Architectural Digest, Bon Appétit,* and/or *Martha Stewart Living,* not to mention the platinum-edition DVD boxed set of *This Old House* (complete with Bob Vila action figures for the grandkids). In those exciting days of yore, these wildcatting, hell-for-leather matriarchs—when not on weekend treasure hunts for vintage fixtures and period stained glass or berry-picking to make that perfect Amish cobbler, followed up by a drum circle at Barb's—pushed through all that legislation that established strict noise and vagrancy laws, banned plastic shopping bags and fracking, turned the nearby swamp into a wetland, founded the Berryweather High Summer Fruit Festival, required all the parks to post informational signs about the prehistory of the long-gone native peoples, and set up both the farmers' *and* Saturday markets. Due to their efforts, within five years our Merryweather was sporting those neo-Arcadian necessities of a yoga studio, a Saab dealership, and an organic bakery selling creations with no calories; the hillsides round about became scattered with housing developments like fast-food boxes dropped from the sky; and flower baskets hung at every downtown intersection. (Flower baskets strategically hung from lampposts are the long-recognized funeral bouquet of every sleepy small town before it is reborn as a Merryweather.)

However, that magical age of confusion and creation ended about ten years back when bud blight struck all the vineyards hereabouts, the winery-tour weekends slowed, and the real estate market flattened. By then, though, Merryweather had settled into its status as an upscale, rural enclave.

This wordy preamble should rivet down the point that, before the invasion of the luxury SUVs and the vegan pet food stores, there was a time when our town did possess "outskirts," acres of grass, weeds, and rusting farm equipment, those bucolic, all-American, red-barn vistas seen in the end-of-the-year calendar sent out by your insurance broker, or acted as the setting for a secret place of inner healing and reconfiguration. This is just what Dr. Phineas Fairfax founded when he appeared in Merryweather just ahead of the rusticating grandmas and, in those "outskirts," far off any main road, set up the Orphis New Life Exit-Counseling Clinic.

With the history lesson out of the way, we should turn to the present, because right now there is a poor sucker tied up in a car trunk, and the air is running out.

CHAPTER I

A DRIVE IN THE COUNTRY, OR NO WALK IN THE PARK

With so much of the land around Merryweather getting buried beneath housing developments, it should have been an easy task to find the Orphis New Life Exit-Counseling Clinic, since it was a sitting duck in a shrinking pond. But this was not the case.

Ms. Mirabella Damson-Freestone (known to her pals and various foreign mercenaries as Bella) was steering her outsized luxury SUV, a snow-white Mercedes G-Class, down road after country road lined with acres of red clover and cow pies, and considering the dire fate awaiting her if she did not find Dr. Phineas Fairfax and his weird little sanatorium.

But at least she would not face the executioner alone. Without taking her eyes from the farmlands past her tinted windscreen, Bella reached a hand back and knocked a wrinkle-free knuckle on the specially constructed corrugated barrier blocking her compartment from the rest of the vehicle. "Hey, kid, how're you doing?" she asked with a ringing voice. "Kid? Hey, kid? Come on now, no playin' possum." (Bella had been spying an awful lot of roadkill since dawn and had decided that the country was no place to be a wild animal.)

Just then, a knock came obligingly through the merciless metal wall, and Bella guessed that since the fellow on the other side was bound and gagged, he must be thumping his head against it.

At least the air holes were working, she thought. She did not want him ending up like the last one.

"Hey, kid," she shouted again as she swerved around a pair of retirees in spandex training for a 35k bike marathon. "Sorry you're still tied up, but the cops did show up, so I had to go for Plan B." In Bella's world, Plan B was Don't Get Caught. "So, you know where this Orphis place is, right?"

No knocks.

"OK, whatever," she said.

At least the little guy was alive and she could return to finding this Dr. Phineas Fairfax character.

✳✳✳

As Bella meandered about this May morning, she could not believe the ignorance of local geography among these locals. At every gas station, roadside tamale stand, and silage-spray-machinery cleaning yard, she would mention "Orphis," "Fairfax," or the ever-popular "Don't you speak English?" only to be met with evasions, sagging jaws, and uncomprehending gazes.

This scene was typical: Bella pulls her albino juggernaut up in front of a spacious ranch house shaded by mighty pioneer poplars. A pair of silos, an aluminum barn, a dog kennel, and sundry other outbuildings populate the background. From around the house, the master of this manse, a man between middle years and old age with a steady and unhurrying gait, walks up to her vehicle. As he comes nigh, Bella lowers her window, props up a smile, and playing the part of the happy wanderer, asks with a bend of the head, "Say, I'm looking for Orphis?"

But our hazelnut baron simply pushes up the bill of his herbicide-manufacturer-man-swag ball cap, assumes a mask of silent cogitation as if spying a threatening cloud on the horizon, and breathes in ominous silence. Bella guesses that he is avoiding the question, and she hauls down her smile like a circus tent, raises her tinted window, and drives off in a cloud of gravel dust.

So, Bella drove on, looking for another lead but feeling none too chipper, not only because this mission had begun with a lack of sleep but also because she knew that the warm air playing about her neck was not due to a malfunctioning air conditioner. No, that steamy breeze was the impatient panting of Dr. Sheena Lypotrope, Electrolyte Demigoddess, the she-demon who had so impolitely wakened Bella about eight hours ago...

✳✳✳

Earlier that morning, at 03:35 a.m., the hum-along ringtone of Bella's smartphone had rudely roused her out of the beauty sleep that Dr. Helsingfors had very thoughtfully prescribed. After flipping a light, Bella brought her phone close to her bloodshot eyes, made out the name of the caller, and groaned, "Ah," an innocent syllable that in this case sounded like the brazen gates into the underworld rustily opening. From her subterranean lair on Level VIII, deep below MAXIFAX Laboratories (located somewhere in the American Southwest), Dr. Sheena Lypotrope, Electrolyte Demigoddess, was reaching out to her.

Blinking awake, Bella sat up in her suddenly much-less-cozy bed, brought the device to her ear, and heard, "Freestone, you remember Fairfax." (When wearing her Empress-of-the-Universe hat, Dr. Lypotrope tended to deploy surnames.)

Bella gave a hypnogogic grunt and mumbled a bald-faced lie. "Sure, I remember Fairfax."

Dr. Lypotrope said, "You're going to find Phineas Fairfax for us," and immediately Bella's handheld beeped as a fresh message with an attachment arrived.

While Sheena Lypotrope carried on detailing What Needed to Happen, Bella sleepily tapped the attachment open and squinted at what must have been an enlarged snapshot, grainy, at least twenty years old, of a young fellow with a ferret face hedged with a ratty red beard. Over a build both sticky and doughy hung an ill-fitting but regulation white coat of a MAXIFAX staff scientist. With little mental strain, Bella deduced that this was Dr. Phineas Fairfax in the old days.

Bella brought the phone back to her ear. Dr. Lypotrope was Maxim-gunning at her a bandolier of precise details, something about "Merryweather," "Orphis," "five a.m. behind the E-Z Fuel Plaza," "Darshan and Felipe," "the plant," "kid gloves," and "get that data, understand, peon queen?" and other bullet points that were probably vital. Throughout this fusillade of information, Bella managed a few yes-ma'am noises, until Dr. Lypotrope capped this expositoria with, "This needs to happen. I want you to have something to look forward to."

Suppressing a yawn, Bella asked, "What do I have to look forward to, Sheena?"

"Dr. Lypotrope."

"Sorry—Dr. Lypotrope."

"I want your next restoration to occur on schedule, Freestone. Tell me, what does Level VII mean to you?"

Bella's pupils widened $1/32$nd of an inch, and she said nothing, her silence as frigid and dark as interplanetary space. Bella did remember Level VII: very subterranean, professional, sterile, and well appointed with spacious stainless-steel tables with troughs to catch any fluids, drone lasers to do the messy work, and walk-in freezers for easy storage, all boxed in by ominously dark, light-absorbing windows, behind which Dr. Sheena Lypotrope might or might not sit enthroned, watching the fun. Imagining just where the laser saw would begin its work, Bella found herself instinctively feeling her neck.

The voice of Dr. Sheena Lypotrope returned like the convex waves of a supernova. "Redistribution's not a pretty word, I know. But if it'll light a fire under you..." And without any parting pleasantries, she hung up.

Bella's handheld then gave her another officious beep with the message We think Fairfax is here and a tiny map, like a misplaced postage stamp. Its road pattern was as meaningful as worm tracks in the mud, with place names in two-point type hovering over intersections of country roads. But one beefy moniker shimmered larger than the others: Merryweather.

"Merryweather, Merryweather...," she mumbled. "Oh, Merryweather." Martie and Baba had places in Merryweather, living the good life, away from it all. Just a couple of hours away, if she laid it on the accelerator. After cursing both her fear of death and ownership of a vehicle with a high-tonnage towing capacity, Bella told herself that after this bit of hatchet work, Sheena Lypotrope would rubberstamp Dr. Helsingfors to work another of his minor miracles—a touch-up on the creases and corners and, while he was at it, maybe a new hyoid bone, whatever that was. (Baba had had hers replaced last year, a reward for having taken out that cryptocurrency trader in Zagorsk.)

After averaging 102 miles per hour up the interstate, Bella had reached the E-Z Fuel Plaza as the dawn began to shimmer over the horizon. And just as she had found a good parking space and settled in to watch the eighteen-wheelers cruise in and out of the fuel bays, her handheld beeped with a text: Head for the field.

Just then, down from the pink clouds of dawn descended a helicopter that splayed out the dewy grith the wind from its rotors. (This particular whirlybird was *Willendorf I,* Sheena Lypotrope's private airship. She hoped to have a whole contingent of them patrolling the skies one day.) While the pilot yelled fruitlessly at her out of the cockpit (Bella guessed that this was Darshan), a second goon (by default, Felipe) was shoving her accomplice out of the chopper like a unicorn out of the side of the Ark. Just then, a sheriff began maneuvering his patrol car through the parking lot of the E-Z Fuel Plaza toward these questionable activities. As the anxious *Willendorf I* rose rapidly away and curled off into the rising sun, Bella—not wishing for any officer of the peace to get wrist strain writing reports—hustled up to the bundled body in the grass, dragged it to the back of her car, and gunned it herself across the field, breaking through a fence and coming out onto some pavement and, she hoped, to freedom.

As she caught her breath and began zigzagging through a maze of country roads (a great way to lose a pursuer but also to get lost), Bella thought that just like her pals Baba and Martie, someday she should get away from it all too—and being lost in a tangle of country backroads, maybe she already had.

✳✳✳

Still no nearer to landing this Phineas Fairfax and stuffing him in her knockoff Leda Marx Cleopatra clutch bag, Bella knew that come sundown Dr. Sheena Lypotrope would expect a report radioactively aglow with success. Fortunately for Bella, back in those girlhood months at MAXIFAX Laboratories (somewhere in the American Southwest), the head of her knowledge-infusing team had jotted down *indefatigable* in the margins of her file. So, even while keeping her eyes on the road (and scarcely missing a small herd of Angus cattle that had wandered from their paddock), she knocked again on the metal wall behind her to rev up the teamwork machine.

Her passenger, though, did not answer.

She knocked again. "Hey, how're you doing?"

Again, no answer.

"How're those air holes?"

But only silence, deafening silence.

Bella sighed. Maybe she should not have kept her down payment low by declining that pesky escape button in the trunk. But thinking that a quick dose of atmospheric oxygen might haul this kid back from the brink, she kept an eye out for a convenient pullout, and lo and behold, what came into view, but a gas station?

Rolling into the lot, she sighted a half acre or so of asphalt at the far end, only to be kept from one of her trademark big-rig swoop parking jobs, because a mid-1990s black SUV was hogging an adjacent parking space. After parking more or less perpendicularly, she stepped out into the May morning, not to find birdsong embroidering the air, but the snorting of passing log trucks, the chugging engines of the local motorcycle club ("The Merryweather Boys" read the steel-stud names across their recently FedExed leathers), and the thumping of an urban bass beat from a jacked-up ghetto ride, its fresh-faced young driver sporting an Future Farmers of America T-shirt and purposely distressed MAGA ball cap tilted microscopically off-center. Bella could not grasp the allure of country life.

As Bella makes for the rear hatch to check on her companion (or hostage), we should award prizes to readers who can most vividly picture our *protagonista*. Carrying home the blue ribbon will be the one who sees a woman in age anywhere from a mature twenty-five to a well-sustained fifty-one. As to race, well, what with years of tanning, bronzers, anti-melanoma supplements, and long lunches at the mole-removal clinic, that is still open to debate. As for build, gaunt in general and somewhat, well, rebuilt, for want of a better word. Atop her stiff, even cadaverous form sits a mess of half-straightened bleach-blond hair, and if Bella Freestone had any wrinkling about the eyes, it is withheld from public view by the strategic armor of sunglasses (the latest in Nigerian technology, not those archaic blue-blockers). Caparisoned for the day in a string top to catch the sun, she accents her top with a caiman-leather belt (the caimans eat some endangered waterfowl, so it was ecological justice to make them into high-end accessories) and below, an above-the-knee skirt exposing a faint purplish cartography of varicose veins. (This skews the odds against her being a mature twenty-five.)

With the awards ceremony at an end, we now see Bella pausing at the rear of her rig with the concerned expression that her passenger might be among either the quick or the dead; that is, he might either scream his head off or be down for the count. Either of these would land her in the clutches of the local boys in blue or Dr. Sheena Lypotrope—and she knew which hands had the crueler claws.

But before opening the hatch, she scanned the parking lot for any pesky witnesses. In the SUV beside her, the driver, some goateed fellow with glasses, was just sitting there enjoying the spring day through his half-open car window. He looked absorbed in an obscure periodical. (Bella guessed maybe *GAL Pal: The Journal of the Modern Guanaco-Alpaca-Llama Fancier* or *¡Bienvenidos!: Human Resources Management of Your Migrant Workers*). Safe enough.

As she opened back hatch, the hot air gusting up into her face left her expecting the worst.

Focusing into the gloom, she made out a young fellow with muffled mouth and hands and feet tightly gyved with zip ties, in a lab coat and sporting thick, sweaty, blondish, unkempt hair and a few days' stubble. He bent his head grumpily at Bella, stared at her through the one lens of his glasses (the other lens and the frames were now bent irreparably out of shape, victims of the recent drop to the ground by Felipe); through the gag he was murmuring something. Bella decided that since their eyes had met, they had formed a professional bond, and she beamed like the captain of the varsity booster squad. "Looks like you're holding up pretty well. You'll need to put on a good show for this Fairfax quack when we find him."

Without much team spirit, the young fellow only grunted.

"Well, you're still alive."

He grunted something else.

"Listen," said Bella, stowing away the pep. "I hum, you sing along. When I come back, we'll strategize about finding this funny farm."

But as she slammed the trunk shut, he let out a muffled shriek, and Bella gave an anxious glance at the SUV next door. The driver rolled his window up, which Bella took as a sign that he did not want to share in the messy domestic dispute playing out in the next vehicle over. Then, to ensure that no drone was skimming by, she took in the blue sky, only to find towering white clouds, bounteous with moisture. *Ugh,* she thought. *Nature.*

Since no one seemed the wiser, Bella headed for this gas station's mini-mart to grub up some nutrition and gave to all who saw her the unsettling impression of a glossy gray shark making for the beach.

✳✳✳

Meanwhile, back in the trunk, the young man, Bobby Lumbar by name, swallowed up once again in superheated darkness, was left wondering whether he would end up on the Death Channel's flagship show, *No One Will Miss Them*.

Then, though, he told himself that It Was All Right.

Staring through what was left of his glasses into the hot plastic darkness, with his thoughts swirling like goldfish caught in a draining sink, Bobby Lumbar held onto the one thought, no, the one *hope*, that maybe *she* was in those shadows, watching him, proud of his sacrifice, praying for his success, and making ready for his homecoming. She was his princess in a petri dish, his pleroma of Pleiadean pulchritude pulsing unseen in the darkness, moving the forces of the world. Certainly, she moved his world.

Yes, Bobby Lumbar would endure all of this, since all of this was part of her will and her wish: the will and wish of Dr. Sheena Lypotrope, Electrolyte Demigoddess.

CHAPTER II
BOBBY LUMBAR, OR TEST-TUBE MANHOOD

Approximately forty-eight hours before, Bobby Lumbar's life was not so complicated.

To alleviate the Atlas-load of student debt he had accrued after trusting what his former hippie grandmother-turned-life-coach had said about the value of a college degree, young Bobby Lumbar, after ranking in the ninety-sixth percentile of graduates worldwide in avian studies, had thrown in his lot with the shadowy but immense MAXIFAX Laboratories (located somewhere in the American Southwest). When he had launched himself on this professional trajectory, little could he have foreseen that not only would he end up as just another lab-coated dink with a lanyard and company coffee tumbler, shuffling about in the vast underground facility, but also that someday he would be able to pad his résumé with both *stooge* and *spy* under Duties Performed.

Bobby Lumbar (known to HR as Robert J. Lumbar and to the senior dinks on Level III as "Booby") had started off his workday in the morning crawl of traffic between two boom cars blasting enough bass to crack the windows of all nearby vehicles. Then, at the gate of the MAXIFAX parking lot, while digging out his ID badge, he had spilled the dregs of his drive-through coffee, decoupaging his only clean shirt with a chocolatey nevus. Then, zooming over the parking lot speed bumps, he had dislodged something vital in the undercarriage of his car. At last, finishing the race to his cubicle in the cattle yard that is Level III, Booby (sorry, Bobby) found that the newest email in his inbox was a zippy note from Doug in Payroll informing him that he was being docked $0.54094 of pay because he had arrived 2.0392877 minutes late. (The ID badge system at MAXIFAX was surgically accurate and was whispered to Know All.)

Bobby's workday had then oozed by with little purpose. After his mandatory morning shift under the flickering fluorescent bulbs in the silent, sterile confines of Lab II(a), Bobby, with slouching spine, had shuffled back to his cubicle, his day brightened slightly by a pursuing happy ball. (These levitating spheres, a playful application of MAXI-Tech, skimmed about the corridors, distributing emissions of full-spectrum light to offset any possible loss of vitamin D, since the inmates at MAXIFAX had so little contact with actual sunlight that they might get rickets.)

Hunched over back at his tiny desk, Bobby had then partaken of his mid-work nutrition while letting a finger skim over his handheld, thus incrementally ruining his posture, his taste, and his social skills, none of which were in the ninety-sixth percentile.

But after a few minutes, Bobby Lumbar laid his device aside like a spent romance, and the same fingers that had tapped and swiped its cracked plastic face quietly drifted down to the handle of his desk drawer and pulled it open with slow, succulent expectation, as if it were the secret portal into a harem.

Just then, his computer chirped and he turned on the screen, ready to please.

A video chat screen, tiny and tight, showed a grainy face, depixelating and reforming. It was Rachael in Reporting. "Where're your reports?" she asked.

Keeping his drawer-hungry hand in his lap, Bobby said, "I'm still on lunch, Rachael."

The poor connection was distorting Rachael's features—already fairly distorted by a recent prismatic dye job and enough piercings to remind Bobby of a hundred-year-old carp dragged out the old fishin' hole, but Bobby still made out her smirk. "You'll flex it at the end of the day," she said with a soupçon of sarcasm. "Dr. Guagamal's asking about them."

Then a second face, desiccated like an aged dill pickle, closed in on the webcam and pushed Rachael aside. It demanded through the static, "Lumbar? Lumbar?"

"Right here, Dr. Guagamal."

"I don't have the latest version of the phylogenetic bracketing report. Where is it?"

"I don't have it."

"Yes, you do have it, young man. I mailed it to you electronically. It is waiting in your email mailbox. No rest for the wicked, young man."

Bobby had heard that line in his youth at Vacation Bible School. He had not recalled being particularly wicked lately (or even any time before that), but looking at his ID badge, he guessed that MAXIFAX knew something that he did not. "All right, doctor," Bobby had mumbled.

"Good," crowed Guagamal. "Now, show me that you can earn a Very Good." Guagamal then shrank out of sight, as if having smelled his subordinate and found him inedible, and left Bobby with a yearning to grasp the handle of his desk drawer and expose the treasure within.

But duty squelched desire, and fiddling with the computer mouse on his Audubon Society mousepad, Bobby clicked open the emails that had accumulated like dust bunnies for b.lumbar@maxifax.com. One from his theistic evolution online chat group he forwarded to his private account—only to immediately receive an automated reminder from Beth in HR about the receiving of private emails in the company email box. He then made himself read through a teary missive from the Diversity, Inclusion, and Equity Committee, or DIE-C. In today's "Hear ye, hear ye," DIE-C was announcing sadly that the plans for the Interrogating Racial Supremacy group were being set aside. (This was stated without explanation, although knowing whispers between the cubicles agreed that since the majority of the workers at MAXIFAX were either East Asian or East Indian, no one understood what all the fuss was about, nor did they frankly care.) Bobby furtively hauled these obsequies to the desktop Recycling Bin, as if nervously dropping a body off of a mountain road. But no sooner had he felt the thrill of escaping a brush with the company's propaganda department than a chat line speedily appeared in the corner of his screen, reading:

Robert, Why did you delete this message? It is very important.

With a sigh, Bobby Lumbar restored the message to its original place, starred it as important, and with an almost disembodied view of himself from above (or maybe it was a happy ball discreetly spying on him) tapped out a nice, noncommittal, and neutral response to DIE-C.

After finding the sought-for message from o.guagamal@maxifax.com, complete with attachment, Bobby slowly, sullenly, and resentfully dragged it to his desktop and commenced his task. Still, his eyes drifted to the drawer of his desk, as if to an unopened jewel box, which none but he could open.

Bobby then endured the drudgery of verifying citations, attestations, font size, line spacing, indentations, superscripting, and subscripting on a report concerning the phylogenetic bracketing of viroid remains in Huronian stratigraphic deposits. (Rachael in Reporting had a slogan: "The More Obscure the Better.") But as he rectified all the extra spaces chamfering the footnotes, his fingers twitched, rebellious, eager, and hungry, and he imagined hearing through the hot cave of his brain a primal voice calling to him, "The drawer...The drawer..."

But after three hours, the end hove in sight.

Having pressed Ctrl+S, he clicked the ←, followed the prompts to Share, and offered up his intellectual tribute up to Rachael and Dr. Guagamal, leaving Bobby his own man until quittin' time, the king of his cubicle for a few golden minutes.

And the king was full of desire.

At last, at last, his hand moved to the drawer, like that of the bridegroom coming nigh the pale silk of...

"Hey, 'sup, Boob Dude?"

Over one of his cubicle dividers there had suddenly appeared a threesome of disembodied heads, like alien moons above the horizon, the thinking, if thoughtless, portions of Jeremy, Ian, and Noah. (On a good day, Toby might also constellate among the heads.) These other young lab coats at MAXIFAX were the juvenile males of the pack, the sluggards and clock-watchers who put in a regular appearance near the close of the day to feed on the social carrion that was Bobby Lumbar.

With his unkempt brown hair, his untrimmed curly beard, and a hooked nose bobbing like a predatory water bird into the brackish pool of Bobby's workspace, Jeremy threw out a well-meated hook. "You comin' by tonight, dude? Toby's finally got *Alaric's Trident*." (For those not among the cognoscenti of the gaming world, *Alaric's Trident* was the new Ostrogothic-Atlantean fusion game, as familiar to this clique as Heisenberg's uncertainty principle.)

Bobby mumbled, "Cool," hoping that that would send them on their collective way.

Now it was Noah who contributed, "Oh, Bobert, the Kepler conference's comin' up."

"Cool."

"Oh, I just heard *the best* joke—"

Ian said, "Oh, is that the one—?"

"Bro, totally. So, a vegan, a PETA signature gatherer, and a dispensary delivery guy walk into this organic brewpub—No, believe me, this is hilarious..."

But before Ian could carry the ball over the punch line, a fresh moon appeared above the cliffs. This was Kevin Chang, one of the actual shining stars (or gleaming moons) of Level III. His social salvo was "Hey, *Homo sapiens*," but Bobby, in no mood for chitchat with these australopithecines, gave a good impression of *Homo habilis* by grunting, "Hey, Kev." (Later, in a hot mist of regret, Bobby thought that he should have given Mr. Chang something like, "'Sup, Peking Man?"—or "Beijing Man," to keep things contemporary—but guessed that the Diversity, Inclusion, and Equity Committee would not have appreciated any equitable inclusion of Kevin's diversity.)

Noah was back at bat. "Dude, d'you hear? My drone—" At this, Jeremy, Kevin, and Ian became as wide-eyed as coyotes snapshot by a wildlife camera. Loud enough for Moniqua and Olivia in the adjoining cubicles to hear, Noah said, "Check it out, check it out. Dude, the drone *breached the security bubble* at the women's penitentiary. Hey, orange is the new pink, you hear what I'm sayin'?"

At this invitation to "movie night," Bobby Lumbar wavered. But in that semi-second of indecision, one of his hands unconsciously moved like a twining passion vine toward the drawer, but with his eyes on Noah, he missed his target and ended up landing on a black notebook occupying some valuable desktop real estate.

"Uh-oh," Ian said, "look out, hot date," and seized said notebook. Opening its front cover, he read out loud,

Chloride Monohydrate Portals in Anatidae Mesothelial Tissues
and their Transfer Rates in 0.05% Mg+ Distillate

"It's my dissertation," Bobby said. "I'm going for my master's online."

"Whatever, bro," Ian said, tossing the notebook back onto his desk with a painfully loud bang that echoed among the cubicles. "Come on, dudes," and the alien moons disappeared from the horizon, leaving Bobby Lumbar alone once more.

Now, he thought, *now!*

Like a paladin charging up to the iron-girdled gates of the troll king's keep to rescue his lady fair, Bobby Lumbar wrenched open his desk drawer and pushed aside outdated instruction manuals, a metric/standard ruler, a rubber-banded bundle of felt-tip pens, an unopened box of white correction tape, two vintage staplers, dental floss, breath mints, antacid, and a small manual pencil sharpener (but no pencils). At long last, he laid a hand on a nondescript binder.

With the reverence of a hierophant about to gaze upon the mysteries, Bobby Lumbar drew forth the binder, laid it on his desk as upon an altar cloth of samite, and—lest its effulgence strike blind the unworthy—opened its cover with a fearful reverence.

Within were several pages of plain paper, all written in his hand, then a map of the nearby nature preserve starred with red and crisscrossed with ley lines, a phylogenic chart of many branches beginning and ending with question marks, and a plastic zipper bag containing a blue thumb drive, a taped bundle of paper, and a second much smaller notebook. Drawing forth this junior notebook—revelations within revelations—Bobby pored over its small acid-free pages, all tattooed with eldritch dashes, slashes, and cabbalistic symbols known only to the initiated (that is, to Bobby Lumbar). Then, from yet a deeper sleeve of this little Moleskine, he slid out a pair of photos, each of a small bluish bird.

These motley objects were his treasure, his quest, the goal of his energies and will, and Bobby Lumbar gazed upon them like a lover contemplating the porcelain curves of a sweet, haloed sleeping face. The thumb drive held images and song recordings, and the paper bundle protected a feather and egg samples, all from *a heretofore unknown bird*, a bird that *he* had seen in the local nature preserve—*twice.*

This would be his discovery, his finding, his gift to the world of science. As he rested his warm, quiet gaze upon his findings, a fire of many flames welled up within him, the anxiety, desperation, and hunger to gather more data, make a video recording, find a nesting site, and map its habits and migrations. Then, he, Robert J. Lumbar, would present his findings to the international ornithological community and join the rarified college of ornithological grandees with a species *bearing his name.*

Sinking into a reverie of future glory, Bobby imagined opening a field guide and seeing his discovery's name rendered in Latin: *B. lumbarensis.* (The *B.* was for Bobby, of course.) Poetry unalloyed.

Returning for but a moment to the mundane world, he gave a periscopic peek over the rim of his cubicle: only a happy ball skimming through Level III, now rapidly depopulating.

But then, the sound of footsteps.

In a light-speed cascade of action, Bobby replaced the photos of the birds, closed his Moleskine, slid it into the plastic zipper bag, and laid the binder in the drawer, to sleep under a sedimentary layer of lonely and unused office supplies. Shutting the drawer, he speedily grabbed his dissertation and set to flipping its pages while feigning a face etched with hours of intellectual effort. Then a woman's voice sounded from the opening of his cubicle.

"Hello there," it crooned. "Could we talk for a few minutes?"

Bobby was telling himself, "Ignore, ignore, ignore...*B. lumbarensis, B. lumbarensis...*" until he had looked up—and found himself staring and staring and staring.

Up to his desk had glided, like a warm ocean tide coated in white, a female of the human species, before whom Bobby Lumbar sat as entranced as a stranded sailor. She was the archetypal exemplar of Woman Prime, eminently suited to answer that request, "Can you make something like this, fellas?" when the male half of the human species put in its order for an object to adore.

Past her pink palpating aura of anima energy, Bobby saw a woman of relatively towering height, her lab coat covering the marble curves of her limbs and torso like glaciers down the slopes of a snowy volcano. Blinded though he was by the alpenglow of her blond hair, her immense glittering eyes like opals, and her mouth, pouting and glossy, as inviting as a cave of rosy corundum, Bobby still heard supercelestial words descend to him through the luminous rays and clouds of hyperalpine glory embowering her. "I was waiting for your little friends to leave."

Despite a hand to his eyes to shield them from her luminescence, he saw on her lab coat, like a piece of airplane wreckage, her name tag, printed in the soulless sans serif type so beloved by organizations large and small. It read:

DR. SHEENA LYPOTROPE

She then leaned forward and smiled. "Oh, what's this?" she breathed with a soft gasp; and with amorphous emotion and a tremolo of palpitations, Bobby watched as her pearly hand settled like a winter swan upon his dissertation and she opened it with the slightest of motions to read aloud, *"Chloride Monohydrate Portals in Anatidae Mesothelial Tissues and Their Transfer Rates in 0.05% Mg+ Distillate."* Clutching at her name tag as if containing her rapture, she purred, "Thrilling."

Unsure whether this demigoddess understood mortal speech, Bobby had mumbled, "That's my dissertation. I'm going for my master's."

"Yes, we know." Closing the notebook and resting her fingertips on it again as if casting a sleeping spell upon it, she slid her hands into her pockets. "Why don't you tell me all about it?"

This invocation of his knowledge, of the endless hours of dissecting geese, ducks, eiders, smews, mergansers, and goldeneyes, of the microscopy, the identification, the double-blind testing, the analysis, the desert bleakness of dead ends, the loss of data, and the accusations of academic plagiarism, all of this Bobby went on to relate, on and on, like epic poetry.

To this Beowulfing, Dr. Sheena Lypotrope nodded with occasional wide eyes, and even a smile and a giggle of apparent interest, for about half an hour, although for Bobby Lumbar it was a sweet eternity. Finally, though, she deftly terminated his rambling with a soft and sultry, "Thank you, Dr. Lumbar."

"Oh." Bobby swallowed, as if to keep forever her innocent mistake like a doubloon in his belly. "I'm not a doctor."

"But at this rate...," she suggested creamily. "Yes, we think you're probably the most talented staff on this level. But maybe you could come with me to Level VIII? That's where you'll find my office."

"Sure," he half panted and, putting his dissertation to his chest, stood up to follow her.

Sheena Lypotrope merely smiled. "Oh, that's sweet. Here..." Sending her hand out like a well-manicured tentacle, she snatched the notebook from him.

"Um." Bobby gulped. "That's really important."

"But the committee might want to see it. You've been to Stockholm for the awards ceremony, haven't you? It's lovely." Clutching his thesis to her ample bosom, she turned about.

Her walk bid Bobby follow, and he began to eagerly do so, until he glimpsed his desk drawer and felt a twitch of guilt. He was leaving his best girl alone at home on a Saturday night.

He called at Sheena Lypotrope's fleeing form, "Oh, I just have to take care of one thing."

But she had answered back lightly, "Oh, whatever it is, it's not going anywhere."

And so, abandoning his cubicle and all that it contained, Bobby Lumbar ran after her, while a happy ball skimmed along overheard, shining a fine dose of vitamin D into his lovestruck eyes.

✳✳✳

What transpired after the romantic elevator ride down to Level VIII, Bobby Lumbar recalled only in a sketchy montage. He definitely remembered the frosty energy drink, downed in manly fashion right out of the can. (Sheena herself had brought him this libation, compliments of the executive break room, already opened and ready to quaff.)

But after this point, Bobby stopped being a reliable witness.

Having drained the energy drink to the dregs, he had felt none too energetic—no doubt from a biochemical imbalance caused by unrequited passion. And as Sheena held forth on the vision of MAXIFAX, that Bobby was part of that vision, a sliver of true blue in the prismatic spectrum of the future, and something about a mission, she began to sway from side to side.

"What do you think of that, Dr. Lumbar?" she asked.

Still trying to focus on her swaying form, Bobby said, "Whatever, anything for the team..."

"MAXIFAX needs you to do this," she said with a moist, melting, hopeless gaze, "And I need you to do this."

Bobby remembered nodding vigorously in agreement, before collapsing onto the floor.

He remembered Sheena leaning over him, her face oh-so close to his, like a starry sky in the eyes of an astrophysicist who had forgotten his key to the observatory. He recalled hearing, like an echo from the depths of a galactic garden, "You will do this, won't you, Bobby?" and he had nodded again, bonking his head against the floor.

"Good," she said, her syllables dissipating into the cosmos, and waved a black notebook before her face like a fan. "I'll just keep a hold of this."

Then began a nebulous memory of getting hustled across the MAXIFAX tarmac to the waiting *Willendorf I*.

✳✳✳

So, as Bobby Lumbar lay trussed-up in the back of Bella's rig like a dead duck in a hot oven, he just knew that Sheena would straighten all this out and apologize and together they would laugh about it over a candlelit dinner at the steak house.

But still, the last sparks of his consciousness posed him one last stumper: If he was the scientist, why did he feel like the guinea pig?

✳✳✳

Meanwhile, Bella Freestone stepped into the gas station mini-mart, marched past the wire stand with the penny-saver paper and the bulletin board with flyers about roofing work and pit bull puppies to the perimeter of the store to collect beverages for herself and her unwilling assistant, then to the center aisles to snag a few plastic bags of processed food with which to refuel herself. (But not the kid: Low blood sugar makes one weak and easily led, a lesson learned obliquely from years of watching Dr. Sheena Lypotrope.) With her tanning-booth-brown arms full of artificial sustenance, she finally made for the register, where the sweaty pack of farmworkers ahead of her at the service deli were ordering their afternoon rations of chicken strips, corn dogs, and barbecue burritos.

While this crew of mud-booted gandy dancers provisioned itself, Bella read the label of the drink bottles and smirked. "No Artificial Flavors." She remembered that field trip to Level V. By the time that the agricultural trenchermen had collected their midday grease bombs and were moving on, Bella found herself actually fretting about the kid in the trunk. But any worries evaporated after she remembered that only dogs and little children were at risk in an overheated car.

It was her turn to support the local economy.

From the other side of the glassed-over countertop collage of scratch-off lottery tickets, the tattooed saleslady greeted Bella. "How y'doin' today, hon?"

Bella dumped down her load, slid her sunglasses up into her metallic blond 'do, and rummaged through her purse for some medium of exchange. "Say," she said, starting up her skit, "I'm just passing through"—she found her debit card—"and I'm trying to look up a friend of mine?" She swiped her card instead of sticking it into the chip reader, smiled an apology, and brushed her hair from her eyes. "His last name's Fairfax?" The card reader was asking about PIN numbers and cash back. "His place is called Orphis?"

"Sorry, hon," commiserated the counter lady. "How 'bout a scratch-off?"

Bella was chalking up another defeat when her smartphone chimed. With one hand tapping on the card reader, the other pushed her phone against her shell-like ears and treated the lady behind the counter to half of a conversation.

"Yes, Sheena...Sorry—Dr. Lypotrope...Orphis. Yes, Orphis." Bella sneaked a sly peek at the lady behind the counter, hoping to see in her face that she knew all about the arcane secrets of Orphis and that quack Phineas Fairfax. No such luck. "Fairfax. Orphis. I heard you the first time, Sheena. Sorry—Dr. Lypotrope...All right. Hey, come on. You know—Yes,

yes, I know that we're still paying off the liposuction. Yes, and if I stopped eating, that wouldn't be a problem. Yes, I bet you can arrange that. Uh-huh. You know, all this time I'm jabbering—No, no, there's no one else here." Bella gave another glance to the lady behind the scratch-offs, whose face was one of patience-at-its-end. "All right. Bye. OK. OK. All right—" The conversation became terminally one-sided.

The woman behind the counter asked, "Sheila Microscope hung up on you?"

Sliding her phone back into her purse, Bella gave a sheepish smile, tore her receipt from its feeder, and headed for the door with her junk food, all while reminding herself that she still had the laser-like focus to get this job done.

And laser-like focus is a grand thing, except when it fails to notice that all this time, behind you in line, has been standing a fellow in a white lab coat, a fellow with a dignified and detached (should we say scientific?) air, who has quickly, carefully, and quietly stepped from the queue, past the rack of Confederate flag ball caps and cannabis-leaf bandanas, on past the wall of shame with the pictures of the shoplifters, and with his head turned to avoid being caught on security camera, has opened the glass doors with just a nudge of his shoulder so as not to leave fingerprints and is now on the move across the parking lot.

✳✳✳

Still in utero, as it were, and breathing air so overheated that it was sterilized, Bobby Lumbar was ready to chew open a jug of motor oil to survive a few minutes longer, when, through the carapace of his prison cell, he thought that he heard...three knocks.

Seizing the moment—symbolically, of course, since he was still swaddled like an overgrown papoose—Bobby Lumbar with his foot started up a percussion like something from one of his grandmother's shamanic journeying CDs but played at high speed.

After one round of this footwork, he heard the crude music of the back hatch unlatching and a crack of light split open the darkness like a

Precambrian dawn shining over Gondwanaland. Then a figure, humanoid and bipedal, blotted out the morning in May, and Bobby Lumbar felt masculine hands lifting him up.

The same hands chucked him into yet another vehicle, onto a marginally more comfortable *faux* leather back seat. Bobby heard the passenger door by his head slam shut loudly, the driver's door open, the soft sounds of a body sliding into the driver's seat, and the engine revving to life. He was on the move again.

From his new vantage, with a seat belt head poking him in a soft place, Bobby made out the back of a man's head, a very fine specimen, its hair thick, coppery, and well trimmed.

Through his gag, Bobby mumbled some thanks to the cavalry.

In a voice made of pipe tobacco, venison, a swallow of bourbon, and windfall apples, the driver asked, "How are you doing, son?"

Bobby managed, "Oo-ah-oo?"

The driver did not answer.

Bobby repeated the experiment. "Oo-ah-oo?"

He received the same results.

Bobby was about to try a different tack (like screaming for help, as if that would do any good), when the driver said, "My name is Phineas Fairfax. And I'm taking you to Orphis."

✳✳✳

Marching back to her great white fortress on wheels, Bella hummed away under the weight of so much liquid refreshment. The blue drink, she knew, would keep the captive in line, since she had sighted midway down its Gettysburg Address of ingredients Yellow 75 (marketed by MAXIFAX under the trade name Illusia®). This little gem was documented as causing aphasia and stupor in 0.06 percent of subjects during initial testing. Bella could only hope.

On arriving at her mutant sugar cube, Bella pulled open the back with a loud "Soo-eee!" only to stand in a mute and paralyzed shock as her drinks rolled about her feet.

The trunk was empty.

The kid was gone.

Bella wanted to blink in disbelief but opted not to. (Her new eyelids had not run through their warranty.) Instead, with agitated fingertips, she immediately skimmed through her contacts in her handheld for any friendly entities within a ten-mile radius.

Bella exhaled with relief as two names materialized on the screen: Baba and Martie. Since they had all matriculated from the same "finishing school" (their little name for Level IV), they were duty-bound to help out an old pal—or so she hoped.

After quickly sending out a desperate Lost my man, Bella forcefully reinserted herself into the front seat, seat-belted herself in with violent determination, and—ignoring a notification from Dr. Sheena Lypotrope, who wished for further words with her—raced on to find this town of Merryweather where they lived.

CHAPTER III

LIFE IN THE WASPS' NEST, OR BABA, MARTIE, AND THE BAG LADIES

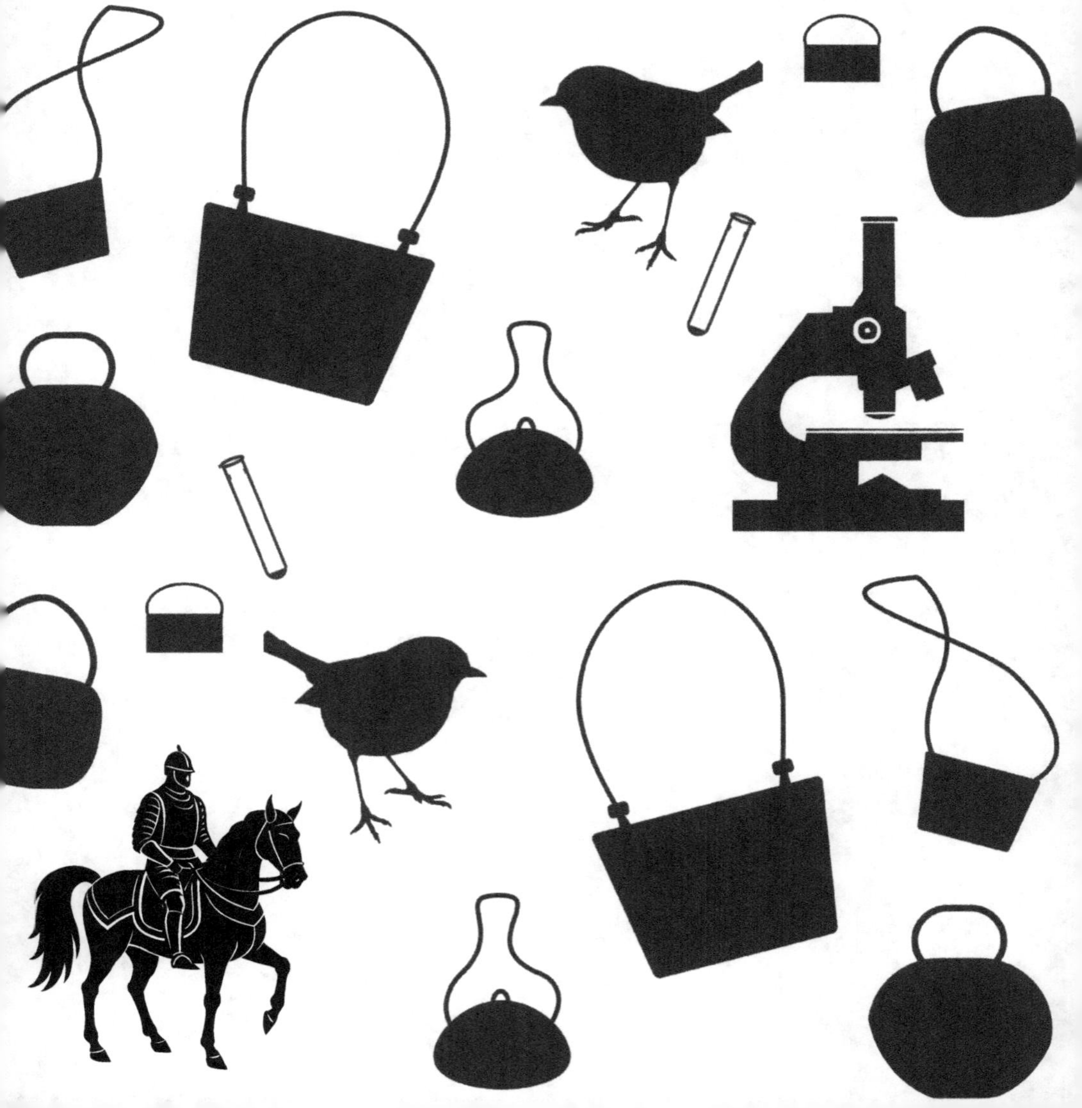

Bella's frustration did not abate as she drove into the throbbing red-brick heart of our lovely town of Merryweather.

Just as our cheery countryside should have endeared Bella to our little corner of heaven, so our town's charming welcome sign should have softened her snarling features. Hanging between charmingly carved posts growing from charming, low-maintenance bedding plants, its lettering, gilded and glinting under the midday sun, charmed the stranger with:

WELCOME TO MERRYWEATHER
THE TOWN THAT'S GLAD TO MEET YOU

But Bella cracked no smile at this welcome, nor during the next twenty or so blocks into the ye olde historic center. Neither the sunshine of May glowing amid the lemony clusters of laburnum, the lavender canopy of jacaranda, and the party-pink blossoms festooning the gnarled old horse chestnuts, nor the gingerbread architecture, nor the sight of power walkers with piston elbows marching into their Arts and Crafts cottages for an hour or so of vlogging in defense of the Merryweather Lifestyle[1] could lighten her mood.

In time, this enchanting quarter of house after house with their dogwoods, lilacs, and fresh crème-spectrum paint jobs gave way to half a dozen blocks of brick-and-mortar cafés, sweet shops, handmade toy shops, and a cruelty-free leather-goods emporium, and as Bella navigated everskinnier side streets, her most pressing battle became how to find a parking place. For crying out loud, she fumed, were they importing people into this backwater? A phalanx of eco-cars had already nosed into every possible space, and a few were snouting over the line into the crosswalks.

---

1 The fire of the ancient mothers had not died out. The spiritual granddaughters of the boozy chatterbox and her friends were now elbow-deep in small-town political activism, besieging town council meetings to demand that Merryweather be preserved in as pristine a state as possible. The word had come down from city hall that a whole block of the charming, old brick-and-mortar buildings downtown was to be hauled down, and after the fixtures and finials were sent off to architectural salvage, the way would be clear for something called Happy Sky Village, a complex embracing one hundred "income-based housing units," a methadone clinic, a needle exchange, a mental health drop-in site, a bottle-redemption center, and office space for various nonprofit and community-based organizations. The ladies, panting hot breaths rank with Gewürztraminer and gluten-free brownie bites, decided that this was not what Merryweather was all about, and so the war had begun...

With the minute hand of the old cast-iron clock on the corner of Quaint and Darling inching toward 12:00 p.m. and spying the fetching neon window sign for her destination, Come All Kombucha (Baba and Martie had both suggested the same place), Bella was left with no choice but to land her craft.

Then, voilà, as the French majors said, she spied an empty spot right in front of the venerable old stucco grange hall, serving now as a venue for both punk bands and the Merryweather Folk Ensemble. With whitening knuckles, Bella parallel-parked between a couple of electric cars, then stepped onto the narrow street with its historic trolley tracks tenderly preserved in place and strode to Come All Kombucha.

Its door was postered over with placards reassuring the customer that any gender was welcome, that love trumps hate, and that the management stood with Compassionate Merryweather, which honors and accepts their homeless neighbors—of whom Bella saw none right then, but guessed that plenty were sure to arrive once the word got out about all the compassion in town. Within the *kombucheria*, broad beams of enduring wood bridged the ceiling, but this sturdiness petered out at lower altitudes, where the walls of aged brick were hung with mixed-medium pieces, and about the floor squatted hefty chairs in environmentally suggestive mid-1970s monochromes around glass-and-chrome tables where tech-savvy twentysomethings sat with generous beverages, indulging their interweb addictions.

Leisurely scanning the room for familiar faces, Bella sighted at the farther end, under a collage of pirated street and road signs, a mop of brilliantly copper-red hair. This was Baba—Charlotte "Baba" Savarin to the uninitiated—and Bella hove in closer.

As the queen of her own glass-and-chrome domain, Baba sat languorously enthroned like an urbane prophetess, her hair a cloud above a shrine, while about her floated fumes like the breath of a great censer, the vapor of her malachite electronic cigarette balanced between spidery fingers that terminated in iodine-orange fingernails. (Bella reminded herself to ask where she got her mannies—that color had to be illegal in this state.)

Around Baba chattered a bevy of women of ambiguous age but youthful attire, no doubt a few local cronies, but with emphasis on the *crone*, thought Bella, since those string tops did not go with those crow's feet. But such was the way. Send up a clarion call about romantic distress and the ladies stampede to offer consolation and advice.

Closing in on the gabbing little group, Bella whipped out her mental score card to rank each woman by her handbag. A Birkin, a Brahmin, a Kelly Bag, and a Swarovski. The hierarchy was clear. Now, she thought, time to eavesdrop on a few strands of conversation to bring herself up to speed.

One was saying, "That reminds me, Marjorie's having a sale this week-end." This was the Kelly Bag, a slightly geriatric number, dressed about thirty years too young.

"Marjorie?" asked another.

"Marjorie?" thought a third.

And a fourth had to explain, "Oh, you know, Marjorie." (Marjorie Mayfield was a local heavy in the estate sale business—and quite literally, due to her addiction to high-end ice cream. But the Bag Ladies were ready to forgive that.)

Like a mourner guessing at the will, another of them knowingly opined, "You know, dead people always have the best stuff." This was the Birkin, a bit young to have succeeded so triumphantly in the Handbag Wars by merit alone, and Bella surmised that there was blood under them thar press-ons.

Then the Swarovski contributed to the symposium. "Oh, and have you heard about that one store, Aire...?" The bevy quieted. "They don't sell anything at all. They just let you go inside."

"And?" Baba inquired, her lone word rolling out from the end of the table like thunder at twilight. Dispensing e-smoke from her e-cigarette, she awaited the response.

"And nothing," said the Swarovski.

"Bizarre," Baba smirked, not quite Delphically, but still communicating her judgment.

The Swarovski must have felt the chill and speedily piped up, "But it's so cool 'cause you don't have to spend any money. You just get to go to this really cool store."

"Wow, that is so cool," murmured the Brahmin Bag. As far as Bella could make out, this lady was a kind of bridge figure, a link in the sisterly chain, necessary filler.

The Swarovski opened her mouth to spring back into the fray, but the Birkin Bag made her parry. "And what about the mountain?" This obviously disrupted the mercantile theme. "I think that we need a mountain or two here. I wanted to post some pictures on Instagram, like, *now*, and a mountain would look just right in the background. But I called the US Geological Survey, and they said it would take, like, a couple of thousand years. I'm sorry, but..."

Recognizing that this could go on for hours, Bella seized her moment and slithered into their midst, sat herself down with a smile, and planted on the table her own handbag—the Leda Marks, and yes, a knockoff, which Bella would freely admit under torture, but, please: Only a student of the craft could tell, and as a free agent, she was not out to impress anyone.

From beneath her crown of sunset-colored hair, Baba announced, "Ah, Bella," and all of the other women sweetly pounced on the newcomer with variations of "Oh, are you Bella?" or "Hi, Bella," or "How do you know Baba?"

"Hey, everybody," Bella returned generically and gave a theatrical scan about the table. "Hey, where's Martie?"

The Birkin Bag said, "Martie's running late," as if explaining away the incarceration of a wayward child.

But just then, a very harried soul hurried up to the table, and Bella smiled: Martie coming in for a landing.

With Bella Freestone being the blond and Baba Savarin the redhead (although her rinse was probably made from discarded pennies), Martie (Lily Martagon Turkscap) was conveniently the brunette. Right then, she was showing the assembled only her head of black, black, black hair, since her face was slumped over into her hands in despairing weepiness. After a dainty sniff of self-pity, she raised her face. No one could have pegged her as belonging to any particular race, color, ethnicity, or DNA haplogroup, but she appeared youngish, her tears and pouty mouth suggesting late adolescence.

The table quieted, awaiting some delicious revelation, but Martie only sniffed again and stared at the tabletop. (She may have just come from watching the mock public hanging at the Merryweather Historical Park and could not rid her brain of the harshness of life during our town's medieval period.)

After a sniffle or two, she wiped an eye and fiddled with her own Birkin bag. (Bella knew that this could upset the ecology of the table, but with extermination looming, there was no time to fret about environmental niceties.) Martie drew herself up, apparently collecting her emotions, only to collapse with a quiet wail. "Why?" she lamented. "Why? Just tell me, somebody."

The other ladies bent incrementally toward her, ready to smother her in sympathy.

"I know I'm late," said Martie with a daub to the eyes. "But I was stuck behind someone *going the speed limit.*"

Bella read the reactions among the ladies: mixed, but a straw poll coming out in sympathy with Martie.

The Brahmin Bag said, "I mean, who does that?" and a pantomime-chorus of nods erupted about the table.

"I know what you mean," said the Swarovski. "I mean, why do those people exist, really?" Then, in a camphor-flame of inspiration, "Those people just need to die. Why can't we just round them up and put them somewhere to die?" Now the nodding was furious. "Or take them to the woods and hunt them?"

The Kelly Bag said, "I'll call Barb. She has some pull in the state senate." One big nod from the Birkin Bag and a hum of agreement for good measure.

"Well," sniffed Martie, wiping the periphery of her eyes to preserve her make-up, "I'm glad someone's on our side."

Bella saw this as a window through which to defenestrate some excess bodies. "Hey," she said, "has anybody heard about the No Store?" and Bella saw in their faces the gaze of wolves scenting a wounded prey. "It doesn't have a name. I mean, who cares about the name? You just want good stuff." At this, she gave Baba and Martie each a quick look, narrow-eyed and confidential, to signal that this was all bosh.

"Oh, where is it?" asked the Kelly Bag, with an almost proprietary desire to be the first from among their little clutch to claim a visit.

Bella took half a beat to concoct an address. "2525, I think. Center Street." During her knowledge infusion sessions at MAXIFAX, she had imbibed that Center Street was the most common street name in the U.S. of A., so she was staking all of her chips that this thoroughfare had to run somewhere across the map of Merryweather.

"Oh," chirped the Kelly Bag, "Center Street's right over there," and seizing her totem clutch, she shimmied off through the hunched-over hipster patrons.

With a chummy urgency, Bella whispered to both the Birkin Bag and the Swarovski, "You'd better go catch her." These ladies made for the door without their handbags, proof of the potency of Bella's powers of persuasion, but realizing that they were each missing a limb, they circled back through the sundry kombucha junkies to claim their high-end appendages with a flutter of apologies, then made a redoubled beeline for the mythical 2525 Center Street.

That left just the Brahmin Bag. Bella looked at her. "Well?"

"Oh, that's right," the lady agreed, and she up and left, chanting the little litany, "Shop, shop, shop."

✳✳✳

Once the threesome was alone, Baba gave a womanly chuckle and sent her fingertips like a bejeweled comb through her coppery locks. "They're just coffee friends. And I wouldn't want to have to arrange any accidents."

"But they seemed really nice," Martie sniffed, still putting herself together.

Now running a finger around the rim of her kombucha cup as if it were a Cellini salt cellar, Baba agreed in world-weary consolation, "And that's all that matters, sweetheart."

"No, it's not," said Bella.

After a protracted drag, Baba said, "But that's why we're here, Bella dear," her words gently rending the exhaling vapor.

"Because you're a real friend," concurred Martie, composed at last.

"And your friendship means so much to me," said Bella with a patient smile. "As memory serves—"

"Memory?" asked Martie, plainly forgetting.

"You were out the day we learned that, sweetheart," Baba explained.

"You don't sound like a good friend, Charlotte."

"Lily," said Baba, remembering her dignity inherent as the eldest of this trio (by about five minutes), "you know I don't like that name."

"Sorry, Charlotte."

During this contretemps, Bella had begun drumming her nails on the tabletop (gently, so as not to undo any recent renovations) and was about to interject her own bit of defiant spite when, in neat mechanical symmetry, Baba and Martie, with faces scrubbed of any brusquerie or bad manners, turned as one back to Bella.

Bella made up for lost seconds. "So, I've lost my man."

Like a court stenographer playing prosecuting attorney, Martie held up her handheld and showed Bella desperate text message as evidence.

For her part, Baba said, "In about an hour I'm having a Skype consult with Helsingfors about my hyoid bone." She gently rubbed her fingers against the undesirable underside of her chin. "So, who exactly are we discussing?"

"Well," said Bella flatly, "I don't exactly remember his name."

"The man of the hour." Martie giggled.

"Or the half hour," as Baba branded the misplaced beau.

"Come on, I have way better taste than him," spluttered Bella. (Admittedly, she had not had much of a look at him, so she might not know what she was missing, but right now she would stand on principle.)

"Maybe not," said Martie. "We haven't seen him."

"And I bet we won't," Baba surmised, checking the time on her device. "But he's missing, and Bella feels pain."

This catty chatter forced Bella to take the quick, if not painless, route. She drove in her spike. "He's one of Dr. Lypotrope's little helpers. And I've lost him."

As if the Almighty had pulled the stopper at the bottom of the Mariana Trench, all girlish teasing drained away. Martie shut her sugary lips, and Baba brought her lethally manicured hand to her own mouth.

"Does Sheena know?" she asked Bella sotto voce.

"No," said Bella, happy to have some good news to report. She gave very spotty recapitulation of the last six hours or so. "Need I say more?"

"No," said Baba, pushing away her kombucha as if it were a bad year. "Please, don't. You know, Bella dear, there are better reasons to face a slow and, I would guess, painful death."

"But I left him tied up."

Not wishing to dwell on this error in judgment, Baba steered the fact-finding back to the facts. "And this place you're trying to find?"

"Oh, I heard her," Martie piped up. "It's called Orphis."

"Gold star," said Baba. "What are you supposed to do at this Orphis?"

"Find a guy—"

"Given your luck with men, dear...But, continue."

"He's called Dr. Phineas Fairfax."

Another change came over Baba and Martie. Their eyes, usually the cynical recipients of so many Belgian cosmetics and regularly scheduled Botox pokings, became fixed and uncertain, and their faces seemed slathered with the cold crème of reality.

Unsure whether to gasp with hope or sigh with despair, Bella said, "So, you know who this joker is?" Another round of uninformative silence commenced, but unwilling to trek across another salt flat of silence, she blurted out, "Say something."

As if trying to determine which end of the hydrogen bomb was the most touchy, Baba asked, "You say the Queen of the Night is looking for Dr. Fairfax?"

"Sheena would like him found. Yes."

Baba began to ask Martie, "Lily, dear, what do you...?" but Martie was looking over the room with as much discretion as a security guard shouting, "Hey, you!" across a parking lot.

Finally, she reported, "I don't see Sheena."

Bella said, "Yet."

"Give her nine hours," Baba murmured. "I doubt she's been aboveground since Obama left office, in which case she'll have to go through red-light treatment before she could take direct solar radiation."

"So, we have a little time," Martie said. "You know, I always thought that Dr. Lypotrope would be happier if she made more friends."

"But if she had friends," Baba speculated, "she'd have fewer people to devour," then ran her Pedicure-of-the-Year-Awards fingers protectively down her own swan-like neck. "Thank you, Bella dear, for involving us in all this."

"Yeah," said Martie, the porcelain sheen of her Kewpie doll face stained with the smear of looming extinction.

Bella counterpointed, "Well, it's not like you had anything to do tonight."

"Excuse me," Martie started, poised to unroll the Wayfair rag-rug of her social calendar, only to remember that she really did not have anything coming up.

Even as she surrendered to the fickle ministrations of friendship, Baba reminded her, "Not only will I miss my chat with Dr. Helsingfors, but I was scheduled for a spell in the sensory deprivation chamber." Suddenly, she was looking strategically past Bella. One of the waitstaff, a young, unspoiled specimen, was moving directly toward their little cabal.

As she closed in, Bella hissed in a quick whisper, "Well, Sheena can deprive you of your senses too."

As the young lady arrived, each of them changed her face to sweetly welcoming (Martie), detached but surprised (Bella), and oblivious and blasé (Baba). The newcomer was female, with light brown skin, dark brown eyes, short black pixie hair (Joan Jett trying to pull off Audrey Hepburn), and a flat stomach, with a handheld device slid into one pocket: all in all, Bella thought, a forerunner of the race of the future. Lifting her triplicate pad and poising her ballpoint pen, she said in a singsong, "Hey, ladies, 's everything all right today?"

With enough verbal sugar to induce early-onset diabetes, Martie said, "Yes, thank you." (The toxic dollop came on the "thank you.")

Bella gave a neutral shrug, but Baba, appearing to notice her at last, said, "We've already got what we need," and took another e-drag from her e-cigarette.

"Oh, I'm sorry," she said, "but there's no smoking here at Come All."

"Come again?" Baba asked, expecting the help to chuckle at the pun, all while she contributed another cloudlet of e-smoke to the immediate vicinity.

"You know, could you take that outside? Thanks. That would be amazing."

Baba gave a theatrical cough. "This," she explained with a nonchalant wave of the device, "is perfectly clean."

"Well, I'd call it an addiction."

"Well, it does keep me thin," Baba said, then announced not at all sotto voce to Bella, Martie, and the next table, "it wouldn't kill some of the staff here to take it up."

At this aspersion against the obvious success of months of eating clean and vegan, any and all cotton-candy dogma about customer service quickly burned away in dripping strings of black bile. "Listen," began the server, verbally drawing forth a flaming sword. "I don't care what you older models think…"

Blowing out another nebula of contempt, Baba said, "I guess we're everywhere now." After a smooth scan of the nearby tables and their trust fund occupants, she asked the upstart, "Is there a back alley we can repair to, dollface?"

It was the server's turn to smirk. "It's a bike path now."

"Complete with bollards at each end to keep the hybrid cars out?"

"Petroleum is the slow murder of the earth," prophesied the help.

"Then they can take you to the hospital in a rickshaw, little girl."

At this point, one side cast aside her triplicate pad like a gauntlet and the other shifted from glamourite to gladiatrix, before each turned herself to the front door and marched through the huddling customers to do battle outside.

CHAPTER IV

BLOOD ON THE BIKE PATH, OR BRING ON THE BIO BAGS

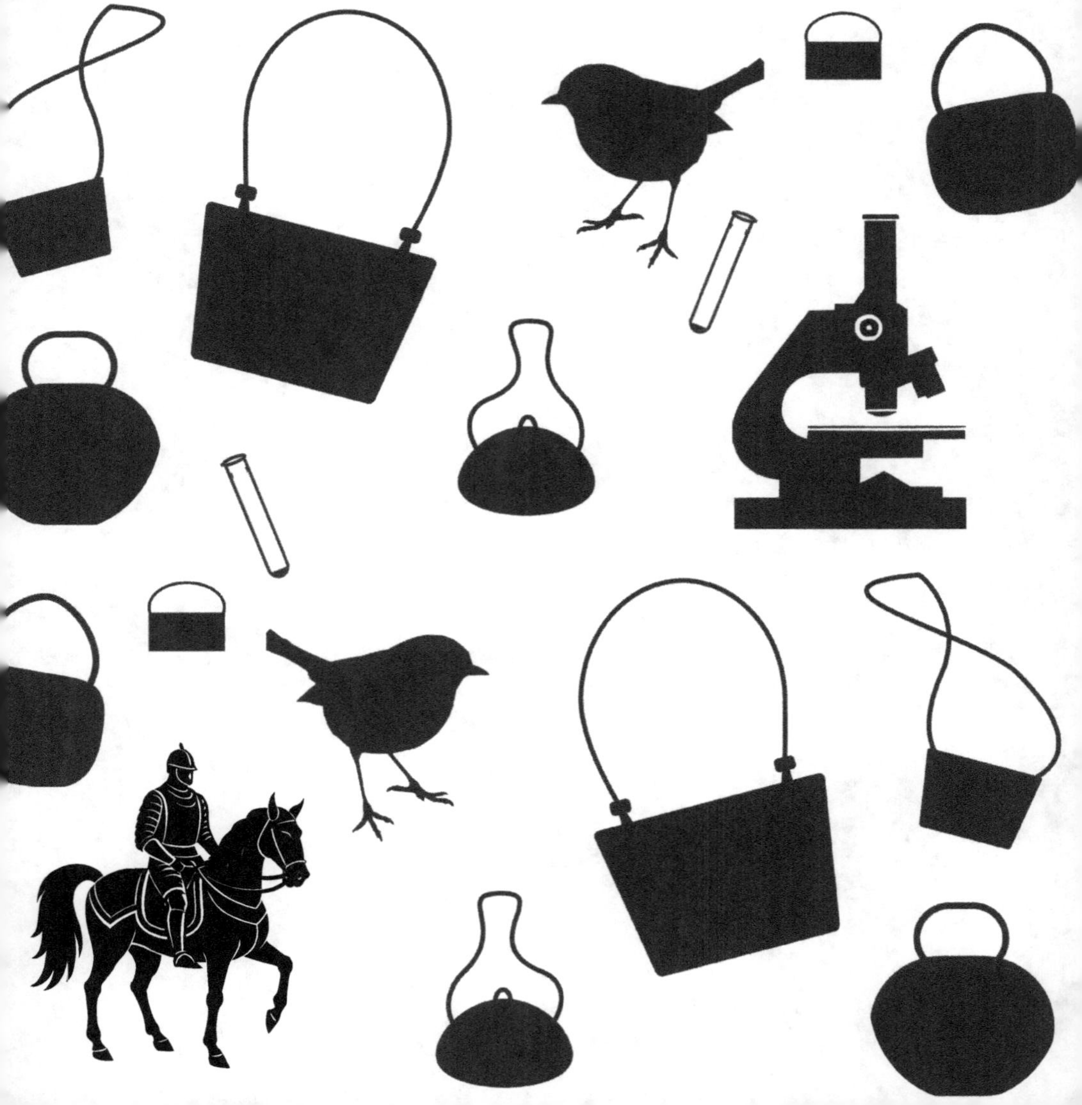

Stepping out of Come All Kombucha, they hung a hard right to the former back alley, with the serving girl passing first through the row of dull if forbidding bollards. (Originally these little concrete pillars were painted in Cascadian blue, old-growth forest green, and guilt-ridden oppressor white, but now homemade anarchist and nihilistic stickers defaced all of this chromatic virtue signaling.)

After giving the girl a glance that she would be there in a jiff, hon, Baba turned to Bella and Martie, who naturally had come along for the show. "Just keep an eye peeled," she said.

Martie jabbed one thumb down, in solidarity with putting the younger models in their place, while Bella, after peeking up and down the street to ensure that no meter maids and petition gatherers were in sight, took Baba's hands. "Save me a hyoid bone, if she's got one," she said.

Baba returned a nod of honor and strode off to combat, her metallic mane burnishing bronze like a helmet fresh from the forge.

While the gladiatrices arrayed themselves over the former through-way, Bella quickly checked her phone for any fresh demands from Dr. Lypotrope. (The phone had felt a bit hotter and might have even been slightly smoking.) Sheena had indeed sent an e-carrier pigeon, but Bella tucked her handheld back into her bag and resumed her pose as one of the breathless groundlings.

***

The affray between Baba and the triplicate princess was mercilessly brief. Deploying techniques from the Silent-but-Deadly school of cat fighting, Baba began by staring upon her opponent with the serene, polished-agate eyes of a cougar sighting a fawn. Then she leapt. The rest was a haiku of efficiency.

It had been an impressive exhibition, and Bella and Martie scurried over the charming old cobbles to congratulate Baba. Although a second-generation unit, Baba had lost none of her programming—nor her vanity, as she strategically ignored the adulation of her fans to smooth her coppery locks with her fingers, now moist with pale metabolic fluids.

They turned to the victim with a consolation prize of sympathy, but after viewing the carnage—a ratatouille of tubing, sensors, and hydraulics—Martie and Bella each tried to hide behind the other.

Not wishing to explain what had happened to anyone (*read* Dr. Sheena Lypotrope), Bella cast another anxious look back and forth: No one was at either end of the alley to complicate an escape. Martie, meanwhile, having overcome her dread and deciding that the slippery remains were not going to jerk back to life and lunge at her, ventured cautiously forward to pillage something for herself; and Baba, done with her battleground coiffure, asked her, "The hepatic transponder, sweetie, if you can fish it out? I'm sure Helsingfors won't mind if I go to the wrecking yard."

Having neatly pocketed a part or two into her Birkin bag and wiped her hands on Bella's skirt, Martie asked skittishly, "Why didn't we know?"

Tucking that all-important hepatic transponder into her own high-end catchall, Baba said with the sobriety of a notary public, "The new ones have a different smell."

"Maybe she heard us."

"No doubt."

"And she might have talked, right?"

"Yes. And"—Baba gave her handiwork a nudge with the toe—"she might have become one of us someday."

"And no one can ever be like us, can they, Charlotte?"

"No, Lily." Stepping back, Baba pulled out her vaping pen, resumed her mid-level dopamine flow, and through a pale cloud, said, "We aren't the same as these newer models. For which we must thank Dr. Fairfax."

And Martie whispered, "Thank you, Dr. Fairfax," as if his name were a trinity of jasmine, sweet pea, and wild rose.

A smart gal who saw this as her Big Chance, Bella up and barked, "So, who is Dr.—?"

But, at their expensively shod feet, the hipster giblets began to move.

In desperation, Martie started fishing through her bag. "Take it back, take it back!"

With a harsh placidity, Baba wearily straddled the wriggling goo and delivered a good heel blow into a crucial zone, taking out the gear mechanism. This, however, did not end all of its writhing, for the young lady's 1973 retro string top, still covering the chassis, began to pup upward, like a little tent.

"What is it?" one of them dared to ask.

Not frightfully large, but frighteningly strange, the object beneath the cloth was moving in a determined motion, rolling or rubbing against the fabric, while Bella, Baba, and Martie, with faces of dread, weariness, and fright, respectively, watched its progress.

Then it found an escape. Rolling under the hem and out into the air, a tiny sphere like a half-ripened cherry tomato popped forth. Floating up into the air, it tested the atmosphere before floating nearer to our trio.

Baba theorized agnostically, "Maybe it's her soul."

Martie sniffled, "But who'd want a soul?"

Ignoring her own lack of daring, Bella whispered, "This is not good."

"Maybe it's just lonely," said Martie.

"No," said Bella. "Somebody get it."

"Charlotte," Martie suggested, "you grab it."

Sighing with dutiful resignation, Baba assumed the mantle of eldest sister, and with the fingertips of her left hand twitching, as if the air was a clavichord and she was playing the first bars of a Haydn divertimento (Baba was the pride of the left-handed Sinister Series, we should report), she stared down the little sphere in a game of cybergenic chicken.

But as her limb shot up like a moray eel at an unsuspecting puffer fish, an electrical sound like a crackling clap of thunder shook through the alleyway. Not only did Baba freeze her hand in midair, but the little floating ball itself twirled about like a planetoid catching the boom of a supernova in the next galaxy over.

While Martie let out a wordless whimper, Bella whispered in wavering tones, "What are they?"

Among the bollards at the end of the alley stood a trio of ominous silhouettes, like mountains at night. Within the darkness of their triangular forms showed their eyes, as lambent as the first stars of night. Were these the revenant spirits of the mothers of Merryweather or entities from the pandemonial tinkertown of MAXIFAX Laboratories, come to strike our

heroines down for shedding the life fluids of one of their experimental
baby dolls?

Like nocturnal waters, this tenebrous triad spilled through the bollards with weird weapons drawn, for the hand of each stranger clutched…a
butterfly net? At the same time, the strangers sent up, like a cloud of con-
fectioners' sugar, a sweet song to summon the floating ball to come and
play. Momentarily, their levitating quarry shivered at the sugar-sprinkled
assault—and in that moment of weakness, this shadowy trio arched their
butterfly nets and made their attack.

One of the dark newcomers leapt, sending its net in an ellipse while
its companions triangulated themselves over the pavement, a strategy that
brought about a speedy catch.

Each one in the dark trio had its butterfly net over the angry ball,
now zipping about like a spherical hornet, pulling its captors back and
forth, to and fro, and hither and yon over the pavement, while the hunters sprinkled the air with marshmallowy gasps at how naughty the little
ball was being.

Suddenly, though, the ball gave a fierce tug and dragged its captors
like a bunch of black parachutes straight into Bella, Baba, and Martie.

As all six tumbled together—with Bella, Baba, and Martie at the bottom
of the heap—they heard a sharp rip-rip-ripping, and with a burst of victori-
ous rage, the ball slit through all three butterfly nets, spit upward into the
air, and slipped away over the rooftops of Merryweather, heading toward
MAXIFAX (somewhere in the American Southwest).

At the bottom of their human hillock, Bella, Baba, and Martie looked
to the three shapes on top of them in mute and anxious fascination, until
fluttering pink-and-plum rose petals of apology, sprinkled in a pixyish
singsong, showered down upon them.

Before they could answer, "Oh, that's all right," the darkly dressed
newcomers stood as one and flowed back, leaving Bella to wonder what
fresh sugary fun was on the boards now.

Said fun consisted of the trio with their torn butterfly nets swirling
around the leftovers of Baba's victim, now oozing like a great amoeba
over the pavement and maybe looking for their chance to get back into

the action. Encircling the futuristic gristle, one of the happy hunters produced, as if from nowhere, a handy broad-billed snow shovel; sent it with a grating scrape across the pavement; scooped up all of its tubes, motors, and fluids; and with a heave, dumped the catch into the broad-mouthed, industrial-strength garbage bag held at the ready by her companions.

The shovel-maiden now turned to Bella, Baba, and Martie, and with her implement upright at her side as if she were auditioning for Grant Wood, she smiled. "Well, we're done here. Thank you so, so much. And we're sorry for the bad surprise. But we have to go now, because Dr. Fairfax may want to see this." And with that name hovering in the air like a preternatural moth batting about a cosmic flame, the other two on the marquee of mystery bunched up the bulging black bag and hefted it up, its bottom sagging, to tote it on to a better place.

The three strangers now departed, lugging their load happily off through the bollards, all the while chattering among themselves like a flock of finches winging their way over a field of Indian summer sunflowers.

Bella, Baba, and Martie were still squatting on the sticky asphalt, like survivors of a wreck stranded on a coral atoll of ignorance, beyond the boundaries of unbelief, saying nothing. But after another mute minute, Bella did ask, "You do know that we were just defeated by a band of nuns?"

✳✳✳

It was Baba who ventured, "So, do we lay this one at the cloven hooves of Sheena Lypotrope..."

"*Doctor* Lypotrope," Martie corrected her.

"...or at the Florsheims of Dr. Fairfax? In any event, I suggest vacating the vicinity." Making herself vertical, Baba brushed herself off and fired up her vaping pen.

Martie stood, too, leaving one-third of our future fugitives still on the pavement.

Bella was glowering up at them, until demanding in a salvo of frustration, "Who is Dr. Phineas Fairfax?"

But Martie gave a sudden shriek. A happy bicyclist was whirring right up the alley-cum-bicycle path, straight for the leftovers of the leftovers of the poor counter girl (a layer about a quarter-inch deep, whitish, maybe a little rosy, with a bit of a gloss).

And sure enough, swerving around Bella without an apology, the insouciant clean-energy earth-lover squished right through the mess, sending fluids up in pinkish spray and pedaling on, leaving Bella's disgruntled face to take the brunt of the soupy goo.

With fluids dripping from her string top and her recent dye job, Bella finally stood and erupted, "Just tell me, who is—"

Baba exhaled some e-smoke. "Dr. Phineas Fairfax?"

Bella nodded with sententious rage.

Baba said, "Dr. Phineas Fairfax is the Maker."

And needing no cue cards to help demystify her pal, Martie told Bella, "Dr. Fairfax is Daddy."

CHAPTER V

NOT OF THIS WORLD,
OR WHERE EXACTLY AM I?

Courtesy of a cracked-open car window, Bobby Lumbar felt refreshed by actual air during a trip over what felt like decently paved roads—until a jolt of force shook his latest conveyance.

This is it, he thought and took one or two of his last remaining seconds to realize what a loss to ornithology that his demise would entail. Never would *B. lumbarensis* grace the pages of *The Handy Guide the Southwest American Birds*. Certain that he was hurtling over a mountain precipice (if he had to guess, an andesite relic of the late Miocene), he knew that within mere seconds he would become the booby prize for the search-and-rescue team.

But no disaster ensued, since the jolt became a rumbly stretch, and Bobby guessed that the SUV had turned onto a gravel road. He smiled behind his gag in dreamy anticlimax. He had another chance to be cited in a footnote.

Then, though, an all but living image of Dr. Sheena Lypotrope appeared in his mind's eye, and her words echoed in his brain in nymphlike, Lorelei tones. "The mission...," they said. "The mission..."

Oh, Bobby thought. *The mission. Dr. Phineas Fairfax. Orphis.*

The car's slowing to a halt interrupted this honey-do list. He heard Phineas Fairfax call calmly out of his window, "Mothers." The rumble of small engines neared the driver's side. "I need your assistance. I've bagged a warm one. Could you meet me at Orphis?"

And the SUV was on the move again.

In little time, though, the SUV stopped, the engine stopped, and Bobby thought that, for a second, his heart stopped. Behind his head, he heard the quick rusty creak of the car door and Phineas Fairfax tell him, "Hold tight, son. This will be over soon."

There followed the rhythmic crunching of gravel that stopped near the car door, Phineas Fairfax's order, "If you'll all gather about here...," and as the crunching of many feet closed in about his head, he saw in the corner of his eye a handful of looming dark shapes, all leaning in on him.

"Behold, miladies," Dr. Phineas Fairfax declared. "A fresh one."

"Oh, a man," muttered one of the shapes, her tone polite, as if agreeing to taste a native staple at a foreign restaurant.

"Oh, a man," pouted another, as if she had just opened an overnighted package and found the wrong thing nested in the bubble wrap.

"Oh, a man," sighed a third, torn and despondent, like a monarchist forced to choose between the Menshevik and the anarcho-syndicalist on one of those ballot things.

"But just think of what we can do with this one," said Phineas Fairfax. "Now, we put our backs into it."

And many work-strong fingers sank deep into Bobby's upper regions and sent him on the thrill ride out of the car headfirst. As his heels struck gravel, a few more hands seized hold and pulled him in a stuttery drag across the lot. (No one had thought to pick up his feet.)

Enduring this stretch of the trip face down, Bobby could see the hems of black and ominous garb, like the draperies from an antebellum funeral parlor. Guessing that this was his destination, he tried to scream through his gag. His latest captors found this amusing.

"Oh, that's sweet," said a woman at his left shoulder.

At this right shoulder, Dr. Phineas Fairfax declared, "I believe he wants someone to come to his assistance."

And all present (except Bobby) shared a pleasant chuckle.

The bumpity-bump along the gritty ground slowed as he heard a door growl open and the hands hefted him over a threshold and dropped him like a feed sack onto a floor strewn with straw, old nails, pills of drywall, wisps of insulation, and shavings from building material no longer legally allowed because of carcinogen seepage when wet.

After another confident command from Dr. Phineas Fairfax, they rolled Bobby over like a Christmas bread in postapocalyptic powdered sugar, and he was facing the ceiling. After spitting up bits of straw, he gave a brief stare to his surroundings: a musty skeleton of two-by-fours and pressboard walls, with a ceiling clad in corpulent exposed rolls of pink insulation, like the morning clouds in Purgatory.

Beetling above him, meanwhile, like forbidding mountain peaks, stood two to four dark-robed women, each fascinated, politely curious, or too horrified to look away. But amid these lesser heights stood another peak, lone and snowy, immaculate in his lab coat, Dr. Phineas Fairfax.

The doctor addressed the women. "I thank you ladies for your manful strength. I can deal with the specimen alone now."

One, like a vegetarian tourist excusing herself after watching the natives sacrifice a goat for her benefit, said, "Yes, Doctor."

Another, like one commander to another: "Yes, Doctor."

And the last, like a teenager to her martinet father: "Yes, Doctor."

So, these three pylons in black slipped away, and Bobby was unsure whether to call them back or be glad to see them go.

Dr. Phineas Fairfax now crouched down beside Bobby. With his knees akimbo and his Tennysonian face lit with an ineffable purpose, he joined his hands, bent forward, and met his captive's eyes. The sunlight through the door gleamed upon his glasses and played like sparks in his deftly trimmed mustache and silken red beard, discreetly pointed but unwaxed. The hair of his head swooped and flowed like an Art Nouveau cavalier's: the figure of perfect maturity, comely serenity, and silent confidence.

"Welcome to Orphis," he said. "I'd shake your hand, but you aren't in a position to do that, are you?" Bringing a hand to Bobby's chest, he took cautious hold of his MAXIFAX name badge as if it was a shard from an archaeological dig. "Robert J. Lumbar. The middle initial's a nice touch these days." His eyes narrowed. "Robert J. Lumbar...The only Robert J. Lumbar I've read of lately was the noted graduate from Faraday-Kage College, in the field of avian studies."

After a second of surprise, Bobby grunted through his gag, reveling in the warmth of recognition. He did not know that he had made it to the pages of anything except as the Level III Staff of the Month in the MAXIFAX e-newsletter. (It had been his turn.)

"As for these..." The doctor tapped a manicured fingernail on the last pitiful vestiges of Bobby's glasses, then snatched them from his startled face, peered through the surviving lens, and rested them back onto Bobby's face with surprising delicacy. "I may have an extra pair. I'll check my collection of those who came before you. It's not as if they need them anymore. But for now"—Phineas Fairfax slid a manicured hand into the depths of his lab coat pocket and drew out a box cutter—"on to better things." Bringing its menacing triangular tip near Bobby's exposed if myopic eye, he asked, "How does this look? Or these, perhaps?" Sliding it back into his pocket, he then took out a pair of medical scissors, their repoussé tips making a jaunty jut, and in a voice more suited to Papa Bear than Goldilocks, said, "This one's just right."

The prisoner grunted out what might have been a question.

Kneeling by his captive, the good doctor, like a tailor drafted as a military surgeon, slid a blade of the scissors under his gag and with alacrity and precision snipped. "Something to say, son?"

"Help!"

"How about a big long one? Make it worth the effort?"

"Heeeeelp!" Bobby screamed as the rats in the rafters scurried off and a wise old barn owl flapped out through the door.

"But, Robert, I'm helping you."

"Heeeeelp!"

"You said that already. So, tell me, Robert..."

"Bobby, Lumbar."

"I'll still call you Robert. Am I right about your place of employment, Robert?"

"MAXIFAX? Yeah."

"In that case, my sympathies."

Bobby's scientific curiosity should have followed up on this, but he only asked, "What are you?"

"One man is many things."

"Who are you?"

"Dr. Phineas Fairfax. I already said that."

"Where am I?"

"Orphis. And soon you will have no desire to leave." He pressed the tip of the scissors to his lips and appeared to be in thought, like a painter deciding that a landscape needed a windmill or maybe a frightful gallows daubed in for interest.

"Help!" yelled Bobby all the louder.

"Silence," directed the doctor.

Ignorant that he was practicing a delaying tactic, Bobby asked, "And what were they?"

"Of whom do you speak?"

"They looked kind of like nuns."

"An excellent surmise. Is this your first encounter with nuns, in the wild, I mean?"

"I've seen *The Sound of Music*."

"Your bona fides are irreproachable. I will say, too, you have more cultural literacy than most of your age cohort."

"But they're all wearing all black."

"And?"

For some undiscoverable reason, perhaps because he thought that the Stockholm syndrome was one of the steps toward receiving the Nobel Prize, Bobby imagined that he and the doctor had built up enough rapport and he could josh around a bit. "I think they look like *demon* nuns," Bobby said.

Dr. Phineas Fairfax transfixed the youngster with a precise and laser-like gaze. The scissor blades hinged open like a barracuda's mouth. "They wear black," he explained with restraint, "because they're mourning for their sins and for this fallen world."

"That's sad," swallowed Bobby.

"Ironic, because I for one find them to be the cheeriest people I have ever met. Those fine women are Byzantine nuns." Snipping the blades of the scissors with slow and sinister effect, he recited from the thesaurus. "Eastern nuns. Basilian sisters. Ruthenian monastics." He gave the scissors another metal-on-metal manipulation, the swipe of the blades like thin wicked hands dusting themselves off for a final crime.

Forgetting the difference between synonym, antonym, homonym, toponym, autonym, eponym, and pseudonym, Bobby blinked and stared in mute dread.

But this silence must have mollified the doctor. "I don't know why," he said with a benign smile, "but I also find nuns to be the most dangerous creatures in the world. That's why I keep a hefty supply of them at hand."

And precisely on cue, a chorus of giggles overcame from the outside. Peering through the doorway was a new band of black-wimpled women, all young, pearl-faced, and thrilling with curiosity. Just then, a mature nun broke through them like the one half of a pincer maneuver in the battle for a little discipline around this place.

The doctor met her at the doorway. "Yes, Mother Deborah?" he asked.

From his plump and juicy worm's-eye view, Bobby made out a gym teacher of a woman, all ready to order the girls to gimme ten and then twice around the track, an august "Sir, yes, sir" nun with a chunky cross about her neck. She informed the doctor, "Euphemia, Agrippina, and Pelagia just got back from town."

"And none of them turned into a pillar of salt, I trust?" said Dr. Fairfax.

"I trust my girls. But they've got something for you. Show him what you found, girls."

But the big "reveal" apparently had to wait, as Euphemia, Agrippina, and Pelagia erupted in a gleeful twitter as each tried to relate what had transpired. The doctor raised a pharaonic hand, and awestruck, the young vestals quieted.

"One at a time," he said.

Euphemia set the scene. "We had just come out of the hardware store with the snow shovel for you..."

"On sale?"

"Oh, of course, Doctor. And then—"

Agrippina suffused the narrative with a spot of color. "Then we went to the backyard bird store"—Bobby cocked an ear at this plot twist—"and bought these butterfly nets."

"Very nice," said Dr. Fairfax. "What then?"

"Well, you asked us to keep an eye out for anything odd..."

"Yes?"

Pelagia put in, "So, we heard these girls fighting behind the kombucha place...," and the first and second threw in their own bits to make a complete sentence.

"That wasn't very nice," Dr. Fairfax said.

Three black-clad heads frowned and nodded rapidly.

"But look what we found," said Euphemia, lugging forward the bloated garbage bag. She rapidly untied the cinch, all three pulled back its mouth, and Dr. Phineas Fairfax stared into its depths.

"We did punch some air holes for it," said Agrippina.

"A good idea," said Dr. Fairfax, crouching and rubbing its bulging sides as if it were an ailing heifer. The contents were trying—without success—to squirm their way out into fresh air. "Well, tie it back up and bring it to the lab, will you, girls?"

Happy to be advancing any cause of Dr. Phineas Fairfax, the young renunciants sent up a cloud of obedient giggles, but at this pink cumulus of enthusiasm, Mother Deborah gave a cough. Her subordinates deflated with a pout, then quietly tied up the bag, still churning and heaving of its own accord, and stepped back.

Craning a cursory look at Bobby, Mother Deborah asked, "But what're you going to do with this one?"

Dr. Fairfax hummed, "I'll address him soon. But not as soon as I'd like." (Bobby thought that "address" might mean cramming him into a secure box and scribbling the postal code of a Third World country across it.) "Robert, please excuse me momentarily."

But as the possible cult leader conferred with Mother Deborah (Bobby heard snatches about "the trapeza for a bowl of lentils and dandelion greens?" and "Ninth Hour" and "vespers," which he thought had to be a new kind of electric car), he noticed on the gritty floor near his face—through what was left of his glasses—a small silvery sphere, just bigger than the average schoolboy marble and almost shining, if darkness could shine. Unlike its billiard ball cousins, it was not in thrall to elementary physics, but rolled here and there, carefully, secretively, and deliberately, almost consciously, without collecting any straw, wisps of insulation, and/ or blobs of owl guano. (Ornithologists think of these things.)

Suddenly, he heard, "Robert?"

Bobby glanced rapidly up at Phineas Fairfax, only to look back at once at the curious little roundling.

"Robert?"

Bobby asked with a gulp, "Yeah?"

"I'm off myself to the lab, where I hope to bring you very soon."

At this, Bobby Lumbar's ankles took matters into their own hands (or feet) and, giving a violent and purposeful kick, snapped whatever was binding them. His wrists made a similar gyrating twist, and to the surprise of all, especially Bobby, he was free, pushing his smashed glasses up his nose, throwing a mad hand onto the strange little ball, seizing it, bouncing upright like a jack-in-the-box, charging straight through the white and black figures populating the doorway, and escaping screaming into the world outside.

CHAPTER VI

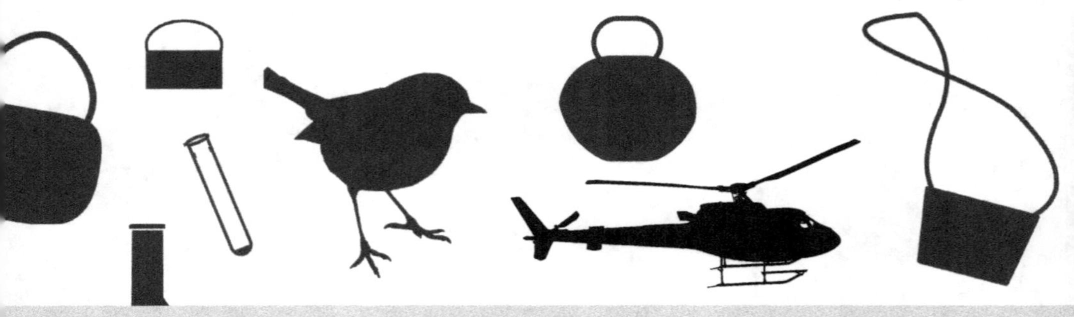

SIMIAN STYLITES, OR JUNGLE GYMNASTICS

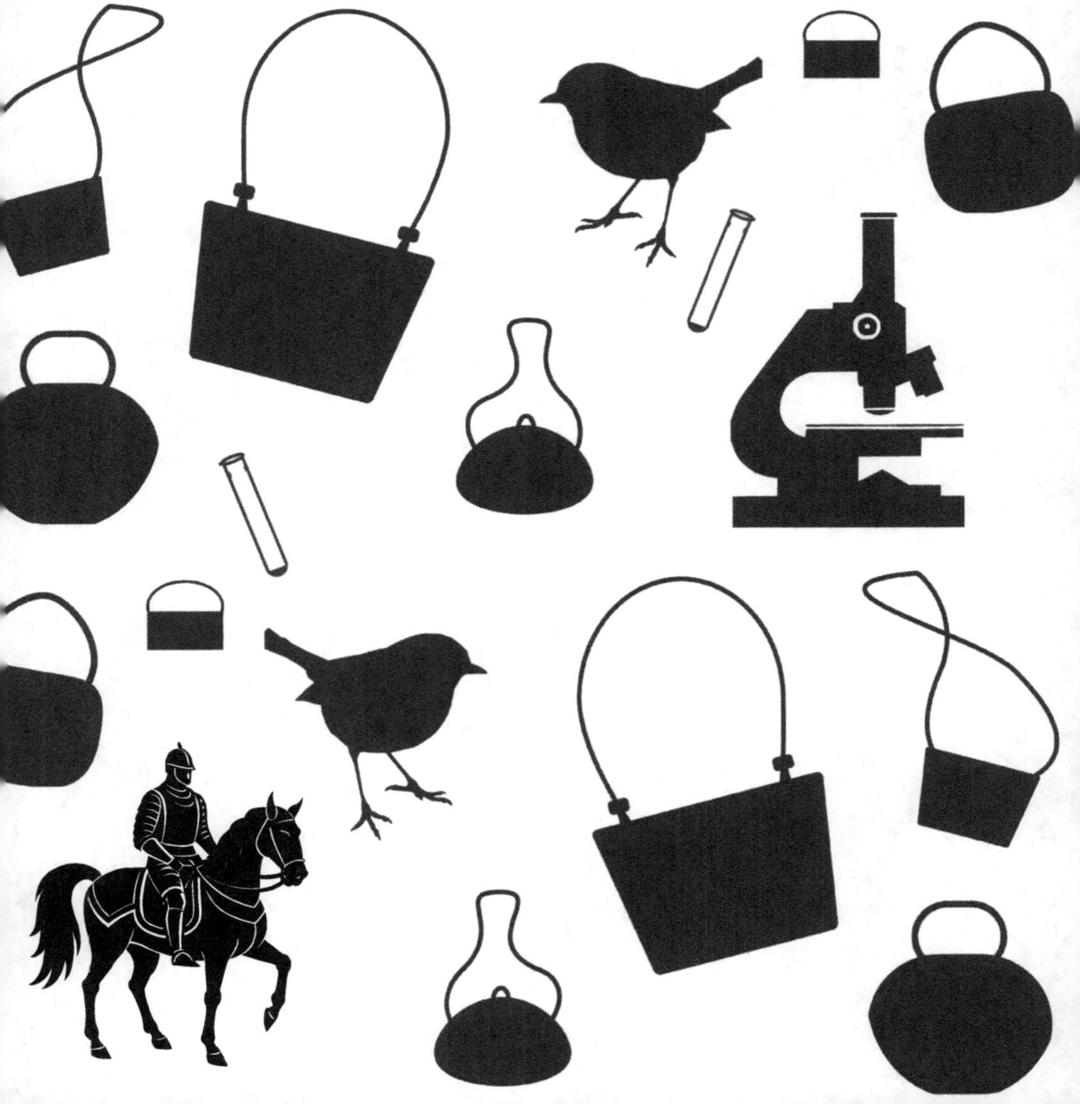

As Bobby Lumbar burst through door, he heard the young nuns cry out, "Oh, he'll get away!" and in the corner of his good eye, he saw their butterfly nets rise to the ready.

In no time he was dashing across the gravel lot outside his makeshift interrogation shack when his Great Escape was cut short as he almost ran right into...a water tower?

Wasting what brief moments of life were left to him, Bobby gaped up at this relic of Americana: a dun-metal tank held aloft on four tremendous legs, its drum like the metal-shop project of a long-forgotten race of giants, and on its top, a neat conical cap pointing to the sky, a subtle touch of chinoiserie in the heartland—or wherever he was. It only lacked the message "Welcome to Our Town"—a bad, bad sign in Bobby's book.

A second chorus of twitters and exclamations bubbled up behind him, and forgetting that story about Lot's wife from Vacation Bible School, Bobby turned to see a high tide of nuns streaming toward him, their vespertine vesture curling about them. Behind them in turn, Phineas Fairfax strode confidently, calling out, "Let us catch him and make him our own!"

On top of this, a strange, small, feminine voice asked him, "Lumbar, are you there? Where are you?" and realized that the ball that he was desperately squeezing was speaking at him. "Lumbar? Can you hear me?"

But just as Dr. Phineas Fairfax and friends were bursting upon him at the rear, Bobby muttered a speedy oath, popped the ball into his mouth like an all-day sucker, laid hands on the ladder up the water tower, and not unlike the wily bonobo, the southern pig-tailed macaque, or even the Guyanan red howler monkey, moved skyward at a startlingly fast pace.

Two minutes later, wincing, whining, whimpering, panting, gasping, and hunched over with exhaustion, Bobby was at the top, standing on the rickety platform running 'round the tower's rusty drum. Spitting the talk ball into one red, blistered, and welty palm, he looked back down to the ground.

Far beneath, the nuns circled about and waved up at him while the doctor, gazing up, pronounced with a hint of prophecy, "Come away, mothers. We can wait. She will do our work for us." So, instead of setting up croquet hoops to pass the time or waiting out the siege in lawn chairs, they all wandered out of sight.

Seeing that, for the first time in maybe a day, he was out of the clutches of anyone associated with MAXIFAX Laboratories, Bobby had a little free time to think, only to have two thoughts flash through his cranium: first, that he had quite neatly treed himself; and second, that this stunt proved that the lower primates were managing just fine, since the bonobos, southern pig-tailed macaques, and even Guyanan red howler monkeys had more sense than to work their way up a framework of superheated metal without a plan for coming back down. This particular *Homo sapiens*, meanwhile, was on his way to extinction.

But before resolving to drop out of his theistic evolution online chat group and/or find Charles Darwin's grave (so he could dance on it), Bobby decided that until Sheena sent the rescue chopper, he should take a gander at where he was, and leaning against the hot iron railing, through his last lens, he did just that.

His first thought was that those flat-earthers must know something he did not. The land all around, like the world around the axis mundi, was a lovely disc in a hundred hues of living, lush, and languorous green, an entrancing nature show of undulating hills drowsy at midday, with gaps here and there in the trees. (Bobby guessed maybe a road or a river, but by now he did not rule out a jagged gulley full of sacrificial victims.)

As for the sky, after a few reverent seconds of recognition that he was indeed a tiny quarkian particle within the onion-thin Ptolemaic layers of physical existence, he watched the sedate parade of cumulonimbus clouds, like silent herds of aerial Holsteins grazing on lush sky-grass. But feeling enchantment taking hold, he gave his head a shake: This faerie-fay gleam would not get him out of here, any closer to the rostrum in Stockholm, or in the steak house with Sheena.

He looked earthward again: The gravel lot was still devoid of all foes, but just beyond the lot and a collection of sheds, barns, dormitories, and what might have been interrogation shacks, he saw an odder and more-than-vaguely disturbing sight.

Bobby made out a shadowy mass of cruel, impenetrable, and over-grown trees stretching away into the horizon. Sharp-winged black birds (Bobby guessed *Corvus brachyrhynchos* or, at a stretch, *Quiscalus quis-cula*) darted threateningly over the coiling trunks and branches that had wildly woven themselves into a single, endless leafy carapace, forbidding and threatening. No doubt, in years gone by, when this water tower stood new in shiny pride, those trees had blossomed in row upon row as the pink-and-white promise of springtime. But at some vague period in the nameless past, the grounds crew must have set down their loppers, leav-ing Mother Nature, never a very tidy gal, to take over with menacing and knotty results: a sleeping beast, hungry and anxious for a snack.

But just as Bobby was telling himself to steer clear of that particular nature trail, he heard, "Lumbar?"

He looked at the palm of his hand. The ball was glowing, a pale pellu-cidum playing over its curving metal shell and pupating into prickly rays. But before it could stab him with some new kind of solidified light tech-nology (who knew what MAXIFAX would come up with next), he heard from above, "Lumbar, up here."

Bending his neck up, Bobby saw floating in the air above a hologram of the head and upper regions of Dr. Sheena Lypotrope, like a bust of Marie Curie—if Marie Curie took her hair and fashion tips from the character development department of a major comic book franchise.

"Sheena," he breathed, as if she were a tank of oxygen hissing at full blast.

As the image rippled, pixilated, and reformed, Bobby heard a garbled, "I've been calling you. Where are you?"

He reached up for her, as if she were a tropical fruit spilling from a cornucopia of light. "Waiting for you," he sighed.

Her face looked perturbed. "This is important. Where are you?"

"With Dr. Fairfax."

"With Phin? Good. What—"

"What do you mean, 'Phin'?"

"Where is he, right now?"

"So, do you want to know where he's at or where I'm at?"

In a tone oscillating between teacher and pupil but veering off toward truant officer, she said, "Where are you right now?"

"Orphis, just like you wanted." He hoped that this little reminder would stir up some girlish gratitude.

"Good. Just a second."

Her image appeared to be scanning the terrain behind him, and Bobby turned about to see what was so fascinating among the gentle hills. Turning back clueless, he was treated to Sheena Lypotrope telling him, "Don't move. Just hold still. Right there. We're getting a shot of all this." The half goddess in the hologram was now fiddling with something in her astral realm, and the ball in his hand swerved and shuffled about, like a lone eye scrutinizing the postcard countryside.

Telling himself that this was just her way of playing hard to get, Bobby pressed on, husbanding that flickering dream of that candlelit evening over rib eye. "Sheena, when can I—" Her hand went up, as forbidding as any portcullis, so he tried, "When can we—"

"Perfect. Perfect," she went on distractedly. "All right, we got that." Then she muttered to one of the unseen entities around her, "Send the terrain shot to Google. What? I don't care. Tell Sundar Pachai we have that tissue sample. He knows what that means. Okay, that's done," she muttered. "Send in the gamma model. No need to get O'Keefe Media Group after us." Bobby did not like the sound of that, since "the gamma model" was code for any of Noah's aerial critters.

With this final directive shot off like an arrow from the bow of Artemis, the hologram deigned to grant him an audience. "So, where's Freestone?"

"Who?"

"Your mission partner."

"It's a long story," said Bobby, experimenting with a technique he had overheard Ian (or maybe Noah) deploy to avoid Dr. Guagamal's more pressing demands for results. "And besides, who cares about her?" he asked, trying to pull off that come-hither cock of an eyebrow and melt his voice into something buttery and beckoning.

"You're on a mission," said Dr. Lypotrope, not unlike an anthropologist explaining a banana to a chimpanzee. "Where's your partner?"

Bobby still attempted to play the swain. "Why don't you come here and I'll tell you all about it?"

Her tone became like chlorine trifluoride, simple and explosive. "Talk."

And Bobby obliged with anecdotes of being the test subject of the effects of gravity on the human body behind the E-Z Fuel Plaza, then the stuffy sessions in Bella Freestone's trunk, and then the rescue (or abduction) by Phineas Fairfax. For color, he wove in a subplot about a bevy of nuns, topping it off with his daring escape, all to find his way back to her.

After this genetically modified cherry-on-top, the hologram partially broke apart and her words crackled like sparks in the air, leaving Bobby to wonder whether she was anguished at his falling into the clutches of Phineas Fairfax ("Oh, my baby!") or thrilled at his daring escape ("Oh, my baby!").

After several tense seconds, Bobby said, "You know, these people are crazy here."

"That's Phin for you." By now the hologram had cleared, and the mid-altitude Sheena Lypotrope added with a smile, "And that's why you're there."

"Me?"

"Yes," she whispered from on high. "You."

Bobby sighed. No doubt that static moments before had been electronic vandalism from Dr. Phineas Fairfax, desperately turning a few knobs in his laboratory somewhere.

Her hyper-angelic face still gazing down upon him, she said, "I need you to stay there, for me."

"But..."

With eyes like the young stars of dawn and a voice like the wind billowing ere the golden rising of the sun, she whispered, "A little longer. Please? I need you to do this for me."

"For you?"

"For me."

His question becoming her answer. "Yes, Sheena," he said. "I'll stay here for you."

"But I do have one more question for you."

"Yes, Sheena?"

"And, please, just keep it short..."

"What, Sheena?"

"What is that...thing behind you?"

Ever the curious lad, Bobby Lumbar turned around but did not find more scenery shots from the Merryweather Chamber of Commerce website. Instead, he found himself gaping, staring, and gasping in dread at a gaunt-faced, shadow-clad, and spectral apparition, a crepuscular fiend at midday, half swept and half crept around the rusting girth of the water tower tank. Dropping its mouth open, it keened out ghostly words like finger bones jabbing into Bobby's ears. "Boy, what are you doing in my nest?"

And showing himself the Guyanan red howler monkey, Bobby Lumbar leapt over the railing with a shriek of self-preservation and shimmied frantically down the hot metal legs of the water tower.

✳✳✳

Back where he had started, but without collecting two hundred dollars and with his glasses barely intact, Bobby, like a very bookish cyclops, gave a scan around him.

The terrain lacked any Fairfaxes and could be easily described as nunless. But squinting back up at that towering relic of the American heartland, he shuddered: the apparition, its mouth open, was clutching at the railing high above him, bending its horrible skeletal head downward, and seemed to be crawling over the railing like a monstrous lemur—a madness-masked Malagasy Madagascarite arboreal horror.

Just then, Bobby heard, "Oh, Dr. Fairfax! He's back! He's back! Oh, stay there. Please, stay there. Dr. Fairfax! He came back down!"

These summonses produced the man, and Dr. Fairfax stepped from around a corner of one of the nearby outbuildings that cowered nondescriptly in the background.

"Ah," he called to Bobby like a conqueror and rubbed his hands together with hearty zeal. "A truly magnificent happenstance!"

While Dr. Fairfax and his be-wimpled cheerleaders and their butterfly nets came ever nearer, and a glance back up the water tower showed
Bobby the welcoming committee climbing sinuously down the rickety legs,
Bobby looked in the only direction left to him: to the orchard of dark,
knotted trees he had seen from on high, now the only way he would get
out of these woods.

So, listening to his animal brain, Bobby made a dash for safety—even
if safety could be found only inside a haunted forest.

CHAPTER VII

DOCTOR'S ORDERS,
OR PRESCRIPTION FOR DISASTER

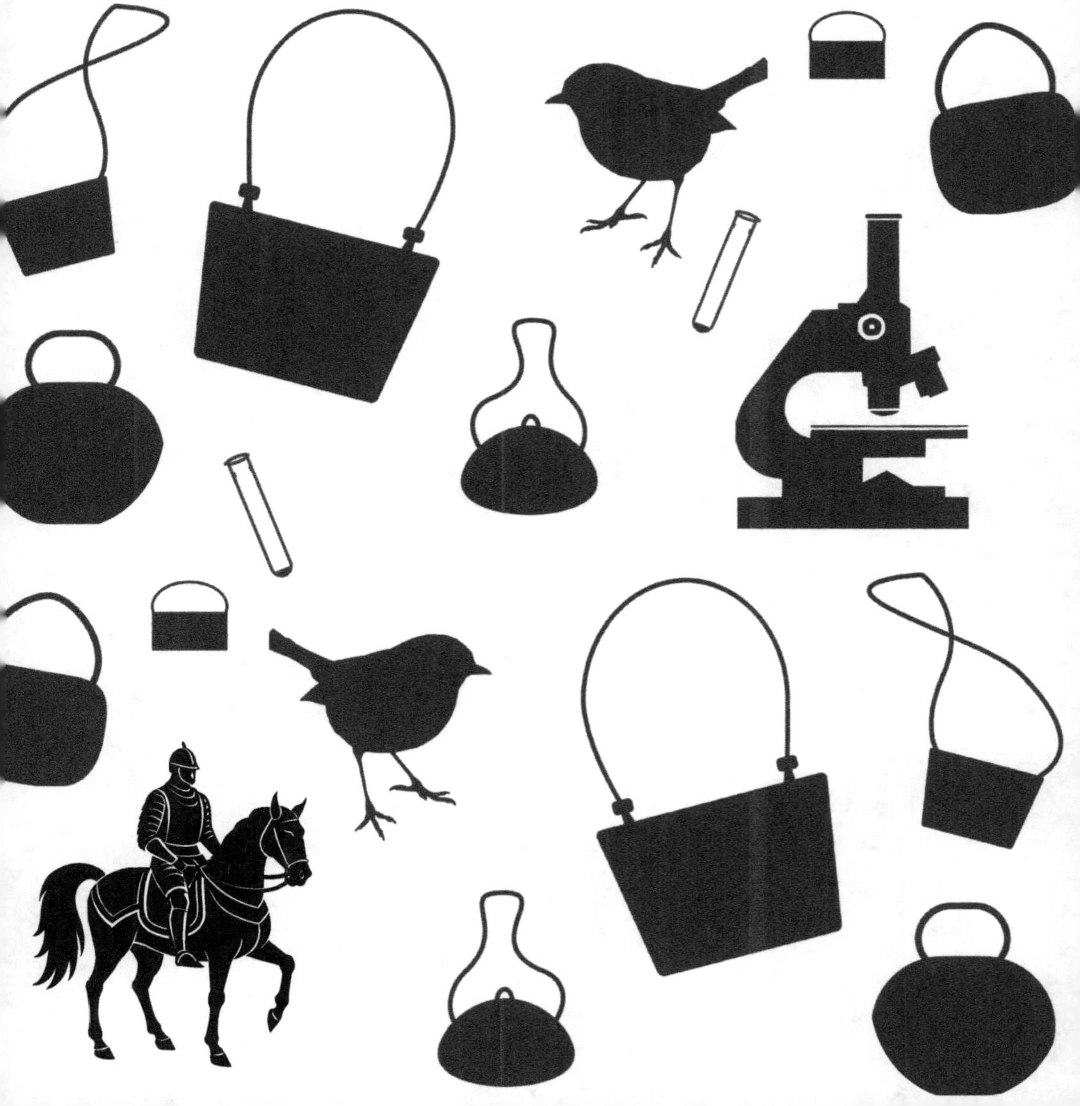

Meanwhile, back in cute-cute downtown Merryweather, Baba and Martie were nursing Bella through her confusion about MAXIFAX, Phineas Fairfax, and any other recent facts.

"Daddy?" she muttered, as if trying out a new accent before an overseas mission, only to deliver another "Daddy?" since the first one did not sound right—and never would.

In all fairness, MAXIFAX dropped the ball royally with Bella's generation of units, allowing them to skip sessions, permitting them unsupervised jaunts of liberty, freedom, and other John-Waynery, all in the name of "building character." Martie was out of class on the day of post-adolescent mind infusion, and Baba was off getting her nails titanium-plated when they were programmed with empathy, and Bella somehow missed the end-of-pupation visit from Dr. Phineas Fairfax in the flesh, that special day when he had explained the facts of existence to them. To be sure, no such slipshod Montessorian nonsense was allowed in the more recent generations. Those young ladies moved in smooth grooves from seedbed to womb room to hypertrophy chamber to their own little minimalist, single-occupancy pens and then to an immersion year of social media and online shopping: sarabands of sameness and minuets of materialism. And all the while, language was kept to words of one or two syllables, with "like" and "so" predominating. (The Rhodes scholars among them say "totally.")

A third time she said, "Daddy?" and it still was not working like a charm.

Baba repeated, "The Maker."

"I like 'Daddy,'" said Martie.

Taking a drag from her vaping pen, Baba scanned the sky. "Sheena could be on the move by now. I suggest finding shelter."

"Who cares about Sheena?" Bella said. (Obviously this new existential conundrum had derailed her sense of self-preservation.)

"That's right," Martie agreed. "No one cares about Sheena."

"And Sheena cares about no one," finished Baba. "That allows her to do away with people who upset her plans."

"Like you," Martie whispered to Bella in as comforting a voice as she could muster.

At this in-kind contribution to the Save Bella Freestone Fund, Bella gave her herbal-infused blond top a shake and came back to reality. "Thanks, Martie. Remind me to donate a cornea to you."

"How about a liver lobe?" asked Martie, exploiting the warm and tender moment for all that she could. "You might not be needing either of them soon."

"Come along," said Baba, unwilling to sit through any more horse-trading. "Survival awaits." And with that, the demoiselles fled the scene.

✳✳✳

But even as they hastily crossed the street, it was plain to all witnesses that they were not pulling off the *tableau vivant* of three devil-may-care, free-and-easy gal pals on a shopping spree. If any stranger came near, Martie sniffled with dread, Baba drew forth her Shaka Zooloo® assegai (with the collapsible, hinged shaft—very handy), and Bella inadvertently begged the stranger, "Take them, take them..."

After a few rounds of this behavior, they found themselves not only avoided by the residents of downtown Merryweather, but they also noticed a mental health van now repeatedly circling the block like a boxy metal buzzard.

When the soccer mom van with the bearded do-gooders cruised alongside them a third time, Bella decided for the group, "Cry time's over. I think that there just might do as a little shelter from the storm."

Bella had spied a stucco storefront with an outsized sign reading FOR LEASE—as well as yards and yards of yellow-and-black police tape forbiddingly festooning it. But the auspicious sign that, the crime scene or not, this was Meant to Be was its address: 2525 Center Street. Was this a prophecy fulfilled or a not-so-simple synchronicity? Without delving too deeply into the workings of an unfeeling universe, Bella veered to the front door, her pals bending their rudders accordingly, and soon they stood before their safe house.

But they did hesitate. Not only was the police tape still relatively taut, but they also noticed evidence of a recent fracas: claw marks striping the window glass, a weblike smash pattern in the front door glass, and the gritty chalk outline of a human figure over the pavement, the line of one hand including a squarish appendage, like a high-end handbag. Recalling the young Birkin Bag girl from Come All Kombucha, Bella muttered, "Well, there's blood under them thar press-ons now. Looks like your friends did each other in, Baba."

"But they seemed so nice," Martie whimpered.

"And that's the Merryweather way," Baba reassured her chum. "But never fear, Bella dear. I think I'm carrying my fake detective badge." Lifting the police tape, she deftly ducked beneath it.

But before she could test the door, a sudden whirring sounded just above their heads. As one, they bent their heads up, to be treated to a bit of performance art entitled *Evil Sphere in May.*

The fugitive sphere that had flown off on its merry way had returned and, just out of reach, was now busily rotating and spinning like a tiny independent planet beholden to no solar body, while tiny eyelike illuminations festooning its shell glowed and pulsed.

As it skimmed about in its interpretive midair dance, Martie, trying to keep up with its midgey migrations, asked, "Can we just ignore it?"

Baba said, "It's not a frat boy, sweetie."

Never averse to a little brute force, Bella said, "Can't we just kill it?"

Martie hummed in agreement like a panelist on PBS (this was as intellectual as she would probably every get), before the dainty sphere pirouetted a few times up and down, then levitated to a place slightly above their heads and, tilting downward, turned its miniscule eyes upon them with a cold and determined focus.

"Bella dear," said Baba, "distract it with your sparkling repartee while I try something." She gave the knob of 2525 Center Street a quick turn. "Locked."

"Just break it down, Charlotte," Martie said.

"But, Lily, I don't want to be arrested."

"You won't when you show them your detective badge."

"And your decoder ring," said Bella.

"And while you're all at it," announced a new feminine voice radiating from the buoyant boisterous little ball, "you can dig out your map to the bomb shelter."

Bella, Baba, and Martie looked up to see the sphere giving birth in midair to a bizarre shape. Bending their dye jobs first one way, then the other, they followed a dangling, upside-down hologram, like a paper doll growing out of its bottom of the ball, until the ball got its bearings and delivered its firstborn into an upright position. Now, with flourishes of lightning amid clouds of magnificent fluorescent dread, as an ominous crackling electrified the air, Bella, Baba, and Martie beheld the image of a strikingly buxom woman in an icily white lab coat: Dr. Sheena Lypotrope, Electrolyte Demigoddess, manifesting herself in the realm of mortals.

What also manifested the realm of mortals was a volley of luminous javelinesque blasts striking the storefront door behind them with frightening accuracy and shattering its antique mechanism. It opened with a sigh.

With the floating ball still smoking, and before any of them could mutter a mushy apology or belabored greeting, Sheena Lypotrope clearly and coldly commanded them, "All right, hags, move it," and Bella, Baba, and Martie turned obediently about and marched inside.

✳✳✳

Bella, Baba, and Martie gathered in a cluster in the middle of a dusty floor, 2525 Center being in the midst of renovation for new occupants, while the talk ball zoomed in behind them, dragging the hologram of Dr. Lypotrope along like a plastic pennant. After a spin on its axis, it delivered another rapid white-hot rat-a-tat blast, now at the inside of the door, not only staining the aged wood with black feathers of char but melting the nineteenth-century wood-mounting screws into smoking streams of hot metal that trickled down to the floor and reduced the rest of its vintage fixtures into a molten magmoid blob.

"While that cools...," began Dr. Lypotrope, as the ball rotated to show their hostess as very much the specter of vengeance. It pointed an accusing digit at Bella. "You, the idiot. You lost him."

"I guess I did," said Bella with a brittle cheeriness, forcing herself to enjoy to the full these last minutes of existence.

"Your stupidity and lack of planning are practically *fractal* in their multi-dimensionality because—and here is the core, the *kernel,* of the message—you did not just *lose* that underling..." Sheena took a second to compose herself.

Martie piped up quietly, "I don't understand, Dr. Lypotrope."

At this grade-school declaration, the ball sent out a warning blast over Martie's head that shattered an unsuspecting light fixture.

The critique resumed. "Our Mirabella Freestone, known to the mass of humanity as Miss Flunky, failed not merely to retain control of her mission partner, but allowed the target of the mission to *abduct* him."

Baba erred by asking, "Is that what happened? Well, that calls for a cigarette break..." But as she slipped a hand into the smart Givenchy number hanging negligently from one snowy shoulder, a precise blast from the ball sliced through the shoulder strap, sending both purse and contents dumping to the gritty floor at her well-heeled feet.

"Savarin," said Sheena Lypotrope, "if you want to enjoy a cigarette, I have a firing squad with your name on it."

Glad that the death ray was pointed at someone else for a second, Bella asked, "By the way, did that patsy have a name? I never did find out. Just curious."

"You can ask him when you run into him in the afterlife."

Martie asked, "I thought we didn't get an afterlife."

"And if you don't learn the value of silence"—a tutorial blast from the ball skimmed by her black tresses and decorated an adjacent wall with a blast crater—"you won't have much of a life here, either." Then, a slight alteration in her tone suggested that she wished to engage the entire group. "Now," she said, "what will we do to bring about a positive outcome from all of this? Hmm? What are some results that might gratify me?"

But before she could enumerate these bullet points in the workplan, Bella asked, "Just a second, Sheena. Can I get my three-ring notebook so I can jot this down?"

"I don't know, can you?" A fusillade of laser blasts ricocheted violently from every surface but petered out shy of causing any flesh wounds. "Freestone, if you're ready to listen and maybe avoid a visit from the boys on Level VII...? This is what I need to happen." Dr. Lypotrope held up three fingers. "See these? These are a clue that *three* things need to happen. They also, of course, match the three idiots before me—or, sorry, the one idiot and two emotional defectives lacking any judgment in the area of friendship."

Suddenly Martie bleated out, "But at least we have friends."

Sheena Lypotrope lay a two-dimensional hand on her two-and-a-half-dimensional bust. "That is so sweet. But if you continue to contribute in any way to this conversation, Miss Turkscap, your friends can comfort you when you're all spending your few remaining days in the bottom of a dark pit. Now, if it's all right with you, may I return to my pep talk?" Martie started to say something but, remembering that she was not supposed to say anything, nodded and hoped that that would not count as talking—or not talking. "Excellent. You know, I think maybe you're the smartest one of the bunch. As I was saying: three goals. Three. Count 'em. First—Are we listening? Good. First, find that brainless *dink* that Freestone lost and bring him back to me. He does not need to be roaming at large, not that he'd survive long in the wild. Level IX would like to have him in for a little conference. Next, the *data*. Let's all say that together..."

Bella, Baba, and Martie muttered in a gray mumble, "The data."

"Good enough. These *data* are really the whole point of the mission, and I'll flesh that out for you little girls later, if I feel like it. But don't hold your breath. So, dink and data. Finally, and this is number three—one, two, three, just like the three mental defectives I see in front of me—the *doctor*. Dr. Phineas Fairfax. And here's where my faith in you is going to shine through, because although I suspect that you will very likely fail utterly on the first two counts, I cannot envisage a scenario in which you cannot lasso a grown man, shove a wad of socks in his mouth, and bring him to me in the back of a meat wagon. So, there you go. Isn't that easy? Simplicity itself: dink, data, doctor. You understand me, don't you? You can all nod now, 'Yes, Dr. Lypotrope, we understand.'"

Bella gave a begrudging nod, and Baba inclined her head in a way that could have been taken as disappointment at the utter dullness of the world. But Martie pressed her lips together and gave Sheena Lypotrope a stare.

Dr. Sheena Lypotrope whispered, "Oh, Turkscap..." and delivered a blast that ricocheted off of one of the surviving light fixtures before taking out a rat scuttling along the wall. "I am sensing the need for a refresher course on the facts of your particular lives. Very well."

The image of Sheena Lypotrope dissolved and in its place appeared the face of a woman like a Victorian doll from *Antiques Roadshow.*

"Isn't she pretty? It looks like she held herself together." Martie brightened at this possible future, while Bella and Baba waited for the inevitable fine print. "But, this willful soul—"

Martie lost points by saying, "You said we don't have souls."

"And at this rate, you won't have much of a body either. Now, examine the following."

The face of the doll woman aged before their eyes, shriveling into a woman of, charitably, advanced years, with glossy swollen bags like bloated tadpoles under her eyes, billions of fine veins like microscopic worms infesting the yellowish whites of her eyes, wiry sprigs of unplucked hairs curling out from her chin and upper lip, crow's feet like the tracks of pterodactyls, and a head of hair reduced to crinkling gray-brown strands like brittle, wintery grass.

Martie shrieked and covered her face, Baba wished that she could blow out a cloud of smoke to obscure this specter, and Bella tightened her lips and blinked over and over but to no avail.

Sheena explained coldly, "This one wanted to age gracefully. It looks to me like she managed the aging part just fine. Her name was Pellagra Johnson, from the Johnson Series. She did everything right. She made us proud. But she wanted 'freedom.' She broke away. She actually imagined that she didn't need maintenance. She did not think that Dr. Helsingfors was her friend."

Martie chirped up, "But Dr. Helsingfors's my friend."

"Because you're a smart little girl who wants to stay fresh. But how do we make sure that we stay fresh?" A general silence fell over the group, which Dr. Lypotrope dispelled. "By remembering our programming, which is...? The first day of class?" Sheena helped them along by rounding her mouth. "O..."

"Obey and spend," Martie burst out with bubbly certainty.

"Obey and *shop*. Close enough. Now, how about you, Coppertop?"

"I think 'Obey and shop' is the answer," said Baba.

"Excellent." Sheena looked at Bella. "Freestone, I'm looking for something that rhymes with...?"

"Obey and shop," said Bella.

"So simple. Modus vivendi and modus operandi, like Dr. Fairfax used to say. Obey and shop. Obey and shop. All anyone needs to do, really. Now, my little drones, what half of this is relevant right now?"

"Shop," offered Martie. The hologram shook its head, leaving Martie to deduce, "Obey?"

The hologram nodded. "You know, Turkscap, you shed a really fluorescent light on any subject. So, with that out of the way, I'm going to let you all in on a little secret. Come closer, come closer. As you've noticed around town, MAXIFAX has been beta testing a new line—far slimmer and more obedient than certain older models. Savarin, that model that you took out earlier today with your rather creaky combat skills?"

"You found out about that?"

"The ball knows all. She was expensive. So, if you survive this mission, you won't be surprised at a drastic drop in your bank balance. But, you know, maybe one of your little friends here will let you sublet her broom closet to live in for the rest of your days. Now, though, to quote Agent Psaki, let's circle back. It's a funny thing about these new models: most of their parts are just the same as in the old models. And in these days of rampant inflation and ecological awareness, sometimes it's better to just reuse old parts instead of leaving a big carbon footprint by manufacturing new ones. And, let's see, where could I find old parts for cheap? Well, I know of three sources right off the top of my head. In fact, I can almost reach out and touch them. To sum up, then—and please listen, because this is the part where I repeat what I've already said: dink, data, doctor. Dink, data, doctor. Dink, data, doctor. And since I've been in brief communication with the dink, we just about know where Phineas Fairfax is holding up. But to help you along, I will be sending you a cartographic projection to help you proceed."

Baba leaned into Martie. "That means a map." Then, primping her hair with topaz-tipped fingers, just to look good for the scaffold, Baba did venture, "And we're to believe that MAXIFAX doesn't have the surveillance technology to pinpoint his location?"

"Savarin," Dr. Lypotrope said flatly to nip any intellectual sparring in the bud, "MAXIFAX has very precise geo-finding tech, but not only is the dink's handheld device in my chopper to prevent him using it inadvertently while in the field..."

"You do think of everything."

"Except how to choose subordinates who can accomplish elementary, core-level tasks like kidnapping and assassination. So, as I was explaining to the slow kids in the front row..."

"Wait a second," said Bella. "You were in conference with Stooge Central and you didn't just ask him where he was?"

"Freestone," asked Dr. Lypotrope, her words like a cape of ice crystals blowing down the fissured face of a mountain glacier, "what should happen now, in response to that question?"

"Oh, wait, wait, I know. A sudden blast of energy should reduce me to a heap of ashes."

"Good guess." The ball delivered a salvo uncomfortably close to Bella's head and took out a half-empty bucket of drywall paste that had been minding its own business on the far side of the room. "It's a good thing that my aim is a little off after this long session of remedial education. But to dispel any mental fog, I'll remind you that the target kidnapped the little dumb-dumb, so, no, he couldn't supply us an address, a weather report, and word on how good the schools are."

"Well, the weather here's really nice right now," said Bella.

"And that makes it a good day to die."

"I'd guess," Baba theorized, "that Dr. Fairfax is using a jamming tech with wide-area distribution? Nanotech, probably. I mean, you've already ruled out channel-hopping and flow jammers, right?"

The hologram flickered before stating with a staccato, sushi-chef efficiency, "You forgot pulsed noise. I'll tell you what, Savarin: When you write that letter of appeal with your mascara applicator from inside the refrigerator on Level VII, you can tell me all the details."

Then, though, just as a sky, on the verge of tossing buckets of icy hail onto the heads of carefree picnickers, might transform into an azurescape of buoyant clouds like vermeilled marshmallows, in the same way did the face of Dr. Sheena Lypotrope take on a welcoming glow. Through a lambent, warm, and enchanting aura, she told them, "Now I need to go and see Dr. Helsingfors. For a consult. You understand. He says in Singapore they're blazing whole new trails with a combination of laser sculpting and Sumatran leeches. But let's not have any tears, because this isn't goodbye. We'll talk soon. And I know that you'll succeed, that you won't ruin this for me, because, frankly"—the gently buoyant clouds were taking on an algal hue—"you know how things will play out, unless there is anything but complete success. It's a pretty word, isn't it? 'Success.' But, if I do not see success, then, I'm sorry to say, I will be unhappy. And in that case, the only people, if you can call them that, who will end up happy will be your little friends from the coffee shop, because any of your parts that MAXIFAX can't use, well, they can. Take a look, right over there."

Who can ken the means by which Dr. Sheena Lypotrope knew that the Bag Ladies of Come All Kombucha were still lurking near 2525 Center Street? But there they were, on the other side of the front windows, their hands spread out over the glass like the sucker feet of tropical lizards and their bulging eyes rotating around and around like ocular tops. Could they see through the darkness limning the outer face of the glass, straining to discover what was so hip, modish, and desirable beyond the doors? Or had they, like scavenging she-wolves, smelled well-aged meat? The mouths of one or two hung open. These ladies were hungry and would feed.

Through the hologram, Dr. Lypotrope said, "One misstep and I will dismantle each of you like a rusted-out Chevy Vega. No. Sorry. They will dismantle you and I will watch. That means I wouldn't just be squatting here like an ape at a garbage pail, ladies. Time to make Dr. Lypotrope happy. And I'm sure you can find the back door." At this, the hologram dissolved as the talk ball, like a planetoid finding itself in the wrong solar system, whirred quietly away up into a vent in the ceiling and disappeared.

Suddenly from the direction of the front windows came a cruel chorus of crash after crash, as the Bag Ladies, like mama trolls at the crystalline ramparts of a castle, were pounding their way in.

"The back door," said Bella, as the windows began to buckle and crack.

"Can I come too?" simpered Martie.

"Of course, sweetheart," said Baba, snatching up her purse with one hand and with the other, like an anxious shepherdess rescuing her ewe lamb, the crook of Martie's elbow.

Seconds later, the ladies had slammed the back door of 2525 Center Street securely behind them—and as an add-on to their group life insurance policy, shoved a couple of greasy trash barrels against it—while from within echoed the final sharp shattering crash of the front windows, followed by the anguished and disappointed howls of women desperate for a few minor organs or a bionic eye.

CHAPTER VIII

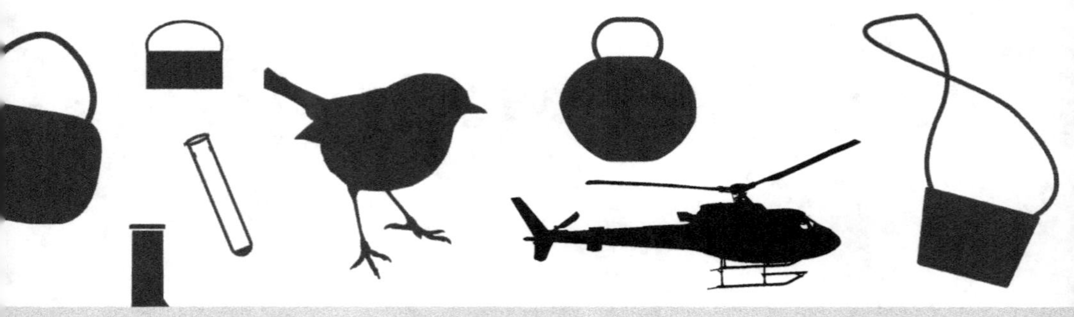

MUDDY PATHS, OR THE HAPPY HUNTING GROUNDS

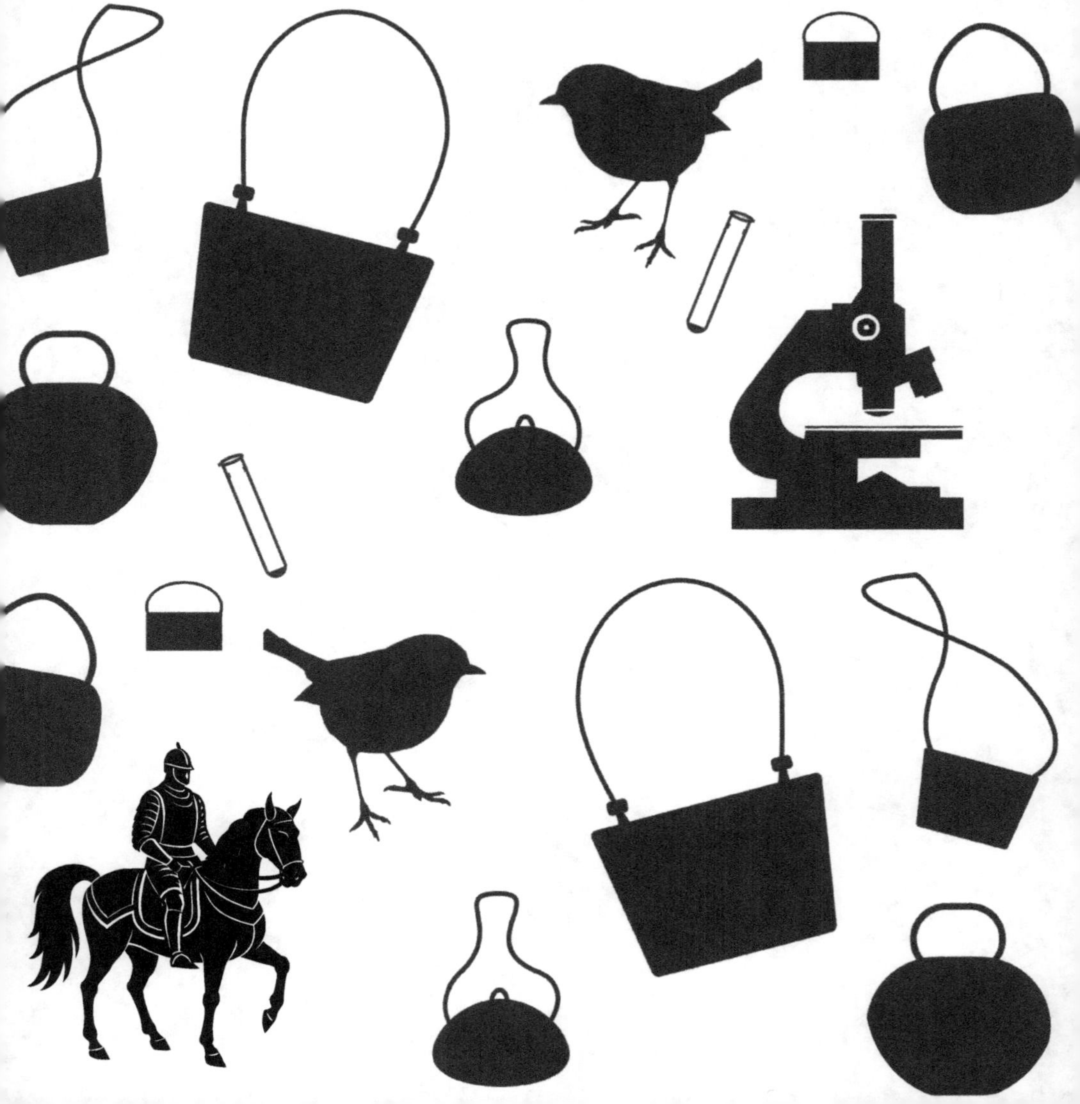

After a desperate dash into the overgrown orchard, Bobby Lumbar hid himself behind the biggest tree he could find, leaned against its hobnail bark, and covering his head with his blistered hands, starting wildly whispering, "*B. lumbarensis, B. lumbarensis...*"

Then, after giving what was left of his glasses a shove up his nose, he took a terrified look around.

The reader should not imagine the trees that seemed to close in around Bobby Lumbar were like those contorted subjects populating paintings by Van Gogh, Manet, Monet, or any of those other Impressionist, pre-Impressionist, or post-Impressionist plein air pigment-pushers.

Not at all.

The stalwarts of this fearsome forest had not known any pollarding, pruning, snipping, trimming, thinning, crowning, or topping for more than a generation and were a threatening, twisting, grasping, and clutching collective knot of bark and branches. As if feeding on mysterious chthonic energies, these many-branched fruit factories had become the hierophants, devotees, and living walls of an über-heathen shrine where lost children—and clueless junior scientists—wandered in but never out, and Bobby just knew that someday, they would post right next to the sign for the Hansel and Gretel Nature Trail, a plaque commemorating the known sighting of that budding ornithological genius, Robert J. Lumbar.

This woeful reflection broke apart like a rotten log when a noisy squadron of utility all-terrain vehicles, each one manned (or womanned) by a nun, roared around a venerable persimmon tree and made straight for him. Each lady held aloft her butterfly net, as pale as a wraith, leaving Bobby Lumbar to imagine the size of the butterflies in these parts.

With an ugly rev of their engines, the ATVs zoomed forward, leapt over a heap of fetid compost, and landed with a splash into pools of muddy slime. In no time, like goddesses of fate mounted on wild boars, the nuns were weaving about him, with each rotation spewing slime and rotten fruit in his face. "Oh, this is so much fun!" one chimed out, before another warned off her sisters with, "Oh, he's crying! I think we're making him cry!" (Actually, Bobby was just holding his hands to his face to protect what was left of his glasses.)

But as their revving and growling slowed to a more conscientious chug-a-lug pace, Bobby spread his fingers and, seeing a goblin track between two trees, dashed past the rumbling machines, to run deeper into the forbidding depths of this hideous fruitopian maze.

After a few quick turns to lose his pursuers, Bobby tripped over a pugnacious tree root and, with a plop, fell face down into a fetid brownish pool. After pushing himself out of this cold slurry, he cocked an ear and, through the crisscrossing branches, caught the harsh zoom of engines fading away. The mawkish sisters with their garden-party assault weapons were racing on.

Breathing with relief, Bobby crept onto a dry patch and tried to remember one of those catchy New Age nostrums supplied by his grandmother in her monthly emails. (She cribbed these from her own self-published ebooks, *Ancient Wisdom/Future Truth* and *Snuggling Up with Mortality*.) The one that came to Bobby ran, "The best way out is through," a pearl of advice all shiny on its surface, but at its core an ugly speck of gritty truth, viz. that Bobby would need to brave unknown acres of ravenous monsters, spiked pits, and, yes, booby traps, before reaching freedom.

But then, like a moth batting against his glasses, came the fleeting cruel thought: that maybe he would never escape this hellish nutyard at all. He imagined a vision of his future self, gnarled and hideous, by day snorting about for half-ripe pears and gnawing on Japanese plum pits. But by night, he would chase incautious teenagers in bellbottoms and polyester tops, his long-reach arborist tools gleaming for one deadly second in the moonlight. Yes, he would end his days as that horrific urban legend, the Pruner...

The roar of an ATV shattered this grim glimpse of things to come, and a four-wheeled war machine reared, spewing goo and belching exhaust, and wheeled up before him. Its dark charioteer was Mother Deborah, and behind her stood Dr. Phineas Fairfax.

Bobby started to run once more, until one misplaced footfall on one particular slimy patch of earth sent him airborne...before landing him on his backside.

The ATV rumbled up and through the engine noise, and Bobby heard Mother Deborah say, "Well, Doc, looks like he still doesn't want to play," to which Phineas Fairfax jumped to the ground, and his unsullied form soon stood looming above Bobby, his lab coat as white as an unsuspected avalanche.

But Bobby crawled madly to his feet and was on the run once again, sliding and slipping up an alley of creaking fig trees, the macramé of their branches blotting out the sun.

✳✳✳

After a sprint worthy of the Olympic track-and-field trials, Bobby Lumbar jigged around a row of quince trees, only to stumble into an abandoned ditch and find his feet sinking into the slime. Clutching the crumbling edge of this earth trough and gritting his teeth, he liberated himself from the muck with a very rude sound, then tripped and clawed up onto solid ground. Looking about, he could not make any sense of where he was, although between the paw-paw trees, he heard from the buzz of many an ATV and here and there the black flashes of the good nuns, their butterfly nets ballooning behind them, ready to bag their bounty. "Dr. Fairfax, Dr. Fairfax!" they were gleefully giggling. "Oh, he's over here! We think he's over here!"

With the pack closing in yet again, Bobby shot forward, deeper and deeper into this slimy labyrinth, and he descended lower and lower down the food chain.

✳✳✳

After another of his by-now trademark sharp turns, Bobby crouched against whatever tree was at his immediate rear.

It was time to practice a little offense.

Moving to the tool-using stage, Bobby felt about for anything to come to his aid. He laid his hand first on an old tomato cage, then a one-gallon black plastic plant pot split down the side, then a pile of spiky rust that had been a box of roofing nails, and finally a more-or-less straight branch. He would find the flint spearpoint later. All that he needed now was the watering hole watched over by a sabretooth tiger and he could star in *Olduvai: The Musical.*

But the public would have to wait for the didgeridoo-and-flat-drum overture, since the prehistoric predators had just shown up. Out of the dappling shade in front of him stepped a creeping pair of immense and drooling dogs with gelatinous ropes of snow-white slobber swaying from their jowly jaws and panting maws.

The two behemoth pooches stomped ever nearer, and the muddy ground seemed to shudder. Bobby gave a gulp that echoed out of the abyss of his empty stomach. As the dog monsters sent up contemptuous howls, Bobby was on his feet yet again and shot straight forward, racing right between the beasts...

...only to stagger out into the brilliant and blossoming daylight.

✳✳✳

Slack-jawed and uncomprehending, Bobby Lumbar dropped his serendipitous spear, gave what was left of his glasses a last shove up his nose, and blinked a few times. My, how things had changed.

Before him spread immense garden beds, a diorama of back-to-the-land bounty: bear-pelt black soil rowed with a rainbow of hot pink and yellow chard, orange nasturtiums, blue borage, white feverfew, rouge red lettuce, pink bean and pea blossoms, and last year's scarlet radishes sending the sweet dregs of their winter sugar up in a confetti of party pastel flowers, and at one end, like a pharmacy next to the green grocer's, grew an annex of yellow, gray, and pale purple herbs. There Bobby saw, sitting on a handcrafted wooden bench, a slender feminine figure draped in a gray veil like a cascading drift of nuclear snow. A chain of luridly sunny daisies held this murky drapery upon her head.

This mysterious person must have heard Bobby stumbling up, because she turned about, her eyes met Bobby's, and she asked, "Are you new at Orphis?"

He felt his feet were sending out taproots to hold him in place, while the rest of him floated to the heavens. "I think so," he said.

"Good. You want to help me make another one of these?" She held up a dainty cross woven of willow twigs.

All right, thought Bobby, *she thinks I'm a vampire—or a werewolf.* "No," he blurted out. "No, I mean, I don't know how. Sorry."

"Well, do you know anything about birds?"

The question was a herald's horn from a far-off mountain crag. Striding forth with vim and gusto, he stubbed his toe on a decorative rock, squelched an expression not suitable for a lady's ears, knelt before her amid the hippie pharmaceuticals, and whispered huskily, "What exactly do you need to know?"

"What kind is this one?" She showed him a smallish box, earlier in its career something for baby shoes but now gaudified with anything that could be swept from the floor of the craft store. Over its lid, a childlike hand (or maybe Chagall or Matisse) had drawn an avian figure with smiling beak and gay eyes winging its way skyward toward a felt-pen figure of a smiling bearded man with a halo and rippling white robe. Golden glitter adhering to tracks of glue suggested heavenly rays descending to meet the birdie soaring now to its eternal nest.

Lifting the lid off of this rainy-day project with delicate fingers, she revealed the paper-product sarcophagus within. On a bed of goldenrod tissue paper lay motionless, as if merely sleeping but perfect in proportion, symmetry, and feather color, a tiny bird. *Ah,* thought Bobby, *Regulus calendula.* In deference to the feelings of the grieving family, he said gently, "It's a ruby-crowned kinglet," and pushing his shattered glasses up his nose, raised his eyes to hers.

She looked away with a smile of gratitude. "Now I'll know who to pray for."

"Pray for?"

"Sure. See?" She stood and walked along a path lined with lion's tail, bee balm, hyssop, and valerian to a tidy patch of dainty graves, each with a willow-wand cross and a heavy, decorative stone to forestall any unwanted desecration by grave robbers (*read* raccoons, possums, and skunks).

"That's very nice," Bobby said with plenty of feeling, before realizing that he sounded like a substitute kindergarten teacher inspecting a Play-Doh dinosaur.

Right then, though, the tour of the necropolis came to an unpleasant end. Staring at him with a leaden expression, her eyes gushed out tears like freshly melted diamonds. "No," cried the mysterious maiden. "You'll ruin everything! You'll ruin it! You'll ruin it! Everything!" and running around him with an indignant sniffle, she crashed against the black form of Mother Deborah, as if the older woman was a portal into oblivion. "Mother!" she sobbed.

And at that moment, all of Bobby's many pursuers were putting in an appearance, both en masse and on foot: the already-mentioned Mother Deborah, then an umbrageous bevy of supplementary nuns breaking out of the untamed orchard and parking their ATVs to cool at the end of a satisfying chase, and at last, with a steady, manly stride, Dr. Phineas Fairfax, the white of his lab coat painfully pure to the eyes. At either side of the doctor loped the dogs that had almost made Bobby their lunch, and as the doctor stopped, so did these monstrosities, sitting immediately on their haunches and flanking him like foo beasts defending Potala Palace.

Bobby looked back at the girl, still cowering in the patient embrace of Mother Deborah, who looked up mutely to tell all present, "Oh, this again." She lifted the girl's chin with a pair of fingers. "That's no way to face the world," she said and, in an act of maternalistic tough love, pressed her away.

The young lady came to a very definite halt and, in a huff, yanked off her veil, loosening a head of deep red hair that unfurled like a tapestry woven with threads of gold that caught the rays of the lowering sun—or that was how Bobby Lumbar saw it.

Still, she pointed at Bobby as if he embodied all that was yucky and cootified. "Just make him go," she sniffled. "Hand him over to Dr. Fairfax." There, with a blank, horrified expression, she realized aloud, "But then I'd have to see him."

Mother Deborah suggested, "You can always look at something else."

"No," the girl insisted, sure that she could bend reality to her will.

"Suit yourself."

Just then, from far away sounded the singsong ding-dong of great bells, and Bobby noticed in the distance a grand cedar-wood chapel, its belltowers balancing a trio of gilded onion domes, just then beginning to glow like candle flames at day's end.

Mother Deborah squinted at the chatelaine watch pinned to her habit, and her face puckered as if she had seen a blob of wax besmirching the chapel tiles. "Well, girls, we've missed Ninth Hour. I'm surprised the earth hasn't opened up to swallow us all whole. Well, we can still fit in vespers." She looked at Dr. Fairfax. "No rest for the wicked. The pilgrimage starts tomorrow, on top of the berry pickers."

"In reparation," said Phineas Fairfax, "I think I can supply a few more souls for the pilgrimage."

"I won't stop you," said Mother Deborah. Then, making one syllable out of two, she announced, "Chapel," and the nuns began to shuffle along after their abbess like the cygnets of the Australian black swan (*Cygnus atratus*, Bobby remembered).

Watching this exodus, the mysterious girl said, "But, don't you want me to come?"

"Yes," said Mother Deborah. "But I don't think that you do."

Suddenly, Bobby yelled out, "Hey, wait a second."

The mysterious girl drew her head back in surprise. Mother Deborah drew her head back in surprise. The nuns in a line drew back their heads in surprise. Even Bobby drew his head back in surprise, until he realized that he was the center of attention. With a nervous crack in his voice, he asked, "So, where am I now?"

"Right here," chimed in one of the young nuns. "That's all that matters." (This bubbling water feature of wisdom was Mother Sulpicia, who had joined the convent after a stretch at a Zen monastery, albeit one of those comfy progressive ones with the diversity prayer flags strung between the electric car charging station and the bank of solar panels. She still had a touch of the Timothy Leary about her.)

Dr. Phineas Fairfax (who had not drawn back his head in surprise) clarified matters. Nodding toward the chapel and a small metropolis of huddling, useful-looking buildings around it, he said, "You're at the Sorbo-Ruthenian Women's Monastery of Blessed Charles of Austria and the Servant of God Zita of the Exarchy of Blainesville. It's also their fruit farm."

"But you said I was at Orphis."

"You were at Orphis, until you insisted on getting some exercise by running away. On the other side of the orchard is Orphis. It is a bit of a multiverse here, I admit, but we've been good neighbors for years, and we help each other out as the need arises." He lowered a warm, firm hand onto Bobby's bony shoulder. "Once more, welcome to Orphis. But," he said simply, "you are free to go."

"Why would he want to?" warbled a nunly voice.

"Well, I certainly don't know," chimed another.

"I think he should just go." The naysayer was the mysterious young woman.

"And maybe you'll get your wish," said Mother Deborah. "In the meantime: Girls, psalms." And with the sun beginning to set and the cool perfume of leaves, grass, and unpruned fruit trees rising into the air, she and her subordinates set off, their butterfly nets limp over their shoulders.

✳✳✳

Alone with Dr. Fairfax and the girl, Bobby for some reason—and he had several to choose from—felt a tentacle of dread slowly twining about him. As the doctor quietly rubbed the boxy head of one of the beastly dogs, Bobby began picturing himself in a gray smock and tinfoil football helmet, going by a new intergalactic name, with a blank look in his eyes and a permanent stoop working the fields, cultivating purple kale for the rest of his days.

He broke out of this vision when he heard, "Again, you are always free to go."

And the girl was more than willing to head up his deportation committee. "That's right," she piped up. "You can go."

The doctor intervened. "I don't think you two have been properly introduced. Robert J. Lumbar, rising star of the science world, Zoe Feldspar."

Zoe's eyes shrank in suspicion, but her crabby mouth managed a perfunctory "Hello," and she unenthusiastically offered a hand. Bobby squeezed it for a second or two longer than society approved. It was small and soft.

"Very good," said Phineas Fairfax. "But the sun's going down, and we wouldn't want to be caught in the orchard at night."

A subatomic spark of self-preservation glowed awake inside Bobby. "Uh, why?"

"Because in the dark, you might end up coming out onto Smithville Road—and no one wants that."

Going to one of the ATVs, the doctor saddled himself onto it as if mounting a polo pony. "I suspect the mothers won't mind if we borrow them." He gave a sharp whistle and called, "Sangreal! Siege Perelous!" and the two dogs dragged their heavy forms over to the ATV and, after a leap, managed to fit themselves in the scooped-out rear double seat. "And by the way," the doctor said, "you might have startled Mother Johanna."

"You scared Mother Johanna?" asked Zoe, her scandalized voice both a mutter and a gasp.

"Inadvertently, I'm sure. You see, Robert, Mother Johanna's not used to unannounced visitors in her tower. That's why she lives there. I'd suggest a simple note of apology. I have an old 1927 Emily Post for your reference. And also, I think you dropped this." He tossed him a small round object in a neat arc.

Bobby caught the talk ball that had so recently channeled Dr. Sheena Lypotrope to him, then instinctively looked at Zoe, hoping that she had been impressed by his dexterous athleticism. Their eyes did meet, then she looked away, as if informing him that, really, it was just a lucky catch (which it was).

Giving the ATV a chuggy start, the doctor asked over the put-put of the engine, "Zoe?" She smiled agreeably at him. "Please come see me in the lab on your return. I have a special job for you." And with a rev of the handles, he and his canine companions zoomed off, disappearing into the trees of the eventide orchard.

Alone with Zoe, Bobby Lumbar felt like a nervous prehistoric lizard ready to take tentative flight and become *Archaeopteryx*—or get swallowed alive. But choosing to spread his wings, he headed for an ATV, prepared to vault upon it like a four-wheeled charger and summon this maid to join him for a gay jaunt under the sunset then filling the sky.

(Bobby had no idea how to operate this or any other small-engine machine, but figured that he could learn by doing.) Before he could make an idiot of himself, though, Zoe marched past him, jumped on one herself, and after a dismissive blow of exhaust, was bumping away alone into the orchard.

"Hey!" Bobby yelled out after her.

The ATV slowed to a stop, its brake lights glowing red like the eyes of a predator.

"Maybe I can ride with you," he said, not decorating the words with a question mark.

The ATV reversed straight backward, and he jumped aside before being flattened.

"Hold on," she said and Bobby complied, conveniently forgetting how things had played out over the last twenty-four hours when other folks had been behind the wheel.

✳✳✳

Upon arriving at Orphis, Bobby followed a very taciturn Zoe into one of the dim quiet buildings, then down a dim quiet hallway to a door where she delivered a series of rapid (no doubt coded) knocks. The doors opened slowly, almost guardedly, to show Dr. Phineas Fairfax silhouetted in the warm yellowish light of a laboratory. (This Bobby knew at a glance—or at a smell, since these places all tended to exude fumes.) He told her, "There's something just for you in the blue tub. Just be gentle. I'll back in a little while." And as she slipped alone over the threshold, the doctor stepped out, shutting the door firmly behind him.

"Come, Robert," and Dr. Fairfax marched Bobby to a drab laundry room, where he gave to him a pile of warm, neatly folded bedclothes squeezed between his manicured hands. "I'm sure they'll fit you. These were Avery's. He doesn't need them anymore."

There then followed a journey to a drab door. "This is your room," the doctor said. "Russell by now should be sinking into delta sleep, so you shouldn't go in, yet."

He then led Bobby straight down the dim quiet hall to a drab washroom. "The water is hot and the towels are clean. Good night." He turned away, his white form dissolving in the gloom of the corridor like the specter that Ian and Noah swore haunted Level V.

After a long spell in the washroom scouring himself clean of his first kidnapping, his brush with death with Felipe and Darshan, his entrapment in the back of that blond's SUV, his second kidnapping by Phineas Fairfax, his escape from his "rescuer," his climb up the water tower, his climb down the water tower, his run through the haunted orchard, and his discovery of the prettiest girl that any madhouse had to offer, Bobby Lumbar, shaven, scrubbed, and clad in Avery's bedclothes, traveled nervously alone back up the dim corridor to his new digs and quietly went inside.

He made out on a neighboring bed, half hidden in the dark, another human male, motionless but snoring—probably knocked out by some proprietary concoction of "all-natural" ingredients from the herb garden. Bobby's own half of the room offered a narrow regulation bed and a miniscule writing desk. On it sat a gooseneck lamp, the cone of its glow onto the desk illuminating, like survivors huddling around a campfire, a bowl of soup, one half of a sandwich, a glass of clear liquid—Bobby hoped that it was water—a pair of writing pens, an envelope, writing paper embossed with

and on a dainty lectern, a volume of Emily Post, copyrighted 1927 by the looks of it.

With as much pluck as he could muster, he penned his awkward regrets to the mysterious Mother Johanna. But between glances at the talk ball, sitting on the desktop and glowing like the first star of night, and searching through the desk drawers for sealing wax and a personal seal for that timeless touch, Bobby also spent more than a little time flipping through the pages in the old, musty tome to find, if he could, any matronly tips on how to compose a good love note.

CHAPTER IX

FLEEING THE SCENE,
OR ESCAPE IS FUTILE

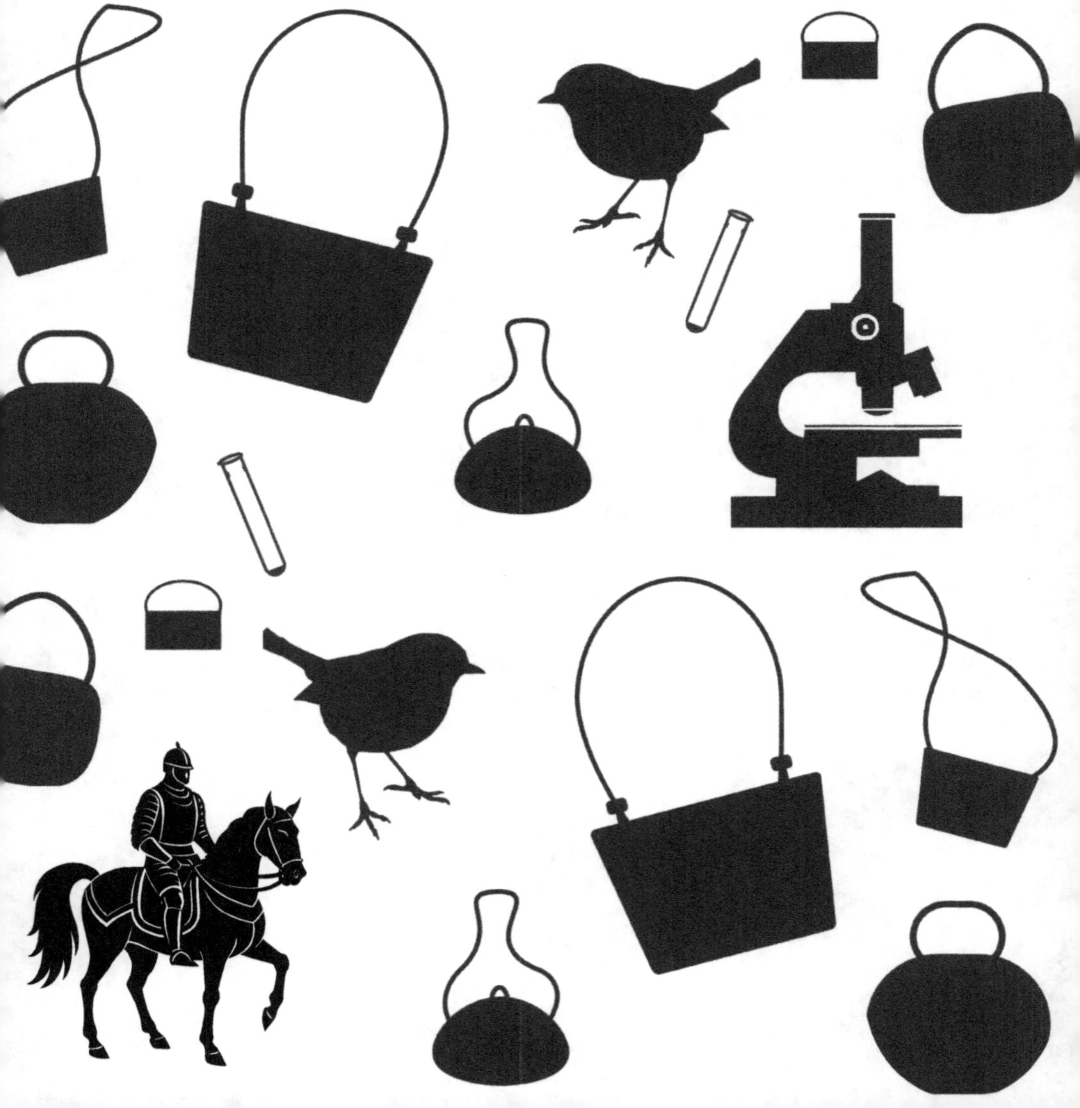

That same evening, back in downtown Merryweather, the three chums marked for death were not in a festive mood.

After their grateful escape from 2525 Center Street, Bella, Baba, and Martie had tried to work out an escape by poring over timetables for any upcoming red-eye flights, camel caravans, or Andaman Island junks departing for obscure corners of the world. They tried texting any "close friends" who might put them up while they had emergency reconstructive surgery done, only to find that all of the big-name social media titans (after a cool word from Sheena Lypotrope...?) had blocked, suspended, and otherwise pulled the plug on their accounts. Finally, they shone a few lights into the corners of the dark web for arms dealers able to overnight express a little firepower, only for a mob of Ad-Bots™, a special creation of MAXIFAX, to pop up over their screens, hiding from their desperate eyes any "questionable" material. At that point, drained of all hope but needing to refuel, they slipped into the Muff-Muff Cupcake Bar, since a situation of so gross a magnitude obviously demanded artisanal pastries.

At their dainty tile-topped table next to the window, Bella, Baba, and Martie, like aged runway models thinking that their figures still mattered, sat picking at a Moon of Heaven, a bulbous lychee nut and lotus root steamed bun, grateful that, for the time being at least, Sheena Lypotrope was ignoring them, since she was having her face-time with Dr. Helsingfors. (And they meant "face-time" literally; although no one wanted to say it out loud for fear of ending up on a missing-persons report, lately Sheena had been looking a bit puffy under the eyes.)

But her appointment must have come to an end, since before any of them could nibble another pill of sticky steamed dough, their handhelds chimed, beeped, and/or trilled in unison: Sheena Lypotrope was emailing them the "cartographic projection" (or "map," in Martie's lexicon).

Opening the message, each lady saw a map (or cartographic projection) encompassing an area generous in size but skimpy on details, with many unlabeled tortuous white lines and meandering blue lines. Already acquainted with Sheena Lypotrope's version of "Oh, it's right down the road," Bella laid her phone down, and Baba, not wishing to squint too long at her screen and risk irreparable crow's feet, admitted, "I have no idea where this place is. Time to call it a day." But it was Martie who provided a bit of childlike ballast. "Why don't we just ask someone?"

"Martie, sweetie," Baba reminded her, "this is Merryweather."

"Where the Good Life Is," chirped Martie, parroting the Chamber of Commerce.

"And...?" prompted Baba.

"...speaking to your neighbors is not part of the Good Life."

"That's right," Baba said, and turning her doomed, swanlike neck to take in the evening street scene past the window, she gave a nonchalant wave to the mental health van cruising by.

Suddenly, Bella whispered, "Down!" and as one the trio huddled down over their lunar dough ball.

"Tell me, Bella dear," asked Baba, deep in the huddle, "why am I losing my dignity in public?"

"Bag Ladies," warned Bella.

"Where?" asked Martie.

"At the croissant trolley."

"But this is a *cupcake* bar."

"Across the street," hissed Bella and bobbed her head at the window. All three carefully rotated their gazes to the glass and peered through the passing electric cars to the May We? Patisserie, the neighborhood competition to Muff-Muff. Through its wide, inviting front windows, they spied a pair of the Bag Ladies surreptitiously purchasing flaky Gallic breakfast rolls in anticipation of their own much-needed midnight snack.

"Hold still," Bella said. "As long as we don't move..."

"I heard that's not true," said Martie, without loosening a single muscle fiber.

"If the end is near," said Baba, rhetorically breaking ranks to straighten up, "then why not a cigarette?"

Dragging her to the tabletop by her metallic orange hair, Bella said, "Down."

"As a favor to an old friend," Baba winced.

Bella whispered, "I'm the only friend you've got right now." After a simper from Martie, she told her, "You know you're more than a friend, honey."

Her simper swelled into "You're mean."

"And cruel," said Baba, patting her hair. "Who exactly are we talking about?" She gave a prairie-dog look across to May We?.

"Frannie and Angela," Baba stated definitively, watching them salaciously overseeing the counter staff nestle their pastry-flour-and-powdered-sugar dietary depth charges into little pink boxes. "Those poor doughnuts won't survive the trip to the front door."

"Oink, oink," whispered Martie, ballooning her cheeks. "Why don't they just glue it to their hips?"

"I know. But if Frannie and Angela operate true to form, they might just dart over here for a second course."

"So, while their snouts are in the trough...," said Bella.

As Baba took a quick après-snack hit from her vaping pen and Martie dropped the rest of the Moon of Heaven into her bag, Bella gave a strafing gaze over the heads of the half-employed sociology majors clogging the other tables for a bit of cover—and, lucky day, heading for the exit was another cluster of carb-loaded ladies, social workers by the sound of them. (Bella had earlier overheard some of their chatter, laced with jargon like "active listening," "people-centered approaches," and "culturally specific programs.") They would work as human shields.

Humming along behind these idealists, Bella, Baba, and Martie rode their wake safely out the door to the world outside. They were just about to slip away, when from across the street shot a pair of keening wails, like banshees in a contralto sing-along. To the tooty medley of hybrid-car horns and the rubbery skid of recycled tires, Angela and Frannie were charging across the street in full-frontal assault.

Armchair tacticians still shuttlecock opposing theories as to why the Bag Ladies, numbering only two, made an assault against foes numbering three, and in a manifestly public place with so many social media junkies on hand, ready to record and post the fracas worldwide. Theory A, labeled the Wolves-Upon-the-Fold, argues that the Bag Ladies imagined that Martie was alone, Baba and Bella being obscured behind a facade of social workers, and the advantage was theirs. Theory B is the Stab-in-the-Back, asserting that a third or even fourth Bag Lady lay at the ready to fall upon our heroines in a pincer movement, but that something fore-stalled their participation—betrayal, cowardice, or lack of provisioning (*read* they had not finished their own cupcakes at Muff-Muff). And, in fact, there exists Theory C, the Light Brigade, which argues that bad intel misdirected Angela and Frannie to charge. But who was the source of this malfeasance? And thus, buds forth yet another sub-school of speculation...

The facts were as follows: Having negotiated the busy evening street, Frannie and Angela, like carnivorous wallabies, made a leap with their bionic legs and landed in the midst of their prey. The melee soon cycloned into a swirl of limbs, string tops, and overpriced handbags. Angela was baying for some segment of internal tubing that she thought Martie could do without; in response, Martie deployed her Birkin bag, hammering it on Angela's nape, ears, nose, and any other zone that might feel pain. Baba, meanwhile, was in a tangle with Frannie, who was demanding a tissue sample. Bella divided her energies between them, forcing a gap be-tween one pair of combatants and then the other, only to hear the first pair fall back on each. Because the combatants were fairly well matched, the rounds of play went on and on, not allowing for a break for station identification.

But as this rock-'em, sock-'em grudge match stretched to its rub-bery breaking point, up drove a black-and-white and out stepped two of Merryweather's finest, Officers Capricia Johnson and Imelda Martinez-Perez, nocturnal blue-blockers in position and batons at the ready.

The rat-a-tat of Officer Johnson's baton on an arts-and-entertainment weekly news box brought about a brief cessation of play.

At halftime, the players did not make an attractive bunch. Those candid shots of the Merryweather Scrumptious Mud women's rugby team lying in the mutilated turf with cleat marks on their faces were like glossy eight-by-ten glamour shots beside this montage of snarling, semiconscious, half-alive, half-dead mugs staring up at the two officers.

Officer Johnson asked, "You ladies awake?"

The bruised faces continued to stare, perhaps with the hope that one of them would volunteer to clear everything up with these minions of the law.

However, since the miscreants were exercising their right to remain silent, said minions of law took things into their own latex-gloved hands, with Officer Johnson latching on to Bella—she was the closest—and hauling her up from the pavement.

"So, what's going on?" she asked, while Officer Martinez-Perez, with waves of her baton, directed the other bedraggled combatants to untangle themselves and stand up.

Once these innocent-until-proven-guilty molls were more or less upright, Officer Johnson began collecting just the facts, ma'am. "Girls' night out?" she asked.

"I wouldn't say 'girls,'" contributed Officer Martinez-Perez.

"Uh-huh. So?"

Martie began story hour by pointing a twiggy finger at Frannie and Angela as the Ones Who Started It All. This accusatory kabuki did not sit well with Frannie and Angela, and within a second our little conventicle of hooliganism had yanked open a butterfly box of excuses, exculpations, and recriminations.

Trying to keep a clear head amid this confetti of claim and counterclaim, Officer Johnson raised a hand to remind them about that right to remain silent, when suddenly from above, a barrage of laser blasts shot down, blowing up the entertainment weekly box in a papery cloud of art house movie reviews.

The officers shrank down to the pavement, and their suspects would have joined them, except that their instinct for survival, enigmatically, was overcoming their instinct for survival. As another rain of blasts bounced about them, Bella, Baba, and Martie, like sheep forced to join the wolves, ran desperately up the street in the same direction as the Bag Ladies, with the shrieks of yet more blasts sounding behind them.

✳✳✳

After a shared sharp right turn, the five ladies stopped for a breather. But any chance for a pleasant spell of camaraderie dwindled to nil when Baba, using a convenient storefront window to inspect her hair, saw that her coppery top of hair was so mangled, misaligned, and half plucked that she could have passed for an old red hen left hanging in the barn. Releasing a vicious hiss of shock and rage, she wheeled about, raised her amber-orange claws, and lunged savagely at Frannie and Angela, ready to seize flesh, hair, and cellulite.

Just then, a crisp superheated sleet of laser blasts was charring the pavement and through the ribbons of smoke rising from the sidewalk descended a talk ball.

They heard, "How long does it take..." These words fizzled out amid pulses of static interference, then crystallized into "...do not like this kind of publicity? I forget whether *gratitude*..." and the words crackled apart again as a hologram of Dr. Sheena Lypotrope shivered into visibility above them. While lacking any dreadful majesty—the neon illumination of Merryweather-after-dusk imparted a more intimate glow—she nonetheless impressed.

Laying aside any desire to strangle each other, our cowering turkey-necked troublemakers guessed what Sheena Lypotrope meant about not liking "this kind of publicity." The videos of their street brawl must have been debuting on the interweb even before the punches had landed. But while Bella, Baba, Frannie, and Angela kept their eyes screwed to the hologram, it was Martie who broke out of their mutual-protection society and, with the fearlessness of the simple-minded, bared her perfectly polished teeth. "Maybe we don't care what you think!"

This contumacious and overweening defiance of the set order of the universe draped an almost cosmic silence over the scene.

"You have no right to bother us! You have no right to chase us around! And you have *no right—*"

But before she could call this final foul, Dr. Lypotrope asked, "Is that so?" and the hologram expanded, spreading and filling the air with streaming ropes of orange and purple energy, like a nebula manifesting unto the edges of the universe. (If Dr. Lypotrope had been trying to avoid unnecessary publicity, she was failing.)

This did not daunt Martie. "Yes, that is so!" she said, and with a quickness that startled all and sundry, she snatched the talk ball from the air.

Sheena Lypotrope's two-dimensional eyes bugged out, and her flat hands clutched and clawed at the air, and with blobs of the hologram oozing from between her fingers, an eye here, a nose there, Martie squeezed her hand tight and yelled at her fist. "You be quiet in there! You talk too much! You need a time-out!" Then, not picky about personalities, she shot a command at the fugitives behind her. "Hey, you there!"

Bella hurried up with that captain-my-captain spirit, and Martie nodded at an entertainment weekly box. "Open it!" she said, but in all the excitement, Bella stood staring at the box as if it were a time bomb running a little fast. "Come on! Grab the handle and pull it open, or do I need to get someone who didn't just have her peroxide rinse?"

Frannie started to offer her services (the envy of her generation of units, she was an actual blond), but at the last second, Bella found her jungle-cat reflexes and opened the door and Martie plunged her fist inside, exiling the ball into the sticky bottom of the box, a ninth circle of mildewed to-go latte cups, ant-covered microwave burrito wrappers, and a mid-1980s hardbound romance novel that no one had read in the first place.

"Now close it, quick!" she ordered, and Bella let go of the handle, with the spring-loaded metal door slamming shut...right onto Martie's delicate fingertips.

"Charlotte!" she bawled, shaking her fingers, which made them hurt all the more.

Baba came to her side. "Oh, honey," she clucked, tightening her lips and examining the injured digits with sigh of sisterly disappointment. Even by neon light, anyone could see that Martie's very recent acrylic extensions, like a gleaming city of marble and statuary, had been in an instant reduced to utter ruination. "And they even had little rhinestones."

"Cubic"—sniffle—"zirconciums."

"Well, heroics have their price. After I have a smoke—"

"But they hurt *now!*" wailed Martie with a deluge of tears. "How can I text with sore fingers?"

"Then I guess you can't. Bella dear?"

Bella had been ignoring her friends just then, because she had entered into an impromptu staring match with Frannie and Angela. No one wanted to be the first to leave, nor did anyone wanted to stick around, lest Officers Johnson and Martinez-Perez give chase—or another talk ball appear, complete with Dr. Sheena Lypotrope in full battle array. It took Baba, ever the mature realist, to announce like a barkeep at 2:00 a.m., "All right, everyone, the party's over. Bella, honey, this way. Frannie, love? Angela, sweetie? There's an all-night poetry slam around the corner. You'll see the sign."

Frannie pointed somewhat to the right, suggesting, "So, this way...?" With an insincere smile, she and Angela retreated to the nearest intersection to dart out of sight. Maybe there was still time for another croissant.

Bella turned back to her *compadriñas*. "Well, does your bus station have a red-eye to Ecuador?"

"Just a second," sniffled Martie. She was trying to balance her handheld on her knees and tap it with her one uninjured digit. "I'm seeing if I can find an all-night mani place."

"All I know," announced Baba, giving her mussed-up hair a pat, "is that in the morning, I'll need a little urgent care at my private day spa. Maybe they can help you out too, sweetheart."

And so, our heroines departed, leaving the lanes of Merryweather all the quieter, save for the blast after blast of a talk ball trying to escape from its glass and metal cage.

CHAPTER X

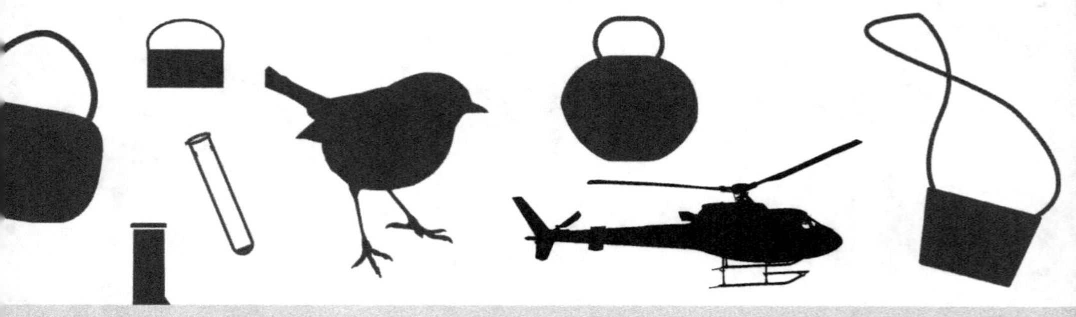

MORNING IN ORPHIS, OR CRACKING THE COSMIC EGG

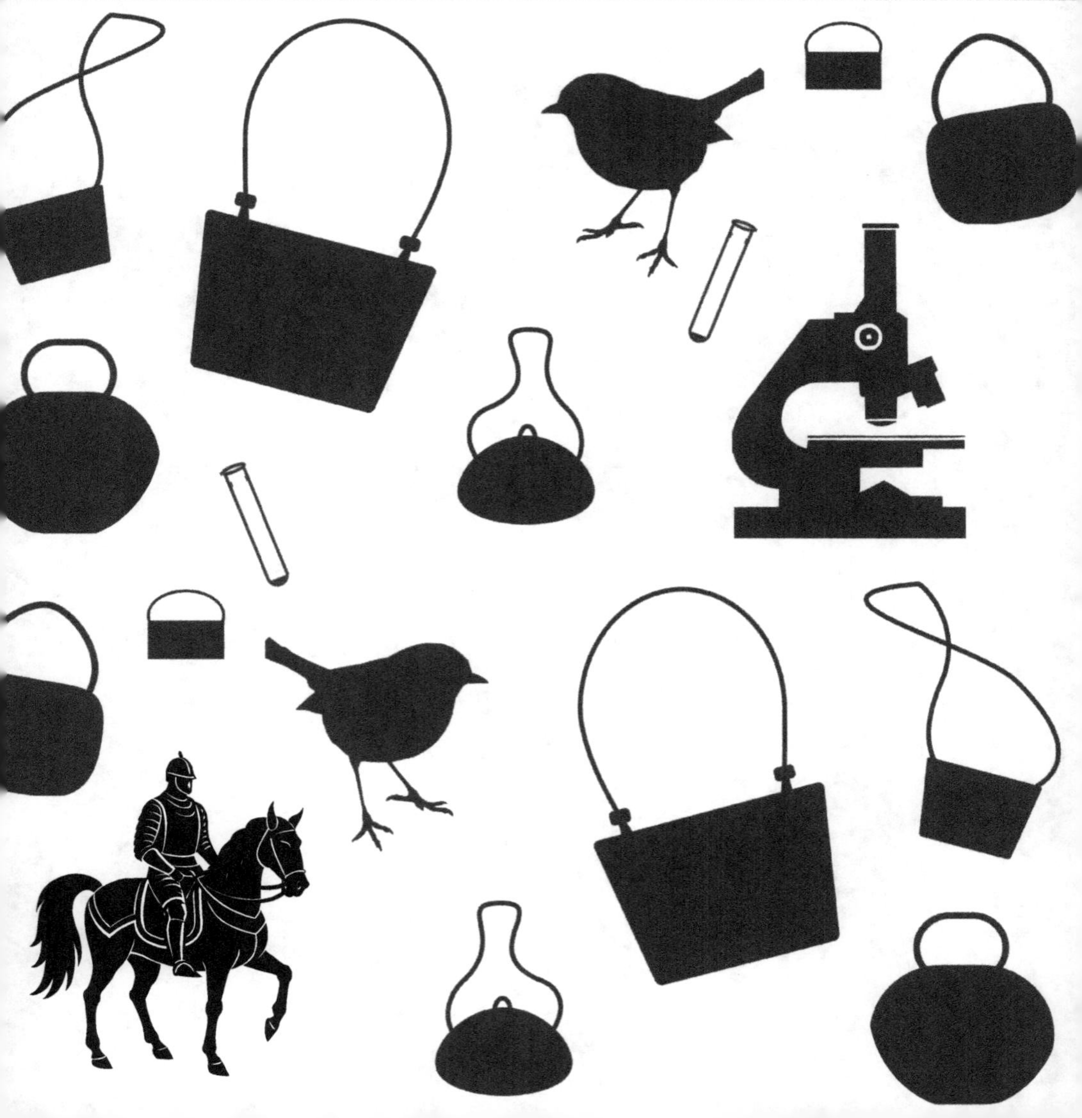

Bobby Lumbar awoke to slanting beams of morning sunlight shining on his face, as if the searchlight of the universe had spotted him, singling him out for further suffering.

But when he saw that the solar system was simply beginning another spring day, he reflexively reached out for his glasses at the side table, felt something strange, dragged his find closer, and squinted myopically at a brand-new pair of spectacles, like a gilded mantis staring back at him. Landing them into position, he looked about for whatever dangers lurked in his new biome.

First of all, the light of morn floating through the polyester curtains dished up for him, like breakfast in bed for the eyes, his roommate Russell's half of the room. Russell had gone, and his bed, negligently unmade, stretched huddled and oppressed beneath a kind of wailing wall plastered with placards, bumper stickers, a basement-printed raised fist on a piece of eight-by-twelve paper, monosyllabic slogans, and silkscreened political posters, all in hues of capitalist-blood red, purity-of-intentions white, and ecological-collapse black.

Other than this left-of-the-Left decor, though, he noticed a tidy pile of new duds on the chair at his desk.

Creeping from his bed, he inspected them: a white Oxford shirt, a clip-on red bow tie, manly foundation garments toxically pungent from a floral laundry detergent, calf-hugging black socks, Florsheims, unpleated beige slacks as smooth as chamois cloth, a pocket protector still maidenly in its crinkly plastic wrapper, and hanging on a hook on the back of the door, like a waterfall down a lonesome cliff, the sartorial coup de grâce: a lab coat.

He then found a triangle of paper sticking out from the velvety folds of the slacks. After cautiously extracting it like a poisoned arrowhead, he read:

Suit up, young man.

—Ph. F., PhD

Having donned this costume, Bobby Lumbar slipped his mea culpa to Mother Johanna in his pocket, tidied his bed and felt slightly superior to Russell, and scanned the terrain to be sure that he had everything—only to realize that he had nothing. He had no idea where his smartphone, wallet, or car keys were hiding (or being held hostage). But what was the loss of security, money, movement, communication, and knowledge, with a talk ball sitting on a corner of the desk, ready to be your pal?

Before he dropped this new friend into a pocket, Bobby gave the ball a quick look—only to find that, like Nietzsche's abyss, it was staring back at him. Over its gleaming silvery surface, an attractive face was coming into view.

"Bobby?" it asked. "I can just see you, Bobby."

"Sheena?" he said.

"Where are you?"

"I'm at Orphis."

"Good. Good. Where's Phin?"

"Dr. Fairfax? I don't know."

"What do you mean you don't know?"

"I just woke up."

She snapped, "And why were you sleeping?" Quickly, her tiny face softened, taking on a halo suitable for a dream sequence or a walk by the lake. "Just find out as much as you can, tiger. You know, all I want is for you to make it out of there alive."

Bobby wanted to ask why he should not make it out of there alive, when a rude and rapid rapping came at the door.

"That's Phin. Don't let him out of your sight. And get him to talk."

A second fusillade of rapping was like a bazooka barraging the door with jawbreakers. "Steffany!" sounded a sharp, ear-stabbing, but marginally feminine, claxon call. "I know you're in there!"

"I gotta go," Bobby whispered into his hand. "I'll tell you what I find out."

"Whatever you say. Just be careful, big man."

As another hailstorm of knocks echoed through the door, Bobby popped the ball into a pocket, shuffled charily to the site of the attack, and with shaking hand, gave the doorknob a twist.

In the doorway stood a squat biped, potentially female, with pastrycook forearms and tree-stump legs, her feet crammed into combat boots, and wearing a T-shirt dismembered of its sleeves and informing 49 percent of the population:

You put the ick in toxic masculinity

Her drill sergeant hair was dyed magenta with lemon-yellow highlights, and the piercings penetrating the different cartilages about her head rivetted down the idea that this lady was no friend to traditional womanly beauty. On top of these, she was goggling at him through a cyclopean black eye, and Bobby felt secure assigning her to the same genus, if different species, as Rachael in Reporting. But as soon she spoke, Bobby knew that any relationship with Rachael was only cursory, in the same way that the luckless day hiker realizes too late that the grizzly mama bear about to devour him has nothing to do with the gentle panda nibbling bamboo shoots.

She immediately tommy-gunned him with, "What'd you do to Steffany? Is she hiding in here?"

Bobby tried a placatory "She's not here right now?" inadvertently asking a question back at her.

"Well, *duh,* beta boy. What'd you do with her?"

Bobby went deeper into the maze. "Well, Dr. Fairfax—"

"Patriarchist!"

Bobby tried to think on his feet but staggered. "I don't know what that means?"

"You sent Russell to the organ harvesters! You and that andronormative hegemonist! Now, what about Steffany?"

Bobby wanted to check with Emily Post (so near, yet so far) for some filler to mollify this harpy, but considering all that he had seen so far, maybe Phineas Fairfax was actually sending his patients via one-way coach class to Wuhan Province.

Now, like a punkified La Pucelle before Orléans, she was charging her figurative postmodern palfrey over the moat. "I know what this place is all about. And I know what you're all about too, little boy."

This was one crossbow bolt too many, and though he felt more than a little embarrassed for standing up for himself, Bobby heard himself say, "Well, you know, Zoe's a nice girl. Maybe—"

This landed like a coconut on a corrugated metal roof. Her already livid face turned as magenta as her hair, the white of her one good eye yellowed with enough bile to match her highlights, and spraying a fountain of slobber, white hot with rage, she brayed, *"Never say that word!"* She delivered a sucker punch into his solar plexus, leaving Bobby on the floor curled up in confusion, self-pity, oxygen deprivation, and inglorious defeat, to the stomp-stomp-stomp of her combat boots fading away down the hall.

In time, though, Bobby did manage to stagger upright and poke his head into the hall.

His assailant was nowhere in sight.

So, he set off, with hunched shoulders and an occasional backward glance, shuffling away in what he hoped was the opposite direction of his attacker.

✳✳✳

Bobby passed door after anonymous door. He guessed that most opened into innocent bedrooms or offices, but with each successive step, as the tread of his new shoes joined with the crackling of the fluorescent light that ran up the center of the ceiling, seemingly into the ultimate horizon, Bobby felt that something about Orphis made the narrative of late-night AM radio seem very, very plausible. He could not shake the notion that one of these unassuming bedroom doors might just open into paradimensional enclaves, places where the Ethereans or the Astralites were perfecting their unlooked-for strike against Plane Primus (a.k.a. dear old planet Earth).

In time, the hallway did end, at what Bobby hoped was a safe, earthbound portal. Daring to the door, he did not plunge into the Omicron Realms, but stepped into the budding springtime morning, warm with sunshine, sweet with the smells of apple blossom, and loud with the mating call of many a bird. How bad a place could Orphis be, he let himself think, with a breeding population of house finches and lazuli buntings inhabiting the shrubbery? So, Bobby innocently took in the cult center that was Orphis.

Surrounding him on three sides was a compound of one-story buildings suggesting the Carter era. To one side he saw a muddy pack of ATVs, no doubt napping before another afternoon of chasing unsuspecting strangers; to another, a stodgy metal-sided barn suitable for weekend carpentry (or to house the generator for that eventual siege by government forces); at his feet spread that not-so-innocuous gravel lot...and at its far end a gravel road curling away out of sight.

Then Zoe Feldspar came into view.

Flitting along, she was singsonging some sort of silly scansion about the clouds of puffy piglet pink that prettify the sleepy sky for those magical minutes before begins this dandy day. (Admittedly, a rough rendering.)

Bobby called out, "Zoe?" but like any giggling, winsome, woodland spirit—or the undiscovered female of *B. lumbarensis*—Zoe simply carried on offering her villanelle to the morn, caroling to the larks and nightingales. (Naturally, Bobby recognized that, based upon the visible woody plant species, neither larks nor nightingales were endemic to this bioregion. But he was more than ready to indulge Zoe's poetic fancies—or anything else she had in mind.)

Before Bobby could warble her name once more, though, she had curled in carefree reverie out of sight around one of the plywood structures.

It is not necessary to plumb too deeply the workings of a young man's mind on a sun-dappled morn in springtime. Yes, seconds earlier, he had been trying to escape—and he was on a mission for Dr. Sheena Lypotrope. But now in battle with (and ready to surrender to) a new and overpowering gravity, he happily set after his pretty prey with a percolating eagerness.

Bobby took the very track that Zoe had just tread, fully expecting to find a field of poppies peopled with frolicsome nymphs and fauns...only to stumble into a sort of terrarium from the Triassic period.

Hoping that he had not been teleported to Gondwanaland, Bobby saw that he had stepped into a spacious patio planted as a tropical diorama of somewhere sticky, malarial, and hot. He was no botanist but recognized swaying banana trees, rustling bamboos, a potted palm, a fig tree or two, a bank of grandiose ferns—and the two outsized dogs he had met in the orchard the afternoon before.

Apotropaic and sphinxlike, they growled in unison, until Dr. Phineas Fairfax, sitting behind them and sipping from a demitasse cup, said, "Sangreal...Siege Perelous...," and they resumed the pose of statues flanking the steps into any county courthouse.

The lord of Orphis was taking his ease in an antique cast-iron garden chair before an antique cast-iron garden table on which gleamed a dainty arrangement of porcelain dishes, all as delicate as peony petals. The glow of the morning dappling the fronds and foliage also showed to good effect the doctor's heathen-red hair, now ennobled and knightly, as well as his glacially white lab coat. He appeared engrossed in a small leather-bound volume of Victorian poetry, while a small breakfast sat patiently to one side awaiting the inevitable. After a last scan, he laid the tiny tome on the table, took a sip from his tiny cup, and gave Bobby a look up and down. "Yes," he said with satisfaction, "your new *toga virilis* suits you. How do you like my little replica of paradise? I'd watched an old film about a planter in the Federated Malay States and thought, why not here? Are you hungry? Let's feed you." Rising, he dabbed his unsullied mouth with a monogrammed napkin.

At this, the dogs sat up in unison for whatever gobbets of food the master was supplying from his Ming dynasty tableware. Under their sagging but grateful gazes, Dr. Fairfax distributed baksheesh of buttered bread while asking Bobby, "Did you pen your missive to Mother Johanna?"

Bobby reached in his pocket and found his homework while feeling the buzz of the talk ball.

"Hmm," said the doctor, gently rubbing his ear. "Maybe my tinnitus is getting the better of me. Well, no matter." He noted the note in Bobby's hand. "Just give it to Zoe and she'll bring it to Mother Johanna with her fan mail."

Those sweet syllables ("Zoe," that is, not "is," "her," "of," "fan mail," etc.) set Bobby back on his instinctive course, like a bird of passage coming out of a monsoon. Forgetting thoughts of nourishment and tinfoil hats, he asked, "So, where is...?"

"Zoe?" Dr. Fairfax pushed his iron chair against the table. "I'm not certain. She did dance through here a moment ago."

Right then, a flock of chipper nuns made their cheerful way around the corner and encircled the doctor. While they wore black habits, Bobby noted a clash about the heads, each sporting a brightly dyed ball cap of cornstalk green and stitched with sunflower-yellow lettering and apple-red piping declaring in state fair barker boldness:

Strange Sisters Fruit Farm

Sangreal and Siege Perelous slapped their tails in unison on the paving stones at these sugary invaders, who were now pummeling Dr. Fairfax with details of the day's upcoming pilgrimage. There would be a tour of the chapel to see the miraculous icon, then a tour of the convent complex, then a tour of the berry fields, and maybe a sermon from Mother Johanna if she looked down from her water tower. The good doctor heard the itinerary with the dispassion of a generalissimo receiving a report that the banana republic next door was being invaded by CIA-backed insurgents, then allowed himself a charitable smile. "You'll have a full day, then, won't you?" At this, the consecrated maidens shared a sigh that Bobby Lumbar thought sounded like, "Yes, Doctor."

But an unseasonable bank of clouds drifted over their sunny faces when Dr. Fairfax said, "You know, though, I have to visit town, so I cannot make it. Robert here will deputize for me." The nuns rotated toward Bobby Lumbar and pouted. "Well, you have a busy day in front of you. Off you go."

This acted as a strong wind on their disappointment and to a chorus of "Oh, yes, Doctor, yes, Doctor," they wove away through the banana fronds, to attack what sounded to Bobby like a very full schedule.

As the rev of ATVs broke through the greenery and then trailed away, the doctor smiled. "It keeps them busy, when they're not interceding for our fallen world."

"What was with...?" Bobby asked, pointing to his head.

"The Strange Sister Orchards. The mothers have to support themselves somehow. It's ironic that even voluntary poverty costs money. If you'll forgive a bit of Merryweather history..."

"Merryweather?" asked Bobby.

"Our town. Not far, as the crow flies," he said, while impolitely failing to show in which direction civilization lay. Then, like a docent from the county historical museum, he explained, "The orchards came to the mothers as bequest. It was a very odd concatenation of circumstances, but in brief: The Evil Smiths—"

"The Evil Smiths?"

"The Evil Smiths. Old Merryweather stock. Not nice people. In any event, the Evil Smiths established this latifundium in the 1970s as the Strange Fruits Company. But the State Agricultural and Fruit Farmers Commission—the most Byzantine cabal of bloodthirsty backstabber and professional revenge killers imaginable—they called it the Stupid Fruits Company, since it was mostly an exotic fruit farm—figs, persimmons, jostaberries, gooseberries—everything that doesn't ship well. Finally, though, their many nefarious deeds caught up with them."

Bobby had already lost the thread of this subplot. "The State Fruit Farmers Commission or the Evil Smiths?"

"The Evil Smiths. About ten years ago, the Evil Smiths needed to escape the country PDQ, and by donating their land to the mothers, they arranged for a tax write-off to provide for future funds while they sit things out in Bolivia growing genetically engineered hazelnut-infused coffee beans. I like to imagine that they were also trying to buy off the Almighty, but on this side of the veil, we'll never know. It's been a chore for the mothers, redeeming the wilderness from all that neglect and misuse. The part of the orchard that you decided to explore yesterday still has not come under the pruning hook."

"Yeah, I noticed," said Bobby.

"Experience is the best teacher. But, since about an acre was mulberries, there was some talk about importing silkworms and spinning cloth of gold like Byzantine ladies of yore." Just then, Bobby started to nod from want of breakfast, but the thought that he had heard the word *Byzantine* twice in one morning saved him from toppling forward. (Maybe the Byzantines were the land-shark riders in *Alaric's Trident*.) "Nine hundred years ago, naturally, such plans were all well and good, but when the driplines have to be checked and the drainage ditches are full of carp, who has time to play at Penelope? Fortunately, Mother Deborah has a head for business. But, come now. Orphis awaits!"

And as Phineas Fairfax energetically exited the subtropical patio, Bobby hurried along, trying to catch his lab coat tails, while Sangreal and Siege Perelous lumbered behind, their drooling jaws at the ready should this newcomer step out of line.

✳✳✳

As the older man moved briskly around one of the buildings, Bobby Lumbar asked, "Um, so why am I here?"

"To assist me," answered the doctor, not slowing at all. "There's work to do."

"Work?" Right then, Bobby felt the talk ball vibrate violently in his pocket, and he slapped his hand on it, hoping that he had hit the Off button.

"Important work," proceeded the doctor, his pace keeping abreast with his presentation. "You'll be good at it, I'm sure."

He arrived at a nondescript outside door and came to a swift halt, forcing Bobby to slam on his own brakes.

"Yes, very important work," the doctor continued, drawing out a ring of keys. "Deprogramming. That is what we do here at Orphis. Come and see." Finding the right key, he slid brass into brass, opened the door, and entered, with Sangreal and Siege Perelous pushing Bobby along over the threshold.

Instead of being lured into Dimension Delta, Bobby found himself in a room decorated from floor to ceiling with framed picture portraits in row upon row, practically coiling around the around the walls like great chains of being—along with the occasional testimonial composed of letters cut out from a magazine. Bobby squirmed a bit, suspecting that he had stepped into "sacred space," as his grandmother would have said, for the room held a hush like a kind of auditory incense, and even the dogs sat on their haunches, like acolytes at the ready.

Dr. Fairfax contemplated the many images with a peculiar reverence before declaring, like a hierophant calling upon the spirits of ancestors, "The Gallery of the Ex-Orphs. Those who have left us. Those who are now whole."

While Bobby hoped that "whole" meant "in one piece," Dr. Fairfax repeated like a chant, "The ex-orphs. See here."

He brought his hand to a photograph of a young, spindly fellow. He was swathed in loose hempen garb embroidered with vivid velveteen red, green, and blue, while from his cheeks trailed a lichenous blond beard. This twiggy yeoman might have passed for a medieval peasant just returned to the garth from a long day of tying up hay ricks, save for the fact that he held close to his breast a pink, plush stuffed unicorn, complete with a rainbow-banded horn, a glitter-sprinkled tail, and a silvery mane woven into French braids.

"This was Chiron," said Dr. Fairfax. "His Christian name was Kyle. The unicorn, he'd explained on his first day, was his spirit animal." Mention of spirit animals reminded Bobby of his grandmother, and if a question-and-answer session on crystal therapy, indigo children, or ley lines came up, Bobby knew that could fake his way through it. "Kyle, or Chiron, held on to certain notions about what he called the realm of Faerie. He was a past master on the flowery field pagans, the dappled woodland pagans, the herb garden pagans, the misty landscape pagans, the towering dark forest pagans, and tropical island volcano goddess pagans. His immersion into the field was admirable, and as a scientist, I couldn't fault his taxonomy. But, as with the case of many who pass through Orphis, what should have remained the pleasant domain of the impassioned amateur became a police state. At first, Kyle dressed rather colorfully, which his parents and his friends forgave. Then came the wand, the daily application of glitter body paint, and his own language, which he expected everyone to know, understand, and use—including the police when he was pulled over for expired tags. Finally, Chiron fashioned for himself a pair of huge hymenopteran wings from plastic wrap and coat hangers, as if he were something out of Edmund Spenser, in prelude to his attempt to fly. Plastic wrap, I am sure you can guess, is not suitable for air travel at any altitude. Thankfully, he landed in a duck pond."

"Chiron sounds crazy."

Dr. Fairfax considered his unwilling protégé not unlike a Roman emperor deciding who should end up smothered in rose petals. "'Fully immersed' is what we say at Orphis. As for Kyle—"

"Or Chiron," said Bobby, to show that he had been paying attention.

"—that incident drove his mother to contact me. As already mentioned, Chiron was brilliant in his métier, explicating with a magisterial depth and fullness the nuances between pixies, goblins, sylphs, leprechauns, and so forth, and he did give a bit of color to the place..." Bobby wanted to say that there was a little too much color already. "However—and this was the sticking point—I could not think how to give him what he wanted," the doctor continued, then murmured, "What he wanted, what he wanted..." Turning from the photograph, he held up a finger like an illuminating flame. "Unless the orph gets what he truly wants, he will never heal."

Bobby wanted to raise a finger of his own to solicit a clearer definition of *orph*, but the doctor was proceeding apace.

"You see, Robert, these kinds of disorders—worldview disorders, we might call them—are like personality disorders. Or demonic possession, now that I think of it. I should ask Father Maximilian about that when he visits the mothers this Sunday."

This mention of weekends and Sabbaths reminded Bobby that he had lost all track of time, but Dr. Fairfax was marching on, his tone piledriving and pistonlike.

"The orph never perceives his problem, while those around him do. So, it's the worried parents that make the call—now and then the grandparents, but so many of them are baby boomers who simply excuse their descendants' little eccentricities. Or the frustrated fiancée calls up in tears, usually after her father has met the prospective son-in-law and given him an F– as a graft onto the family tree. Now and then, a compassionate boss reaches out, but usually not, because typically the orph is simply 'let go' and moves on to alienate the next unsuspecting employer. But whoever seeks us out, they discover that Orphis brings about much-needed healing, because it is so simple. At Orphis, we don't drill holes in anyone's heads, and we don't 'talk things out.'"

"So, what...?" Bobby began to ask.

"The people who come to Orphis are perfectly sane," said the doctor. "They simply live in unreality, and here at Orphis, we give them reality. Here at Orphis, we give them what they want. So, I saw that Kyle sought authentic paganism—no reconstruction, no racially sensitive Heathenry, no pastiche altars, no complimentary New Age newspaper in the library lobby. No, he wanted what he imagined polytheism was, at its most frank—howling at the moon, baying through the storm, license at the solstice, and smoking heaps of sacrificed cattle before a three-faced idol."

"That sounds nice?" Bobby half asked, blotting out the holocaust of cows.

"So Chiron thought. It *sounded* nice. So very many things sound nice, like marriage or collectivization, until one truly experiences them." (Bobby guessed that his host was a bachelor and entrepreneur.) "The solution came to me one afternoon when Chiron and I were having an innocent chat—and, no, not in his homemade language. He was cataloging inter alia the prehistoric crimes of the local Indian tribes, saying they had infringed upon the 'mythopoeic terrain' of the Baxwbakwalanuxwsiwe', not to mention displacing the Qoaxqoaxualanuxsiwae..." (Bobby did not even bother asking.) "And then the scenario rose before mine eyes. It would be a dicey proposition, mind you. I had to cash in favors at the morgue and with the lady at the raptor center, and ask our graduate Evan to don a chef's hat and cedar-bark loincloth. But it worked. Chiron got what he wanted and went back to being Kyle. He does still sign his Christmas cards 'Happy Solstice,' but he's holding down a job as the floor manager at the electronics store and now completely refuses to eat red meat in any form."

As Bobby squelched any desire to ask what exactly Chiron/Kyle had endured, but like a majordomo showing dynastic portraits to the hoi polloi, the doctor had moved on down the gallery.

"This orph is..." Bobby hoped that "is" meant that the poor sucker was still alive, even if walled up in a cavity under the work shed with a tube to deliver nutrients to him. Bobby did not catch this one's name, but did hear, "Initially, he had a relationship with his handheld device, which evolved into ethnic identification with it. In time, he was saying things like 'I'm feeling really analog today' and 'My motherboard really wounded me.' He concocted a history of cyber-trauma and requested a cyber-therapist. Here at Orphis, you should know, no communication devices are permitted. To prevent escapism. The orph must experience his emotions. You understand." Bobby nodded, while suddenly recalling the narrow line between escapism and escape. He gave a furtive look around for a half-open door. No such luck.

The doctor stepped up to another picture. "And this is Lola. She was an early orph."

Before this portrait of redemption, a shocked, appalled, and amazed Bobby could only mumble, "Wow..." He was cringing before a photo of a woman in her middle years who, while posing for the camera in the most minimal of wardrobes, was still sufficiently covered for public display, being completely etched, painted, stenciled, decorated, muralled, and gaudified with a seamless panoply of tattoos and piercings, like a walking jungle world of body art: koi fish, cartoon characters, neo-political emblems, the American flag upside down, roses, lilies, nasturtiums, and hollyhocks in bloom, and so on.

Dr. Fairfax said, "Lola was a sad case when she came in. Without painting too detailed a picture, if you'll excuse the expression, Lola sought attention and had spent all of her trust fund money on pole-dancing lessons, tattoos, and piercings to bring this about. To her credit, she did become the state champion aerialist three years running and also taught a class on this particular skill at Merryweather Community College."

Bobby said, "That sound nice?"

"Lola thought so. However, her efforts to become the cynosure of all eyes backfired when she sallied forth into the marriage market and realized both quickly and painfully that none of the men that she wanted wanted a woman that looked, well, as you see. In one quixotic, last-ditch campaign, she thought that she could unroll some canvas to decorate, and so she began to eat and eat and eat in order to make more skin for more tattoos."

"That doesn't sound nice," said Bobby, pushing up his glasses while thinking that he should have taken them off to avoid what he was seeing.

"To her credit, Lola recognized that couldn't very well go back. In fact, she couldn't go anywhere. She had spent all of her money, and none of the, let's say, establishments would hire her on, even as a gag act. On top of that, she'd become too prone to the effects of gravity, to phrase it charitably, to teach her classes. So, Lola came to Orphis."

"Did you give her what she wanted?"

Dr. Fairfax inhaled half stoically, as if both accepting the ways of universe and readying to do battle against them. "No, someone else did," he confessed, and leaving unspoken the details of that professional partnership, strolled along to the next photograph.

He resumed the rhythm of his script. "And this is our Greta."

Bobby now considered a smiling blond, posed sitting on the same antique iron chair that Dr. Fairfax had been warming minutes before. He thought that she could be someone's grown-up sister, until he remembered that creating that "family feeling" was the standard operating procedure among charismatic authoritarian pseudo-father figures.

"We love our Greta," the doctor said, then energetically announced, "Let's go meet her, right now!"

As the dogs loped along after him to a door at the end of the room, Bobby quickly followed too, if only to avoid being left in this room with only Ex-Orphs for company.

✳✳✳

After a sharp turn first here and then there, men and dogs stepped into a fragrant and well-lit kitchen. "Greta, milady!" Dr. Fairfax called out. "Food for this knight errant!"

At the end of a counter laden with ceramic mixing bowls, old jars full of grains and beans, a row of copper pots, and a few mid-1950s cookbooks, the pretty blond woman from the photograph looked up from a pair of gal-vanized pots that roiled forth steam like a pair of nuclear cooling towers. She wore a country apron, and her pleasant face was moist and pink; one of her hands held the pale carcass of a chicken and the other a lengthy cutting knife.

She raised the rubbery carcass for the doctor. "Will this do?"

"Yes, indeed," he said and took the liberty of perusing the contents of the cauldrons. Coming along behind, Bobby peered around the doctor into pots quietly bubbling with brown rice, turkey, celery, and carrots. "One for orphs and one for the dogs," the doctor said. "Good plain food. Robert, this is Greta, one of our most successful graduates. Greta, this is Robert. He will be assisting me henceforth." (For Bobby, that "hence-forth" had a metallic ring to it.)

Greta dreamily informed Bobby, "You will love it here at Orphis. Just like I love it." And she repeated, emphasizing each and every syllable, "You...will...love...it...here."

Dr. Fairfax placed a protective hand on her shoulder. "But you did not always love Orphis, did you?"

"No," said Greta, wilting a trifle, until she beamed with sunny pride. "But I was a fascinating case, wasn't I?"

"True. But tell Robert what you were when you came to us."

Her bashful smile ran a bit in the wet heat. "I was a diversity junkie."

"Please, tell Robert all about it."

Greta stirred one pot and then the other, staring into their steam like a native healer summoning the dead from her cauldrons. "I was going for my degree in computer science."

"Very useful," said the doctor.

"We need women in science," Greta smiled wanly.

"I could introduce you to one that might take the shine off that apple. Be that as it may, your time at the state university did not serve you very well, did it? Or, should we say, you didn't serve them very well?"

Like a guest on a late-night talk show, Greta told Bobby, "I hacked the mainframe computer system of the university."

"And?" prompted the doctor.

"And I changed the word *university* officially to *diversity* on their website and all of their electronic correspondence."

"And they didn't like that, did they?" Before Greta could verify these freshman hijinks, the doctor smiled through his beard. "No, they did not. But the administration was in a bit of a bind, wasn't it?"

As if a possessing spirit was taking over her being, Greta fervently insisted, "Their website said that they supported free speech in all its forms."

"Nonetheless," said Dr. Fairfax, "they decided that they could not countenance cyberterrorism."

"That's what their lawyers called it," Greta muttered bitterly. Then leaving off her Witch-of-Endor impersonation, she took up an up-until-then-unnoticed meat cleaver. Running a moist thumb down its edge, she whacked a leg from the chicken carcass, gave it a corkscrew twist, and dropped it into a pot.

"That one will be for us, won't it, Greta? The dogs shouldn't get poultry bones." (During these reminiscences, Sangreal and Siege Perelous had been staring with pleading faces toward the edge of the kitchen counter as if it were the gold bar of Heaven.) The doctor bore the story forth. "So, the school expelled Greta."

With eyes deeper than waters stilled at eventide, Greta sniffed, "But, we need more women in science."

"Cooking is chemistry," said the doctor, his voice like fresh caramel oozing over a buttered pan. Unconsoled, Greta carried on marinating in her inner agony until Dr. Fairfax said, "Tell Robert what finally brought you here."

Fixing Bobby with the eyes of a secular prophetess decrying the transgressions of the electorate, Greta declared, "My sister's wedding was not diverse enough."

"And why was that?" asked the doctor, his detached curiosity belying the fact that he had heard the story a thousand times and had read about it in the papers when it had first occurred.

With a little embarrassment, she said, "Well, my sister's white."

"Just like you," said Phineas Fairfax, keeping her roped to reality.

"But I tried," said Greta, veering toward tears.

"Greta," Dr. Fairfax murmured, "you're on a one-way road to the future now."

"But the groom was white too," she bleated, trying to blame the victim.

"Yes: Bryan," said Dr. Fairfax in clarification. "But why not tell Robert about Devin?"

Her face brightened. "Devin was in my affinity group. He was so cute."

"I'm sure that the fellows in Cell Block D think so too." The doctor told Bobby, "Devin was a key player in Greta's scheme, since he worked in the home improvement department of a large hardware and home goods chain store."

"He got the paint," said Greta, playing tour guide through the past.

"Which they're still trying to get out of your grandmother's lace."

"But that was a relic of generational wealth."

"Which you will not be partaking of, since your father used your inheritance to cover your fees here." Dr. Fairfax told Bobby in a confidential tone, "Greta now has nowhere else to go, you see, so I keep her around to help about the place."

But Greta was going on, nostalgically soaking up the glow from that one day of glory. "Devin got the sprayers too. Now, those were fun."

"A rainbow of latex and acrylic lacquer," said Phineas Fairfax.

"And enamel," said Greta. "I had the enamel." She looked poised to regale the audience with her eye-witness reportage of what should have been the most special day of her sister's life, until she sniffed, "Oh, but it was all so *racist.* Her dress was white. And the walls inside the church were white."

"Not when you got done with them," said Phineas Fairfax.

"And her bouquet was white."

"But maybe orange blossoms are supposed to be orange—and black."

"But I didn't do anything wrong."

"Well, your sister wasn't happy. Or your mother."

"Or Daddy," Greta sniffed. "Or Grandma."

Dr. Fairfax nodded his head in time to the catalog of the wronged. "Nor the groom."

"Bryan."

"Yes, he gave you a good shove out his car when they dropped you off."

"That gravel hurts."

"I think it was a good start."

Trying to veer the searchlight away from herself, Greta said, "Oh, tell him about Amber."

The doctor's voice dropped an octave or so, even as he raised his head. "Amber was not one of my triumphs."

"Like Lola?" said Bobby, joining in the conversation and so missing a chance to dart out of a nearby doors for a go at freedom—after abducting Zoe, of course.

"You've met Lola?" Greta asked.

"Not exactly," said Dr. Fairfax firmly.

For a single juxtaposed moment, Greta tried her own hand at playing the healer. "Well, you did try with Amber." She told Bobby, "Amber lived across the hall from me. I wasn't as bad as she was."

Quite aware that Greta was still holding the cleaver, the doctor said, "We'll just say that Amber also celebrated diversity."

"Tell him how you got rid of her," said Greta, like a little girl anxious for the good part of the story.

"You mean how I 'sought her healing.' Amber's story was in many ways similar to Greta's. But while I was crafting a plan for her healing, she happened to see a story on the community access news program."

Greta said, "That's when you decided no phones or TV."

"No news...," began the doctor.

"...is good news," finished Greta.

"The broadcast reported that Merryweather Hands and Hearts, a local nonprofit, was sponsoring the resettlement of a band of refugees from the A'aribono province in South Nubia. What no one had told Merryweather Hands and Hearts..."

"Or Amber," added Greta.

"...was that these particular A'aribonoans were claiming refugee status to escape the latest round of tribal revenge killing at the hands of their neighbors from the Tusawwaram region."

Greta told Bobby, "Dr. Fairfax's really good with names."

The doctor went on, enunciating clearly. "All that Merryweather Hands and Hearts needed to hear was that they were fleeing political violence, and so the band joined our happy town. In any event, Amber ended up very much enamored with them, falling in love with their colorful veils, their spicy soups, their flatbread, their drumming, and such like. She could not rein in her adulation for these people."

"He means she wouldn't shut up."

"So," the doctor continued, "to give Amber what she wanted, I contacted the Refugee Resettlement Program at Merryweather Hands and Hearts, and they put me in contact with the front man of the band about arranging a marriage for Amber to his teenage grandson back in the home country. I told Amber that if she truly wished to celebrate diversity, then she must embrace it to the full. 'The political is the personal,' as the bra burners used to say. But rather than hopping out of the corner that her logic had painted her into, which is what I guessed would happen, Amber felt bound by her principles to accept the boy. Through my contact at the South Nubian consulate, I understand, she still has not risen above secondary wife."

Greta, back to stirring the pots and smiling with the triumphalism particular to spectators of gladiatorial games of the heart, told Bobby, "That's 'cause her dad never sent any grenade launchers with her dowry. That's what happened."

"For what it's worth, though," said Dr. Fairfax, "Amber does stay in the good graces of the village council, what with the current exchange rate, and the permanent veiling keeps her from getting too badly sunburned. She's picked up enough phrases, too, to talk to the midwife when she comes for that yearly visit."

"How many is it now?" asked Greta.

"Children are a blessing, Greta. I've been told. But let's finish your story. Tell Robert how you came to see the world differently."

Greta gave a moist smile. "Dr. Fairfax sent me to work in a public housing building, with a free apartment and everything."

"Twenty-four hours a day of living in the rainbow. Every single race, ethnicity, and identity imaginable."

"Because I wanted diversity," Greta admitted, her smile weakening and her eyes turning glassy as she took in the terroir of the past. "You might not know this, Robert, but all those diverse people? They don't care about diversity."

"That's the truncated version of events," clarified the doctor. "You did attempt your multicultural Winter Celebration, didn't you?"

Quietly stirring the pot, she stared into its celery-strewn vortex as if contemplating the wreck of a beautiful ship. "They kept calling it a Christmas party."

"But you'd gotten what she wanted."

Suddenly sobbing aloud, Greta dropped her spoon and fell at Phineas Fairfax's flawless Florsheims. "Yes, yes," she gasped. "You gave me..." Her words were lost in the knots of the rag rug under his feet, until loud and clear she choked out, "...just what I wanted."

Benevolently staring down at this worshipper, the doctor whispered, "I gave you nothing. You found it yourself. Come, Greta, rise. You have so much yet do to." While Bobby wondered whether this meant that she had to reshingle the barn, Greta stood up and, brushing her face clean, returned to the pots as if nothing untoward had transpired.

"That was a nice story, wasn't it, Robert?" asked the doctor. "Well, we'll leave Greta to captain the vats. Here. Break your fast." And taking a ceramic bowl of fruit from the counter in his broad and veiny hands, he offered it to Bobby. But even while Bobby was choosing from among the mango, the hardy kiwi, and the dragon fruit, he heard, "Come along, then. It's time for a little deprogramming."

✳✳✳

They were soon moving down another hallway lined with doors. But while Phineas Fairfax moved forward with a silent, clear-eyed focus, Bobby kept stopping at door after door to read the quaint square wooden nameplates fixed beside each. Each nameplate contained a Polaroid snapshot of the occupant, a name, and an occasional pressed flower or cartoon sticker (such things a touch of individuality to the reeducation camp). When he caught the name *Russell*, he thought, *Oh, so that's what Russell looks like,* upon seeing the young black man in the Polaroid. But when he saw *Robert* on a sticky note beneath it, Bobby realized that not only had he come full circle, but he also had no idea where he was.

Hustling around the next bend in the labyrinth, Bobby found Dr. Fairfax standing before another door. Playing against type, this one was not labeled at all, but had four great savage diagonal lines marring its face, like the slashes of a bizarre two-clawed creature. Bobby thought it might read "XX."

The doctor quietly took a slow breath, perhaps preparatory, perhaps meditative, but definitely suggesting that it might be his last, then tapped on the door.

His knockity-knock might as well have been the heavenly hosts barging through the front gate of Beelzebub's condominium. With a rush of air, the door wrenched open and Bobby saw with both horror and relief—since it is always pleasant to see a familiar face—the young so-called woman who had sucker punched him not too long before.

Dr. Fairfax was detached and seigneurial. "Ah, Madison. Good morning. It looks like you have a real shiner there."

"It's Steffany's fault," she snarled.

"And how did you and Steffany come to blows?"

"I told her I hoped an old-growth forest would shade out her organic garden."

"Fightin' words, if I ever heard any. May we come in?"

"'*May we? May we?*' Your question is a power modality. Etiquette was a creation of hierarchical systems to impose control structures specifically upon the feminine cohort through—"

Dr. Fairfax breathed out like a solar deity dispelling a cloud of hellspawn. "Etiquette was the creation of those who wished—"

At this, Madison, unwilling to abide by the rules of civil debate—or any other rules, Bobby guessed—up and spluttered, "You just don't get it, you're so stupid!" and answering a question that no one had asked, she shrieked, "No, *no,* I don't care what you have to say!" then threw up her arms like a pair of buffalo horns and chanted, "Pig! Pig! Pig! Patriarchy

Pig! Fry 'im like bacon!" Then she trained her eyes on Bobby. "And you brought the patriarchy trainee," she seethed. Holding a curled fist up at his face, she sneered, "But I realigned his power modality already."

Holding fast to his main mast amid the tempest, the doctor said, "This is Robert, Madison."

"And this is a *she-only* space, gender fascist."

"Come, Madison, this isn't the nineties."

"Hitlerian androcrat!"

"And Herr Hitler was a vegetarian socialist freelance artist who loved dogs and wanted to ban smoking. At least there's no one like that running around these days."

Rejecting such blatant mansplaining, Madison shrieked, "Colonizer! Colonizer! Land back for the gynarchs!" She summoned a defensive and defiant growl. "Where'd Steffany go?"

"Steffany's on her camping trip."

"So, she gets *her* freedom."

Drawing out an antique watch, the doctor clicked it open and hummed. "By now, I'd say that freedom is the last thing on Steffany's mind."

"And Russell?"

"He's at his job," he said, replacing his watch, "which is part of his healing."

"How much of a cut do you get, wage slaver?"

"I congratulate him on sticking it out this long."

Still on the hunt, Madison pointed at Bobby. "Oh, and he said the word 'girl' in front of me!"

Phineas Fairfax said, "I understand that there are far worse words than that, but our governess never let us hear any of them." Madison looked ready to erupt in a pyroclastic flow littered with a few of those forbidden syllables when the doctor, apparently uninterested in beefing up his vocabulary, asked, "What else should he have said?"

"Woman!"

"Well, had you behaved like one, he might have said 'woman.'"

After a second to decide whether this was an insult, Madison brayed, "And I want my phone."

"As you agreed when you came here, you will get it back, if you leave. And maybe someday you will leave, Madison."

"But there's nothing wrong with me."

"Your mother doesn't think so—and she's a woman."

Sidestepping any dangerous deductions, Madison snorted, "Whatever."

To this filler, Dr. Fairfax lowered himself to her enraged face, his golden glasses glimmering. "Madison, don't you want to get better?"

And even as he gazed in benevolent certitude at Madison with her lemony-purple hair and her Army-Navy cast-off couture, her face quivered, her spittle-sprinkled lips writhed, and she burst out in dribbly tears, her black eye like an overripe plum oozing its juice. Executing a quick retreat, she slammed her door behind her.

But as the door vibrated in his face, Phineas Fairfax said, "Ah, Robert, this will be so easy. On to pleasanter pastures. We should go see Zoe now," and he set off down the hallway with Sangreal and Siege Perelous lumbering along at his sides, leaving Bobby to follow hastily on, lest Madison slither out and deliver a murderous Parthian shot.

✳✳✳

The doctor and his canine entourage lit before another door. "Robert, please keep back so that we don't overwhelm Zoe."

While imagining any number of ways to overwhelm Zoe, Bobby did step back as the doctor delivered a gentle rapping on this chamber door.

The young lady inside promptly opened it.

Clad in the mournful ensemble from the day before, complete with her veil, now fully covering her face, something to wow 'em at the cenotaph, Zoe looked like a grieving mushroom off to the requiem for a beloved chanterelle who never returned from the frozen gourmet pizza factory.

"Good morning again, Zoe," said Dr. Fairfax. "This is quite a change. Earlier, you were positively Terpsichorean."

She gave a deep, doleful sigh that blew the tulle about her face like the tattered curtains in a decrepit mansion.

With the clarity and care of a superpower interpreter translating a nuclear disarmament treaty on live television, the doctor asked, "Did you like visiting the laboratory last night?"

The lacey black heap that was her head nodded.

"You liked that new job, didn't you?"

Another motion, up and down.

"You're a good helper here. You're free to go into the lab whenever you wish."

"I can do lab work too," Bobby chimed in, remembering his old life at MAXIFAX Laboratories (a life that now felt very, very far away, somewhere in the American Southwest).

"No, Zoe needs to learn this task alone." He asked her, "Were you scared of what you saw?"

The black head swayed back and forth.

She's so brave, Bobby sighed and imagined the adventures they could share at the wildlife refuge: tagging sandhill cranes for migration studies, a laughing escape from a sudden hailstorm, and a few hours of digging out the roots of invasive Japanese knotweed as the sun went down—those knuckle-biting moments that bind two hearts into one.

The doctor asked her, "What do you have planned for today, Zoe?"

Setting two pale hands under the dark and delicate lacey liminus that hid her face, she lifted it and Bobby sighed again. He did not know that the sun could rise twice in one day.

But her melancholy tone was a cloud. "The garden," she told him, as if condemned to a nickel mine above the Arctic Circle. Suddenly, she asked, "Oh, maybe I could make it a little crematorium?" and her face seemed to brighten with the flames of immolations to come.

"Zoe," Dr. Fairfax asked, "don't you want to get better?" Before Bobby could tell him that there was nothing wrong with her, Phineas Fairfax suggested, "You can help Robert. He needs to bring his note to Mother Johanna, and I know that you can coax her down for a visit."

Zoe's face, lambent as she imagined the smoking offering of so many deceased sparrows, now dimmed. Like a disconsolate sexton with a busted shovel and a plague wagon on the way, she looked at Bobby with doubtful and dubious eyes, while Bobby himself bounced his eyebrows invitingly and gave her what he thought was a morning-fresh smile.

This must have worked some magic, though, and like a young heifer remembering that daisies lined the path up to the slaughterhouse, she said, "All right."

"We'll be waiting for you on the patio," said Dr. Fairfax. "But do stop by the lab again on your way."

"All right," she mumbled again and closed her door.

And Bobby sighed a third time. *The sun sets so early in these parts...*

"Come along, Robert," said the doctor as he and the mighty dogs made for the end of the corridor. There, he opened a door, and the light and scents of May spilled into the hallway.

But Bobby did not follow at once and rejoin the world of sunlight, birdsong, and growing things. Instead, he simply stood, in an eternity of solitude, uncertain, looking at Zoe's door and wondering dumbly where the wonders of the world truly lay.

✳✳✳

In time, Bobby did tear himself away and joined Dr. Fairfax on the patio amid the subtropical greenery. With the heat of the day coming on, Bobby in his lab coat did feel a bit like a linen-suited colonial on the veranda, minus the whiskey and splash, but he whiled away the interminable minutes until Zoe arrived, by giving the talk ball in his pocket another swat to keep it quiet.

While taking in the pale, toothy fronds of a honeybush, Dr. Phineas Fairfax said with sober confidentiality, "Robert, you may have noticed certain things about Zoe."

Bobby would have lingeringly related every single detail that he had noticed about her, but the doctor's focus differed. "In Zoe Feldspar's chart, I have penned the diagnosis SA-NOS: Starry-Eyed, Not Otherwise Specified." Then, resting his face near the cream-colored blossoms of a Japanese persimmon, he murmured, "Ah, like unguents. But, Zoe: very tender, very dreamy. She dresses in mourning because she finds life hideous. For those of her psycho-emotional type, life can too easily peter out at the door of the opium den or in the clutches of the mob." He bent his attention to the Antwerp blue berries of a *Mahonia x media,* then stroked the head of one of the dogs. "Oblivion or the mob, oblivion or the mob...And we don't want that. But perhaps you'll cure our Zoe. In fact, I'm sure you will. And here she is."

Bobby perked up. He had expected her to look like a window display from the Nihilists' secondhand store, but instead, she was guarding herself against the world in garb that was anonymously unisexual—denim jeans, a plain T-shirt, and athletic shoes that were aged and holey, all topped off by a ball cap advertising the Strange Sisters Fruit Farm. (Her red hair was disappointingly bridled into a ponytail, leaving Bobby to imagine its cinnamon strands dancing free in the summer wind as he chased her through the wildlife refuge...)

Just as at her room, her mood blighted the sunny day. "Do I have to?"

"I need to spend some time in the lab," said the doctor, "and then I have to go into town. But I had another thought. After helping Robert deliver his note to Mother Johanna, you should show him a few of the sights." Bobby wanted to blurt out that Zoe could show him anything she thought he might like, but the doctor had an itinerary already in mind. "I thought the convent, the berry fields, the fruit stand, maybe the old ice house."

"Yes, the old ice house," said Bobby, thinking that he should put in his two cents.

"And the pilgrimage starts today. And there's the view from the Smithville Dike. So, to help you pass a pleasant hour, I asked Greta to put together a little something for you."

And whistling a commanding ditty at the dogs, Sangreal swayed to attention and made for the far end of the patio, to disappear behind a stand of scarlet-flowered salvia. (Siege Perelous sat unmoving, content to have his ears scratched.) Soon the first dog reemerged bearing in his saggy, soggy jaws a wicker picnic hamper festive with ribbons of blue, pink, and lavender. Lumbering back to his master, the dog thudded the hamper at his feet and sat back with a squat, ready for payment in the form of a beef neck bone. Having paid off man's best pack animal with something cow-flavored from his pocket, the doctor said, "And these, I think, will help as well."

Now the doctor drew from a pocket of his lab coat both a monogrammed handkerchief (to wipe the slobber from the hamper handle) and a pair of field glasses, suitable for sighting a migratory flock of arctic terns that had blown off course. These he handed to Bobby as if bestowing the keys to the convertible.

As suavely as he could, Bobby took the binoculars, then turned to Zoe, his happy, hopeful, open face inviting her on a friendly stroll. But she had already snatched up the picnic hamper and was making straight for the water tower, looming in the distance like an intergalactic spider awaiting its prey. This left Bobby to hurry on after her, which he happily did.

CHAPTER XI

ANYTHING FOR BEAUTY,
OR THE BOTTOM OF THE BARREL

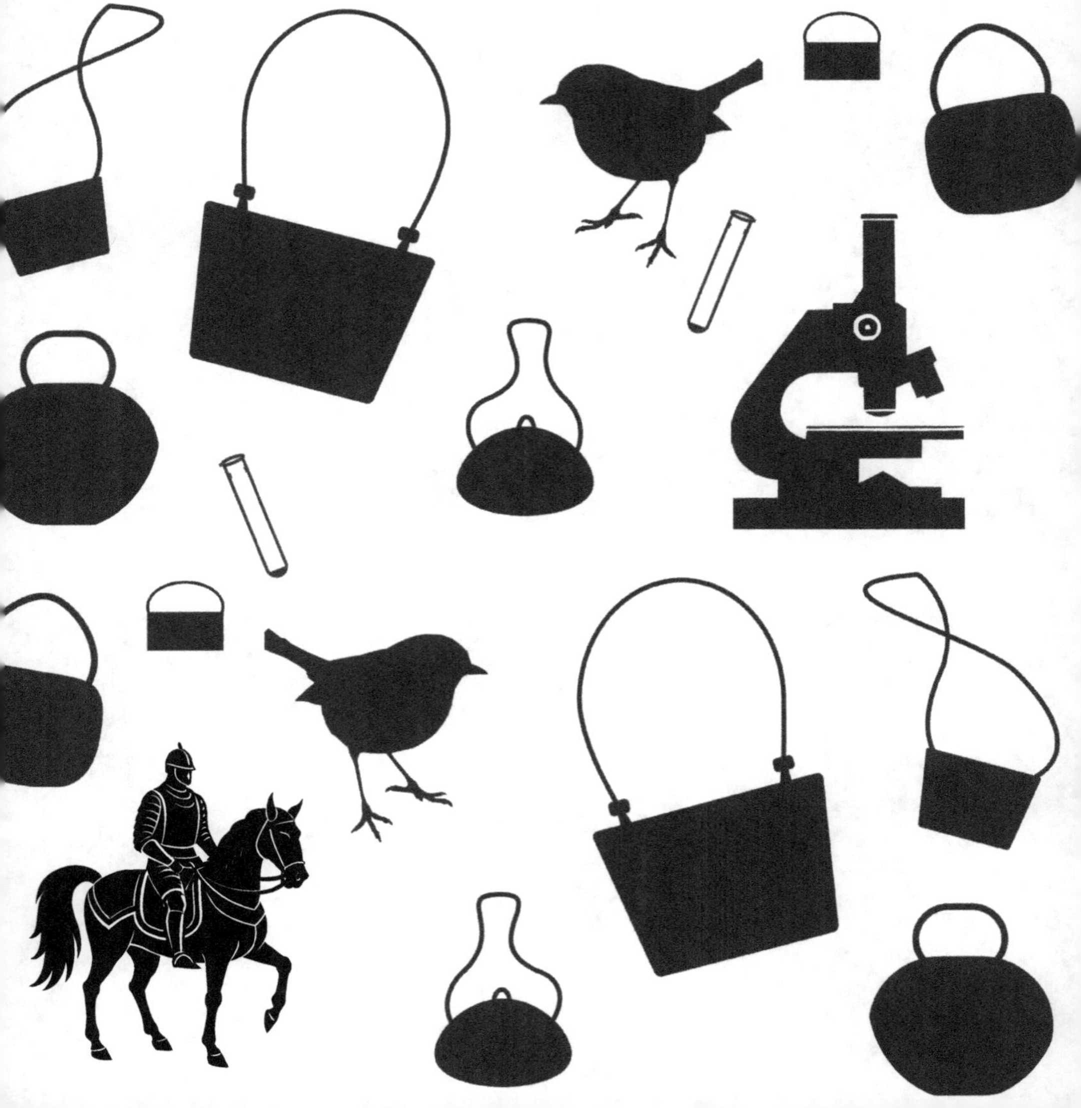

While the morning sun was reminding most of Merryweather that another sixteen hours of the good life was at the starting blocks, no such siren song sang into the shell-like ears of Bella, Baba, and Martie.

Our threesome had passed the night in an impromptu sleepover at Martie's pied-à-terre at the Riverside Commons Condominiums, where Martie showed her ignorance of good hostessing by leaving Bella and Baba to make nests for themselves in either her single minimalist armchair or on the kitchen island, whichever they liked, while she herself curled up on the queen-sized futon.

As the first light of day peeked through the window treatments, Martie stepped out of her cubicle of a bedroom as fresh as a newly misted house-plant, while Bella and Baba creaked into a semi-upright position. After a scarcely veiled threat to give this place half a star on a couple of prominent travel websites, Bella nudged aside a vertical window slat and scanned the street below, while Baba unwrapped Martie's boo-booed hand, bandaged in swoop after swoop of gauze and looking like an outsized cotton swab. She propped a pair of vintage cat-eye half glasses made from Galapagos tortoiseshell into position and peered at the devastation.

Martie asked, "Will they have to cut it off?"

As Baba shook her head with "No, you'll live to text another day," Bella turned back from the window, fairly certain that Dr. Sheena Lypotrope was not lurking behind a potted shrub in the building's patio.

"So, where's the coffee?" she asked.

Forgetting her fingers, Martie sang out what had to be a jingle from local FM radio: *"Crazy cup, crazy cup / It's the cup that keeps you up! / Crazy, crazy Chaos cup!"*

Bella blinked at this one-woman sister act, while Baba, with her blasé tolerance of out-of-towners, told her, "Chaos Coffee, dear. It's where we always go. And after that"—she was wrapping an apricot silk scarf into a turban around her much-maltreated tresses to hide them from the public's gaze—"we're off to my private little day spa for an emergency treatment."

✳✳✳

Down in the concrete cavern of the condominium's parking garage, Bella and her pals spent a significant slice of time solving the intricate puzzle of fitting three bodies into a vehicle designed for two. (No one was willing to curl up as a sweaty ball in the rear compartment, thank you, which still smelled of Bobby Lumbar.) In the end, Bella slumped behind the steering wheel, Baba enthroned herself in the passenger's seat, and Martie sat uncomfortably on her lap like a futuristic collectible doll.

As Bella fired up the ignition, she asked her hostess, "What happened to your car, Martie?"

"Oh, I left it downtown," said Martie, shifting herself about to find a position that was a little less uncomfortable. "I'll pick it up someday. I didn't want to get in trouble with the carbon police by driving it too much."

Bella gave Baba a look to confirm this bit of fabulism, and Baba nodded her head with a narrow, cynical eyes that told her, "Welcome to Merryweather."

"Whatever," sighed Bella, and as she mentally made her plan to escape the compassionate clutches of the carbon police, she also made a hard sharp turn out of the two parking spaces that she had occupied, sending her white monster right through the parking lot's protective gate arm and taking out the keycard reader. Even as Martie shrieked about that coming out of her resident fees, Bella poo-pooed her. "Believe me, there are worse things in life—like trying to sleep on a kitchen island."

Not having had her morning visit to Chaos Coffee, Martie could not give a snappy retort, but Baba was maintaining focus and played navigatrix. "A left here, dear."

Bella swept up a side street while Baba scanned the street signs. "Let's see...," she murmured. "Go straight." Bella accelerated as two lanes of oncoming one-way traffic swerved aside to let her charge through. "And how about a right, up there?"

Bella complied as her friends' heads bonked against the passenger-side windows.

Patting her head through her turban to make sure that it was still attached, Baba said, "Bella dear, let's remember Jenny and not relive that tragedy" ("Jenny" Genoise Batterbowl was one of their fellow graduates, whose head accidentally unscrewed itself on an amusement park ride. Only MAXIFAX's ownership of the local news affiliate managed to get the story buried.) "Now," she went on, "let's head for the second red. Then look for the line of cars wrapping around the cute little shack with the funky sign."

"Oh," Martie chirped up, "when we get there, can I have the fair-trade hot chocolate? I'll treat next time."

Baba mused, "And I think the twelve-ounce macchiato with the coriander sprinkles and white chocolate coffee bean would hit the spot. Oh, and Bella sweetie, you don't mind if I light up, do you?"

Bella shook her head with resignation and zoomed on, a threat to all and sundry, judging by the screams of the horrified pedestrians in the crosswalks and the blast of a horn from the trash truck that she had faked out. But as Baba inhaled in languorous ecstasy and glanced into the side mirror at a power walker running for her life, she floated the suggestion, "If it helps, Bella dear, I hear they even serve decaf."

✳✳✳

Bella's rancorous energy coughed to a stop as her SUV joined the eight other caffeine-and-sugar-syrup junkies in the drive-up at Chaos Coffee. But soon enough, once she and her friends were loaded with hot cups of caffeine, Bella practically stood on the accelerator, rolled over a concrete curb, and charged through Chaos Coffee's landscaping, to drive on to Baba's "private little day spa."

As they headed up the street, Baba raised her cup between sips to guide her along, while Bella envisioned just what Baba's "private little day spa" might be. She thought maybe a dainty, renovated cottage behind a bamboo-stick fence with a maze-like walkway of riverstone pavers through a Zen fern garden and an entryway becalmed by the mellow tones of wind chimes; she went on to expect that after that short Taoist stroll to the front door, there would follow a few hours of quiet physical manipulation, and maybe a bout with hot stones or volcanic mud.

Such a fantasy, though, was nowhere in sight.

Instead, they were lumbering up the six-lane mega-thoroughfare of Smithville Boulevard, the commercial gut of Merryweather: block after block of used-car lots, Chinese restaurants, a movie theater converted into a mega-church, secondhand store donation centers, and satellite clinics for every major health system. (The ancient mothers of Merryweather had not gotten around to tweaking the zoning laws to forbid either chain stores or chain-link fences.)

After they had zoomed past a brand-new public housing complex (Smiling Skies was the intended name), Baba raised her cardboard cup a last time and, after licking a macchiato mustache from her upper lip, told Bella, "Right over there, dear, on the left."

After an eighty-nine-degree turn hard across three lanes of traffic, Bella bounced her rig into the parking lot of the Royal Village Mini-Mall and hit the brakes in time to avoid crashing through the front windows of a carpet-and-flooring emporium. Martie, though, did lose control of her Chaos Coffee carbon-offset cardboard cup and slathered Bella's dashboard with the dregs of her hot chocolate, which leisurely trickled into the workings of the car stereo and onto the floor—and since the place was already a mess, Baba littered the floor of the cab with her own empty cup before disembarking (or escaping) from the passenger side with Martie.

While reminding herself to find a car wash and a new set of friends, Bella donned her high-end Nigerian shades, stepped out onto the cigarette-butt-studded parking lot, and shuddered at the mercantile wasteland before her.

Most towns can lay an embarrassed claim to some version of the Royal Village Mini-Mall, where none of the businesses bother to declare how politically aware their owners are. Here, the dolled-up anchor store was Darcy's Doubles, the sandwich board on the sidewalk reassuring passing potential patrons, "Our Machines Blessed Every Day." Next door was Pawdicure Pet Grooming, then Samarkand Market with ropes of dried ghost chilis hanging in the window like vampire bones, and then the Green & Clean Laundromat. The eye went on to meet the carpet and flooring store (its front windows still intact) doing next to what Bella deduced, with inescapable horror, was the end of their quest: Lovelies Salon. In Baba Savarin's brain, she realized, "private little day spa" was another way of saying "unmentionable relic from ages past."

Having eyed the place herself, Martie shuffled up to Bella. "Should we go in?"

"Not without a hazmat suit."

But Baba was already on the defensive. "This is the only place that still stocks my color: 'Brazen.' Otherwise, I'd need to fly to Bogotá." And after a fortifying drag, she patted her locks through her turban and strode purposefully to the entrance.

Apparently willing to die on the hill of undying friendship, Bella and Martie unenthusiastically brought up the rear. But before any of them could cross into Lovelies Salon, the morning sun was suddenly blotted out; a stumpy white bus seating fourteen had cruised up alongside the building and, with an asthmatic cloud of diesel exhaust, had chugged to a stop. Blazoned along the side of this great pale purveyor ran the name:

Summerfield Estates

The passenger door quickly creaked open to disgorge about a dozen elderly but spry ladies sporting various degrees of good posture, all of them dressed, if not to the nines, then to the eight-and-a-halves, with wrist-length polyester tops and pleated pants, nail polish gleaming like bull's blood, brooches like scarabs, and hair like clouds of cotton candy, all to go and get a touch-up from Mr. Phipps, or whomever the overlord of the curling tongs was at this place.

As this troupe of Mimis disembarked, Bella overheard a seamless prattle about grandchildren, great-grandchildren, husbands, dead husbands, the untimely death of a neighbor down the street, an estate sale by Marjorie Mayfield, macular degeneration, and recipes for brisket.

She muttered to Martie, "Silver tsunami warning."

"Is that what we'll look like?" Martie asked innocently. "Well, at least you've got a good start."

Before Bella could shoot back a comparable dart, the alpha grandma had turned back to the bus and called inside, "Andreas, how long do we have today?"

Out of the bus a man's voice, with a weighty German accent, said with a flourish, "But how little time you will need, since you are already so lovely?"

This revved up the titters to a high pitch. The driver himself now hopped out, and Bella saw a squat, tight-bodied old man in an athlete's jumpsuit c. 1962 and a freshly shellacked crew cut. With ramrod posture, he marched straight to the door of Lovelies Salon, opened it in an obligato of chivalry, and nodded to each of his elderly charges as she passed inside. Bringing up the rear on this trek to the fountain of youth was the alpha grandma, who, after a second or two of banter with him, received a courtly kiss to her hand. "Oh, teach my grandson to do that," she fluttered. "When will you be back?"

With steady but teasing gaze, he whispered, "One hour, my lady," and waving a cooling hand before her blushing face, she floated inside on a cloud of flirtatious vapors.

Baba, appointing herself the alpha female of a second group, sauntered up to the door and offered her own hand for a little continental treatment. But the old fellow's aristocratic solicitude did not, sadly, extend to these newcomers. After scanning them up and down, he barked, "You try to look like young, strong girls, then you are to act like young, strong girls. The door is there," and aimed an indicating digit at the portal. With that, he marched back to the bus, which soon was chugging out of the parking lot, leaving behind only a toxic nebula of exhaust.

Martie shouted through the gray cloud, "I am not *trying* to look like a young, strong girl. I mean...Wait a second. Bella, hop in your car and go after him. Right now."

A cooler, or at least well-mentholated, head prevailed. "Focus, please," Baba said. "Simone's waiting for me," and accepting the burden of opening her own doors, she strode into Lovelies Salon.

After shuddering in surprise at seeing Baba Savarin live by someone else's timetable, Bella and Martie shuffled in behind her against an escaping wave of nail polish fumes.

With the customers from Summerfield Estates clogging the queue in front of them, Bella, Baba, and Martie settled in to patiently absorb the atmosphere (along with the acetone fumes). A placard behind the happy head of the plump receptionist told Bella of the styles available from the hands of the veteran staff: the Martha-Hillary, the Faded Glory, the Swan Song, the Mama Bear, the Pixie Dowager, and that hardcore standby, the Football Helmet. Needless to say, she cringed as she overheard Martie asking Baba which one might look good on her (Martie, that is).

Fortunately, the ladies peopling the path to the front counter turned out to be regular Ritas, and soon most were whisked off to the station of a gal who had been sculpting their locks since the early Reagan years.

As Bella and Martie neared the counter, they were treated to further revelations regarding Baba Savarin. Gone was any studied indifference or weary commentary on the foibles of her satellites. Slipping her turban up for the receptionist to take in the damage, she then leant over the counter, and her battered tangerine mop drooped over her face like a ragged veil. Over a much-scribbled-upon eighteen-month desk calendar of appointments, whispered words with the receptionist wended back and forth. After rubbing out her own half-smoked unfiltered cancer stick, the mistress of the time slots nodded, reached over, and patted Baba's hand to console the haggard soul. Bella and Martie made out, "It'll be fine, sugar. Simone'll take care of it. Just like new." They thought that they had also heard a stifled sniffle of gratitude, but would never know, for after rearing her head, Baba gave her mane a shake and strode away to Simone's station, abandoning her companions, whom she knew were old enough to entertain themselves.

Seeing Bella and Martie, the lady behind the counter told them, "Sorry, girls, you'll have to wait."

"Oh, that's all right," said Martie. "We want good haircuts."

Bella swooped in. "Oh, look, Martie, magazines," and after slipping a Canadian quarter into a cardboard Easter Seals placard on the counter and snagging a petrified mint patty, she hustled her friend over to the floral-pattern couches to take in the late 1980s decor and the rows of dryer domes soon to house the ladies from Summerfield Estates.

A few stylists must have been on strike, since Bella found herself shar-ing a couch with a twosome from the bus, waiting their turns with Simone or Mr. Phipps. After skimming through a *People* magazine from 1997, she thought to pass the time—solely for entertainment value, of course—by eavesdropping on the conversation of her neighbors (Connie and Edna, she had gathered so far).

Connie, full of faith in some unnamed miracle cure: "Oh, they just did wonders for Kyle—Kyle's my grandson. He's holding down a job now and he doesn't think he's an elf..."

Edna, with a voice roughened by decades of unfiltered cigarettes: "Oh, that's good, that's good."

Connie, stirring the pot a bit: "But the fellow there who runs that outfit, he's quite a character, you know."

Edna: (Nodding)

Connie: "He's funny. You know, *funny*, not funny."

Edna: "I've met him."

Connie: "Oh, yes, at Andi's house, that's right."

Edna: (Nodding again) "At the Christmas party."

Connie: "Oh, but what's his name?"

While Bella was waiting for the plot to flesh itself out, Martie next to her had discovered *Coverlets and Counterpanes* magazine and, with eyes like sunflowers on a bright prairie morn, was happily declaring, "Oh, Bella, look, this is so neat. Oh, look at that—a pay-per-view Laura Ingalls Wilder retrospective's coming up. When did this issue come out?"

But just as Martie was scrutinizing the cover for a date, Bella heard, with crystalline clarity through her other ear, Edna say, "Phineas Fairfax."

"Fairfax, that's it," said Connie. "Phineas Fairfax. 'Funny Phineas Fairfax,' that's how I remember," and on top of her, in a kind of conver-sational polyphony, Edna said, "That's cute."

But Bella, desperate for a solo performance, decided that audience participation was now in order. Ignoring Martie, who was showing her just the cutest cross-stitch pattern for a corncob doll's dress, she butted in. "Oh, I'm sorry, did I hear you say Phineas Fairfax?" In her eagerness,

Bella's aim was a bit off, and she ended up putting the question to Edna, who drew back with a look that said, "Who's asking?"

With a smile as saccharine as a sugar-free butterscotch drop, Connie said, "That was me. Do you know him? He's a real character, isn't he?"

"*Tell* me about it," Bella sighed, then swatted Martie's hand away. (She was not in the mood to hear about taffy-pull parties for fun and profit.) "I haven't seen him in *years*. So, where's he at now?"

"The same place he was before. You know—"

"Oh, don't tell me," Bella theatrically fretted and even tapped her lips once or twice. "Oh, where is it...?"

Before Connie could contribute the answer, though, Edna had fixed her eyes like gunsights on this newbie. At Lovelies Salon, everybody had known everybody since the old girdle-and-panty-hose days. With the icy calculation of a veteran bounty hunter, she asked, "But what's your name, sweetheart?"

Deploying her own jungle cat quickness, Bella said, "Oh, my name's Sheena." Hearing this self-preserving untruth, Martie's mouth gaped open, as if she had found that she had accidentally served Aunt Belva's thimbleberry cordial to the visiting parson. (Something to that effect was a plot point in the latest installment of *Lily, Pioneer Rose,* serialized quarterly in *Coverlets and Counterpanes,* and Martie had just begun to immerse herself in its serpentine plot.)

Edna recognized in Bella's too-brisk and oh-so-glib reply a defensive shield invisibly on the rise. But to coax her to open the gates, she gave a glance down at the younger woman's half-exposed lower limbs and their incipient webbing of varicose veins. "You know, hon, they can take of that here."

"Oh, I'm sure," said Bella, trying to push her hemline a little lower. "Time marches on. Guess it's time for slacks."

Connie said, "Wait 'til you get to my age."

"Speak for yourself," said Edna, not removing her riveting gaze from Bella.

But Bella was undeterred by any stink-eye. "So, Phineas, he runs...Oh, what's the name of that place?"

"You know," Connie said, probing her handbag, "my friend gave me this when I told her about Kyle, and I think it has his address." And from the hodgepodge of necessaries and incidentals collected over the last forty years, Connie drew out a dog-eared but still legible brochure. "Here you go."

"Oh, let me see," said Martie, making a grab at it, but Bella swatted her hand and snatched it herself while making a mental note to apologize to her pal sometime during the next calendar year.

Before giving it a scan, Bella asked, "But you said your friend knows him?"

"Oh, sure. You can ask her yourself," and as a graduate of the "Oh, she won't mind" school of fine friendship, Connie dug yet again through her handbag to find her flip phone. Soon she was tapping along through her contact list. "Just a second. Ronnie—Her name's Ronnie, and she's an *angel.* I have her on speed dial."

Edna butted in. "Connie, maybe you should..."

But Connie was on a roll. "You know, since Kyle got me this thing on sale at his new job—he is *so* responsible—I've forgotten every single phone number I ever knew." The phone was at her ear. "What's your name again, dear? Sheena?"

Bella nodded rapidly. The party on the other end must have answered, since Connie raised her eyebrows and smiled. After mandatory chitchat, she told the unseen Ronnie, "Well, she's asking about that doctor friend of yours. Yes. Phineas Fairfax. She says she used to work with him. Would you like to talk with her a second? She's right here." Bella (or Sheena, for the time being) put forth a hand to take the phone, when Connie stuck up a fast finger. "Oh, Ronnie, that reminds me. Did you talk with Bev? Oh, and Sue? Yes, yes. Well, you know Anne-Marie and Phil said that Sam and Nelva had told them everything about Greg, which is really...Hmm-hmm? Yes, *yes,* I know. Oh, I know, I can't believe it either. In this day and age—or maybe I shouldn't be surprised."

Bella was waving her hand, signaling that she was all set to talk with Ronnie now, when Baba reappeared, much more composed and ready to resume the flight to safety. Before any niceties could flit back and forth, however, a strange woman's voice called over the row of humming dryers and hunched-over nail technicians. "Connie? Connie, I'm ready for you!"

"Oh, I'm up!" started Connie and, standing up, flipped her phone shut. Not noticing the expression of pain coming over Bella's face, Connie asked Baba, "Oh, you see Simone too? She's a wonder, isn't she?"

Baba nodded, proudly petted the fringes of her coiffure as if it were an immense blossom, and smiled with an almost transcendental bliss, perfuming the waiting area with her ecstasy.

"Well, my turn." Right then, though, Connie noticed Bella staring up at her like a galley slave getting chained to the sinking ship. "Oh, honey, I'm *sorry*. I forgot all about you." After giving a look at the far-off Simone, who was working through a tub of hand wipes to get the orange hair dye off of her fingers, she told Bella, "Johnson. Ronnie Johnson. At the Belleweather Bungalows. You know where they're at. Everyone does. Oh, and if you like to bake"—Connie threw another placatory glance at Simone—"she has the best recipe for pecan pull-aparts. To die for."

And with that, she slid her phone into her purse, waved back to Simone, and sallied forth for her weekly touch-up.

Bella wanted to chase after her, even if that meant risking being taken for a customer of Lovelies Salon, but was fenced in by Edna, Martie, and Baba.

Still engrossed in the playful misadventures of *Lily, Pioneer Rose,* Martie was not appreciating the poignancy of her friend's plight, or her own, entangled as she was in the fate, destiny, and/or doom of Bella Freestone; Baba was still afloat on empyrean clouds of joy, knowing that her hair would be once more the envy of the kombucha klatch set, or maybe she was under the influence of copper poisoning from all of those discarded pennies; and Edna was sitting with polyester pants, legs crossed in a seamless unit, and displaying an air of relief that her pal Connie was no longer blabbing at this dubious newcomer.

But Edna did help Bella along. "What's the brochure say, dear?"

Bella was not sure what this old broad's beef was, but she played her part. "I'd better take a look, shouldn't I?"

The brochure's glossy cover depicted, of all things, a serpent coiling about an egg painted with stars and moons and a couple of comet-like squiggles. Underneath this escutcheon, in very prominent golden letters shadowed in purple blue, ran the legend *Orphis New Life Exit-Counseling Clinic*. Opening this propaganda, Bella found a pitch for a spiritual pyramid scheme, with keywords like *realignment*, *essential reality*, *liberation*, and *return to reality* glinting through the text like will-o-the-wisps floating over a fen. Finally, on the penultimate fold of this broadsheet, the prospective sucker was treated to a studio portrait of a clubman figure in a white lab coat, beneath which ran the caption:

DR. PHINEAS FAIRFAX

Bella balked in surprise. Taking out her handheld, she pulled up the small grainy snapshot of the young Dr. Phineas Fairfax. Comparing the figure on her phone to the man in the brochure, Bella saw that other than the hair color (of which Baba would approve), the ginger simian in the first photo bore no relation to the polished and professorial arch-male in the brochure.

"Finding anything good, dear?" asked Edna with a challenging lilt.

At this point, Baba was coming down from her cloud of bliss to touch ground, figuratively speaking, and said, "Allow me." Snatching the flimsy publication, she perused it like the buffet menu at a North Korean reeducation camp.

At this, Martie said, "Oh, let me, let me too," tossed away *Coverlets and Counterpanes* (thus condemning herself never to know what became of the wild turkey that walked into the spelling bee), and captured the brochure from Baba. "Oh, look, right there." She pointed. "Look, look, look."

Bella now reclaimed it and examined the bottom of the last page. "Well," she said, as if noticing the fine print in a stay of execution, "a PO box."

Baba now matter-of-factly took another turn with it. "The main post office is downtown. I say we should..."

But Bella gave Baba a narrow warning look. She knew that Baba could deceive the likes of Frannie and Angela with a shower of glittering cynicisms, but this Edna with the polyester pants came from tougher stock—she probably even wrote out personal messages in her Christmas cards—and, even without built-in MAXIFAX-brand translation software, would see through the most casual of banter.

Bella took the brochure back and slipped it into her bag. "Let's go see that Ronnie Johnson first."

Edna said, "She's a lovely lady."

"At the Belleweather Bungalows, right?"

"Everybody knows where those are."

"I don't," Martie said.

"But you're not everybody," said Bella, then reassured her with, "you're somebody. Well, I guess we're done here."

"I guess you are," said Edna. "Bye, then." But as Bella stood and herded her friends to the entrance, Edna asked, "Oh, and it was Sheena?"

Bella turned her head, nodded generously, and gave a parting wave, thankful to be getting out of range of Edna's scanners.

But as her SUV peeled out of the parking lot and onto the hot and fast arterial of Smithville Boulevard, Bella and her companions could not know that back inside Lovelies Salon, Edna had drawn her own flip phone from her own handbag and was telling a German acquaintance, *"Andreas? Es ist Edna. Warnen Sie den Arzt...Was? Ich weiß es nicht. Ihr Name ist Sheena..."*

CHAPTER XII

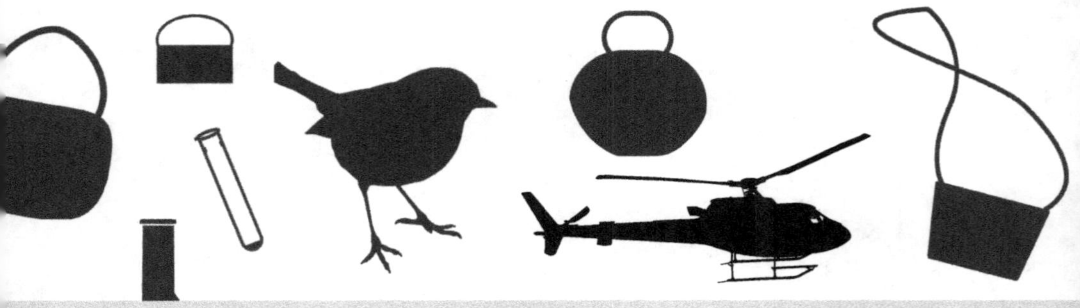

A SPRING IN HIS STEP, OR THE VERY MERRY MONTH OF MAY

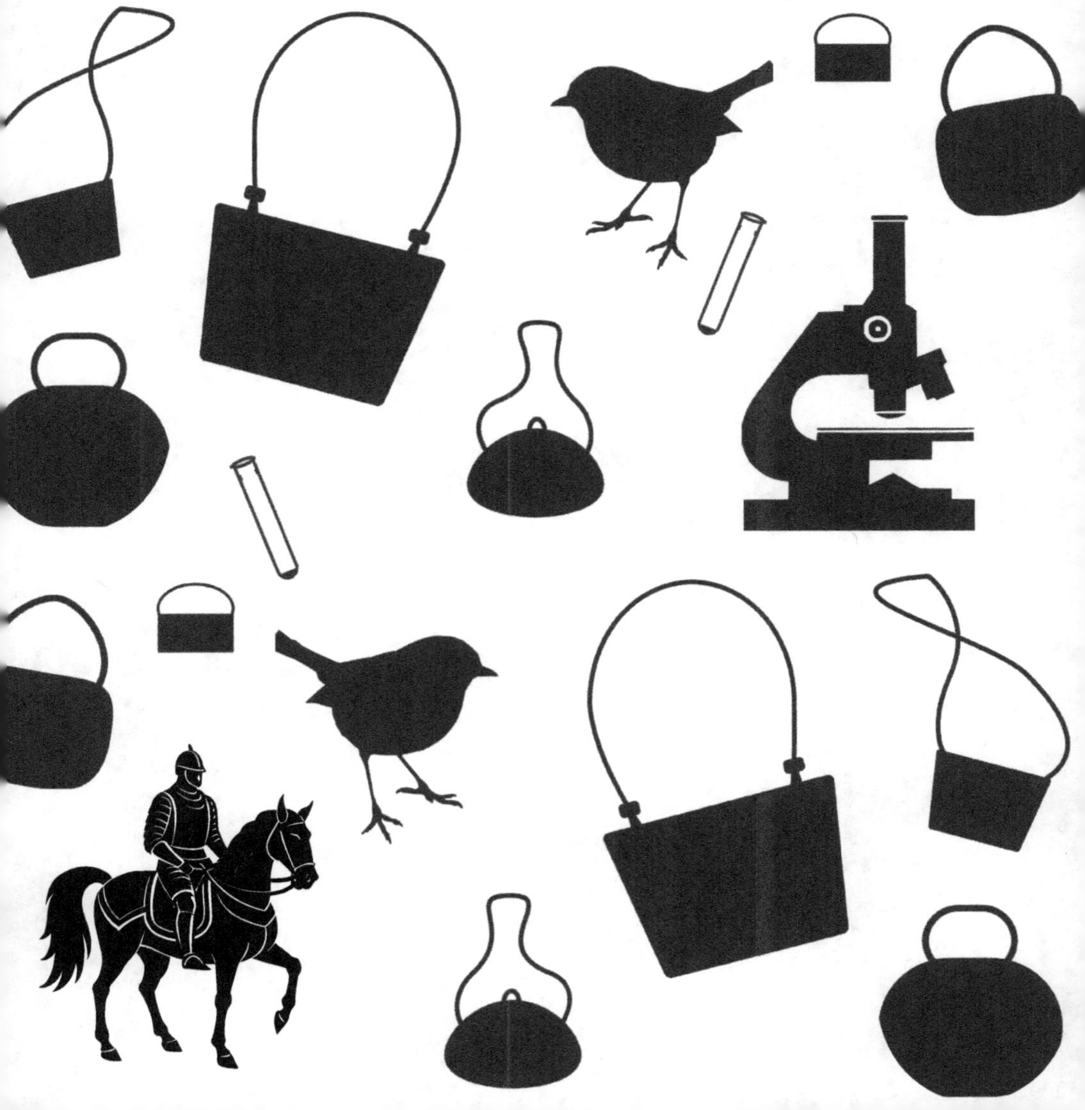

For Bobby Lumbar, the walk with Zoe to Mother Johanna's water tower hermitage was both painfully short and blissfully brief, but in no time, they were at the water tower.

Setting down the picnic hamper, Zoe called up into the sky, "Mother Johanna! Mail!" But while Bobby stood by smiling anxiously, all four of his eyes fixed on her, Zoe kept her peepers peeled up the beetling height of the tower...when from the summit, a sharp and rippling shriek rent the morning air and Zoe leapt directly into Bobby's arms.

When she realized that she was staring into Bobby's face, Zoe gave him a smack and extricated herself from his arms—until a second shriek sounded from above and she ran straight back to her new hero. (Little did she know that with all his strength he was refraining from throwing her over his shoulder right then and there and making for the nearest wildlife refuge.)

A third time came the shriek, now spiked with the words, "The boy and the girl!" and Mother Johanna's menacing form, like oleaginous radioactive waste taking on humanoid form, began to creep slickly toward them down the creaking superstructure of the tower.

Knowing that he had to put on at least a show of bravery, Bobby stiffened his back, shoved his glasses up his nose, and as this entity slithered down the water tower, closer and closer, he barked up at her, "Hey!"

The Medusa herself, perhaps surprised at this resistance, perhaps planning her angle of next attack, paused in her descent. Zoe, though, gave Bobby a fresh swat. "Don't you talk to her like that," and she squirmed from his protective embrace, but not before digging into his lab coat pocket and retrieving the letter of apology.

By now, Mother Johanna had neared ground level. But rather than taking that next crucial step in evolution and standing on two legs, she stopped two or three rungs from the jungle floor, hung from a crossbar, and swung about in midair, before coiling back and crouching on sweat-sock-swaddled feet overhead, just out of reach.

Finally, however, she did bend down, down toward Bobby's anxious face, and with her own visage hidden in its cowl like a beast in its cave, she began to...sniff.

Bobby whispered to Zoe, "Give it to her."

"Mother Johanna," Zoe said, and with a censorious glance at her traveling companion, "this is from him."

With a hiss, the hermit sent out a hand gloved in black, only its cracked fingertips exposed to the air, like the burnt branch of a tree. Snatching up the letter, she dragged it into the depths of her cowl and, after a grunt, sniffed at the paper. Following many mutters, she raised her head, her cowl still obscuring all traces of her face, and a gargled word came forth like a solitary bat. "Mine...?" Then dragging the letter into the abyss of her pitchy garb, with a swirl of her robes, she raced hand over hand up the metal of the tower, as if she were fleeing the dark side of the moon, to disappear behind the bloated bulk of the reservoir high above.

After a minute of staring with unblinking eyes, Bobby shook his head and returned to the here and now. "What about her fan mail?" he asked Zoe. "Dr. Fairfax said you had to give her her fan mail."

"I have to get it from Mother Deborah," she said. "So, are you, like, done embarrassing me?"

He said, "Uh, you're supposed to show me some other stuff too."

"Whatever," she said and tromped off toward the orchards, yelling to the sky, "Come on, if you're coming."

And with the talk ball vibrating again in his pocket, Bobby ventured along after her.

✳✳✳

This morning, the jaunt under the trees was quite the pleasure, not only because ATVs and mad scientists were nowhere in evidence, but because Zoe was guiding him through the section of the orchard that had been pruned, redeemed, and rehabilitated, rows of apples, pears, apricots, and almonds, their tidy branches in full flower, snowy and rosy, pink and pearlescent, and haloed in swarms of buzzing bees. Bobby breathed their perfume in a peaceful ease.

This Shangri-La did lose a bit of its charm, though, since his tour guide had forgotten how to talk. Hoping to generate a little human connection (especially with this human), Bobby thought of pointing out the high concentration of crown sparrows and starlings feeding at the humus layer of the trees or that he hoped that the slow-release granular fertilizer that the mothers had hosed up and down the rows did not lead to nitrogen toxicity. But realizing that a bulletin from the EPA was not exactly the heart-fluttering billet-doux that a girl would cherish to the end of her days, Bobby stuck with the tried-and-true "This is really pretty," and was about to add "...just like you" when they came out from under the blossoming bowers and Bobby found his need for human connection very much fulfilled—filled to overflowing, in fact.

They had set foot into the convent's parking lot, a dusty expanse of packed earth and gravel, just as at Orphis, but while the chapel, with its Baroque onion domes, was taking pride of place in the background, the immediate foreground was dominated by a pair of tour buses and a milling crowd of brochure-toting pilgrims. These pious travelers were of that age when a lot of life had been seen and the next life was right around the corner. The standard uniform for these Medicare beneficiaries was (for women) the print blouse buttoned to the neck and the pleated denim slacks and (for men) the Guayabera shirt and khaki shorts, with the occasional Hawaiian or golf shirt with flat-front chinos as exceptions.

Very quickly, the commanding black buzzsaw of Mother Deborah appeared, cutting a deep delve into the assembled. "All right, folks," she announced with gusto, "who's ready for an e-ticket to the pearly gates? Remember, we may not know what the morrow may bring"—several sober nods amid the assembled—"but what a lineup we've got for today!"

From the back of the crowd, a big-bellied grandpa with a Vietnam veteran cap, padded hunting vest, and military tattoos on his melanoma-specked lower arms cried out with rough, emphysemic piety, "Blessed Symeona, pray for us!"

Mother Deborah knew when to improvise. "Roger's got it right. Blessed Symeona of Blainesville..."

And the crowd called out cheerily, "...pray for us!"

"And Blessed Symeona wants to thank you all right off the bat for considering the purchase of some of our official Strange Sisters®

merchandise, just like that young lady back there's wearing." (Mother Deborah helpfully pointed out Zoe, who smiled and gave an uncharacteristically cheerful wave.) "After all, when the stooges of Antichrist are throwing you off a cliff, you'll want to have that ball cap on to cushion the fall." This vision of things to come caught everyone's attention, and they nodded and whispered among themselves. "And at those pearly gates, St. Peter won't know whose side you're on unless, like the cool kids say"—she made air quotes to assure her hearers that she was still speaking English—"you're 'tricked out' in a Strange Sisters® fleece vest. Do you think that young Dr. Kildare back there stands any chance of attaining to the beatific vision without a Strange Sisters® fleece vest?" Bobby saw that the mistress of ceremonies was now pointing him out, and he shrank a little behind Zoe while the crowd squinted at this soul doomed for the Pit. (Later, over a cup of comfrey tea and an organic scone, Mother Euphemia told the author that this dramatic merchandising pitch resulted in sales of fifty-five percent to the group. Mother Euphemia is the convent's number cruncher, when not harvesting propolis from the hives behind the generator shed and doing small-engine repair. The convent is a busy place.)

With that word from our sponsor duly done and everyone's engines nicely stoked, Mother Deborah said, "And now, off we go...," and like an obsidian spearhead leading on the horde, she charged to the chapel.

With the spotlight off of the young couple, Zoe told Bobby despondently, "Come on. Dr. Fairfax thinks you should see this. He thinks you're stupid or something."

And she scampered off toward the chapel, with Bobby of course following her. Maybe he would find a little supernatural aid.

✳✳✳

Despite their crosses of arthritis and bulging discs, the pilgrims shuffled along happily enough to the oaken doors of the chapel of Blessed Charles of Austria and the Servant of God Zita. There, a pair of cheery mothers with heavenly smiles and Strange Sisters® fleece vests welcomed them as one by one they entered the shadowy depths of the shrine. As Zoe and Bobby stepped up, though, she held up her hand at Bobby.

"Do *not* embarrass me," she said. "Don't *say* anything, don't *touch* anything, and if you can hold your breath so you don't spread any germs, that would be a *big* help." And with that, she plodded on to the chapel doors.

Deciding not to ask why he was the walking disease vector, Bobby marched up to the threshold and was all ready to cross into that "sacred space" that his grandmother liked to talk about, when he felt the talk ball buzzing in his pocket and he came to an annoyed halt.

But as he was about to mumble, "Just a second," Zoe drew her own conclusions.

"You're *possessed*," she gasped. "Father Max said that people who can't walk into a church are supposed to be possessed. I *knew it*. Mother Deborah!"

Bobby waved his hands for her to keep it down—she should not disturb the nice people inside—but she was shrieking, "Mother Deborah! He's possessed! He's possessed!"

To the stomp of pilgrims stampeding back to the doorway, Bobby stammered out very loudly, "No, no, I'm not possessed."

"That's just what a possessed person would say!" Zoe sniffed in horror.

Bobby was scrounging through the sofa cushions of his brain for an argument to counter this Kafka trap as the pilgrims came spilling out onto the chapel porch. "Who? Who?" they asked.

"Him! Him!" Zoe shuddered, pointing at Bobby.

Eager for a show of levitation or revelation of occult knowledge, the pilgrims hungrily circled 'round. (The unspoken consensus was that anyone who refused to set foot in the shrine of Blessed Charles of Austria and the Servant of God Zita and venerate the icon of Blessed Symeona of Blainesville should be strapped to the nearest tree to wait for Max von Sydow to show up—as long as his supernatural bodily strength did send them flying in all directions.)

Mother Deborah's awesome presence quickly filled the doorway, her displeased expression showing that this bizarre little sideshow was not on the itinerary. So, even while Roger in the Vietnam War ball cap was pointing at Bobby with a knuckley and accusing forefinger (or what was left of it, after that accident with the power saw back in '79), Mother Deborah, as if hosing down the fervid crowd with holy water, doused any additional drama by grabbing Bobby by the scruff and dragging him straight over the threshold and into the chapel.

When there ensued no foaming at the mouth or ornate curses in Chaldean, the crowd deflated a bit, and a few of the true blue devout looked ready to shuffle back to the bus to sulk. But to forestall any moody changes of heart, Mother Deborah took Bobby in both hands, heave-hoed him into an upright position, and declared, "See what the prayers of Blessed Symeona of Blainesville accomplish! And that's what you came for, wasn't it?" (At this point, she whispered to him, "Play along, junior, and I'll slip you a free jar of marionberry jam.") And as the pilgrims' faces brightened like votive candles, a few nodded with certain smiles, as if in the know that this thaumaturgy was just part of the tour.

Dropping Bobby with a thunk, Mother Deborah went on to point at some folk art in a candlelit corner at the opposite end of the shrine. "But what do we got here?" she asked in rhetorical grandness. "That rood screen right there was smuggled out of Slovakia *piece by piece* over the space of *fifty years* in the steamer trunk of a traveling trained bear act from Bratislava..." Several sets of half glasses tilted to get a better look, and she shuffled her audience away from the younger generation and their antics.

Zoe stared down at Bobby, still on the mosaic floor. "Well?" she asked.

With a look of horror, Bobby pointed back at the chapel door. "Hey, is that guy possessed too?" he asked, and with Zoe's head turned, he scampered upright.

While Zoe was asking, "Who? I don't see anyone..." Bobby gave the chapel the gander—and immediately felt that he should slip back outside. This was not because of what might be lurking behind that girandole candlestand or those red-and-gold processional banners, but because his modern soul was not acclimated to anything so lovely and gentle. Everywhere over the brass and carved wood played a limpid, guileless light, wandering almost angelically between the clerestory of high leaded-glass windows, then from tier upon tier of red candle glasses, their flames like the eyes of cherubim, quivering and quavering before the gilding on a score of saints' faces. (The grim expressions on icon after icon left Bobby guessing that the inhabitants of Paradise knew a putz when they saw one...)

Having toughed it out for fifteen seconds in this jewel box, Bobby heard Zoe say, "I know who you saw. I bet it was one of the *Shadow* People." She peered with narrow eyes up at the ceiling in case the dark shape had flown into the rafters. "They talk about them on Sea-to-Sea Radio. Come to my room at about two a.m. tonight and..." Bobby immediately brightened, glad to sign on as a research fellow for that project. But with a pout, Zoe remembered, "Oh, but I gotta be in the lab at two a.m. tonight."

"If you need some help...," he said as meltingly as he could in church.

But like a conductor pulling a lever, Zoe changed the track of the conversation and announced the next stop. "Come on. You have to see the icon."

With several specimens close at hand, Bobby wanted to ask, "Which one?" when out of the luminous shadows echoed the voice of Mother Deborah. "And this," said the mistress of ceremonies, "is the miraculous icon of Blessed Symeona of Blainesville."

"It gushes myrrh," Zoe told Bobby.

Before the young man of science could ask what precisely "gushing myrrh" was all about, Zoe was hustling him to the end of the impromptu queue of patient pilgrims now forming to see the miracle-working picture.

And Bobby soon discovered that *patient* was the operative word.

What should have been like a brisk receiving line was actually a traffic jam of the afflicted, with fully half of the pilgrims in the thrall of some painful bodily ailment (think synovitis, bursitis, arthritis, sciatica, or bulging discs). This kept them from delivering a devout prostration, which was exactly what each was trying to accomplish.

Bobby leaned into Zoe. "What's going on?"

Her frustrated sigh was like a monsoon wind. "The whole reason for the pilgrimage is a chance at a miracle."

His time in his theistic evolution online chat group now came in handy. "What miracle?"

"Blessed Symeona of Blainesville"—she said the name as if he should know exactly whom she was talking about—"is the patron saint of knee problems and bulging discs."

"Why is she the patron saint of knee problems and bulging discs?" asked Bobby to the audible creaking around them of many a joint and the grating noise of bone upon bone.

Breaking ranks, Zoe went to the stand of complimentary brochures by the chapel doors, found her prey, and came back. With a look suggesting that this would count as both a birthday and a Christmas present, she slipped the tract to Bobby. With no movement among the faithful in front of them, Bobby had plenty of time to indulge in some not exactly light reading entitled, *The Glorious and Martyric Death of Blessed Symeona of Blainesville, by an Anonymous Sinner.*

Without a detailed retelling, this vita related that Blessed Symeona of Blainesville started her days as Dey'neesha Collins of (yes) Blainesville. After composing a scholarship-winning essay on the history of royal women nuns in Ethiopia for her Head Start program, Dey'neesha received a free ride scholarship for the nearby community college's phlebotomy program but put these plans on hold when she "heard the call." After roughing it in a convent in the Northwest Territories, she was tonsured under the name Symeona (there being no St. Dey'neesha), although her aunties in their Christmas cards spelled *Symeona* with an *i* instead of a *y*. She had to bear this cross but briefly, since on a visit to the world of running water, electricity, and social media (i.e., civilization), Symeona strolled up onto a so-called peaceful protest about some very important contemporary issue and in her idealism tried to debate with the angry blue-haired college sophomores by invoking phrases like "You are made in the image of God," "Love your enemies," and similar dusty slogans of worldviews gone by. This hate speech induced a clutch of pale-faced soy junkies to take their mostly peaceful, obscenity-scrawled signs and unceremoniously thwack first on Symeona's kneecaps and then on the rest of her. This led to Symeona's permanent removal as a participant in future counterdemonstrations. Before the end of the day, she was legally declared deceased by the county coroner, before the end of the following day she was proclaimed a martyr by the Ruthenian female monastics' blogosphere community, and before the end of the month she was held up as the patron saint of bad joints after Mrs. Glencora Fitzpatrick of Bloomington, Indiana, had asked for her intercession during a bad bout of lumbago and experienced immediate (and so far, permanent) relief.

Slipping this edifying (if not too cheery) snapshot of contemporary college life into a front pocket (and hushing the talk ball again), Bobby could see the human traffic snarl in front of him a bit more sympathetically. And with a sizable segment of the line now kneeling on the floor and sending up humble appeals for relief, he caught a glimpse over their prostrate forms of the gilded image: a smiling young black woman in a dark nun's habit, clutching a protest sign that read "Love your enemies, bless them that curse you."

Paned over in glass and lying at a comfortable forty-five-degree angle, as if perpetually bedfast like any other sufferer, the icon rested on a wooded stand carved like an ornate tree trunk. Most of this loving craftsmanship, though, was obscured by ex-votos from her devotees (silicone models of knee joints and the like) and taped-up testimonials of healing sent from Zagreb, Sierra Leone, and Tierra del Fuego, among other foreign parts, while 'round and 'round the stand itself twined a cross-stitched banner from Mrs. Glencora Fitzpatrick of Bloomington, Indiana, herself, and about its varnished roots, wax tapers and candles were melting into self-abnegation. The final festoonery, crammed around the icon's frame and into all the corners against the glass, was a cushiony coronet of cotton wool, like pillows or clouds, soaking up a flood of glistening, gambogian trickles like greasy rosewater. (Bobby figured that this was the gushing myrrh, which contributed to a Christmas-in-May feeling, what with the frankincense smoke lingering from last Sunday and the gold glinting from every other icon, lampstand, and chandelier in sight.)

Eventually, the devotees had risen from their prostrations, and each one plucked a myrrh-soaked cotton ball from the icon's glass. As a helpful nun then gently directed the pilgrims to a back door for a springtime "hay ride" to the U-pick fields, Zoe informed Bobby, "You're done here. Come on," and made for the back door herself.

***

There followed another stroll undisturbed by any disquieting small talk. After several minutes of maneuvering among the sundry small buildings that made up the convent, our pair came out at the weedy fringe of a cultivated field. Zoe opened her hand to the distance and with as much verve as a wind-up doll coming to the end of its clicks, she told Bobby, "And those are the U-pick fields."

Bobby was glad that Zoe was still holding that picnic basket, because he might have dropped it, for into the midday horizon, in an endless vista, swelled acre upon acre of sweet, fragrant, weedy, dusty, wholesome, and cornucopial rows of growing goodness: tiny berries, red, blue, purple, pink, and burgundy, row upon row of knee-high sunflowers, row upon row of green-leather maize plants, rows of U-pick flowers coming into bud, and finally row after row of pumpkin and squash coiling up trumpeting golden blossoms amid their prickly tendrils.

Then, though, Bobby slid his glasses up his nose to make sure that he was seeing what else he truly was seeing: amid the berry bushes he saw *people*, scores and scores of *people*, *people* filling little plastic buckets with little fruits, scores and scores of nameless saviors, any one of whom might have stowaway seating where he could discreetly curl up and get out of this place. (And he was more than willing to take the plunge one more time...)

But how to reach them?

At this point, an uninviting invitation came to the rescue, as Zoe told him, "Come on, this way," and set off between the two rows of white and yellow raspberries.

He quickly caught up with her. "So...?"

"So?" she asked.

He knew that he had to play it cool. "So, what do you think of stowaway seating?"

"It's gross," she said and turned up along a row of pink blueberries.

Since that tack had not worked, he tried, "So..."

"You said that already." She ran her hand over the top of the bushes, sending half a bucketful of blueberries bouncing down to the ground.

"So, do you like it here?" he asked.

"It's all right. Where'd you grow up, in town or in the country?"

Surprised at her interest, but worried that getting any more acquainted would interfere with his escape plans, he risked it and played along. "Mostly in town. But my parents left me at my grandmother's a lot, and she lived outside of town."

"Did she have a farm or something?"

"Or something." Bobby did not think that his grandmother's New Age retreat center with the wooly-thyme-and-Corsican-mint labyrinth counted as a farm, although one November afternoon an entire day retreat accidentally meditated itself into a vegetative state.

Zoe stared up at the sky as she walked along, as if reading off skywriting. "I grew up on a farm, so I love this. Well, maybe I used to love it." Just then, she resumed the chilly mask. "And here you pay for your fruit."

They had reached the commercial heart of the Strange Sisters operation, a spacious pavilion of plastic tarps where two nuns (Mothers Thecla and Nitriana) sat at their folding-table checkout stand with a ten-key and manual scales at the ready, like sharp-eyed Venetian traders in an Ottoman port. In front of them ran a phalanx of hand-painted price signs reminding the world of the juicy bargains on offer. On either side stood racks selling heirloom seeds and "Heaven Scent" handmade soaps, while from a cast-iron "tree" hung old-fashioned glass wasp traps like great glassy figs. (When she dwelt "in the world," Mother Nitriana had been the regional glassblowing champeen, and Mother Deborah knew a great product tie-in when she saw it.)

A line of neo-urbanite foragers waiting to cram the convent's coffers had already formed, reaching back into the pink blueberries. But even while Bobby was scoping out a likely free ride from the mothers-of-two inspecting the heirloom seed rack, Zoe unilaterally decided, "This is boring. Come on."

But Bobby was busy trying to catch the eye of a compassionate day tripper who might have room in the trunk if she taught the kids that life ain't easy by making them walk home; and just as he was asking, "Uh, excuse me, miss—" a flatbed truck pulled up alongside the checkout with a sudden squealing of brakes and a cloud of dust that floated away like a tattered hope.

The driver's door creaked quickly open and, like a spill from an India ink factory, down jumped Mother Deborah. "No one fall off?" she called up to the bed, now an ad hoc passenger section. Crowded on this unfenced platform sat a happy band of the more limber pilgrims reliving their (hopefully) rosy childhoods. (And any who might have fallen off were not there to report the fact.)

"And where are you kids off to now?" she asked Bobby and Zoe.

Thinking that the abbess and Dr. Fairfax maybe shared a telepathic bond and knew each other's schemes, Zoe moaned, "Aren't I *done* yet?"

"You're only done when you're dead," said Mother Deborah.

"Then when do I get to die?"

"Not yet."

"Can I go back to the lab?"

"When you're done with Herbert here."

"Robert," said Bobby.

"But what else can he want to see?" She sighed.

Happy to solve a dilemma, the pilgrims now piped up as travel guides. One said, "There's the giant ground sloth skull at the mini-mart on Brownbag Road."

Another carrot tossed into the pot was, "And the two-headed calf at Farmberg Farm gift shop."

A third poked her nose into the discussion. "And the haunted cannery."

But a fourth fomented controversy with, "But the cannery ain't there no more."

"The ghosts don't know that. The foundation stones make a pattern that traps 'em in this vortex."

"Those were those convicts, escaped from the chain gang."

"No, they were from the state hospital."

"No, they escaped the pen and *then* they hid in the garden shed at the looney bin and *then* they ran to the cannery. My son-in-law's dog is in die-rect dee-scent from the hound that treed the only one they caught."

"Well, that fella was lucky. The other ones, they hid in the vats over the long weekend and got overcomed by fumes or somethin' and ended up in a pallet of Bing cherry pie filling goin' to Cochin-China."

"I thought it went to Thailand."

"Siamese people don't eat cherry pie."

"It was for the naval base in Guam."

"Close enough."

"And the captain of the ship cracked open a can and went insane."

"And the ship's still sailing up and down the Mekong peninsula." (This was Roger's contribution.) "But you can only see it on a night of a second full moon."

Mother Deborah was about to intervene when a muffled line of plainchant sounded from one of her pockets. Pulling out a much-knocked-about handheld, she put it to her ear.

"Yes, Phineas? Oh, they're right here. I never saw two kids more happy. No, really." Lowering the device to her breast, she told Bobby, "He thinks you should go to Smithville Dike for your picnic. You can't beat the view of the housing development." At this addition to the young travelers' itinerary, old Roger the Pilgrim pointed with what was left of his hand to the north. Squinting in the cardinal direction provided, Bobby made out a lengthy heap of grass and trees, something like a burial mound for prehistoric kings, if in ages past enormous mutant caterpillars had been lords of the land.

The sages on the flatbed held forth once again. "Back in the old days, floodin' was bad."

"The flood of '74, that was the one."

"There's the plaque about it at the rest stop."

"Can't I just go back to the lab?" Zoe whined.

"When you're done," said Mother Deborah, clarifying all uncertainties and turning her about to face Bobby.

Zoe held up the picnic basket. "I've got food."

Bobby wished that all eyes were on him, to see the sacrifice he was making. But Mother Deborah was reading a fresh text on her handheld, the pilgrims had fallen into heated contention about the virtues of Epsom salts versus camphor oil rubs, and most of the mothers-of-two were making off with their blueberries and handblown wasp traps for the parking lot. Thus defeated in the age-old feud between freedom or food, Bobby gave a last stare at the parking lot, abandoned this chance at escape, and marched off with Zoe to the enjoy the view from Smithville Dike.

∗∗∗

A stone's throw from the U-pick checkout began a crude gravel road that ran on for a quarter mile before losing its identity and turning into a path of potholes. After another hundred feet, it gave up any kind of self-respect and turned into a long, wide path overgrown with Scotch broom and butterfly bushes. Up this botanical garden of invasive species, Bobby and Zoe started to bushwhack, but without machetes, pocketknives, or any other self-respecting sharp metal edge, they were near surrender (they had gone about a hundred feet or so) when, seedy, sweaty, and panting, they broke out through thistles and rusty farm equipment to discover before them a slope of high green grass shot through with millions upon millions of smiling white daisies.

Too worn out from bushwhacking to care about personalities, one asked, "Smithville Dike?" and the other answered, "Smithville Dike."

But as Bobby was making the observation that this was more a down than a dike, since dikes usually aren't so vertiginous, Zoe with the basket started stomping up through the daisies, snatching handfuls as she climbed.

When Bobby had finally caught up with her on the grassy summit (his Florsheims were not marketed as hiking boots), he saw her sitting beneath a crown of chancrous old apple trees, too hag-ridden to make fruit and just content to watch the world breeze by, setting up their picnic.

Tramping over to her, he tossed his lab coat on the grass, gratefully sat down, tucked his clip-on tie into his pocket, yanked off his Florsheims, and tossed them into the grass, all while smothering the talk ball still seeking an audience with him.

Before she could ask why he was making himself so comfortable, Zoe, with that strange and innate sense unique to her, said, "Oh, look," and cupped up from the grass a tiny dead birdie.

"What is it?" Bobby asked.

"What do you care?" she asked, petting the little victim as she sighed.

Bobby took that as the bell for another round of romantic pugilism, but he made ready to play up to his strengths (such as they were) and, pressing her hand open a little, said, "Just let me see. Ah. *Troglodytes aedon.*"

Zoe immediately folded her hands around the tiny victim like a living shroud. "This makes me sad."

"I'm sorry," he said, still operating on the theory that any conversation with her was good conversation.

Her mood, though, suddenly sprang from the grave. "What's that?" She was pointing to a hazel thicket. "A bluebird."

Imagining himself as the ornithologist attached to a special forces unit, Bobby dug out Dr. Fairfax's field glasses and with silent efficiency brought them to his eyes. He noted on the bird's plumage a bluish cast, but also a lack of prominent thoracic or periocular markings. Lowering the glasses to his chest, he told her, "Yes, it is. Thank you."

"Does that kind die very much?"

Bobby was not down for the count. Yet. "Did you hear that?" he said. "That tapping?" He brought the glasses to his eyes again and trained them on a cottonwood. "Hey, it's a *Melanerpes formicivorus*. They're—"

"It's a woodpecker," Zoe told the expert and started unpacking the picnic basket as if it were her last meal onto his lab coat, now spread over the grass as a tablecloth.

Hanging on the ropes but not tapping out, Bobby tried an interpersonal left hook.

"You mind my asking, why'd you use to love the country, but not now?"

She was taking out fruit, a pair of sandwiches, peanut-butter brownies, and a red-plaid patterned thermos and was trying to array them over his coat, but with little success. Then she said, "'Cause there'll be no more country left," and pointed off beyond the convent.

Peering a third time through the field glasses, Bobby expected to spy a field of chemically treated cabbages, nothing startling to the simple -minded, but deeply grieving to the heart of Zoe Feldspar. Instead, he made out past the convent a gang of objects blighting the neighboring acreage: a mustard-yellow backhoe like a pterodactyl, the boxy mobile home headquarters of a site manager's office, a row of turquoise honeypots like pods budding from a radioactive waste dump, and a rippling plastic banner that read "Future Homesites From the Mid 500s." Over what had once been fields, now shorn of greenery and crushed flat, there shot into the horizon, like the perspective lines for a city of the dead, a grid pattern of tight rectangles for zero-lot-line "luxury homes."

Bobby lowered the glasses, unlooped them from his neck, and cast them aside like a warlord banishing the enemy's messenger from his sight.

"Do they know what they're doing?" he muttered.

"I dunno," Zoe said. She had set the dead birdie back into the grass and now was trying to stand a pair of plastic cups upright.

"I mean, did they make an ecological survey to maintain core loci of native habitat?"

"I dunno."

"Are they maintaining adequate greenspace?"

"Maybe you should ask them. But all the birds are going to die," and her voice sank as she envisioned so many dainty headstones studding the sidewalk medians in front of the new homesites starting in the five hundreds.

But before Zoe submerged deeper into her mire of morbid fantasies, Bobby suddenly became prophetic, his golden glasses like polished gunsights as he envisioned age-old nesting sites and flyways falling under the backhoe. "Do you want all the birds to die?" he fumed.

"I don't want to talk about it," she said, dully folding back the waxed paper from two very chunky chicken-salad sandwiches.

Then, in a burst of indignation, Bobby stood up and loomed over her, blotting out the sun's light with the stubby tower of his righteous rage. But before, in his furor, he chucked his chunky chicken-salad sandwich into the grass—chickens not being an endangered species—a buzzing sounded in his pocket.

Sliding a forceful hand into his trousers, Bobby Lumbar seized the noisemaker and hurled it like a bloated marble off into a clump of wild saskatoons—while forgetting that those heavy metals and electronics would not do this bioregion any favors.

"Now," he said, "where was I? Oh, yeah. The birds..."

At this, Zoe held up to him an apple, its glossy skin at once as red as rancor, as yellow as moral cowardice, and as green as eco-righteousness. "Here," she said.

Not taking his eyes from this gleaming fruit, Bobby pulled off his glasses, slid them into the front pocket of his sweaty Oxford shirt, and knelt in front of her. Chaperoned only by the breeze, he set his hand on the apple, wove his fingers in with hers, and with a firm pressure, lowered it from the space between them. "I just don't want you to be sad," he said, his unspectacled eyes strong and fixed on her. Then, remembering something that a guest lecturer to his theistic evolution online chat group had said, he brought his face oh-so close to hers. "And you know what else?"

If Bobby's eyes would not leave Zoe's, now hers would not leave his. "No," she said. "What?"

"The snake said it tastes good," and he kissed her.

CHAPTER XIII

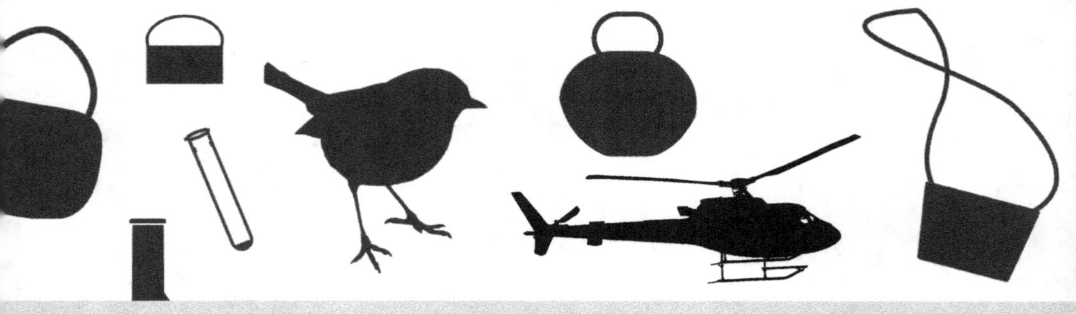

DINOSAUR HUNT, OR LIVING FOSSILS

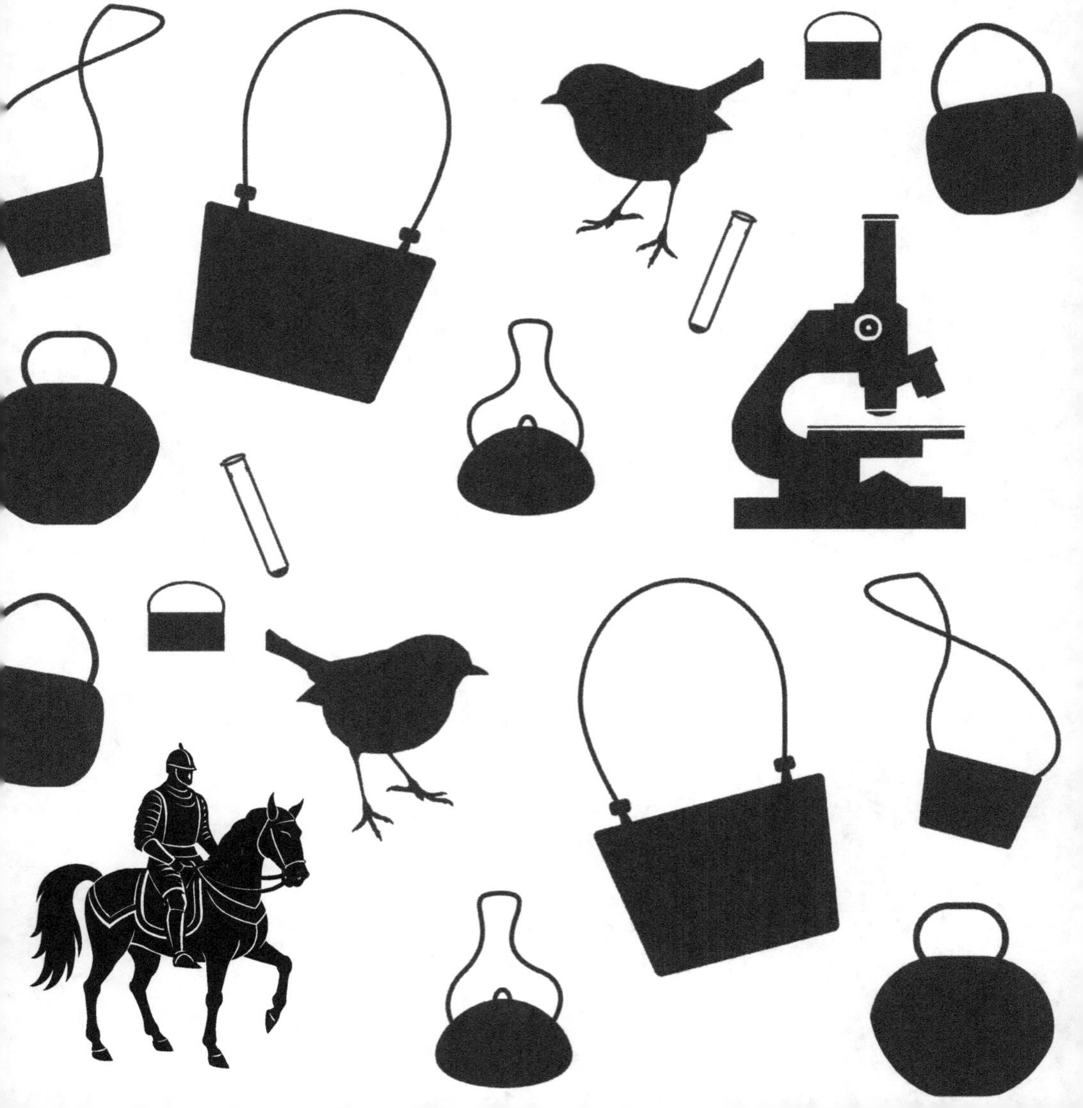

En route to the Belleweather Bungalows, Bella, Baba, and Martie concocted a scheme that would not work.

Bella would wring out of Ronnie Johnson the whereabouts of Dr. Phineas Fairfax, while Baba and Martie staked out the post office in case anyone resembling a red-haired, red-bearded man in a lab coat came to pick up his junk mail and chitchat with the stamp collectors. And should this plan fail (and the bookmakers at Merryweather Meadows were giving good odds that it might), the ladies would regroup and gun it for the nearest international border before Sheena Lypotrope was any the wiser.

This deployment of their scant forces should have caused even Sun Tzu to smile, until personalities asserted themselves. First, Bella announced that she alone would be driving the getaway car. (She blamed the fine print in her insurance policy.) Then Baba argued that she should be the one to interview the mysterious Ronnie Johnson since she (Baba), as the long-recognized doyenne of Merryweather's women-at-mid-life social machine, had all the necessary charm and trickery to draw out whatever was needed. And in a final blow to efficiency and teamwork, Martie groused that she did not have any ideas right then, but they had better listen to her when she did. With this nail in the coffin, all recognized the need to proceed as a unit.

✳✳✳

On reaching the Belleweather Bungalows, Bella scanned the building's sign with narrow eyes. "Should I sue the landlord for using my name without permission?"

"But your middle name's not Weather," said Martie.

"And your last name's not Bungalow," said Baba.

Bella forced herself to hum that this was so and then considered the structures themselves.

Despite the name, the Belleweather Bungalows were not quaint stucco cottages sitting away from each other in cozy if polite autonomy, but a complex of brick quadraplexes held from the public by a fence akin to a line of iron spears and secured by the inevitable locked gate like a sort of metallic granny knot.

Baba waved her vaping pen at draconic coils of razor wire looping viciously down the upper line of the fence. "That's a bit *de trop*."

"The Girl Scouts probably raid the recycling bins," theorized Martie.

"That may be," said Baba. "Now, who are we looking for?" Going to the call box, she set to scrutinizing its tiny, typed labels. Drawing her topaz-tipped finger downward, she murmured name after name. "Scaramangia Wilberforce, Daphne Mazareon, Poppy Mecanopsis, Jicama Pickle, Fruity Lampsa, Artemisia Sage..."

"Faster, please," said Bella, glancing down the sidewalk while hovering behind her friends, who, if they were real friends, should be willing to be used as human shields.

With a ripple of fear in her quiet voice, Martie ventured, "Charlotte, are the people here...?"

"Are they what, Lily?" asked Baba, without looking up from the call box.

"...old?"

"We don't use that word, sweetheart," said Baba. "Ah...But how many Johnsons can there be? Rickettsia Johnson...Pellagra Johnson, crossed out. Phylloxera Johnson...But what about Eurynome Johnson?"

"Eurynome sounds like Ronnie to me," said Bella and, reaching around her, gave the call button a good press.

"Do you have a story ready for the old girl?"

"You said 'old,'" gasped Martie. "But, you know, I think I could live here someday."

Bella started to say, "I bet they don't have kitchen islands..." when a voice crackled through the intercom grill.

"This is Ronnie?" it said.

Baba gestured at the box, inviting Bella to work her magic.

The voice crackled once again. "Hello?"

Tossing her hair, Bella moved into position. "Hey," she told the intercom, "I'm looking for Ronnie Johnson?"

Silence, then another crackle. "This is Ronnie."

"Umm...Connie at the salon said that I should talk to you?"

Deciding to get into the act, Martie reached around Bella and, invading her purse, pulled out the brochure for Orphis and shook it in her face. This earned her both a smack on the hand and a hastily mouthed, "Thank you."

"Yeah," Bella went on, "Connie at the salon. Liver Pills, or whatever it's called. From Summerville, I mean. That's where she lives."

"Oh, Summerfield," said the intercom. "Yes, Connie. I know her. You know her?"

"Yeah," Bella said. "She said you know Dr. Phineas Fairfax and maybe you could help me get in touch with him?"

The summer-storm static that had been sounding through the box suddenly silenced.

Bella froze. "Hello?"

"Just press it again," Martie said and reached around her to do just that, when the lock disengaged and the iron gate quietly swung open before them.

✳✳✳

Once they were inside the fence, the gate closed behind them—seemingly by its own power—with a dull, subdued, and chilling clang.

Lighting up her vaping pen for a revitalizing puff (since it certainly was not a crutch in the face of anxiety or fear), Baba said, "She lives in number five, as I recall. Well, someone, blaze a trail."

Bella said to Martie, "Lily, Pioneer Rose?"

Martie shook her head. "I'll ride shotgun, thanks."

Baba rapidly found herself on the receiving end of a look from Bella. "I remembered the apartment number."

Rolling her eyes at the poltroonery of her bestest buddies, Bella fixed her shoulders bravely back and, with perfect posture, trod to the quadraplexes.

After a benign amble between some grandmotherly rhododendrons, our trio stepped into a sunny courtyard, a cheery little piazza boxed in by the apartments, very open and tidy, but, Bella thought, a setting that also made them sitting ducks.

"That Buddha statue there, by the birdbath...," she whispered to Martie. "What do you think? Throwing stars or a katana longsword?"

"Bella dear," said Baba, inhaling another dose of clarity while perusing the "Thank You For Not Smoking" sign next to the water meter. "Please focus."

"Oh, I need to go back and get my hot chocolate," said Martie.

"No," Bella said. "It's still in my speakers. Just start counting off apartment numbers, if you can manage that."

After sniffing at being bossed about, Martie dutifully stomped off, loudly reciting, "A, B, C, D..."

Bella gave a commanding look at Baba, who mouthed, "Oh," and took up the search in the other direction.

Bella was searching out the units before her when she felt a tug on her skirt. "You looking for someone?"

Looking down, she saw a recumbent bicycle powered by a petite little woman of many years wearing metallic orange spandex, a helmet advertising the Base Camp Bungee Brawl, reflective goggles with projecting side mirrors, and (to complete the lifestyle fashion package) a banner like an immense, rippling dorsal fin behind her ergonomic seat that read "Happy Hags Cycle Club."

The happy hag asked again, "Who you looking for?"

Not wishing to complicate the conversation with too much chitchat, Bella said, "Ronnie Johnson."

"Number 5," verified the fresh-air enthusiast. She started to report, "Right over—" when a sharp, girlish scream rippled through the air, and Martie, her arms vibrating like machine parts that had lost their tensioners, came running madly toward them.

"It's after me!" she shrieked and rushed around Bella, no doubt assuming that an old friend would take the brunt of any frontal attack.

"What's after you, sweetheart?" asked the cyclist, her goggles almost glowing at a threat to the peace and quiet of Belleweather Bungalows.

"I don't know!" Martie sniffled, pointing up the way she had just come. "Just go kill it."

(Bella's eyes bugged at this bandying of the *k*-word in mixed company— but then, if Scaramangia or Artemisia or whomever this was would keep the cops busy...)

"Not here at Belleweather!" snarled Scaramangia (or Artemisia), and with the war cry of "Full lane!" she pedaled off down the walkway after the threat.

Martie asked, "Is she gone?

"She's gone," said Bella.

Martie whistled up the opposite way and from around that corner emerged Baba. Joining them, she said with well-modulated satisfaction, "I love a good diversionary tactic. But now, if you will both follow me..."

Bella felt compelled to ask, "So, no one's chasing you?"

"Here?" said Martie. "Chatty Cathy there had to sit on a bike just to leave the house."

Having rounded a nearby corner, they found Baba drawn elegantly up next to a door complete with the number 5 in well-aged metal. "Bella dear," she suggested, "when you talk with this lady, a little savoir faire, you know, the seamless delivery?"

"I know what I'm doing," Bella reminded her, and after peering down the sidewalk for any oncoming recumbent bikes, she made ready to politely rap the knocker when Martie spoke up.

"Oh, this is so cute." She was enraptured by a dubious object d'art hanging from the eves near the door: an antiquey cast-iron triangle and rod, something from ye olde village smithy. "It's like in the story of the hired hand and the Holstein calf. Let's see if it works."

Baba started to explain, "It's not a blender," but Martie had already giddily grabbed the rod and was giving it a nostalgic, unmistakable, and loud rattle.

"Oh, it works!" she beamed. "It works! That is so neat."

To its dying echo, Bella asked, "And you're allowed to operate a motor vehicle?"

"Well, they said I shouldn't," said Martie and added, pointing the cast-iron rod at her, "But if you tell anyone—"

Martie's threat, though, was lost to posterity when all around them, apartment door after apartment door opened and shadowy heads peered out, only to shrink back cautiously, like jungle tortoises, returning to shelter.

Then the door of apartment number 5 opened in front of them.

Before any greetings were exchanged, Bella Freestone, out of some atavistic female instinct, had to judge whether Ronnie Johnson was prettier than she was. She decided that she definitely had been, say, when the wagon train had first pulled the parking brake in these parts. Despite her many years, though, Eurynome "Ronnie" Johnson still possessed that envy-inducing narrowness of nose, a swanlike neck, almost aerial cheekbones, expertly proportioned eyes of violet, and a creamily innocent and unsullied complexion, probably from avoidance of Mr. Sun. At one stage in her career, her hair had been dark, but was now wintery gray and gathered back. Her sense of fashion had parked itself in the cul-de-sac of the loose, airy, and comfortable, draped as she was in a handwoven purple shawl, of vicuña wool or the lint from the llama ranch. In Bella's stern book, all of this suggested that she had given up the fight.

"Ronnie...Johnson....?" Bella asked unevenly. Maybe she should have let Baba handle the introductions after all.

"Yes, that's me," she answered without a change in her waxy expression. "You called from the gate. You know, you don't look like the Sheena I knew."

Bella blinked and swallowed, but before Baba and her savoir faire glided onto center stage, Martie nudged around Bella and smiled hello. Ronnie Johnson smiled back at her, with only her mouth moving to indicate pleasure at this new acquaintance.

Martie asked, "Can you tell us about this?" and waved the Orphis brochure at the lady's face. Bella snatched it away and glared at Martie to retreat, which she did.

"Well, look at that," said Ronnie Johnson, taking the literature from Bella. She ran her silken fingertips over its glossy cover and stared at it as if scanning a barcode. Still gazing at it, she said, "Come in. Come in, won't you." This was not a question. Bella had decided that there was something odd about this gal, but since Dr. Lypotrope was probably already warming up the laser scalpels and soliciting buyers on the dark web, this particular mystery would have to remain unsolved. So, she made haste to cross the threshold, with Martie and Baba coming along to help fill up the room.

There was not much to say about the room, other than it was so airy and light that Bella was unsure whether to let down her guard or reach for a shank. In one corner, a boxy television set played that old cable-TV standby *Are They Still Alive?* while in another brooded a shrine of candles and incense sticks burning before pinned-up clippings from a fan magazine, c. 1986. (During her "casual" stroll about the chamber, Baba found this to be a shrine to the sacred triad of Bibi Besch, Delta Burke, and Linda Evans.) Along a wide wooden windowsill sat pot after pot of begonias, while from the window frame above hung spirit catchers, bundles of sage, and a dozen cut crystal spheres on fishing line that caught the sunlight and cast little splinters of prismatic light over the white semigloss walls. Other elements of decor in Ronnieville were an expansive hanging of native design, framed pictures, a bookshelf overpopulated with paperbacks from *The New York Times* bestsellers list, and three closed doors placed at strategic points.

Ronnie Johnson waddled across the floor, leading Bella to speculate that if this lady had not exactly graduated from fetching nymph to full-blown fertility goddess, she was certainly cramming for the exams. Reaching an ottoman covered with mailer ads, Ronnie Johnson brushed the junk mail onto the floor, pushed the cushiony cube over to a well-lit breakfast nook, and crawled around it into the nook herself. This nifty alcove, which could have served as the sunny setting for a pancake commercial, was instead crammed to bursting with a gigantic cushiony chair and pillows of exotic embroideries. Depositing herself on this upholstered cloud, Ronnie Johnson reached over to a vintage stereo lilting forth misty, Celtic vocalizations and, turning a silvery knob, brought about an inviting silence. Before indulging her visitors, however, she took from atop one of the speakers a still-dewy eighteen-ounce can of beer and partook of a luxurious and lengthy swig. (Bella noted in the crevasses alongside the cushions of her nest the many empties that must have fallen since sunrise.)

Having returned her libation to its resting place, she said, "Sit there, sweetheart," meaning the ottoman.

Bella proceeded with caution, remembering a similar setup when she made that professional call on the Maharani of Melishwar. But since it did not look like Ronnie Johnson had the facilities for a tiger pit that might suddenly gape open in the middle of the floor, she took a chance and sat.

Ronnie Johnson leaned forward, and in a voice as delicate and benign as the light of dawn through the leafy borders of a springtime woodland, she said, "So, what about Dr. Fairfax? Who's he going to help?" She was staring just past Bella's shoulder.

"Help?" asked Bella, wanting to peek about to see what was so fascinating.

Ronnie Johnson nodded with a narcotic grin, then aimed her gaze directly at Bella. "Will Dr. Fairfax help you?"

"No, not me, I'm fine. It's..." Taking a chance to see what might be going on behind her, she turned her head and saw nothing out of the ordinary, but also a suitable victim. "No, it's my daughter, Lily. Here, Lily, come here," and dragged Martie toward their hostess. "Lily's not a well young woman."

"There's nothing wrong with me," Martie started to fuss.

"You see?" said Bella, giving Martie a meaningful squeeze to remind her not to derail the mission. "And, you know, I was very young when I had her."

Ronnie Johnson hummed. "I understand." Then, staring past her again, she asked Baba, "And who are you?"

Baba had been doing a bit of recon throughout the room and was just then picking through the knickknacks on a shelf. "You know," she told Ronnie, "I just love your place."

"Thanks." Ronnie Johnson smiled. "But you are...?"

"That's Charlotte, my mother," said Bella, quickly staking out the genealogy before anyone tried to peg her as older than she absolutely needed to be.

Baba borrowed a line from Bella. "I was so young when I had her."

Ronnie Johnson nodded sympathetically. "So, Lily, why do you need to see Dr. Fairfax?"

"We just want to help her," Bella answered on her behalf.

"But there's nothing wrong with me!" spluttered Martie, not realizing that this was what she was supposed to say.

"Oh, sweetheart...," said Bella, petting her hand and sighing with false concern. "I don't know, is it a problem not to have a problem?"

Leaning out of her sanctuary, Ronnie Johnson patted the ottoman. "You sit here, next to mama." After a nervous look at Bella, Martie made herself become at once the cynosure of their hostess's attention.

With eyes like amethyst inlay, Ronnie Johnson let her sight wander over Martie's black hair and flawless epidermis. "You are so pretty, honey," she whispered, then rested her hand on Martie's cheek. Martie wanted to cringe at this contact with decay, until Ronnie Johnson murmured, "So pretty," and Martie gave out a smile of true pleasure.

"See?" She smiled at Bella. "Even weird old ladies think I'm pretty."

"Oh, honey, no," gasped Ronnie Johnson and stroked her young visitor's face as if smoothing a tablecloth before a dinner party. "No, no, don't smile too much. And don't cry. Or laugh. You'll just ruin it."

"That's always been my philosophy," said Baba.

"And always wear a hat outside. The sun is lethal. And preservatives: Dr. Fairfax told me years ago that one should eat as many industrially produced foods as possible, since their preservatives keep you young and supple. See?" She put Martie's hand against her own motionless face.

"You're so soft," Martie said with wonder.

And as Ronnie Johnson and Martie joined one another in founding a mutual admiration society, with their hostess now letting her hand drift down Martie's cheek as if stroking the plumage of a dove, Baba leaned in behind Bella. "Is it just me, or has this lady not blinked once since we got here?"

Bella took several seconds of her valuable time to determine whether this was so—and to her dread saw that it was.

Bella knew to push things along. "So, how do we find Dr. Fairfax?"

"Just go to his place," said Ronnie Johnson without taking her eyes from Martie. "It's right outside of town."

"But where exactly...?"

Martie started complicating the schedule by chatting with her fan club of one. "I really like your music."

"Thank you, sweetheart," said Ronnie Johnson.

"Do you have any Dan Fogelberg?" Martie asked, trying to remember a classical composer.

Ronnie Johnson nodded and continued to stare (unblinking) at her. "So pretty..."

"Or Carole King?"

"Of course."

"How about Gordon Lightfoot?"

"Would you like me to put them on? Oh, I know what you would like. Are you hungry?" She took a protracted swallow from her tallboy. "Would you like something to eat, honey? Maybe you'd like a pull-apart?"

"Oh, a pull-apart sounds yummy," Martie said. "Can I, Mom?"

While Ronnie Johnson quietly reminded Martie not to smile, Bella stroked her "daughter's" hair indulgently. "You bet, honey. Have two." (Bella could have stood for a snack herself but knew that she would never keep her figure by eating.)

Crawling out of the breakfast nook, Ronnie Johnson guided Martie to one of the anonymous, unopened doors. Before they had passed into this chamber of mystery, though, Baba, standing before a bank of photographs on the wall, said offhandedly, "Quite the cosmopolitan, weren't you? Where was this?"

"Oh, that one?" said Ronnie Johnson. The photo showed rugged scenery, yurts, and Bactrian camels in the background, and Ronnie Johnson touched her lips as if to rouse a memory. "Oh, that was the camp of our dig along the Altai Range. It was lovely. Curds made from mare's milk. They're very good for you." Baba hummed in acknowledgment and added one more thing to her list of forbidden foods.

"And how about this one?"

"I think that was Bhutan. We were digging up blue and pink poppies."

Familiar with law enforcement in Central Asia after that incident at the Mongolian border with those dinosaur eggs in the bottom of her tote bag, Baba suggested chummily, "Interpol might call that poaching."

For a flicker of a second, Ronnie Johnson lost her airy stare, her face tightened, and she might have even blinked. But like serenity returning to the silver face of an alpine lake, she said with dispassionate pleasantry,

"Not if they don't catch you. But Lily's hungry. Come along, Lily. Let's get you something." And she led Martie on through the door.

Once the door had quietly closed, it was Bella's turn to whisper to Baba. "What do we think?"

"I'm not sure," Baba said. "I just hope this won't be us in the future."

Bella said, "If I end up listening to Enya..."

"Charlotte Church for you. But never fear, Bella dear. We play nice for a few more minutes, she spills the beans, we play nice for another few minutes after that, and no one gets hurt."

Baba went back to scanning the life of Ronnie Johnson in photographs. After a mental notation that there was not one image from girlhood, no cameo snaps with grandma, no little Eurynome in a bassinette or christening gown, etc., she came to an image of an old-fashioned graduation group.

This memory, rectangular and panoramic, blazed with glaring color. The day it captured must have been a sunny one, to judge from the shining faces and squinting eyes of six rows of smartly dressed young women, all very chirpy, but with a certain brittleness suggesting that they were unsure of what was going on. In the background hung a canvas sign propped up on tent rods that read "Johnson College," while at strategic points in the front row, several of the girls held up with nail-polished fingertips a sagging sign that declared, "Merryweather or Bust!"

"Bella dear," said Baba, "do you see what I see?" and she pointed an iron-oxide fingertip to other participants present on this happy day: scientific types, all in lab coats, to the left and right of the young ladies.

Bella murmured, "Wait a second..."

Repeating her move at Lovelies Salon, she took out her handheld and found the photo of Phineas Fairfax. The pear-shaped, scraggle-faced MAXIFAX factotum on her phone's screen was undeniably one of the fellows flanking these graduates of Johnson College. Squinting through his glasses and grinning as stiffly as the young women, he held to his chest a white three-ring notebook as big as half of the Ten Commandments, the black marking-pen letters on its cover reading "Wonderful World."

"And," said Baba, pointing to another lab-coated attendee of that long-ago day, "behold."

At the opposite end of the front row stood a young woman, also in a lab coat and also squinting into sun, but without a smile or any other expression hinting at membership in the human race. Above this beauty-magazine poker face hovered a thundercloud of blond hair, while beneath her lab coat, boxy shoulder pads defied those foolish enough to desire conference with her.

"Do you remember history infusion day?" Baba whispered, her orange hair almost blazing to a molten and metallic tangerine at the horror that this discovery was summoning from within her. With a rapid scan, she peered about the room, taking in detail after detail, like a detective sighting every bloodstain at a mass murder scene. "The Johnson Series," she said.

"First-generation units," murmured Bella, "put out to pasture."

Suddenly a hideous shriek clawed through the closed door, and Bella and Baba swung about. The door slammed open, striking the wall, shaking the pictures, and sending the graduation photo crashing to the floor, as a screaming Martie tumbled sobbing into the room. "But all I wanted was a pull-apart!"

At once, Ronnie Johnson appeared behind her, an industrial pizza cutter shining in her arthritic fist. "Pull-apart!" she bellowed. "Pull-apart!" Staggering forward, she lunged after her prey, only to have the kitchen door swing back and slam into her unblinking, if impeccable, face.

To the vicious scraping of a pizza cutter on semigloss paint, Bella, Baba, and definitely Martie yanked at one of the assorted door handles in their immediate vicinity, with the desperate hope that they were grabbing the right one, pulled open a door, and rushed through it.

They had not opened the right door, for in their haste to find the outside world, they had rushed into a hideous chamber of doom.

With the traitorous door closing behind them, they stood petrified, the glimpsing witnesses to a terrorscape of artificial body parts. Mannequin torsos awaiting the spring line stood about like the habitués at a fiberglass nudist colony; on workbenches of plywood and pressboard, heads for wigs were lined up like jurors at a death-by-decapitation trial; and in each corner squatted resuscitation dummies, mouth-breathing for all time. But most horrible of all, above their heads, swinging to the sinister centrifugal air streaming from a ceiling fan, Bella, Baba, and Martie gaped at what seemed to be a colony of pale plastic bats: dozens upon dozens of unclothed baby dolls, gibbetted and hanging by their necks, their hundreds of half-open kaleidoscope eyes peering down at them and begging for release.

Beneath this mesentery of dread, Bella, Baba, and Martie huddled as one—until Bella heard Martie inhale, no doubt to deliver a whopper of a cry for help, and she clamped down on her friend's ready-to-scream piehole.

But while her first hand was busy, with a finger of her other hand Bella slowly pointed at the gap below the still-closed door that both trapped and protected them.

This slender space showed a band of light, simple, benign, and reassuring, the sunlight in the room on the other side—until there appeared small, shifting shadows, like feet. Then to their ears came the sharp sounds of the something sniffing.

Bella tightened her grip on Martie's anxious organ of free expression, while Baba, with the care of a black widow making a nightcap for her paramour, began to cautiously probe into her bag.

"This is not the time...," Bella started to whisper.

But after a glance that told her, "Wait and see," Baba drew forth a corner-store cigarette lighter and then a travel-size canister of disinfectant spray. These she raised to the ready.

Immediately, the door gaped open, and Ronnie Johnson charged through, her fingers reaching ravenously at them like the heads of a hungry hydra and her glossy gibbering lips fulminating with hungering hydrophobic foam.

At once, Baba ignited the lighter and sprayed the disinfectant, and a flame flew forth in a flag of fire at the raging face of their foe.

As Ronnie Johnson fell back with shrieks and howls, patting her singed hairline and smoking eyebrows, Baba hooked Bella with one hand, captured Martie with the other, and hauled them both through the open door.

Quickly selecting door number two, they were in the outside world once more.

But after only one breath of springtime air, they heard a shriek from behind.

Ronnie Johnson had reached her front door, sunk her claws into the frame, and was hanging forward, her violet eyes bulging like rotting eggplants. Then, falling on the iron triangle bell that Martie had naively rung minutes before, she beat its rod back and forth, clang-clang-clanging a summons through the grounds of the Belleweather Bungalows, while from her sagging mouth, like the exit door out of the underworld, escaped a cruel invitation. "Spare parts!" she shrieked. "Spare parts!"

She had rung the dinner bell.

From the door of every dwelling around them emerged head after womanly head, each panting in a throaty hiss that drifted in a poisonous mist through the rhododendrons, "Spare parts...Spare parts..."

Like hellish buffaloes smashing their corrals to splinters, like infernal kine at whose cruel tread the ground burst into flame, with a dreadful herd instinct, the residents of Belleweather Bungalows burst out from their quadraplexial caves and, with surgical saws in hand, set on the three strangers. At the same moment, to the cruel resonance of the bell's clang-clang-clang and the bovine call of first-generation units hungry to be young once more, around the corners of the buildings, recumbent bicycles wheeled forth in a charge, their banners fluttering.

"Spare parts!" Ronnie Johnson screamed again.

Bella and Martie raced away to the main gate, leaving Baba to deploy her short-range flamethrower against the onslaughting slough of slavering Belleweather Bungalovians. After a sweeping, right-to-left barrage that caught many a hair-sprayed hairdos, the attacking wave fell back with howls, imprecations, and mad pats to their crackling Faded Glory, Swan Song, and Mama Bear hairdos. Hurrying on, Baba joined Bella and Martie to navigate the rest of their escape route with their persons still intact.

They reached the iron fence, even as their pursuers, in a fervid chorus of harsh ruminant bellows for "Spare parts..." broke between the shrubbery. Martie sobbed, "Cook them again! Cook them again!" and Baba shook the can of disinfectant, but heard only an empty rattle, as Bella shook the locked gate as if choking a murder suspect, and down the walk the smoking harridans, their mouths wide to devour, their hands raised to clutch and rend, stomped closer and closer.

This would have been the last moments of our heroines, had not a van from one of the more bloated transnational delivery companies then pulled up, and its well-groomed driver, complete with electronic clipboard, stepped out and came to the gate.

Through the fence, this unexpected hero asked Bella, "Johnson?" Just as Bella was about to deny the charge, Ronnie Johnson's hungry neighbors came into assault range, only to stumble to a stop and drop their anxious hands. Mr. Delivery Man blandly asked the same question at them all through the fence. "Johnson?"

"Which Johnson?" asked the leader of the pack.

"Um...," said the driver, tilting his clipboard to get the sun off of the screen. "Pellagra?"

"Oh, she's gone," said Ronnie. "But I'm her sister."

Mr. Delivery Man held the clipboard and its stylus through the gate. Ronnie came forward and, in a heroic display of self-control, politely refrained from seizing Bella while scribbling on the screen. After swiping her fob at the electronic lock, the gate closed with a heavy clunk, and as Mr. Delivery Man handed the bulky box through, Bella, Baba, and Martie with unapologetic smiles gingerly slipped out into the bright, free, and marginally saner world beyond. The gate shut behind them with a wonderfully metallic finality.

But even after our heroines secured themselves inside Bella's rig and the perimeter bubble had been activated, they heard a loud but muffled, "Excuse me?"

Martie lowered the passenger window an inch, and all three of them peered over the glass toward the iron fence. Still holding the misdelivered package, Ronnie was staring at them with her own unblinking eyes, behind the barrier of black rods. "Next time...," she called to them, and the hungry herd around her nodded in ominous unison.

Martie called back over the window glass, "Maybe we can do lunch?"

"Whatever you want to call it."

Baba whispered to her pal, "Let's not get our date book too full, sweetheart," and with the press of a carnelian finger, she raised the car window to bolster their lines of defense. "Bella dear," she asked, "the accelerator?"

With an alacrity and pep that would have scored her a constellation of stars with any on-demand ride service, Bella floored it.

As they turned a corner and danger sank out of sight, Baba, almost clawing through the bottom of her purse for a cigarette butt, muttered to herself in self-reproach, "First-generation units..."

"Put out to pasture," said Bella, zooming up the narrow residential lane and clipping more than one side mirror.

"So, does that razor wire keep them in...?"

"Or everyone else out?"

Martie, though, was looking into the side mirror up the street behind them with wondering, cautious eyes. (She was not squinting, of course, since in spite of it all, Ronnie's Johnson's skincare advice was sound, and henceforth she would never, ever risk additional wrinkles.) After they had put another block or so behind them, she sniffled, "Charlotte?"

Baba had found a bent and sad little leftover of a past nicotine fix and was now enjoying whatever it had to offer. "Yes, sweetie?" she asked, relaxing into a more expansive mood. "What is it?"

"I don't think I want to live there."

To this, Baba responded with a slow and silent drag, and Bella nodded soberly at her friend's wise choice.

But as they turned a corner to survive the rest of the day, our trio of course could not have noticed that as the delivery van pulled away from Belleweather Bungalows, a mid-1990s SUV had pulled up. Out of it had stepped, with two mastiffs in tow, a tall, well-groomed man in a lab coat, his face a handsome mask of fatherly concern. Nor, of course, had Bella, Baba, and Martie seen him go to the gate and the many women within, still fretful, confused, and disappointed, herd up to the fence, where he reached through and affectionately petted each one on the head, before they unlocked the gate and not only let him enter but also allowed the great dogs in to herd them back to their comfortable pens.

CHAPTER XIV

A TANGLED WEB, OR STUCK ONCE MORE

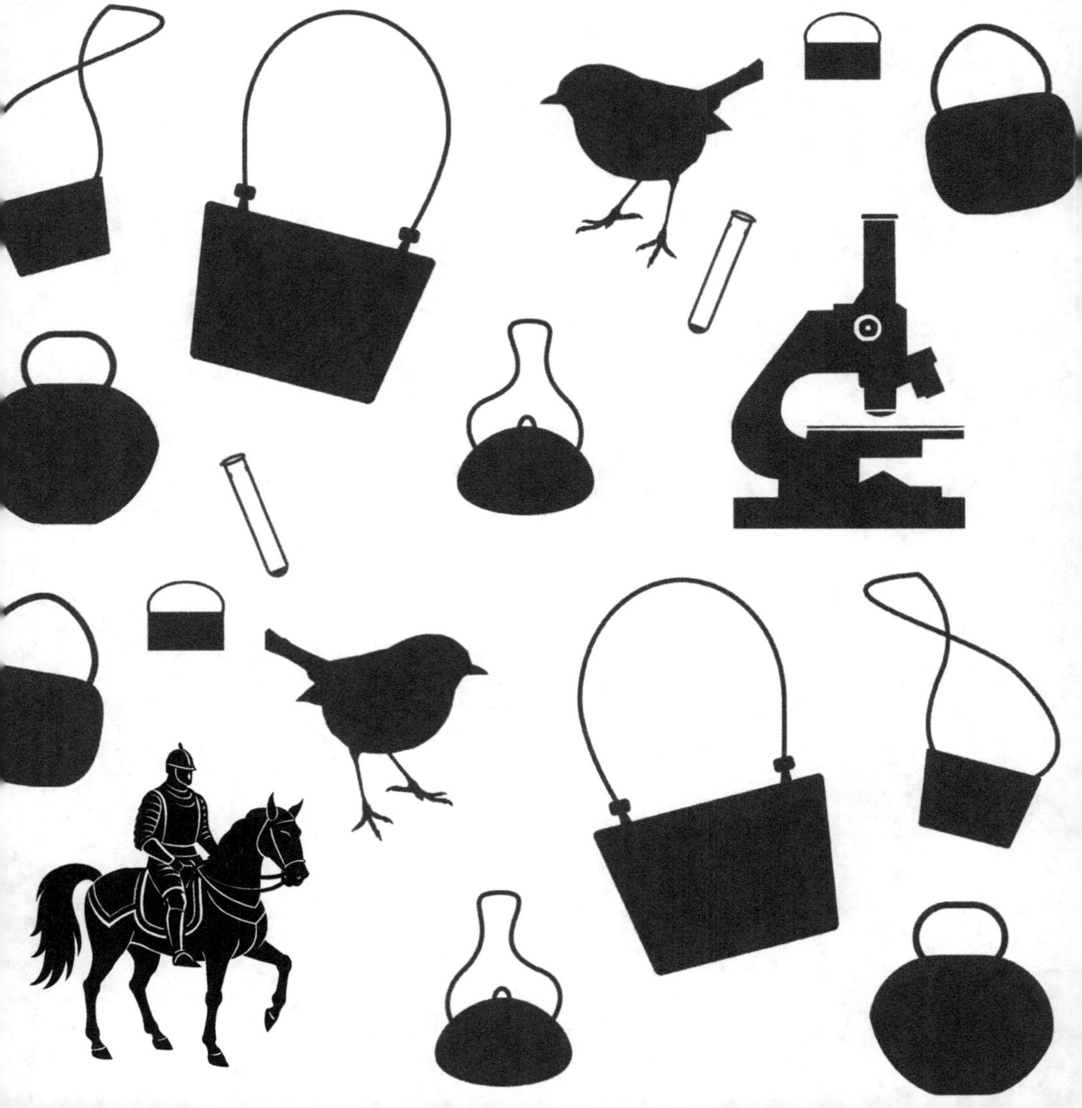

For Bobby Lumbar, with his bow tie jutting up out of his front pocket, his lab coat hooked on two fingers over his shoulder, and his Florsheims dusty and scuffed, the evening amble back to Orphis with Zoe at his side was a flickering montage of the ideal end to a perfect day.

The spring fields about them were billowed by the breezes, silken cirrus clouds wove the warp, woof, and weft on the loom of the sky, swirling swallows swooped over quiet fields gilded in yellow light (the same ones billowed by the warm breeze), and the tread of their shared footfalls and their braided half words of desire, tenderness, and silliness said so much, all to the pop-song percussion of one heart, perhaps his, perhaps hers, or perhaps both together.

As this goliard and his lady strolled on hand in hand, up alongside of them like friendly dragons rumbled two flatbed trucks, one driven by Mother Deborah, the second by Mother Euphemia. Their happy pilgrims on the truck beds all wore brand-spanking-new Strange Sisters Fruit Farms ball caps, were swilling diabetes-inducing pop from small vintage glass bottles, and sang in cheery chorus, *"You are my sunshine, my only sunshine..."* Mother Deborah poked her head out of the cab to say her bit about the gladsome day and something about having been all over heck and back, but for Bobby, any words, verses, meanings, and messages merely skimmed away like fireflies on the evening breeze.

As the flatbeds rolled on down the dry, dusty day-warmed road, the elderly pilgrims lifted their little flagons in convivial appreciation and belted out another bar of *"You'll never know, dear, how much I love you..."* and Bobby and Zoe waved them goodbye, as if bidding farewell to something far away and pleasant, like the setting sun. Meanwhile, the same sun seemed to linger, bending the bylaws of the universe, illumining all the land and the eventide apple blossoms that bounced in the breeze like strawberries-and-cream clouds.

In time, they arrived hand in hand back to Orphis, where the water tower stood now like a gentle guardian giant. They ended where they had begun, in the doctor's semitropical patio, leaning on the iron furniture and watching the last hummingbird of the day dart about, sipping its nightcap of ambrosia and nectar.

An usherette arrived to throw the lights up on this pass-the-popcorn moment.

Madison came stomping around a corner, and the hummingbird zipped away without finishing his drink.

"Hey, beta male! Yeah, you, the soy addict!" She charged up and jabbed a piece of paper at Bobby as if it were orders to report for the wrong end of the firing squad. "I went to Russell's room to rescue him and that was on the door." Then, sighting Zoe, she snarled, "What are you looking at, snowflake? They finally let you out of lockup? Or did you chew off your tracking device?"

Before Bobby had a chance to (maybe) stand up for his lady, Zoe herself closed in on Madison's face, leaving only two or three microns of breathing space. She purred for all to hear, "You know, I wonder…"

Not liking this sudden intimacy, but refusing to blink, Madison tightened her face into a pouting pucker of self-defense. "What do you wonder, snowdrop?"

"I just wonder how you'd look in a box."

"And who's gonna put me there, you or your new girlfriend here?"

Just as Bobby realized that his manhood was being impugned, Zoe chirped up. "A box. Just a box. But no flowers. 'Cause no one will bring any flowers to your grave."

Madison's face shifted toward rage-red. "Yes, they would."

"Because," Zoe elaborated, "no one will show up"—at this, Madison blinked several times—"even to see you dead in a box." Madison's blinking turned into squinting, but Zoe stood her ground. "'Cause nobody loves you! Even when you're dead in a box!"

Madison's mouth gaped open, almost threatening to swallow Zoe whole, but instead she screamed, "No! No! Somebody'll love me!" and in a cyclone of wailing self-hatred, she spun away and escaped, the ground shaking with her every stomp.

Zoe reverted to her innate gentleness. "You know…" She came near Bobby and waggled a finger near his lips, threatening not to touch him. "I have to go to the lab soon."

Up for any kind of experimentation, Bobby asked, "Can I come too?" and leaned forward to kiss her fingertip.

She drew back her offering. "Not this time."

"Then can you tell me what you're doing there?"

"Maybe someday," she said, then stepped into the twilight.

But Bobby reached out and with a "Hey, you, come back here," and drew her back against his Oxford-shirted chest. She gazed up at his now-rugged features. (The cosmetic effect of the growing darkness and all that...)

Just then, the slam of a distant door shook through the dusk. She said, "Russell's come home."

"That's not Madison?"

"She slams the door different than that."

He wanted to tell her what wonderfully intelligent ears she had (they were still at that stage when anything was a compliment), but she finally laid a finger on his mouth and let their eyes meet for only a moment before giving him a solitary kiss. Then slipping silkily out of his arms, she scampered off into the sweet strange gloaming of the day, leaving Bobby unsure whether she had just stolen something from him or had made him a wonderful gift.

Bobby sighed and felt the air becoming rich about him, either from miracle or magic, and lift him from the pavement of the patio. A moment later, when he had seemed to softly descend back to earth, he was certain, as if of an immutable and unassailable law like gravity, a strong nuclear force, or electromagnetism, that even if she was not *B. lumbarensis,* in Zoe Feldspar he had sighted the bluebird of happiness and heard her sweet song.

With his feet feeling the pull of the earth again, Bobby read the note that Madison had so rudely delivered. (Maybe this in-home delivery service was her distorted way of trying to make friends, but he had his doubts.) By the combined illuminations of Venus, a half-moon, the glow of his own enamored heart, and a security light set off by a skunk heading for a misplaced dog dish, he made out:

I await thy coming.

—Ph.F., PhD

And so, with a happy and manly step, like a masterful lion for whom the world was his golden domain, Bobby strode forth to find the doctor.

✳✳✳

The note had not included a map, so to root out the doctor's room, Bobby had to jiggle a dozen or so doorknobs about the maze that was Orphis. (Greta from the kitchen did not like him poking his head in her door; she was curled up watching disc 1 of the One Love Channel's award-winning Doing the Work trilogy: *Chocolate Frosting,* an interracial holiday romantic comedy about a pastrycook and a small-town snowplow driver who save Kwanzaa when an ice storm traps the children's ecumenical caroling club in the run-down organic fruitcake factory.)

In time, though, Bobby did find a solid clue (the word *Office* tacked to a door), and after a jaunty knock, he heard, "Come in," and ventured into the preserve of Dr. Phineas Fairfax.

There was little to see in the doctor's office, since with the coming of darkness, the blinds had been dropped and the curtains drawn. By a small dimmed lamp or two, Bobby still made out, as if on a charcoal sketch on black paper, the suggestion of a door, probably leading to the cellars where the bio-vats steamed and bubbled; a spacious desk with a sturdy maple wood chair, both no doubt from the Manhattan Project Collection™; photographs, diplomas, and certificates covering the walls in tier upon tier; and like volcanic layers of knowledge, shelf upon shelf of books and books, not to mention boxed sets of long out-of-print academic journals. (Their contributors probably had either college reading rooms or small craters on recently discovered planetoids named after them.)

In the light of one lamp, its stained-glass shade like a kaleidoscopic flower on a brazen stem, the master of this shadowed den, swathed in a green satin dressing gown florid with paisleys and trimmed in cinnabar red, lay upon a chaise longue of brass-studded blue leather. One of his hands entertained a cut-glass tumbler one-quarter filled, while in the other he held a dusty scientific journal of indistinct provenance.

The doctor raised his glass toward a nearby chair upholstered in plush purple. "Sit, Robert, if you wish to. Would you care for a nip? In vino veritas, you know." Still happily drunk on love, Bobby shook his head. "So be it. Forgive this lapse into restrained escapism. It eases my professional weariness. Here"—he offered him the magazine—"a glimpse into a bygone time." Speckled with mold spots, it was the 1975 summer issue of *Rural Entomologist Quarterly,* complete with the gripping cover story "Engorged Nymph and Questing Tick: Three Comparative Studies."

Bobby returned this storybook, then sat on the purple plushness. The doctor inquired, "How was your day?"

Lacking a white board, a blister pack of permanent markers in pink and plum, and a bundle of three-by-five cards to help him describe the indescribable, Bobby fell back on a variation of that old standby. "Just fine."

"Excellent. Mine, for its part, was productive. I just returned from town a little while ago. So, tell me, Robert, what's been going on at MAXIFAX?" Bobby knew that "Not much" would not work, but Dr. Fairfax saved him by stepping into the breach. "You know"—he took a sip of the needful—"I'm sure that things have changed markedly since I did my time there. Tell me, though, is Sheena Lypotrope still haunting the hallways?"

Grateful for a yes or no question instead of short answer, Bobby said, "Yeah, she's on Level VIII."

"In most organizations, the employee ascends." He lifted his glass. "But at MAXIFAX"—he lowered the tumbler below the border of his divan—"he is dragged into the pit. So, Level VIII? I visited Level VIII once or twice, purely as part of my professional enrichment, you understand. Do you know Sheena well, I mean, as well as an organizational hierarchy permits to the plebs?" Before Bobby gave himself away by grunting in agreement, his host continued (after another dose of the well-aged), "I suspect you do, but you don't fraternize. That's good. Hold to that policy. You know, if you'll forgive the expression, Sheena's quite a gal."

Bobby wanted to say, "Not compared to Zoe," but the doctor went on developing his theme.

"There's something—how would you say it?—Jungian about her, *transcendent,* if you haven't noticed. Alluring, like the mysteries of the cosmos.

But you shouldn't trust her as far as you can throw her. You know, I was the one who got Sheena her job there." With his glass, he indicated a color photograph just beyond the light of his many-colored lampshade.

Leaning out of the plush purple chair, Bobby bent toward an ill-lit autochrome of happy mixed bathers on a pebbly beach. Dr. Fairfax directed his gaze. "Sheena's the little blond on the big rock with the trowel and the sand bucket." Bobby located the pale water-fairy in a red, white, and blue swimsuit. "That's her family and my family, the summer of 1976, I think, long before she pupated, if that's the right word."

Bobby stood up to look more closely from this seaside flash from the past. The doctor said, "The light switch is over there," and having flipped the switch, Bobby could take in a few neighboring pictures. He made no further sightings of Sheena Lypotrope but was quietly stunned by one of a family grouping, the most startlingly attractive clan he had ever seen. All of its figures shared the same peerless Edwardian facial structure, piercing gazes, ramrod postures, willowy waistlines, and no doubt unmuddied bloodlines.

"The Fairfaxes," said the doctor. "Or *Fairfaces*, in the Latin—the only language worth speaking in, sometimes. It's a joke *en famille*, if you'll forgive my French, that you cannot even remain in the *gens* Fairfax without a title of some kind. So, I am Doctor Phineas Fairfax. My sister is Dame Phoebe Fairfax. We have a brother somewhere in the missions who is Monsignor Philibert Fairfax. My uncle was General Pharamond Fairfax. His daughter, cousin Felicia, married her title, but did manage to keep it after Felipe died in the plane crash. We forgive her since she gives us free run of the villa. Ah, Majorca in spring...But you've been there. My father is Ambassador Frederick Fairfax. My mother's name is Phaedra, née Goodtruth, of the Woonsocket Goodtruths. I'm sure you know them."

"And what's her title?"

He took another swallow, perhaps to drown any impulse to send his squires to burn down this peasant's hut. "Mother."

Bobby sat back down on the purple plushness. "How'd you end up at MAXIFAX?"

"Ah, well that's quite the tale. But if you'll excuse a little storytelling *ab incunabulis,* it was a case of misapplied brainpower. I matriculated from Far

Uttley, or Futtley as we boys called it, when I was fourteen, I think. Maybe sixteen. For about a week, I thought of being Farmer Fairfax, growing all sorts of edible species, then even of being a priest—Father Fairfax—but I couldn't stomach a life of felt appliqué banners and guitar Masses. By the time I was eighteen years old, I'd already earned my PhD in histology, with a minor in neuronal cartography. I think that the committee said I had created the science, not ex nihilo, naturally, but I did lure out its ungerminated inevitabilities. Yes. By the time I was twenty, I think, I had that second PhD in primate genetics, and it was then that MAXIFAX came calling. The lesson from volume I of this bildungsroman is never be too smart."

Deciding to ask later what Roman buildings had to do with the story, Bobby did start to ask, "So, what about Sheena...?" and quickly tacked on, "Lypotrope, Sheena Lypotrope?"

"Sheena," repeated the doctor. "Not quite the same saga, but graduated from Futtley's sister school, Stifflehurst. She had the same quality of mind as myself, and before too long she was a rising star in microengineering and robotics." He raised his glass once more to indicate the constellation. "I'm sure that she gets a royalty on every bit of nanotech that hits the shelves. That reminds me: Has she been successful in her quest?"

Bobby hoped that he would not take his blank stare as curiosity.

"Is she holding decay at bay? When I knew her, she was doing an exemplary job at erasing the tracks of time. At this point, I'm sure, she must be like a human life raft. Toss her in a lake and she'd float, her mass being mostly aerosol and silicone."

Bobby now wished that he had taken that drink. Hoping that he was not opening a can of mutant worms, he asked, "Why'd you leave MAXIFAX?"

To this, perhaps in begrudging tribute to unspoken (or unspeakable) truth, Dr. Fairfax raised his tumbler, then took an eradicating swallow. "You know, I do believe I heard Russell come home. You should go and at least say hello before he leaves us."

"When's he leaving?" Bobby asked, maybe less out of curiosity than a desire to have the room to himself.

"If I can judge by the slamming of a door, I would say very, very soon. And do remember: Russell is great friend of the oppressed."

✳✳✳

Having checked off his visit to the village headman, Bobby made his ways through the halls until he found his bedroom door gaping open to show his roommate caught up in a storm of activity.

Leaning over his narrow bed, Russell was cramming saggy T-shirts and masculine unmentionables into a money-green plastic shopping bag marked "Mart-Mart," its logo spasming and twitching each time Russell shoved another fistful of clothes into its durable but biodegradable depths.

Unsure whether Russell had heard him arrive or was just not bothering to notice him, Bobby gave a quick, "Hey."

Russell forced another wad of shirts into the bag. "Hey."

"I guess we're roommates?"

"Not for long, bro," he said. "Here, you want this?" He curtly proffered a T-shirt, only to decide for him, "No, you don't," and tossed it with desperate negligence to one end of the bed, where a heap was forming. From what Bobby could see, this mound was a political kitchen midden, composed of bumper stickers with their defiant but simplistic slogans, buttons to armorize any de-sleeved denim jacket, former silk-screened posters now torn into fourths and eighths, and finally, slamming into it like a polyblend meteorite, this T-shirt.

Russell broke off his hasty packing and stared at the wall. "Bro, you ever been to Mart-Mart?"

"My professors said—"

"Whatever," interrupted Russell, knowing how that song ended. "But, bro, have you ever *been* to Mart-Mart? 'Cause, like, today I *saw*, I mean, like, really *saw* the People." His tone was as topsy-turvy as a seesaw on a planet without gravity. "The *People*. They are *at* Mart-Mart, like it's their breeding ground or watering hole or whatever. Tell you what." He looked at Bobby. "Next time you got a spare nuke, give it to me and I'll set it off in the food court."

Russell then carried on for a good fifteen minutes expatiating on Mart-Mart's bread-and-butter clientele. ("I mean, do those apes have to leave the house in just a pajama top and pink thongs?") Then, after shoving the heap of disused political posturing into the center of his bed, he gathered up the corners of the bottom sheet and, like a boy readying to run away from home, tied it tight with a black lanyard printed with red arrows and an inscrutable acronym.

Slinging the bundle over his shoulder, Russell took up his Mart-Mart bags in his other fist and with a "See you 'round, bro," departed into the half-lit hallway.

In some small way, Bobby was now the master of his own tiny domain.

✳✳✳

Considering the day just passed, Bobby by rights should have just slumped off into sleep, with visions of Zoe dancing in his head. But as soon as he had turned off the gooseneck lamp on the bedside table, he made out a throbbing orange light on the closed door opposite his window.

Donning a convenient pair of slippers (snipe as one might about Phineas Fairfax, he was still an admirable host), Bobby went waddling in his pajamas out onto the gravel lot, where a bonfire, a tidy mountain of flames, was blazing up and painting all the buildings in the compound with a warm wash of heat and light.

Coming near the conflagration, Bobby made out two silhouettes and the light of the flames glinting through the cut-glass tumblers in their hands. Reaching this pair, Bobby took a place next to Russell, who in turn stood by Dr. Phineas Fairfax, both watching the auto-da-fé of Russell's *rejecta*—his placards, posters, and effigies of politicians departing into the night like gray moths of ash and sparks, his Weather Underground action figures oozing into the gravel, his unbumpered bumper stickers spitting green and blue flames before shriveling into nothingness, and a T-shirt with the word *Peace* superimposed on a fist of violence being licked into annihilation by tongues of fire.

"Robert," said the doctor, before taking a sip from his glass.

Russell, however, stood mute. In the glow of this holocaust, the flames dappled the whites of his eyes with orange, pink, blue, and green.

"Russell," the doctor said, "you're not the first one to discover the lumpen proletariat and that the human race is a great disappointment. Will you keep on at Mart-Mart?"

Maybe of the mind that the Manichaeism of the People vs. the Power had been neatly kneecapped, Russell walked up to the fire and drained the dregs from his own glass onto the flames, summoning a column of fire like a magical sword. Then, tossing his glass at Bobby (who caught it, thank you), he took up his Mart-Mart bags, turned, and wandered away down the drive into the night.

Phineas Fairfax did not turn his head to watch where Russell was headed, but simply watched the flames perish. Their expiring light gleamed on his glasses, until at last they left to the night merely a hot mound of debris, crackling and coiling, orange, black, and brittle.

"Give 'em what they want," he said in whiskeyed serenity. "Maybe someday, he'll come back for his phone."

✳✳✳

After a night of more-or-less restful sleep, Bobby Lumbar rose with the sun and donned his Oxford shirt, chinos, bow tie, and lab coat. (During the night, these had been folded, pressed, and placed in neat order along the edge of Russell's bed by persons unknown.) Then, sliding open his window to take in the possibilities of the day (which he hoped would be more time wandering with Miss Zoe Feldspar), he felt a bit disheartened when the only gift on offer was the smoke from Russell's nocturnal sacrifice, its pungent heap still sending up a gritty gray banner of residual fumes, like the last gasps of a dead cause. Beyond this slag, however, the trees were touched with sunlight, great swaths of sky were a hopeful blue, and several indigenous species of birds were flitting among the shrubbery. Now, if only he could hear Zoe speaking his name.

"Bobby?"

He drew back.

But that was not Zoe. Had the spirit that had animated Russell's Angela Davis doll returned to life to strike down her destroyers one by one?

"Bobby? Let me in."

This was a woman's voice, whispering from the bushes outside the window. Sliding the window shut, he dragged the curtains over and moved to the door, his plan being to find Zoe, throw her over his shoulder, and then maybe find a good exorcist—even Father Max would work.

But just as his hand was landing on the doorknob, a tap-tap-tap sounded from the discount glass behind him.

"Oh, Bobby," came a plea through the flimsy curtains. "Let me in. Please." But before he could turn the knob, the window shattered, and the talk ball that he had chucked into the weeds on Smithville Dike whirred into the room. In no time, the little fellow was floating underneath the ceiling fan and unfurling like a banner the shuddering, shifting image of Dr. Sheena Lypotrope.

"Oh, Bobby, you're all right," she said, her good wishes crackling and carbonated as they came through the ether. "I've been—"

"Why, look, everybody," said Bobby. "It's Sheena Lypotrope," and with a smirk, he snatched the talk ball like a succulent metallic grape and gave it a toss or two (Sheena's eyes bugged in surprise at this), but the lady of the hour soon regained control by whatever power she possessed and sent the ball back upward to hover near the protective blades of the ceiling fan.

With her shocked and offended image now projecting downward (and the fan blades rhythmically chopping it apart over and over), she sniffled, "I didn't like that, Bobby. I thought—"

"And I"—he made a grab for the ball, but it inched up out of reach— "did not like being kidnapped."

"Bobby, why are you—"

"I'll tell you what, old lady..." Bobby heard her sniffling briefly turn into a gasp. "How about I not report you to the cops and you get on with grooming some other newbie? And while I'm at it"—he went to the door and opened it wide—"maybe I'll yell down the hall for 'Phin' and tell him what's going on?"

"Bobby, please," Sheena said. "What's wrong?"

"Nothing at all, Sheena girl."

"I thought I was more than that to you," she whispered. "Can't I make it all right?"

"No, you can't. I'll tell you what though...Hey, but what is this?"

"What's what, tiger?"

Pinned to the open door hung a fresh note; this he rapidly entrusted to his lab coat pocket.

Sheena asked, "What's that, Bobby? Who's it from?"

"It's from the department of None of Your Business, Sheena," he said, shutting the door and giving them a little privacy. "But I'm sure you want to know what'll make everything all right now, don't you?"

A distant and malevolent laugh rippled through the room as the ball descended, made straight for Bobby, and hovered before his spectacled face. As it throbbed with light and subtle heat, the hologram of Sheena Lypotrope became crystalline in its clarity and detail. Her voice flattening into something like the dialect of androids, the queen of Level VIII told him, "No, I don't want to know, because I will tell *you* what will make everything all right, you insignificant peon."

Whatever fuel that had been stoking Bobby Lumbar's lèse-majesté immediately ran dry, and he broke out in a chilly dew of anxious perspiration.

"I dislike repeating myself," said her stern face. "But for the mentally deficient, I make an exception: What is in that note, Booby Lumbar, and who is it from?"

Without taking his terrified eyes from her icy and demanding gaze, Bobby fiddled rapidly through his pockets, spilled assorted objects like his self-respect onto the floor, felt what had to be the note, and with a shaking hand, offered it up to her.

Opening her hands like a tiny see-and-say, she said, "Story time. Now."

With another gulp, Bobby tried to unfold the note, dropped it, picked it up as Sheena rolled her eyes, and managed to unfold it. Turning it rightways (it had been upside down), he started to cram it back into his pocket when Sheena Lypotrope reminded him, "Show and tell, dumb-dumb."

Bobby read the message aloud:

No rest for the wicked.

—Ph.F., PhD

"Time to focus. What have you found out?"

"Nothing?"

"Where does he keep all his data?"

"I don't know?"

"Where's his lab?"

"I forget?"

The hologram showed signs of displeasure. "Where's his office?" That one Bobby did know, but Sheena interposed, "You probably don't know that either."

"No, no, I know." Then, though, as if this one little quantum of knowledge was a glowing coal catching the kindling of his all-but-dwindled-away dignity, he said, "But I won't tell you."

The angry light from the hologram far outshone Bobby's little ember. "Won't? As if you have free will?"

Remembering a song from Vacation Bible School that went, *"This little light of mine...,"* he gulped. "No, I won't tell you."

With a sigh, Sheena took her eyes from her subordinate and commenced working on something at her end. Without meeting his eyes, she explained as she went about her task, "When I hear the word 'no,' Lumbar, my antennae rise. I feel forced to imagine, unnecessarily, I'm sure, that there's a lack of trust between the parties involved. So, you don't trust me, do you? That makes me sad. So, while I take a breather and collect my thoughts, why don't you take a quick look at what your little friends from Level III are up to?"

The image of Sheena Lypotrope dissolved, to be replaced almost at once by a close-up live stream of several young male figures in lab coats: Noah, Ian, Jeremy, and even Kevin Chang, all of them bound, thrashing about to get free, and sobbing on and on (and on) to an unseen presence, "Let us go, please. We're sorry, just let us go."

The voice of Sheena spoke, offering narration.

"Your little friends are having a grand old time at their weekend-long remedial training. I think this one's called GenderWise Communication in the Work Setting. Moniqua and Olivia complained about something, and as a woman, I understand their feelings." Bobby saw Noah dragged away from his fellows by the rubbery hands of an AI bot, be forced to bite down on a tube of lipstick, and have his head held down to a huge sheet of butcher paper with the heading "My Male Privilege" as a female voice ordered him to start writing. The voice of Sheena then asked, "Aren't you happy you aren't with them?"

Bobby was ready to nod, since Ian, Jeremy, Noah, and Kevin had never done him any real harm. But again, he muttered, "I'm not going to help you."

"Oh, really?" he heard. "That's disappointing."

The image from Sheena's creature cam dissolved, and she returned to view, with a dark square object in one arm like a rectangular baby. "Can you tell me what this is?"

"That's my dissertation."

"No," she said, now holding it up with both hands. "This not your dissertation. The world knows all it needs to about electrolyte transmission in geese." Opening it to him, she first showed him a hand-drawn map of a nature preserve, then another of a phylogenic chart. Closing the notebook, she drew from her lab coat pocket first a blue thumb drive, then a taped bundle of paper, and at last, a tiny photo of a small blue bird.

"That's my bird!" burst out Bobby. "That's my bird! That's *B. lumbarensis!*"

"Is that what you want to call it? Science will weep after it has a good laugh. But what is this?" Her image was replaced by a rough motion clip of a small bird, brownish but streaked noticeably with pleasant blue around the head and neck, bouncing happily amid the thorny branches of a bush common to the American Southwest.

"That's the female!" Bobby gasped. "That's got to be the female! Where did you find her?"

"No, this is not the female. This is a fake female. I made it on Level IV in our CGI department."

"But why—"

"MAXIFAX is now prepared to announce in an upcoming posting on social media that its employee Robert J. Lumbar had discovered a new kind of little blue bird..." Bobby should have felt glad at this, but something told him that this would not end well. "But then"—the image of the so-called female *B. lumbarensis* was quickly exchanged for that of Sheena Lypotrope, hypocritically daubing her eyes—"we will have to announce that tragically this so-called female twittering on a branch in the lonely woodland is calling in vain for her lost mate, her true blue lost mate, who will never come to her, because the last male of this hitherto unknown species of little bird was killed and dissected by Bobby Lumbar, all in the name of science. Another species perishes. I expect you to be torn to small pieces before you can make it across the parking lot."

Bobby spluttered, "People who care about science won't believe that."

"People know nothing about science, nor do they care about facts. Remind me to release a benign skin rash or respiratory ailment from Level VI and see how many people run screaming. Therefore, if you do not find what I am looking for, this pathetic junior college excuse of yours to get your name in a peer-reviewed journal—" She slammed his research binder onto an unseen surface, and Bobby shuddered that she might have broken his eggshell sample. "Or, now that I think about it, I'll need to publish an article one of these days. You know what they say. Maybe this little birdie of yours deserves to be called *S. lypotropensis.* Yes. That has a very nice ring to it."

And at that, the hologram disappeared and the talk ball dropped to the floor with the thud like a boulder fallen from a cliff.

For a few of Bobby's anxious heartbeats, the ball did nothing, neither rolling, weaving, careering, nor taking again to the air. Instead, it transformed.

With a metallic grinding and squealing, the talk ball swelled and bloated, its metal skin cracking along its seams, before sending out the first of one, two, three...eight huge gangling, gleaming many-jointed limbs, shaggy with black wire hairs. With a rough hissing, this clanking monstrosity drew back, only to send two of its manifold hooky appendages straight at Bobby and snatch him up off the floor. As uncountable eyes, each one holding the face of Sheena Lypotrope, bulged out over its bristling surface and glared at him, it gave him a good shake. "Are you listening?" he heard Sheena shout. "Do you understand the English? I'm not using great big words, am I?"

Bobby thought of nervously bragging about understanding both Elvish and Klingon, but instead just gave a nod.

"Then do what the doctor says. This is what will happen. Tonight, after Mr. Sunshine is gone to bed, Mama Sheena will reappear and we, you and I, will take a little walk to see what we can find. And with that, Dr. Doofus"—the talk beast dropped Bobby on the floor—"you are now free to enjoy your day."

And without any further to-do, the ball shrank back to more loveable dimensions and shot out the hole that it had made in the window, while Bobby, still on the floor, gave out a sigh like the rush of gases from a hot-air balloon at mid-altitude.

It was time for him to start his day.

CHAPTER XV

HARVEST OF SOULS,
OR SO, WHAT DID YOU REAP?

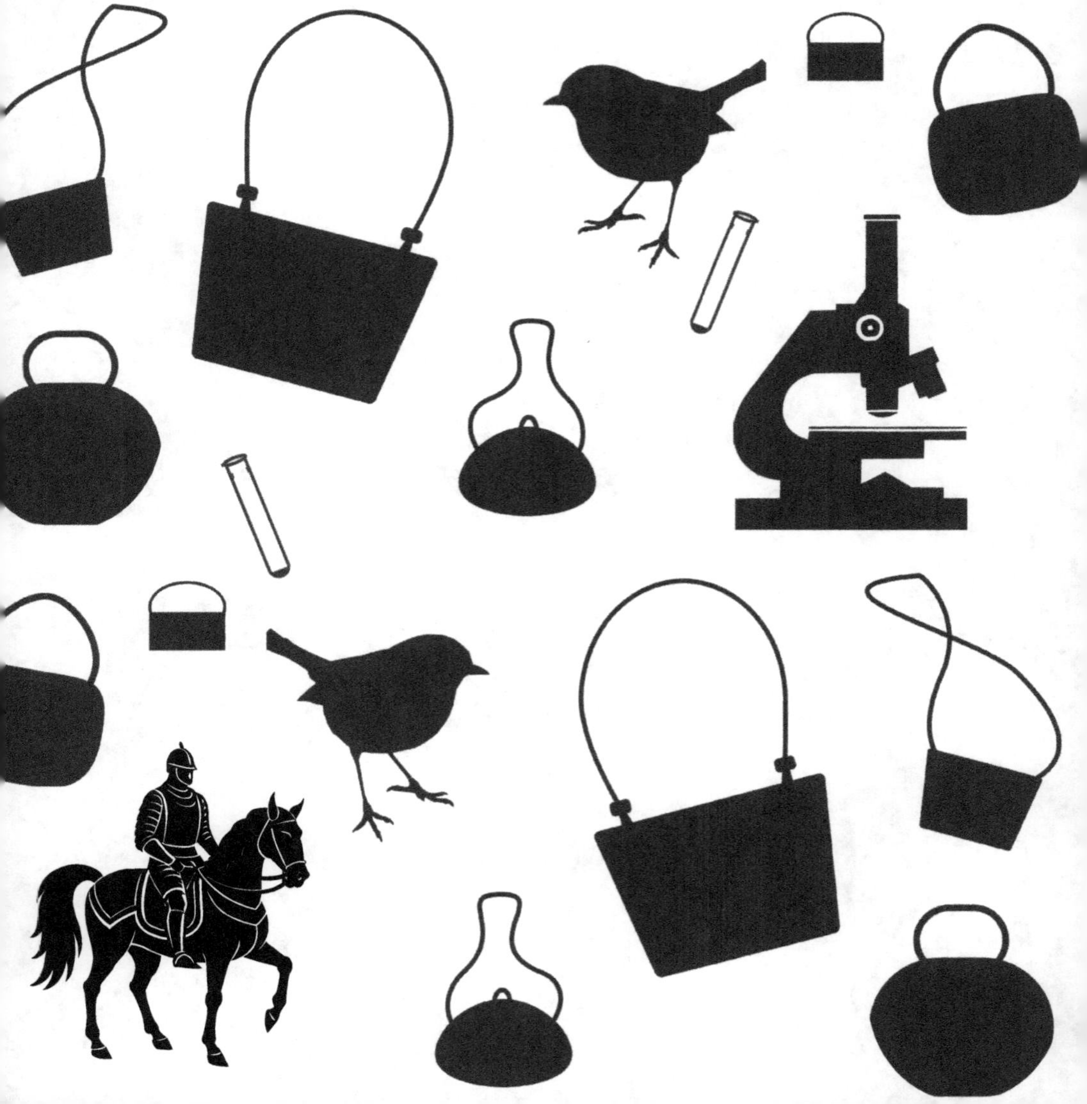

With images of both Zoe and Sheena Lypotrope Jell-O-wrestling for space in his mind's eye, Bobby went in search of Dr. Fairfax.

He began in the kitchen but found only Greta standing over a gigantic midcentury mixing bowl. On seeing Bobby, she gave a horrified and guilty shudder and told him in a rapid and repentant voice, "We're having chocolate cake. I swear, that's why I was watching that movie. We're having a chocolate cake, don't you understand? Here, here, see?" and she showed him a tub of powdered cocoa as proof of her innocence.

"Say," said Bobby, "do you know where's—?"

"He's in the lab," she spluttered. "He's always in the lab. Just please don't tell anyone. It's a really cute movie, really. Here." She shoved a carton of free-range eggs at him to buy his silence.

Bobby gently returned the hen fruit to her. "It'll be our special secret," he said and slipped out, thankful—or maybe mortified—that he was getting the hang of this place.

✳✳✳

Bobby almost ran right into Dr. Fairfax as he was stepping out of the laboratory.

In place of the mellowed raconteur of the previous evening, he saw a cool pillar of ratiocination. "Ah, Robert," said the doctor, closing the door firmly behind him. "You look a bit *distrait*."

"Uh, can I see the lab?"

"Not yet. Zoe's busy in there. But she did say that she wishes to speak with you soon."

"But—"

"Right now, we must advance Madison's treatment to the next phase."

"Madison?" Bobby envisioned any treatment with Madison as requiring a bunker lined in lead.

"Fear not," the doctor reassured him, sensing a quavering resolve. "We are not gladiators saluting Caesar. Not at all. You know that my formula has always been, 'Give 'em what they want,' but in Madison's case, I think a different tack is in order. A little homeopathy, I think. And if we're lucky—or I should say, if Madison is lucky—she should be dyeing her hair back to mouse brown before sundown. But this way, please. We have a guest in the office."

✳✳✳

In the doctor's office, now in the daylight quite spacious and professional, Bobby found himself staring at the middle of a very broad T-shirted torso of a young man.

"Robert," said Dr. Fairfax, "this is Evan."

Bobby risked developing neck strain searching upward to find the top of this towering muscular form, with ten-gauge piercings in his ears and a drapery of yellow barbarian hair draping over his cannonball shoulders.

"'Sup, bro." Evan's booming voice descended upon him like thunder, as his avocado-sized Adam's apple bobbed up and down the tower of his thick, veiny neck. Bobby reflexively offered his hand, and Evan crushed it almost into pulp.

As Bobby stifled a whimper and cradled his traumatized paw, Dr. Fairfax explained, "Evan is going to solve Madison's misunderstanding of the relations between the sexes. I should explain that Evan and I use the same gymnastics trainer—in fact, he'll be here tonight. *Mens sana in corpore sano.* Isn't that right, Evan?" Evan grunted agreeably, if not in agreement. "But, most importantly," said the doctor, "Evan is one of the most successful exitees from Orphis. Evan, tell Robert why you stayed at Orphis."

Evan grunted, "I was a foodophobe."

"The clinical term is 'orthorexic.' Evan was our very own valetudinarian, weren't you, Evan? Please tell Robert about your former relationship with food."

Evan's delivery was as pasty and inedible as overcooked organic breakfast cereal, leaving Dr. Fairfax to coax him along through the big words. Nonetheless, Bobby heard the saga of this young man whose board became all the bleaker day by day, as he cast away foodstuff after foodstuff. According to so-called experts, whom he rashly believed, dairy caused bloating, eggs clogged his arteries, wheat swelled his belly, soy increased his estrogen, beef deforested the Amazon, salmon filled him with mercury, water put him at risk for electrolyte depletion, and (deep breath) bananas, oranges, salt, leafy vegetables, brown rice, asparagus and bananas (again), tree nuts, broccoli, peanuts and liver, shiitake mushrooms and sardines, nuts and seeds of any kind, tofu, oats, avocado, almonds, eggs (again), shiitake mushrooms (again), and pumpkin seeds would sooner than later induce toxicity in (another deep breath) potassium, retinal, thiamin, riboflavin, niacin, pantothenic acid, biotin, ascorbic acid, ergocalciferol, tocopherol, calcium, phosphorus, magnesium, sodium, and zinc, respectively. The "experts" had said so. But the days of this draconian regime were numbered as his wedding approached. (Bobby wanted to ask whether Greta played a walk-on in this part in the story, but he held his tongue.) Evan's fiancée had been a sweet little vegan girl who seemed to understand, but when he told her that because of his diet there would be no wedding cake and then told the priest that they had to have gluten-free Communion wafers, well, his parents hustled him off to Orphis.

The doctor completed the narrative. "As I have told you, Robert, Orphis uses certain techniques to bring about healing, and in Evan's case, Mother Nature acted as a sort of professional consultant. Evan, as a result of your dietary purity, you ended up suffering from, let's see…rickets, softened bones, early-onset congestive heart failure, bleeding gums, anemia, inflammation of the tongue, beriberi, edema, translucent skin, goiter—which first we thought was his Adam's apple—night blindness, brittle hair, mental slowing, and cretinism. These last two still we're addressing with a daily Brazil nut extract, aren't we, Evan?"

Evan had been nodding rhythmically to the litany of ailments. "Dude," he grunted at Bobby, "selenium's, like, my best friend."

"We were able to get you stabilized, Evan, on rainwater and ninety-five percent cocoa chocolate bars shipped in from Ecuador on the backs of a condor that rode up the Pacific current." Here, the doctor confided to Bobby, "Greta had been three credits away from her minor in ethnobotany, so she was a great help. But, Evan, as I recall, you had that brief bout with only greens and stems, and all that plant-based nutrition." Evan nodded grimly. "Now, as you see"—the doctor opened a hand wide—"his protein shake runneth over."

With both humility and pride, Evan told Bobby, "I'm on a sweet Ostarine-Ligadrol stack, dude. My leucine levels are, like, through the roof."

"Cool," said Bobby, thinking that he had better play along, lest he end up as this big fellow's newest protein source.

"And in the end," said Phineas Fairfax, "for your graduation, you had a trencherman's helping of gluten, dairy, eggs, wheat flour, and chocolate."

"And it was good," said Evan, as if reading from a teleprompter.

"Sadly, your fiancée declined to take you back."

Evan shook his head but did not seem too distressed.

The doctor went on. "I understand that she found solace with a bio-chemist for a large transnational agribusiness, which shall remain name-less, and is now the marketing director for livestock products. But that was her loss. So, are you ready?"

Evan bobbed his head.

"Yes, you are," said the doctor. "You just be yourself and then the feast, because Greta's already baking Madison's goodbye cake. Now, come on, tiger. I got some fresh meat for you."

✳✳✳

Our masculine trio wound their way through Orphis's many hallways to Madison's door, where the pair of Xs, immobile and unassailable like woman warriors defending the zenana, so defiantly marked off her domain.

Hoping that he was there just to observe, Bobby held back from the line of fire, but when Dr. Fairfax formed them up in a row, he placed Bobby smack at number two in the line of sacrificial victims, while for reasons unexplained, he allowed Evan to loom in the background.

"Your smartphone?" the doctor asked Evan. Once it was in his hand, he fiddled with it at length. "You turned off the location feature like I told you?" he asked. "You didn't tell anyone you were coming here?"

Evan nodded.

"Good boy. Remember, her name is Madison." Then, holding the smartphone like a mystical tablet, Phineas Fairfax took his ritual breath, let repose his wide shoulders, knocked up on the Xs, murmured to himself, *"Delenda est Carthago,"* and stepped back.

They heard Madison snarl from the unknown country beyond, "What is it now?"

"Madison, it's Dr. Fairfax."

"What do you want?"

"Well, I discovered a little video that I thought would entice you. Someone named Mandrew Gates, or something, some kind of international manosphere influencer, whatever that is, is acknowledging something he's calling his internalized gynophobia, because...Well, I'll let you see. My, this is truly startling: four hundred thousand views in the last two hours."

"I knew that guy was fake," Madison barked from behind the door, and to the resounding stomp of her booted rhinoceros feet, the door roughly opened. With a narrow, predatory gaze, the pupil of her one good eye a black pearl of hostility, she focused on the doctor. "Show me, show me. Where is it? Show me."

But before she could snatch the smartphone, a beetling shadow fell across her face, and looking up, she found that one good eye widening as it gazed upon the solar initiate that was Evan.

"'Sup?" he said. "You Maddie?"

And she collapsed like a pink organdy dress.

Phineas Fairfax whispered to Bobby, "I think that we should leave them alone for a while."

Gratefully concurring, Bobby departed with him down the hall. Only after they had rounded a corner did he see the doctor smile beneath his incomparable mustache.

✳✳✳

Back in his office, Dr. Fairfax said, "One down. That leaves Steffany"—he drew out his watch—"who should be here soon."

Bobby raised his hand.

"Yes, Robert? A question about Steffany? Or Zoe?"

Bobby would have happily passed the day in a Q&A about Zoe, but said, "No, the other one."

"Steffany. Well, what to say?" Phineas Fairfax glanced at his watch once more. "The best I can say is she is, or by now was, profoundly eco-sensitive. A few broad strokes should suffice. Steffany is from Segue and so ended up a victim of the dogma churned out by the Greater Merryweather Educational District, the summer parks and rec programs, all the usual suspects. In hindsight, everyone should have guessed that things would not go well for Steffany after she landed herself repeatedly in the hospital for hypoxia from holding her breath for extended periods, since, by her lights, she was breathing out carbon dioxide and thus increasing global warming. Then she discovered the joy of recycling. For love of mother Gaia—the earth, that is—Steffany happily recycled any item or material that the municipal government told her to, but then went on to develop her own list of victims. She took to peeling the plastic windows from return envelopes, recycling those, then mailing the envelopes back to the company with the request that they reuse them. At her job, she rummaged through the paper recycling box for these abominations and ended up storing about fifty pounds of them around her desk.

"With this sort of bent, understandably, she could not maintain any romantic prospects, and after making lonely-hearts videos on something called TikTok, she started to fill her empty personal life by making the rounds of all the hair salons and barber shops in the tri-county area for their clipped hair. Human hair, as you know, makes an admirable addition to any compost pile when it breaks down into constituent nitrogen. But, living in an SRO, Steffany did not have a compost pile, and being so wrapped up in collecting hair and taking envelopes apart left her without any friends who might have a compost pile. Therefore, she ended up bringing the hair to the office and used her lunch time to go to compost bins in the neighborhood to add in the hair. She was arrested twice for trespassing. The crisis came to a head after she set up her own special compost tub in the break room. Her Gaia Box, she called it. The Gaia Box was very inoffensive, all collaged with pictures from old Nature Conservancy newsletters.

"One day, though, Steffany witnessed a coworker putting the office coffee grounds in the garbage instead of the Gaia Box and told said coworker that Mother Earth might want a frappuccino too. Her coworker yelled very loudly for all to hear that the green police were coming to get them all and, opening up the Gaia Box, dumped a handy bottle of bleach into it. The security cameras caught the rest. Steffany was put on administrative leave, but to pass the time, she started on a statewide hair-gathering binge, complete with a trailer and old garbage cans saved from the landfill as vessels for her treasure. Thankfully, before she had bankrupted herself on the fees for the trailer, her employer found our literature and, since they appreciated her as a worker, suggested that a few weeks at Orphis might help."

"It takes just a few weeks?"

"No." He looked at his watch a third time. "It usually takes but a moment."

That moment must have come, since down the hall rippled the pulsating sounds of crying and sobbing, as from a tourist who lost her phrasebook just when she needed the powder room. To Bobby's startled expression, the doctor said, "Steffany just came back from her camping trip, where Mother Nature took her in her loving embrace."

The office door burst open and through it staggered a young woman, panting and dirty, with superficial scratches down her drawn face and shaking arms, and a sharpened stick in one blistered hand.

"Steffany," said the doctor, "how was your quality time in the woods?"

"That was mean," she hyperventilated.

"But that's what you wanted, to dwell in the arms of Mother Gaia."

Steffany screamed, "But Mother Gaia doesn't care about me!"

"But you love Mother Gaia."

"You left me alone out there!"

"With Mother Gaia. And a sharpened stick."

"And what was I supposed to do with it?!" she shrieked and jabbed it at his face to bring home her question.

"Hunt for your food, forage for roots, or even set up a simple sundial."

"And who was that goon who threw me over his shoulder and brought me back here?"

"My contact from Special Forces."

"Whatever. I don't care. Just get me out of here!"

"So, do you think it is time for you to leave Orphis?" Coming hard on the shattering of her weltanschauung, this question landed like an insult. "Yes," she snarled, "yes." She looked ready to use her sharpened stick on someone. "I am done here."

"Then why don't you tidy up and have some dinner? Greta is making one of her incomparable chocolate cakes."

"Food?" She swallowed.

"Real food. The decadent fruits of a decadent human civilization. But just so you know, Madison's with a friend in your room right now."

And with that, Steffany raced off to wash off any signs of intimacy with Nature.

After a stroke of his beard, the doctor hummed and said, "I think I should stay on top of this. I didn't like the way she was holding that stick. But, Robert, feel free to go and find Zoe. She should be out of the lab by now." And so the doctor left, both the office, to follow Steffany discreetly to her room, and also Bobby, to his own devices, which meant finding Zoe.

✳✳✳

Bobby's quest for Zoe ended on the patio, where, happy in her Strange Sisters ball cap, she was the object of adoration for Sangreal and Siege Perelous, snoozling at her face, while she kissed their muzzles.

As Bobby stepped closer, she smiled at him, a simple and silent act that both unmanned him and filled his frame with vigor.

"Hello," he managed to say.

"Hello," she said, then told the dogs, "Now you go over there." But just as Sangreal and Siege Perelous were trudging off with a shake of the head toward a shady spot, they suddenly burst out in barking, as a screed of human snarls, screams, and hisses filled the air. As Zoe put her arms about Bobby, Steffany charged terrified around the corner with Madison, clutching the other girl's sharpened stick, hot on her heels.

"He's mine!" shrieked Madison, before pouncing on top of her like an obese puma and trying to get at her neck. To escape, Steffany fled away toward the orchards, and both were out of sight.

Dr. Fairfax calmly emerged onto the scene up a flagstone path between two stands of bamboo.

"That was unintended," he said, more amused than discomfited, as distant screams and cries of combat blighted the morning. "From what I gather, when Steffany arrived at their room, she greeted Evan with a simple 'Hi, there,' but that was enough for the teeth to come out."

Now Evan lumbered onto the patio in the doctor's wake. Seeing Zoe, he told her, "'Sup?" and Zoe merely said, "Morning," before looking fondly back up at Bobby, who was clutching her just a bit tighter.

Phineas Fairfax told Evan, "Well done. *Der Kommandant* will be here by seven, so I suppose, make for the arena, and make sure that there's plenty of chalk."

Evan shambled back through the bamboo, only for Madison to drag herself onto the patio from the other direction. Between her fingers hung several strands of sweaty hair, and her own dye job now enjoyed a patch or two of bloodred. In that inscrutable diplomacy that women hold dear, Zoe avoided looking at her recent sparring partner, instead letting the doctor ask, "Yes, Madison?"

"Come on." She smiled with a pant or two. "You know my name's Jessica."

"It was before, I understand."

"Oh, it always has been. That other stuff, that was just an experiment."

"With the male half of the species as your guinea pigs?"

She said, "Can you take me to town? I need to get some hair color."

"That color?" he asked, indicating the strands between her fingers.

"Oh, this is Steffany's." She opened her hand and, with a breath, blew her trophies to the breezy wind.

"Is she still among the living?"

"She's all right. But she won't be any more trouble. I mean, she under-stands what's going on. She was always a real softie, though. No, I need my real color."

"Then you'll be leaving Orphis soon."

"Well, duh. Me and Evan..."

"Then I'll warm up the chariot," the doctor said.

"Is Evan coming?"

"No, he has a project he needs to work on for me."

Madison lost her easy manner. "Then maybe I should stay here?"

"No, I think you need to get some hair color. Let's go to town."

CHAPTER XVI

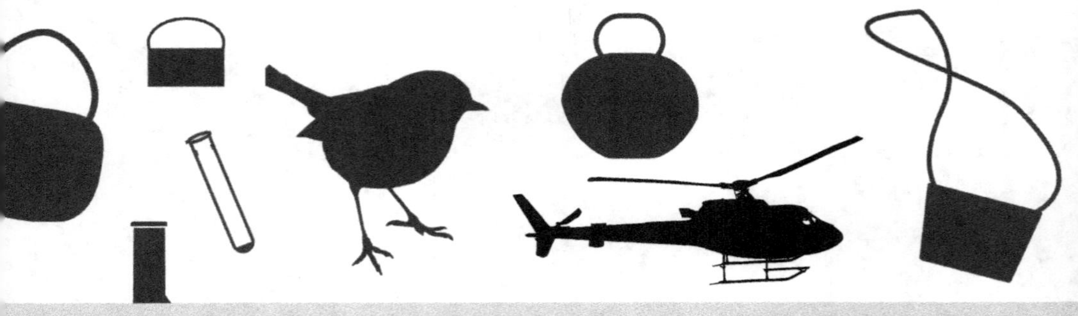

NEITHER SNOW NOR RAIN, OR WHATEVER THE WEATHER

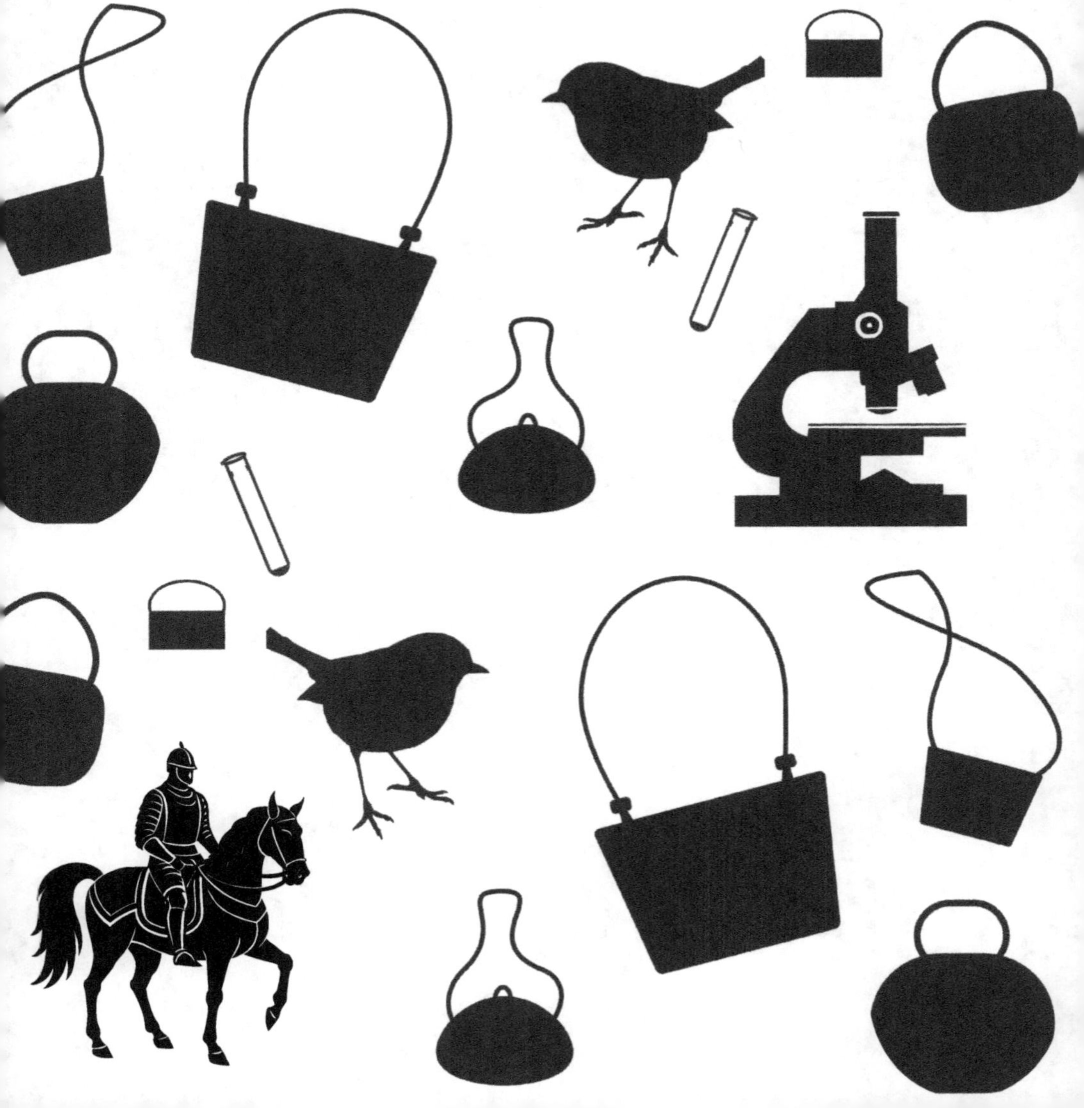

Some readers might entertain the thought that in times past, archaeology had been a thriving pastime in Merryweather, what with the pioneers breaking sod and digging up old Balthazar Himmelfügger to see whether he did swallow all of his gold coins before the malaria got him.

But lately, that kind of spadework had lost its charm, and those on the lookout for tumuli, flint scrapers, and sacrificial victims drowned in a bog would need to push their shovels into the packed layers below First Street, where the most ancient settlements lie smack beneath the United States Post Office (serving Merryweather, Smithtown, Smithburg, Echoville, and Alveola).

As we had seen, one day previous, Bella, Baba, and Martie, having escaped being trampled by the bovine inmates of the Belleweather Bungalows, were left with one single slender thread on which to hang their hopes, a PO box at the Merryweather post office. Once Bella had white-knuckled her rig into a parking space directly across from this architectural artifact of the WPA, they gave it the once-over. Of red brick, it featured a single pine tree as landscaping, under the tree a single park bench for R&R, and along the crown of the facade, equally spaced concrete Art Deco gargoyles that Bella was certain were ready to swoop down upon her. Baba's assessment of this New Deal busywork was, "Retro, very retro," while Martie asked, "Is this where stamp collectors are buried?"

Thus, they began their vigil, waiting for Dr. Phineas Fairfax to put in an appearance.

✳✳✳

By the end of the first half hour or so of their eagle-eyed stakeout, though, Martie was squirming, Baba was setting a recurring timer on her phone to alert her to cigarette breaks, and Bella was looking for a facial-recognition app on her phone to alert her when anyone with the same bone structure as the photo in the brochure came within one hundred yards.

To their credit, they eventually penciled out shifts of equal length, although the demarcations were a little porous, what with the extra half hour it took Baba to finish her stroll to the vape shop, or that quiet hour or two Martie spent at Maids in the Shade shopping for new rhinestoned, cat-eyed sunglasses and a spacious sun hat to keep the solar flares at bay.

For over a day, they toughed it out, each taking her turn scrutinizing every philatelist and government employee shuffling in and out of the red-brick edifice. Even after closing time, they lingered, with the thought that if the lobby was open, a mysterious a figure as Dr. Phineas Fairfax might just manifest at the midnight hour to collect his junk mail.

But no mad scientist arrived.

＊＊＊

By the coffee break of the second day, tempers were beginning to fray like a vintage cashmere scarf. Bella tensed with dread at the arrival at the corner of the city bus (Merryweather's own "Green Machine" fueled by solar panels, little wind turbines, organic ethanol, and high property taxes), then at the passing of every recumbent bicycle, and of course at the appearance of the Merry Minds mental health van. Martie, for her part, had lapsed philosophical, with nostrums along the lines of "If people wrote letters, this place would have more business," and "Oh, I know! Let's send him a postcard. Then he'll come and get it." Finally, since they were stuck together, Bella had decided upon a No Smoking policy, forcing Baba to sit through her shifts with the binoculars without that succoring puff.

Sometime in the midst of this, Martie announced, "Well, I'm bored," and donning her spiffy new sunhat and convertible-ride shades, slid out of the white beast and sauntered down the block to cavort in the historic bronze fountain of Corylus and Avellena. (When a ripple of rioting had disturbed the peace of Merryweather some time back, these Gilded Age personifications of the hazelnut tree survived being dragged to the nearby river because none of the goggle-eyed idealists could connect them to "social injustice.")

After this, Baba suggested, "Why don't I spring for an early lunch, Bella dear? Mongkut Mas, I'd say, that little hole-in-the-wall Thai-Guatemalan-Rumanian fusion tapas bar. As long as you don't know what's in it, it's a journey to another dimension."

For the sake of team cohesion, Bella let Baba clock out of her shift, which left her alone to scope out first at the post office, then at the gender-neutral meter maids working the line of cars behind her, and back to the post office, whose gargoyles, she was sure, had to have cameras set in their eyes and funnels of paralyzing gases ready to billow out from their gaping mouths.

But Bella did not get to gnaw on these possibilities too long, since Baba soon came back through the passenger door with white plastic bags weighted with *tom yum goong, piloyada antigueña, som tam,* and a to-go serving of *tres leches* cake in an unrecyclable plastic clamshell. Ceremoniously handing Bella a cardboard tub of *gaeng keow wan,* she said, "Any developments?"

"Nothing so far," said Bella, waving at the mental health van before attacking her piece of curried poultry with her spork.

At this point, Martie reappeared at the window, still in sunglasses and broad-brimmed chapeau, and tilted her face up at a slight angle. (MAXIFAX had specialized Martie with a bionic nose, after all.) In a tone disturbingly like the ladies at Belleweather howling for spare parts, she inhaled, "Cake..."

"Of course, sweetie," Baba said. "How was the fountain?"

"Wet."

"Startling. Here, sustenance." Baba handed her a little tub of *ciorbă de burtă* through the window, then patted her lap for her to join them inside the cab. This Martie did while demonstrating real acrobatic finesse by holding all at the same time her soup, her plastic spoon, and her phone to try to text—then screamed out, "There he is!"

With a grotesque mess of garlic, lovage, sour cream, and parsnips coating the interior of Bella's vehicle and decoupaging the dashboard, Martie snatched Bella's Leda Marx knockoff bag, rifled through it, retrieved the Orphis brochure. Flipping its folds, she found the photo of Phineas Fairfax. Pointing wildly from the paper to the post office, she shrieked, "There he is! There he is! There he is!"

As Baba calmly snatched the brochure with an adagio of the hand, Bella spied across the street a masculine figure with perfect posture, a red goatee, and a painfully white lab coat exiting an unassuming black mid-1990s SUV (which she thought she might have seen before…). But Martie was already clawing her way headfirst out of the driver's-side window, over Bella (and spilling her *gaeng keow wan* all over her lap, as well as the driver's seat) and screaming, "Daddy! Daddy!"

But the mysterious man had passed into the post office, like a daytime specter into an abandoned mausoleum.

Martie by now had tumbled headfirst onto the street and was now upright and looking about like a chicken dropped from her roost, Bella had climbed out of the cab and was almost on top of her, and Baba was swirling out of the passenger-side door through a last-second cloud of whatever she could rifle out of her purse. Soon enough, they were on the move, like three carefree pals on their way to find out the overnight rates for a package to, say, Capetown or the Outer Hebrides, to anyone who cared to notice them (this being the meter maid, anxious to have the driver out of the vehicle before she pounced).

But Martie disturbed this seamless masquerade when she gasped, "Bella, it's your friends."

Bella would not have called them friends, but toward the post office now approached that trio of nuns from the bike path-slash-alleyway behind Come All Kombucha. Happily sugaring the May morning with their cheery birdsong prattle, their return left Bella torn between either revenge (bopping them on their button noses) or survival (lassoing Dr. Phineas Fairfax to hand him over to the Lady with the Laser Saw). But finishing her scamper across the street and onto the sidewalk, Bella chose door number two, since maybe these were not the same happy busybodies of a few days ago. Good thing for them that they all looked alike, she decided.

Martie brought to naught this act of strategic self-control when, even as Baba was smoothly opening the bronze doors into the post office, she skipped to the doctor's SUV and started chatting up a repellent fat, young woman with magenta and lemon-yellow hair in the passenger seat, clutching a small paper bag from the health and beauty aisle. Her opening ran, "Oh, are you our sister?" but before any embarrassing interchange could transpire (maybe this Quasimodo *was* some relation...), Bella hooked Martie's arm and dragged her through into the post office, barely hearing the merry monastic voices say, "Oh, look, look, it's Madison."

✳✳✳

Inside the small-town federal establishment, all was frighteningly quiet, save for the iron timepiece on the wall rhythmically clunking off the seconds. Yes, people were moving from counter to counter, and now and then the scratching of a complimentary pen on a little chain added to the ominous countdown from the massive clock, but Bella still dreaded that any noise from her and her companions would alert the whole world to their arrival.

This did not stop Martie. "Is this like church?" she whispered to Baba.

"Maybe," came the low answer, "so use your dreamytime voice now," and to keep Martie busy, Baba guided her over to a glass-covered corkboard covered with mugshots.

This left Bella to nostalgically remember that day, long ago at MAXIFAX, when young Dr. Guagamal had slipped into the VCR a clunky VHS tape entitled *The Post Office and You.* In this virtual field trip, fresh-from-the-pod Bella had learned about stamps, stamp collecting, zip codes, and that it was illegal to knowingly ship explosives, a cautionary reminder she recalled time without number since she was loosed upon the world. But she had also learned about the magic of the "post office," or PO box. So, immediately downloading all of the necessary facts from her life skills bank, she listened discreetly for the slide of small keys and the click of small locks.

In no time she detected this mechanical chatter around a nearby corner, but before she could make her way to this chamber of secrets, Martie was squealing happily for all to hear as she pointed out a grainy live-action photo on the corkboard. "Oh, Charlotte, there's a picture of us! Look!"

Baba herself got into the act. "That was before Simone had worked her magic. They'll never recognize me now."

"And get a load of Frannie," Martie softly clucked. "That croissant was already starting to show."

Bella executed a grand jeté straight at her friends to tell them to keep it down, only to hear from the main counter behind her, "Hey, Doc."

Making a cautious pirouette from the corkboard, Bella saw at the main counter the man in the lab coat chatting personably with a worker in his regulation light blue button-up, handing over a white plastic tub of rubber-banded bundles of mail. With this trove now in hand, he made for the exit.

Stealing a line from the drone at the counter, Bella said, "Hey, Doc."

The man stopped but did not turn around. He did, though, make a sound like a greeting smothered in its cradle, then resumed his march for the exit.

As happened previously in this history, two events now transpired simultaneously to cause consternation and confusion. Martie saw reflected in the glass on the corkboard the man in the lab coat and reflexively yelled out, "Daddy!" At the same time, the doors of the post office opened, and the nuns they had seen outside swept in with their own calls of "Oh, Dr. Fairfax! Dr. Fairfax!" and surrounded him with a ring-fence of cheery protection. Thus enclosed, he was able to step out, as the bronze federal-forge-issue doors creaked shut behind both himself and his chipper little rescuers.

Bella wanted to curse any man who hid behind the skirts (or wimple) of a woman, but opted instead to seize Martie and Baba and haul them through the exit. But in those two seconds demanded to open the bronze portals and reenter into the sunny world outside, Phineas Fairfax was already smoothly backing out from his parking space and gliding up First Street, on to points unknown.

And with a recently printed neon yellow parking citation twirling off the windscreen for the litter patrol to find, Bella, Baba, and Martie were very soon in hot pursuit.

But the dark tutelary spirit that guided the ways of meter maids must have wished to avenge its follower, for just as Bella was gunning it up to a yellow light, a flatbed truck like a battleship on wheels broke into the traffic in front of them, blocking their view of the doctor's escaping SUV.

A cheery wave attached to a black-clad arm dangling hand-knotted prayer rope suggested who might be driving this obstruction, and slowing with a screech dangerously near to its back bumper, Bella uncharitably laid on the horn. But in an act of doing good to those who wrong you, however, the driver of the flatbed then gunned her own engine to move along and spewed out a horizontal mushroom cloud of brownish exhaust wide enough to blot out the sun.

It also blotted out Bella's line of sight. (Baba, though, could only appreciate the piquant note it gave to her cigarette, surreptitiously enjoyed at her half-open window.) To escape this death cloud, Bella swerved into oncoming traffic, ironically a smart move, as it gave her a chance to gun it in front of the nuns in the flatbed, until she made out the mental health van drifting through the intersection right before her.

In a new act of kindness, the nun commanding the flatbed gunned her engine a second time to get out of the way of the impending disaster and ran a red light, leaving Bella to slam on her brakes, while the Merry Minds van, with a swirling screech of tires, axles, and undercarriage, tumbled into Mongkut Mas's outdoor patio.

(To ease the concerns of our readers, "Todd" and "Jodi" came out of this tumble all right, being thrown into gaping prep pots of *tom yum* and *caldo de gallina,* respectively. The whole segment even ended up on an educational video still shown in driver's ed classes throughout the Merryweather School District and at traffic court.)

With the road now clearer, Bella gave an aggressive foot massage to the accelerator, and they shot up what was left of First Street before it curved to become (in succession) Beaumont Street with its coffee table book Victorian and Queen Anne houses, Beaumont Boulevard with its spacious tree-shaded industrial parks, and finally Beaumont Road with its back-to-the-land llama farms and unincorporated acreage, blissfully ignorant that it would soon become a series of housing developments. All the while, the flatbed truck and the black SUV were racing on ahead of them.

✳✳✳

Having passed the green-waste recycling company with its steaming hill-ocks of bark mulch, the semitruck repair yards, the livestock auction yard, and a sign to the dump, Bella, Baba, and Martie knew that Merryweather was not simply in the rearview mirror but apparently lost forever. Their targets, though, had not veered off course, until the brake lights on both the SUV and the flatbed glared cherry red, and they made a quiet, country turn to the right, up a gravel lane.

Bella in turn smoothly depressed her brakes and with her companions left Beaumont Road to chug up the ruts of Belmont Road Lane, or so a hand-painted sign informed her. (The official sign was hanging on the back wall at Come All Kombucha, between a couple of mixed-media pieces; but Phineas Fairfax, rather than call the highway department and alert the authorities in any way, shape, or form as to his whereabouts, had simply handed the inmates at Orphis slats of wood and sample cans of exterior paint found at a garage sale and told them to enjoy an afternoon of art therapy painting up new signs, the eventual winner to be chosen by lot.)

Maintaining a frustrating distance, Bella followed the other vehicles in a dusty caravan, winding between scrubby trees and weedy fields, until the flatbed slowed to a stop.

But before Bella could lay on the horn, one of the mothers had hopped from the cab (from the driver's side, making the chance of this rig moving all the less likely) and came back to Bella's car.

Before Bella could concoct a serviceable explanation, the nun asked with a smile, "Good morning. Are you coming to join the pilgrimage?"

Martie asked over Bella, "Does that mean you're having pumpkin pie?"

Baba carried the ball up field. "Why, yes. I love a good prostration."

The nun asked, "Or are you trying to get to the U-pick fields?"

"No," said Bella, as if ordering to-go food from a laminated card, "a pilgrimage is fine. Whatever."

"Oh," said Martie, "what do you grow in your U-pick field?"

"Anything you want, sweetie." (Even though Martie was hiding those emerging crow's-feet behind her new cat-eyed sunglasses, the much younger nun sensed that she needed a little motherly attention.)

"And, uh, how do we get there?" asked Bella, bending her neck not-too-discreetly around the flatbed to see whether the SUV was still in sight up the road. (It was not.)

"Just follow us and we'll take you there."

Leading the witness, Baba asked, "So, we just keep going forward?"

"Oh, you don't want to go up there. That's private property. Just follow us and turn when we turn. This is the back way, but you'll make it. See you soon."

And she hurried back to the flatbed to lead them on up the road.

After thirty seconds of eating the flatbed's dust, Bella said, "If she goes left, we go right." After said seconds, as the scrubby trees on either side had given way to tidy fields of orderly berry bushes and obedient fruit trees, the flatbed's left-turn signal began to blink, and Bella congratulated herself on guessing exactly how this would play out.

And when the flatbed eventually made its wide and leisurely turn, Bella gunned it straight forward only to screech to a stop, bouncing Baba and Martie about like bobbleheads.

The road opening before them forked not only to the left and right but also to the left of center, like a ballot with too many candidates, and no clouds of dust to mark the path of the SUV.

A pair of old creosote fence posts nailed with hand-painted slats gave dubious guidance. One, with an arrow to the center or maybe left read,

<SSFF DELIVERIES

...while the second (with no arrow) stated,

NONE WILL EMERGE UNCHANGED

"I don't want to change," whimpered Martie. "You won't let me change, will you, Charlotte?"

"They'll have to get through me first, sweetheart," said Baba, flicking her lighter and founding it juiceless.

"Will you tell Sheena that?"

"Those can be my very last words, if it'll make you happy."

"You know, I think it will," said Martie, comforting herself.

Bella, though, was too busy seeking her own survival to entertain either despair or self-sacrifice. "Let's try this way...," she said and turned her white behemoth up the road marked for deliveries.

✳✳✳

Years of delivery trucks had crushed the road to the convent's loading dock into a chain of potholes as wide as moon craters, which made for a slow and unpleasant trip. But soon enough, the road not only smoothed but also opened into a wide lot, where here and there other nuns, like black Christmas trees, were moving about. About them stood several humble, but severe buildings, like penitents at the end of a long fast, but overtopping them all rose an otherworldly structure with domes straight out of a fairy story or an AI sci-fi concept movie trailer—probably a site used by the shadow government for experiments in interdimensional travel, thought Bella, to snap pictures of the shadow government site with the golden dome for posting to online paranormal message boards.

Ignoring the sign that read "Shipping/Receiving," Bella drove around the grounds a bit.

"I think we're off course, Bella dear," said Baba.

"Just getting the lay of the land," said Bella.

Martie asked, "Are they going to try to eat us here too?"

Baba said, "Just as a snack, honey."

"Because I'm not big enough for a meal, like some other people."

"That's right. Is the scenic tour at its end?" Baba asked Bella.

"No," said Bella as she scanned each architectural nook and cranny in sight. "Because"—she made a sharp but careful turn into a gap between a small building and a jungle of Japanese knotweed and blackberries and into an empty patch of ground behind it—"it's time for recon, girls."

But after picking her way through the knotweed and setting out on their latest adventure, Martie gave a dainty snort. "What's that horrible smell?"

"Fresh air, sweetie," explained Baba, firing up an unfiltered Turkish she had found in the fold at the bottom of her bag. "It's not nice, is it?"

"No, no," Martie said, with more curiosity that annoyance, "*that* smell?" and like a bird dog, she hurried on to find her prey. When Baba and Bella caught up with her (they did not want her wandering at will), they found her in a sunny yard strung with clotheslines, where black robes swayed back and forth in the breeze, like an art installation from the former East Germany. Martie was running her petite nose over one of the robes stiffening in the sun, only to shrink back, then cautiously close in again.

"Sodium carbonate," she diagnosed, and doing another passable impression of a bloodhound, smelled another habit. "Disodium tetraborate."

"Ah, washing soda and borax," said Baba, translating for Bella, who had missed the Household Chemistry and You infusion session. "Homemade laundry soap. You remember, sweetie, the nice old lady who visited us on Off-the-Grid Day."

Martie gasped. "You said 'old.'"

"Then please wash my mouth out with disodium tetraborate."

"But that was fun." Martie smiled as she remembered tanning hides and tending a beehive.

"As I remember," said Baba, "Granny Earth Mama never made it back to her commune."

Martie swallowed her smile. "What do you mean?"

Rapidly finding a handy euphemism, Baba said, "She went into the compost business, sweetie." (MAXIFAX had funded a nationwide Off-the-Grid Day as a false flag to catch and eliminate anyone who knew how to live without debt, paid cash, did not watch television, and generally "made do." After all, the transnational yeast industry paid MAXIFAX good money to ensure that *no one* made her own sourdough starter.) Baba now asked, "And our next move, Grand Master Bella...?"

While Bella did not like to think of her pals as pawns, she had thought a move or two ahead. Taking a pair of habits from the line, she handed them to Martie and Baba while intoning that age-old tribal wisdom "Black is very slimming."

They both understood that it was time for a crash diet, but it was
Martie who gave as good as she got. Snatching her new outfit, she up and
told Bella, "Then maybe you should put on two of them."

✳✳✳

No sooner had Bella, Baba, and Martie cinched their wimples and imagined that they could blend in with the other ravens in the tree, than
making right for them came a towering and authoritative figure. (Bella
decided to call her the Big Nun.)

"Ah, girls," she said briskly, cutting through any potential nonsense.
"Both St. Anastasia's Academy and the Homeschool Cooperative just
dropped off two school buses of the little tikes. We'll just divvy 'em up
into thirds and you can trade 'em off for the rest of the afternoon. Spread
the love around. I hope you like little kids. And what's this all about?"
Snatching Martie's new sunglasses off of her startled face and her new sun
hat from her head, the Big Nun pocketed the one and spun the other off
onto the springtime breeze, never to be seen again. "Not regulation. Now,
where was I? You"—Baba—"you can do the hay ride. You"—Bella—"oversee
the berry-picking, then show 'em how to make a raspberry brown betty."

"Cook?" asked Mother Bella.

"And while it's baking," said the Big Nun, "give 'em a tour of the
beehives and the guinea fowl yard. Meanwhile, Mother Model-of-the-Year
here..."

Martie was about to waggle a cubic-zinconiumed fingertip at the taskmistress, until not only her single bundle of brain cells reminded her not
to blow their cover, but Bella spoke up. "Wait a second. How come I get
four jobs?"

"Because I see potential. But Covergirl here can help you with the beehives. Anyway, someone'll need to distract the attack swarm."

Martie must have expected something with a guitar and a campfire
and went on to commit a venial sin by saying, "But I'm allergic to bees."

"Suit yourself. You know, the vet said the water buffalo's going to calve
today, so you can help him. Just remember that the rubber gloves go all

the way up to elbow—and use good deep breaths if you have to do mouth-to-mouth. That sometimes happens. The kids'll love that. Hey," she said, noticing Baba's quickly dwindling Turkish cigarette, which Baba had forgotten she was holding. "Let's not be selfish, now," and snagging it, the Big Nun took a sensual drag. "It has been a *long* time. I needed something for Confession anyway. Well"—she crushed the fag under the toe of her steel-toed boot—"come on, then. You can't say you're gonna be bored today."

CHAPTER XVII

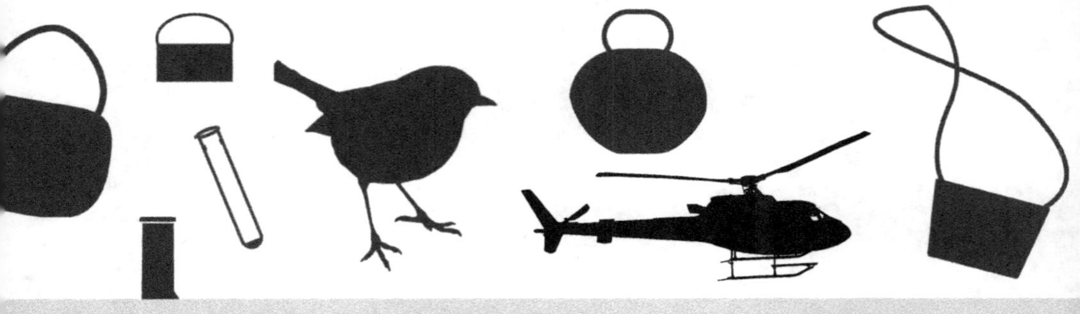

ORPHIS BY NIGHT, OR A LITTLE BEDTIME READING

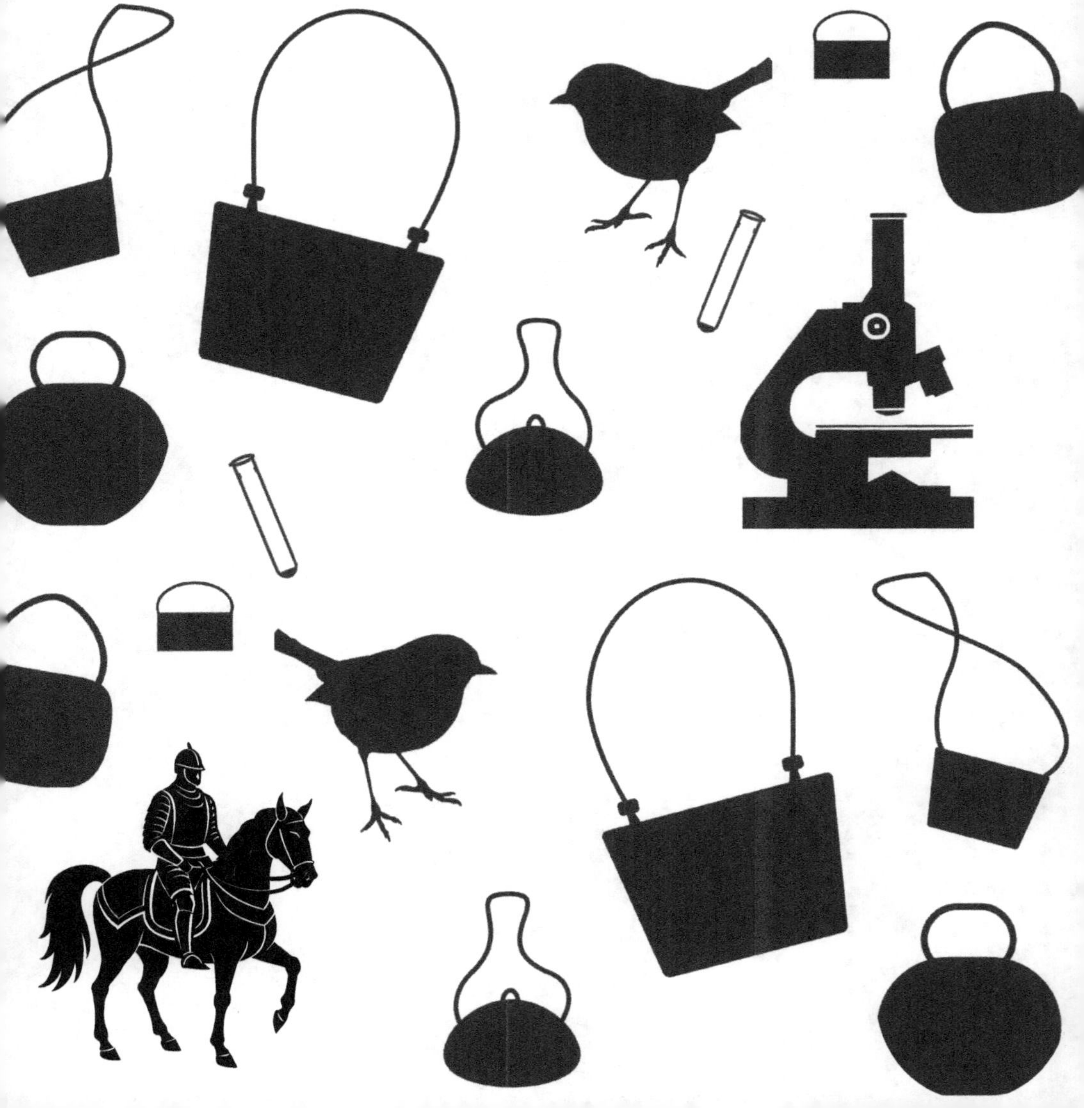

At the goodbye dinner for Steffany and Madison, Bobby Lumbar might not have been the most witty and glittering contributor, but he was not the only one.

At the spacious round dinner table, Dr. Phineas Fairfax himself sat silent, like a king circleted with a crown of success and armored in a breastplate of moral certitude, with his Sangreal and Siege Perelous at his feet. With her head swathed in a scarf to conceal the raw patch acquired during that heated misunderstanding with Madison about romantic property rights, Steffany would have regaled the group with spine-tingling cliff-hangers about rubbing sticks together and gathering berries, but she was too busy gorging herself. Evan communicated in an inarticulate high-protein mumble, while Madison, mooning over his statuesque form, confined herself to cooing dove-like replies in the vein of "Oh, branch-chain amino acids are *so* cool" or "You know, I *always* do a four-on, two-off split routine." (To her credit, Madison was making a go of it. The color from her eleventh-hour medium-brown dye job suggested more motel bedspread than tried-and-true rodent pelt. Also, if her resuscitated fashion sense—she had filched a blouse from Steffany's drawer—was not exactly Givenchy, it would have to do. In the end, she was certain that with enough forearm strength and leg stance, she could reel in Mr. Evan.) Greta, meanwhile, was teetering on the edge of tears, since her masterpiece, a three-tiered German chocolate cake, carbuncled in sugared jewels of fruit, like a castle from a prediabetic production of *Lohengrin,* was still untouched. (The dogs, however, occasionally made a longing stare over the edge of the table at it, with an occasional glance at their master for his leave to charge through the plates, tureens, and gravy boats and devour it. But chocolate is bad for dogs.) And as for Zoe, she must have thought that Bobby was being the strong and silent type; but then, she knew nothing of his upcoming interlude with Dr. Sheena Lypotrope.

With the meal winding down and everyone still confined to subdued chitchat, poor Greta looked ready to drag her sweet brown creation to her breast and wall herself up permanently in her room with it, to view *Chocolate Frosting* over and over again for all time, until Phineas Fairfax saved the day—and Greta's waistline. He quietly asked for her masterwork to be served up and the remainder reverentially divided in quarters: two as viaticum for Steffany and Madison on the morrow, one as payment to Evan for services rendered, and one as a thank-offering for his trainer who was coming that night. With eyes blinking in gratitude, Greta muttered, "Oh, yes, Doctor," slid her magnum opus through an obstacle course of blue willow china to her breast, and lugged it into the kitchen for dissection.

To rectify the restrained mood of dinner, things then got busy. Phineas Fairfax whispered to Evan, *"Der Kommandant,"* and the Nordic giant rose and disappeared through the kitchen door as an anxiously sighing Madison watched him go. Through the same door, but into the dining room, there then billowed Mother Nitriana, who beckoned Zoe to come with her. Now Bobby was watching his beloved depart, but the doctor told him, "The lab. An experiment that cannot wait." Finally, Madison and Steffany scampered off together, all rancor apparently a thing of the past, to pack their bags for their respective adieu come dawn, and of course to fill the quiet hours of night with gossip and romantic mutual support. (Not having a beau was as burdensome as having one, my sources inform me.)

This left Bobby Lumbar and the doctor, who smiled, "I hope that you aren't allergic to dish soap, Robert."

✳✳✳

Soon they were staged at the kitchen sink, Bobby washing, Dr. Fairfax drying, and both looking past the frilly curtains in the window to the quiet world outside.

The evening sun was just retiring behind the crown of the orchard trees and leaving in light only the higher half of the world, a pure cloud or two, a translucent moon waiting in the wings, and naturally the water tower, bright with a rich, reflective glow.

Through his fogging glasses, Bobby smiled at this tableau of blue, gold, and white, when he saw a flatbed truck full of pilgrims rumbling away from the water tower and noticed the silhouette of Mother Johanna, like a figurine of blackened bronze, climbing up and crawling back over the rim of her lair.

Phineas Fairfax had noticed her as well. "Mother Johanna's one of the finest women I've ever met. She's really like a baby bird."

Having met both Mother Johanna and numerous baby birds, Bobby wanted to challenge this comparison, but instead went back to scrubbing the innards of a *saucière.*

Dr. Fairfax explained, "The mothers bring her food and water and whatever else she needs. And the pilgrims love her. That truckload was the second one today. Yesterday, while Zoe was showing you about, a line of them circled around the tower twice so that each could have a chance to speak with her."

Still swirling a soapy rag over the Oriental pine trees and pagodas, Bobby gave another look. The sunlight had just caught her gloomy shape creeping out of sight behind the bulky, bulbous blackness of the tower's tarnished dome, and he had to wonder whether she climbed down at night to haunt the grounds, until the dawn forced her back into her cave in the sky.

This vision, poofed into nothingness when Phineas Fairfax flipped on a light switch and brought the wonders of the filament bulb to the kitchen. With ranks of squeaky-clean chinaware now at rest in the drying rack, he patted his hands dry, draped his towel over a faucet knob, told Bobby, "You're a free man 'til sunrise," and left him without another word.

The time for Bobby to enjoy some unsullied autonomy was all too brief. Almost at once through the window glass in front of him he saw levitate upward from the branches of an heirloom rose bush outside the talk ball, its many tiny eyes glowing to life before staring impatiently at him.

He heard through the window, "Come on, junior. I'm sure you know your way around by now. Show me what's going on. And if we get caught, you're the one that's going down."

✳✳✳

The starting bell with Sheena Lypotrope would have rung sooner if Bobby had just crawled through the window to join her. But since Phineas Fairfax, like a latter-day Daedalus, had designed his healing center like a maze to disorient, trap, and confuse its inhabitants, Bobby was stuck following a roundabout circuit of hallways, footpaths, and stands of bamboo rustling in the sunset breeze before he reached the talk ball, still outside the kitchen window and humming with displeasure.

It swirled up before his face, and the voice of Sheena Lypotrope commanded him, "March."

Not about to admit that he still had not gotten his bearings either inside of the buildings or out, Bobby knew enough to fake it. "We can try the lab."

"Then move it," said Sheena.

They had not made much headway around the perimeter of the buildings before tripping a security light, to which the talk ball returned a small, but deadly, obliterating blast. Leaving a smoking rag of metal and wiring hanging from the wall behind them, they came near a well-lit square of glass. Sheena told him, "Stay here," and the talk ball positioned itself craftily in one corner of the window.

It soon returned, the lights over the ball throbbing in confusion. Sheena's voice shuddered, "There was a short, fat girl with a bedsheet on her head and another one covered in bug bites."

"That's Madison and Steffany."

"Then what's that window over there? Go look."

After tripping another soon-to-be-obliterated security light and startling an unidentified critter that scuttled into the crawlspace, Bobby crept close to the window and crouched down before poking his spectacled face up for a look.

Through the slap-dash window frame, Bobby made out Zoe holding something near to her bosom. But before he could gather further facts, an obscuring form suddenly blotted out the scene. (Mother Nitriana was his guess.) Ducking down, he scuttled back to the talk ball hiding by a downspout.

"Well?" Sheena asked flatly.

"It's the lab."

"Any computers or file cabinets?"

Being from that younger generation unacquainted with file cabinets, checking accounts, or manual-transmission cars, Bobby gave what he hoped was a safe, broad, and diluted answer. "No, just a cryostat, an embedding station, some slide-stainers—oh, and tissue processors." Every lab had those, but in that glimpse of one and half seconds, he would have sworn that he might have seen a diaper pail and a mobile with clouds and stars hanging from the ceiling.

Just then, a harsh, ursine grunt like the voice of a strange and hungry beast sounded from somewhere. Bobby tried to shrink to three sizes smaller to join the vermin in the crawl space, but as another guttural bellow of pain and rage rippled through the twilight, Sheena cackled, "I want to know what that is. I hope Phin's copyrighted the genome sequence, because if he hasn't, I will. It came from that way. Take a look, then come back."

"What if I don't want to?"

Producing a high-gauge probe out of its round, little body, the talk ball gave Bobby a poniard jab. "Sometimes what we want changes," Sheena said through it. "Now move it," and the ball jabbed him straight over to the great aluminum pole barn.

✳✳✳

The tall sliding door of the barn was open a few inches, its padlock hanging from its handle like a security guard sleeping on the job, and here Bobby knelt. Through this well-lit gap, he heard a third beefy cry, this time as strong and cruel as lead superheated to its gaseous state, and Bobby wanted to fall back to save himself from atomization, until quiet returned. Then he leaned forward and, keeping himself as low as possible, peeked through the gap into the barn.

What he beheld was not so much *The Island of Doctor Moreau* as it was *Jason and the Argonauts*.

The barn housed neither a clandestine printing operation, a caged assortment of revivified sauropods, nor bubbling bio-vats that might turn Orphis into a superfund site. Instead, Bobby was peering into a gymnastics studio, fully fitted out with parallel bars, rings, horizontal bars, a pommel horse, and as many mats as a shogun's castle—as well the warrior screams to match any samurai champion charging into the fray.

Bobby saw Evan practically crawling through midair to work the rings, while on the pommel horse a disturbingly well-proportioned Phineas Fairfax was executing round and after round, like a weather vane of deltoids, latissimus dorsi, and chalky hands.

To one side stood a short but hard-bodied elderly man in half glasses and holding a clipboard, like an angry insurance investigator at a train wreck coming right on an earthquake. (Bella, Baba, and Martie could have pegged him as the bus driver who had chauffeured the matrons of Summerfield Estates to their weekly touch-up at Lovelies. He liked to keep his days full.) While Bobby was more than impressed by the doctor's athletics, the coach's face began to prophetically redden, even before Phineas Fairfax, his palm five-eighths of an inch too near the curve of the pad of the horse, slid off and thudded onto the floor.

This failure excited from the oldster a blast of German that would have sent the troops back to Stalingrad for another go. English returned to the conversation when he barked, "Go! Stare at that!" and pointed at the wall to a half-cracked mirror, like a window to the world of truth.

Phineas Fairfax panted, *"Ja, Kommandant,"* and straightening himself, marched to the looking glass, where with a sagging mouth and dulled eyes he stood sucking air and trying to outstare his reflection.

"What do you ask of the failure you see there?" demanded the trainer.

And Phineas Fairfax muttered, "Don't you want to get better?"

"Again!" barked the old man, and Phineas Fairfax staggered to the apparatus, shook his shoulders out, and leapt onto the leather charger once more.

Bobby watched the doctor perform what to his untrained eyes were precisely the same movements, but now concluding with an elegant and firm-footed dismount.

With a deep chuckle, the old man slapped him on the back. *"Arbeit macht frei, ja?"*

And Phineas Fairfax nodded. *"Ja..."*

Suddenly, a pair of drooling muzzles crammed through the opening in the door and Bobby fell back, then scrambled away on his hands and knees. Over the threatening barks that lingered over the coming night,

Bobby missed out on the following exchange: *"Was passiert hier? Est is ein Skunk?"*

"Nein, wahrscheinlich ein Waschbär."

"Oder vielleicht Sheena...?"

Once Bobby had dragged himself well out of range, the barking dwindled to quiet growls somewhere in the dark behind him. Now, though, the talk ball had skimmed up to his face. "What'd you see?" demanded Sheena in a whisper.

"Nothing. He's busy with some friends, I guess."

"Phin doesn't have friends. All right, keep moving. And don't tell me he doesn't have an office somewhere."

＊＊＊

The tour of the innards of Orphis, as complex as any bodily system, seemed to fascinate the talk ball, which whirred and spun about, clicking and snapping like a cicada, recording as much as possible to silo back at MAXIFAX. It came to an end when they arrived at Phineas Fairfax's office, its door predictably locked. But equipped for any contingency, the talk ball sent out a fine needlelike tool that probed the keyhole. Within seconds, both it and Bobby were inside.

"Shut the door," said Sheena. "And don't turn on the lights. I should've started here." Leaving Bobby to his own devices—or abandoning him to his fate—the ball spun about the room, brushing the darkness with a delicate web of pinkish light like the feelers of an undersea creature as it crept from fixture to fixture, from plush purple chair to chaise longue. "Look at all this junk. What about the desk? Check the drawers."

Bobby did as bidden, but soon the talk ball was pestering him aside and scanning its pink light over wooden trays of office supplies and hanging files coded by color. Their tabs were written in an idiosyncratic script, doubtless of the doctor's own making, and while Bobby guessed that these were just old natural gas bills, he did let himself also wonder whether one might spell out "Zoe Feldspar."

"Close it." The ball skimmed about, hissing in frustration. "Phin is insane. He's not leaving anything around for anyone to find. Where's that door go to? Try it."

This was the door that Bobby had noticed in the shadows during the doctor's whiskey-warmed bout of bonhomie the night before. A try at the knob showed that the Orphis security squad had neglected to lock it, and Bobby and his aerial companion slipped into the unlit chamber.

Bobby sensed that like most potential crime scenes, this room needed only a bar or two in minor key to put the audience on edge, but save for the dull thud of Bobby's bumping into a piece of furniture in the dark, the room was fairly quiet. After a rosy-hued scan of the walls, the sphere flew to the light switch, where its negligible body weight was able to push it upward like a miniscule Atlas and so brought a little light to what must have been the doctor's sanctum sanctorum.

The furnishings in this snuggery mirrored those in the office. The ceiling seemed held aloft by pictures, paintings, photographs, and shelf after shelf of books and books and books. The doppelgänger to the blue leather chaise longue was a bed cloaked under a crazy-quilt bedspread of pastel scraps, doubtless from generations of debutantes' gowns. A few antiques also survived in this lost valley: a cheval glass tilted to show the most imperious reflection possible, a Chinese wardrobe lacquered in cinnabar red (probably to match the trim on his dressing gown), a cellaret protecting a suite of favrile vases like melancholy maiden aunts, and a troupe of small bottles with peeling foreign labels.

But the oddest feature was a mid-1950s aluminum road sign of a chipper salesman with a perky finger raised in reminder. It said:

"Give 'em What They Want!"

With the talk ball's sensors greedily aglow, Sheena told Bobby, "Remember, you're looking for *data.* Data, data, data. Just show me what you find, and I'll tell you if it's any good. You'll be looking for a computer, thumb drives, even floppy disks, if I know Phin."

"Why don't you just look for yourself?" Bobby whispered back at her.

"What did you say to me, dink?"

"Look for *yourself.*"

"If you *ever* get back to MAXIFAX, you'll be joining your friends on the next weekend diversity training. Now, repeat after me..."

And Bobby set off snooping about the room, muttering, "Data, data, data..." as if calling for a cybergenic kitty-cat. (He had heard that this was a—literal—pet project in development on Level V.)

Bobby's first stop was a wall mosaicked in diplomas, from Arcadia and Dartmouth, among other places. (He half expected to see one from the Acme Correspondence School of Psychiatry.) Passing these by, he crept along to an over-enlarged photograph, colorful and garish: a candid shot of the revels at a winter-solstice-Yule-post-Hanukkah party at MAXIFAX, with scientist after scientist in red Kris Kringle hats swilling from landfill-clogging plastic cups, as their Coke-bottle glasses and pocket protectors shimmered and gleamed like candles on a Dickensian tree.

The talk ball floated up to it. "Oh, I remember that party. What're those there?" It aimed its light to a line of three-ring binders stretching down a bookshelf like an honor guard. Tilting his head, Bobby read the spine of the first. In heavy marking-pen it read:

VONDERFUL VIR

"Is this what you want?" he asked.

"No," said the ball, and while its blade of light took in the corners of the room and the depths of a hippopotamus foot wastepaper basket, Bobby slipped the binder from the shelf and opened it.

Glued to the center of the first page sat a solitary Polaroid photo: mostly of the camera flash filling a bathroom mirror, but in the bottom half of the glass a bloated, fig-like abdomen, the embarrassing epitome of the "before" picture.

The ball had returned and skimmed its light over the page. Sheena sniffed, "He was always such a slob. Helsingfors would've needed a year to make any headway at all."

Keeping to himself what he had seen in the pole barn, Bobby flipped through the pages. Each was heavy with Polaroid pictures, the bodily flaws in each scrawled with blue ballpoint as, on each successive image, the ink ran out. As a surprise, one of the pages suddenly fell open toward the floor in a lengthy, fragile roll of many folds. Like a clumsy scroll of forbidden wisdom and cabbalistic rites, bandaged over with delicate yellowing tape, this looked to be the day-by-day record of the doctor's weight loss, like an EKG of adiposity. After gingerly folding this artifact back into place, Bobby went on to a plastic sleeve protecting a printed list of exercises: pullups, dips, and planchet, then rarified exertions like "progression with iron cross, progression with handstand, progression with L-sit, progression with straight-arm rings, crucifix hold, planche Maltese on rings..." Bobby found that he was inadvertently squeezing his own sedentary-lifestyle paunch.

A new divider, its manila face marked with "Sartor Resartus," divided one historic period from another. The archaic Polaroids gave way to intermediary three-by-five matte-finish photos: a thinner and still younger Phineas Fairfax holding a pair of wrinkled black puppies, the names "Goth" and "Magothy" in silver marking pen wriggling over them like phosphorescent worms; Phineas Fairfax with the German coach; Phineas Fairfax trying on clothes in a high-end shop; a studio portrait of him with a waxed beard, handlebar mustache, and a Homburg hat like a finial on an Old World lamppost; a dinner table densely populated with glowing china, glinting cutlery, and glittering candlesticks; a vast empty lot sprouting frames of two-by-fours from gaping rectangular foundations; etc.

Bobby quietly returned *Vonderful Vir* to its place and noticed on the shelf above it a Polaroid camera, several packages of old foil-wrapped film, brick-like biographies of Cary Grant and Cecil Beaton, two editions of Emily Post, and three editions of Amy Vanderbilt.

On the shelf of binders, the next was a slimmer and marked *Daily Word.* Inside, Bobby found page upon page of sentences, three each for *ambit, pleonasm, anabasis, ramify, bissextile, aeolian, isinglass, aquarellist, oubliette, autodidact(ic), amphigory, grimthorping, bathypelagic, ideate, paregoric, baneful, temerarious, banquette, suffragan, basiliscene, graustarkian, belvedere, hawser, billingsgate,* and so on...

The neighbor to *Daily Word* was *Gourmet*: cuttings and cuttings from the eponymous magazine, pasted on to wide-ruled pages, recipes for *fricadelles de boeuf avec viand cuite, chou rouge mariné, fioavanti, patte de l'oeurs, fourderaine, ailerons de dindonneau farci en chaud-froid,* and so on...

Sheena Lypotrope had silently been reading all of this over his shoulder. "Boring, boring, boring. What're these?" Like a frustrated hornet looking to break into the honeybee hive, the ball went on down the bank of binders, only to almost shriek, "Yes! Here! Here they are!"

Bobby stepped to the other end of the shelf and read on one spine, *Wonderful World,* then, next to it, *The Johnson Series.*

The talk ball was zipping frantically back and forth, its lights glowing with ecstatic glee. "Open one! Open one!"

Bobby took the fattest binder (*The Johnson Series*) and found on its first page:

MORPHS (FEMINOIDS)

Scarcely containing her fervid joy, Sheena sniped, "Turn the page, you moron, turn the page. I know what they're called."

As Sheena breathed in his ear with slavering excitement, Bobby turned page after page, the first few bedoodled with characters from *The Micronauts* and *The Teen Titans*, then came to chart after chart in chiffon colors, like slices of a summer-picnic pie, and then well-ordered plastic tabs sinking into the distance. These marked off thick sections dedicated to the globella, the globulus, and the globus, followed by the Monax v1, v2, v3, vs1, vs2, and vs3, then descriptions of the protomorph, metamorph, polymorph, quasimorph, cryptomorph, pseudomorph, and paramorph.

As Bobby worked through the binder, Sheena whispered, "Ah, it's all there," and with many a hum and click, the talk ball wove back and forth over leaf after leaf. But for Bobby, begrudgingly turning page after page, all of this jargon, terminology, drawings, and blurry photographs, so briefly sighted, glowed enticingly like will-o-the-wisps, drawing him on into the bogs and swamps of the most bizarre of scientific endeavors before he became lost.

As soon as he closed *The Johnson Series*, the talk ball announced, "I can't get it all right now, but it's a start. But you're gonna make off with all of these in the very near future."

Just then, the sound of the door to the office opening in the next room interrupted her schemes.

"Just grab it!" she said. "Just grab it and go!"

But to the barking of dogs and the voice of Phineas Fairfax asking Sangreal and Siege Perelous what was wrong, Bobby dropped the binder and dashed out through the nearest door he could find.

***

He and the talk ball had spilled out onto a path that ran through a stand of banana trees whispering in the night like witchdoctors and thence onto the doctor's subtropical patio. To cover his tracks, he did scurry back and, hunched over to stay downwind from Sangreal and Siege Perelous, had delicately shut the door to the doctor's bedroom, before hurrying back to his taskmistress.

Out of the moonlit branches of a tree peony, Sheena said, "I'll be back. For now, your job is to keep an eye peeled for your mission partner. I finally got her back on track."

"Sheena," said Bobby, "I don't think—"

"Good. Never think. Hey, who's that?"

And to the whir of a talk ball making its escape off through the moonlit Ming dynasty landscaping, Bobby turned to see nothing except a slight silhouette slipping around a corner and into the dark.

***

At the same time, at the Sorbo-Ruthenian Women's Monastery of Blessed Charles of Austria and the Servant of God Zita of the Exarchy of Blainesville, and under the eyes of the miracle-working and myrrh-streaming icon of Blessed Symeona, evening prayer was well underway. But in the back of the chapel by the tract rack, oblivious to the melodious chanting of delicate, dovelike voices hymning "the gladsome light" and "the holy glory of the Father Immortal"—and missing out on Mother Deborah's basso profundo—three nuns that no one recalled meeting before this day, but who had definitely earned their stripes by putting in a long day's work, lay slumped together in a heap of fatigue, drool, and exhausted snoring.

"Mother Belladonna" (that is what she had called herself), her fingertips purple from berry-picking, was curled up and clutching a beekeeper's hat like a teddy bear. (Because of her white beekeeper's suit, no one could see the fine dusting of flour on her habit, proof that, yes, she had slaved away in the kitchen over that raspberry brown betty.) Similarly, "Mother Martina" had not bothered to pull off her heavy rubber boots caked with the barnyard, nor her elbow-length rubber gloves and rubber apron, both stained and slippery with bizarre and viscous fluids. As for "Mother Babulia," at first glance she had made out the best, but closer inspection showed that her orange-tipped fingers were frozen into a permanent clutch, and none but she could feel the hot throbbing in her forearms, now swollen to the dimensions of bowling pins after steering the big rig around and around (and around) the orchard grounds, only to have to haul out the industrial jack when she blew a tire at the far end of the back forty. (The most exertion that Baba's own car ever demanded of her was a press of a button to make it parallel park itself.)

Once prayers had serenely concluded, most of the nuns glided with nary a sound to the next item on their centuries-old agenda, which was dinner. But a handful did gather around these somnolent sisters, the soft sound of their serviceable shoes rousing Mother Belladonna awake with a start. (She had been dreaming about rank upon rank of home-school students with faces like Little Orphan Annie line-dancing straight toward her to either the Tommy Dorsey band or Fauré's *Requiem* playing in the background.) As if being called on in class, she pushed herself up and, with blinking eyes, called out, "Hypostatic Union! The Council of Chalcedon! Dithelitism!" but then reverted to her usual cagey mien and nudging awake her companions to share the moment.

Mother Martina mumbled something about a gigantic baby bottle and a native-patterned blankie to wrap little Hugo in (little Hugo was the water buffalo calf she had helped see into the world), while Mother Babulia was getting ready to ignore any No Smoking signs, only to realize that her hands were too stiff to hold a cigarette.

The Big Nun was the tallest among the benevolent if dark Stonehenge of figures looming around them. "I'll bet you worked up quite an appetite," she said.

Martie, a little confused from low blood sugar and thus mixing up her scenarios, pointed at Bella with, "Oh, she's my mother. My name's—" but Bella tossed her beekeeper's hat at her.

"Time for trapeza," said the Big Nun. "Mother Euphemia'll need some help dishing up."

Pretty certain that trapeza did not involve a couple of tall ladders and a wide net manned by clowns, Mother Belladonna whispered to Mother Martina, "I think it's a free meal."

Suddenly, an extra standing stone joined the Stonehenge, and this new and cheery mother reported chattily to the Big Nun, "Mother Deborah, when I was delivering food to Mother Johanna, Dr. Fairfax gave me a message for you."

Bella's ears pricked up, Baba knew enough to simply hearken attentively, but Martie did her own bit of butting in. "Oh, we know Dr. Fairfax. He's—" and Bella helped along her vow of silence with a hand over the mouth.

Not to be blown off course by these shenanigans, the Big Nun asked, "And what's he need?"

"He has a bus of old friends coming by tomorrow and wants a tour of the chapel and the grounds."

"Hmm," cogitated the Big Nun, as if a sea mist had come across a familiar coastline. "Well, we've got plenty of hands now, haven't we? Mother Belladonna..." Bella tried to muster a perky smile. "After trapeza, how about you three head for Orphis and get all the details. Let him know that you'll be glad to play tour guide."

Bella made ready to raise a hand to pose a strategic question, when Baba asked with an easy delivery, "So, just the high points, or maybe throw a free a cappella concert, you know, an impromptu responsory or two in plainchant?"

"You're thinking some prostopinije with the kontakion for the feast, or maybe a stavrotheotokion?"

Baba said, "Or how about an apolytikion in psalmodic hexameter?"

"Or, you know"—the Big Nun wagged an inspirational finger—"a heirmologic prokeimenon. You know, why not? If they like it, we'll record a CD."

"Oh, nobody does CDs now."

"Then mp3 for download. But be sure to push the tote bags and coffee tumbler insulators. We've got boxes of those. Well, chow time," said the Big Nun, and she and her fellow Stonehengians set off through the chapel door into the newborn night.

Eventually our ladies were upright with stiff joints outside. Using their senses in concert (Bella listening for the scuffle of sensible shoes on a stone path, Baba looking for alterations in ambient lighting as the door to the eatery opened, and Martie sniffing for vegetarian entrées and homemade dish soap in the kitchen), they managed to stagger to the trough. There, each guiltlessly gluttonized on slab upon slab of amaranth and quinoa loaf, soy paste fritters slathered in Szechuan horseradish, and ladle after ladle of sweet oozing lignonberry compote, washing it all down with vats of lemon balm tea and an extra-tall almond-milk, raw-egg, and bumblebee-honey smoothie.

After this refueling, the Big Nun escorted them staggering with their bloated bellies, under the peeking, pale light of so many countryside stars across the grounds of the convent, until the Big Nun said, "Well, here we are, girls."

"Here," they discovered, was the rough borderland of the parking lot, where it met what might have once been a pear orchard, but now might have been the habitat for gargantuan post-nuclear fruit weevils (the ones with the luminous eyes and antennae that shoot rays that reduce their victims to organic applesauce).

"I know, I could just text the doctor," said the Big Nun, "but you know how he is. He turns off his flip phone at sundown. Low tech, no tech. If only I had that kind of guts. Well, you know the way."

Bella was about to politely protest that she did not know the way, when she remembered Dr. Sheena Lypotrope and her laser saws.

"But it's dark in there," Martie said.

"And perfectly safe," declared the Big Nun, like a saleswoman before a doubting customer. "Do you think Blessed Symeona will let you down?"

But before Martie could mug it up by asking who Blessed Symeona was, Baba gave her a pat on the back and a confident nod. "You know it's perfectly safe, Martina."

"And Blessed Desdemona is with us," said Bella.

"That's the spirit," the Big Nun agreed, then said, "Hey, Babulia, remember, charity's a virtue," and from the Baba's recovering fingers slipped the cigarette that she thought she had been keeping protectively out of sight. "I'll just keep an eye on this for you. Well, off you go."

Fortunately for Baba, she had another cancer stick in her stash. This was a good thing, for as she and her friends crept forth into the impenetrable gloom of the haunted orchard, with the Big Nun calling through the trees to them to "just keep going straight, girls," that cigarette gave out their sole guiding light, a tiny orange glow on a sweet but paltry torch, as long as it might last.

Meanwhile, the Big Nun was chuckling, "That'll keep 'em busy," and drawing out her handheld, she tapped out:

> Three strange ladies coming your way

CHAPTER XVIII

THE COURSE OF TRUE LOVE,
OR WHERE WILL THIS END?

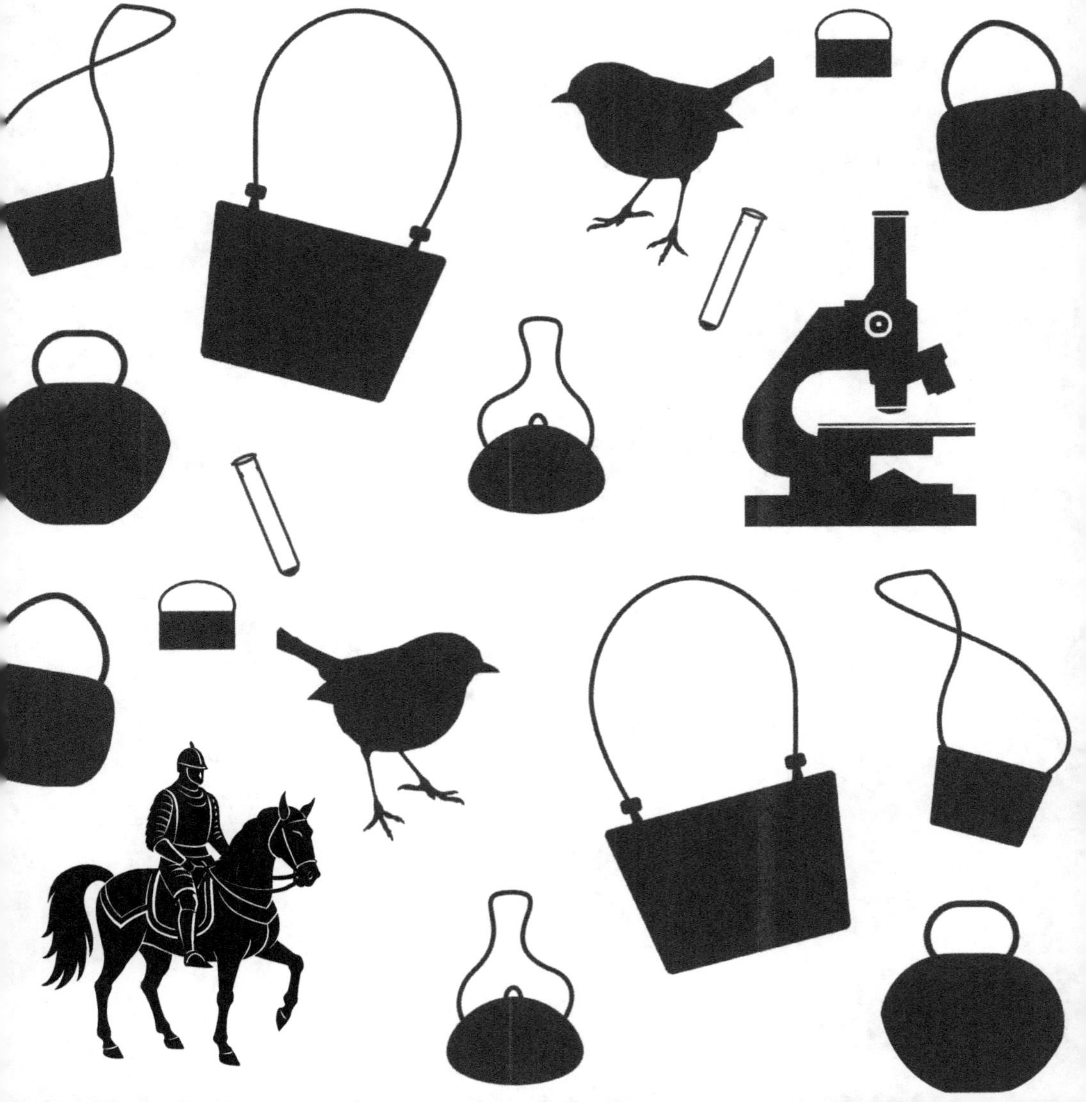

After that anxious night of espionage, Bobby Lumbar could only yawn and blink as he stood next to Dr. Phineas Fairfax as they saw off Steffany and Madison, now leaving to begin life back in polite society.

They were all gathered in the gravel lot, where Greta merrily cranked out "Those Were the Days" on a hurdy-gurdy, while Phineas Fairfax, like a prince consort bestowing decorations to a colonial delegation, flawlessly executed the Return of the Smartphone. But Madison—like Bobby—was not the picture of dewy freshness. Coming off of a graveyard shift of gossiping with Steffany, she was forcing herself to keep her eyes open and smile while giddily leaning against Evan, towering beside her and fiddling on his phone with his online macros calculator.

Steffany, swaying like an old-growth redwood ready to collapse onto unsuspecting campers, was not much better. But as soon as her father drove up, she managed to slip a felt hat over her temporary bald spot, then staggered magnanimously over to Madison, hugged the nearest part of her body, muttered something about fall weddings being really pretty, and crawled into the back of her father's sedan, where she lay down and returned to the wonderland of sweetest slumber. Seeing this, her father looked dubiously at Dr. Fairfax. But as long as his daughter was not trying to sell the family's beach house on the sly because the sea levels were on the rise, nor did he have to come up with bail money because she had been caught stirring a fifty-pound garage bag of human hair into the neighbor's compost tumbler, all was right with the world. So, with the doctor giving an encouraging wave, he drove his offspring away.

Lowering his hand, the doctor quietly told Bobby, "Just one more and we shall no longer be *in loco parentis*." He raised his voice. "Madison?"

She gave no response, either because of her blissful rapture at clinging to Evan or because she was slipping into REM sleep. He tried, "Jessica?" and her eyes cracked open. "You know, if you don't want to wait, Evan can drive you back to your mother's trailer."

As her dream man continued swiping on his phone, she bounced off of him and put a hand to her mouth. "Mommy can't see him, not yet! We're not that far along."

"But you won't tell your mother—"

"Oh, Mommy can't know anything. She'll—"

"But I think I hear her coming right now."

And around the bend in the drive rumbled a beast from country-and-western myth: a full-sized maroon pickup truck blasting a Tim McGraw club mix, with side mirrors as wide as elk antlers. Over the cab, a double row of red, white, and blue halogen search lamps flashed in unison. All four jacked-up tires featured LED wheel-ring lights. Flame fixtures in chrome ran down the sides from hubcaps to brake lights, and the running boards flashed with amber lights. Both Old Glory and Stars and Bars rippled from the back corners of the bed, and a Betty Boop bobblehead in a cowgirl hat was fixed to the dashboard. The driver's hands held a double-sized, glam pink plush steering wheel with rhinestone spokes.

As this juggernaut ground to a halt and the birds within earshot flapped away in shock and awe, the line-dancing club mix mercifully silenced and out of the cab, landing like a meteor, came a potato-shaped woman with cropped hair, angel-wing upper arms like saddlebags, and a tie-dyed Gadsden flag shirt that dared all comers, "Don't Tread on Me."

The newcomer looked first at Dr. Fairfax. "Doc," she said.

"Maggie," replied the doctor.

Then Maggie gave Madison (née Jessica) the ol' up-and-down, then cut to the chase. "Your hair looks a little better."

Sounding as if trying to give the right answer, Madison muttered, "I like it too," and pet the back of her head a few times.

"What's going on with your eye? Who'd you fight this time?"

"She's gone."

"'She?' That's a switch. So, you still hate men?"

"I don't know, Mommy."

"Well, why not?"

"I don't know."

"You know, Rob's taken off with Sue Syverson. I heard they're hiding up in Echoville."

"Echoville's pretty." Madison smiled like a travel agent trying to keep her job.

"Won't be when I get done with it. Well, if you're comin', come on." But as Maggie turned toward her rig, she caught sight of Evan still browsing online for estrogen blockers and anticortisol chewables. "Is he single?"

Madison rotated her gaze like a ship's gun between her mother and Evan. Her one good eye blazed with a possessive glow. "No, Mommy. No, he's not."

"Well, who do I have to run over to snag him?"

"That would be me, Mommy."

"You?" Maggie looked at Phineas Fairfax as if he was handing free bottles of snake oil with each used car the customer managed to tow off the lot. "So, that's what I paid good money for, so she'd think she's a five?" Now she spoke at Madison. "You know something, it ain't that you hate men. I think maybe it's the men that—"

"You know, Mommy, why don't you just run back to your sudoku and your *Y&R* and your Lil' Debbies? 'Cause *this one is mine!*"

Her mother charged at her on farm-boot feet. "Young lady, I did not raise you—"

"Since when did you ever raise me? And I'm not a lady: *I'm a woman!*" and hooking Evan's enormous arm, she dragged him toward the truck. "You, you're coming with me!" (Evan had been chuckling over a meme with a Maori warrior finding an Easter basket full of emoticons and did not notice that he was being entered into evidence.)

At this, Phineas Fairfax laid a hand on Bobby's shoulder in a silent invitation to leave the scene, but did add in a slight spoken coda, "Evan can take care of himself."

So around a corner of a building retreated the doctor, Bobby, and Greta (who also had sensed the mood crackling in the morning air). Meanwhile, the monstrous pickup roared awake, a pudgy hand crammed a timeworn Sarah McLachlan cassette into the stereo, and very soon, Maggie found herself running ragefully down the road into a cloud of dust, her cries of "That's my truck, young lady!" resounding through the morning trees, while in the passenger's seat, Evan finally looked up from his handheld, wondered where he was off to, and popped his daily Brazil nut extract to maybe boost his IQ a few points.

✳✳✳

Having left Madison and her mother to resolve their differences like grown women, the doctor and Bobby ambled along pleasantly. The morning sun was warming the foliage about the compound, the bells of the chapel beyond the apple trees rang out to remind the mothers that the first sub-urbanites were coming up the road to the berry fields, and a soothing breeze danced winsomely about them like a happy maiden.

Unfortunately, just as they reached the patio for an al fresco breakfast, a very unhappy maiden made her appearance.

"Good morning, Zoe," said an unruffled Dr. Fairfax. "You missed Madison's and Steffany's departure. But—you seem to be scowling."

Zoe stomped to a stop in front of Bobby and, fixing him with eyes like a two-pronged pitchfork, curtly accused him, "You."

"Robert," said the doctor, "I should see Greta about breakfast. I shall see you soon."

Once he had left (or abandoned) him, Bobby thought that the doctor might indeed see him soon, but on a slab in the mortuary. Especially when Zoe asked him with the sharpness of a papercut, "Who's Sheena?"

"Nobody," answered Bobby, then repeated, "Nobody," in case her dangerously precise hearing was off.

"I heard you last night talking to her."

"Where?"

"So you were talking to her."

"Where was I talking to her?"

"What are you hiding???" (Her delivery deserved three question marks.)

"I'm not hiding anything. Sheena's just...She's just someone I know."

Before hearing Zoe's response to this "explanation," we should put aside that much marked-up freshman textbook *Interpersonal Communication* and pick up another old standby, *Chemistry 101.* In *Chemistry 101,* we discover that physical substances exist in varying states of matter depending on ambient temperature. If the air becomes cold enough, a gas becomes a liquid and a liquid, in turn, a solid: a somewhat hackneyed example is that of the morning dew that may coat the autumn pumpkin as frost, only to rise as invisible steam with the dawn's early light. Hypothetically, then, what changes might occur to a solid should the temperature plummet to a truly abyssal frigidity, the kind of shiverfest found at midnight near the north pole of a gas giant in the outer arm of a lesser galaxy on the fringes of the known universe? Although the authors of *Chemistry 101* never pursued this hypothesis, the reader should, because this change of state was now coming over Zoe's gaze as she heard Bobby's "explanation" about the mysterious Sheena.

"Well, then," she said, her eyes as hard and bright as the ball bearings in a semitruck's brake wells seconds before the blowout, "if you know her, then I guess you don't need to know me." And with that she curled off, her red hair chasing behind her like a flock of bloody birds done with the dead body.

✳✳✳

During this painful repartee, in a grove of golden bamboo around the patio squatted three very weary and muddy nuns. The festive chase that Bobby had endured a few days prior was as naught compared to the sinuous, indirect, pointless, undirected, and stupefyingly endless, mucky wandering that Bella, Baba, and Martie had suffered as they felt their way between the trees under the glowing stares of so many hairy creatures. At long last they did drag themselves blinking and shivering into the rising sun and, with their last sparks of energy, saw that they had reached their destination. Gratefully had they curled up in a patch of semitropical bushery to catch a little shut-eye—only to have their breakfast nap interrupted by the lovers' tiff described just above.

So, while not in the mood to exactly enjoy this record breaker on the romantic Richter scale, they could now report to Sheena Lypotrope that they had discovered the dink.

After rubbing her eyes and looking around for an espresso stand, Bella whispered, "That's him."

"I can see why you lost him," said Martie. "But she's really pretty."

"And," Baba observed, "it seems she's heard about Sheena."

"But maybe you just weren't what he was looking for," Martie told Bella. "I mean, you're way too old for him. For anybody, really."

Bella was about to rectify this distorted version of recent events, when Baba calmly reported, "Bella dear, your man is on the move."

And indeed, Bobby had started to trudge away in a sulking hangdog slouch. Bella hissed, "Who's got that net?" and Martie pulled out a butterfly net that looked suitable only for nabbing a northern swallowtail or a dragonfly. But recalling something from their Wise Sayings infusions session about "any port in a storm," Bella snatched it and charged through the golden bamboo, with her pals at her heels a second or two later.

Their assault did not seem to surprise, nonplus, or startle Bobby Lumbar. Either too forlorn to care or taking this as just another curiosity on offer at Orphis, he stared at them before offering a limp, "Morning. Which ones are you?"

Bella let the butterfly net sag like a wet blossom after a downpour, but it was Martie who saved the day. "I'm Sister Mister and this is—"

"Hey," said Bobby, noticing Mother Belladonna, and slowly raising a finger. "You're, um..."

Right then, the beefy voice of the Big Nun called out through the honeybushes, and she appeared around the corner. "There you are. You talk with the doc yet? Well, it doesn't matter. I just texted him. And Sister Priscilla's about in tears looking for that butterfly net." She reclaimed it from Bella. "Well, I hope you're up for another full day."

Glad though she was that the Big Nun had shown up as the one-woman cavalry, Bella wanted to say that, no, she was not up for another full day. But the rescue squad was already sounding off the schedule. "I got a last-minute call from the Happy Hags—you know them? Well, you will. They'll be making a pit stop to carb-load on candy corn before their annual 50k. So, Belladonna, you can man the farm stand for a while." This news about Belleweather Bungalows' own gear-grinders putting in an appearance was not encouraging, but before Bella could ask for a reprieve, the Big Nun was rattling off her next shift in the salt mines. "Then you'll need to spray the pigweed coming up in the kiwi arbor. I think it's about two miles square, but you can knock it out before vespers."

Martie piped up, "Oh, yesterday was fun. How about a yak this time?"

"No, sweetheart," said the Big Nun, "no yak yet. But, you know, the kids would love that. I wonder how much they're going for? Or maybe we could get a Highland cow and call it an 'American yak.' No, there's been a coyote lurking around the chicken coops. How're you with a .22?"

"Ask her about her throwing stars," hinted Baba.

"And that reminds me," said the Big Nun, "got any more of those unfiltereds?"

"That was my last."

"You don't know what you've got 'til it's gone, I guess."

"Tell me about it," said Babulia. "But have you ever thought of a side gig with organic tobacco? I mean, if you're going to have an 'addiction'..." She made air quotes of her own.

The Big Nun took on a distracted look. "You know, that would sell." But leaving aside past vices and future profits, she resumed the mantle of command. "Tell you what, since you've got the feel of the wheel, you can steer the big rig up to the hermitage we're building—a little surprise for Mother Johanna. Don't tell her. The paving stones came in yesterday. We haven't graveled the slope yet, but just chain up..."

At this, Baba held up her hands in a stiff, immobile pose.

"Yep, that's right. Ten and two. Say, where've I seen that color?" She closed in on Baba's fingernails. "Oh, right, during that mission year in Bogotá. Well, come on, girls..." In no time she was hustling her errant little chicks away, leaving Bobby Lumbar to his own lonely devices.

But even as Bobby heard Mother Deborah call genially up the water tower, "Hello, Mother Jo!" and the hermit shriek her own greeting back down at her, he was thinking again that he had seen that one nun somewhere else.

✳✳✳

Quite unlike the messy trek of the night before, Bella, Baba, and Martie made their way safely through the orchard behind the Big Nun like three lambs skipping along after Mary—or Little Red Riding Hood. This tiptoe down the primrose path, though, turned out to be tiramisu before a serving of cold broccoli. As soon as they were back in the forced labor camp that was the Strange Sisters Fruit Farm, the Big Nun was reminding them to "offer it up," since not only was the weather threatening a possible downpour (rain smocks were in the robery, if they could find Mother Preobrajenska to let them in) but, as promised, they also saw arriving a contingent of recumbent bicycles, the spry and spandexed Happy Hags, with Artemisia Sage from Belleweather Bungalows pumping away at the pedals right there at their head.

✳✳✳

Bobby Lumbar joined Phineas Fairfax at breakfast. While picking disconsolately at his meal, the doctor sat quietly improving his already capacious gray matter with a yellowing dime-store volume, *The Jakesman of Mosier.* Between turning its brittle pages and taking sips from his Ching dynasty coffee cup, the older man quietly observed, "Zoe seemed vexed." But before Bobby sought any romantic advice from a confirmed bachelor, the doctor said, "I'm having some old friends visit the convent today for a short tour. It might take your mind off your troubles if you came with me and acted as my factotum, amanuensis, omnibus, what have you."

Bobby gave a nod of agreement, since this would give him something to do instead of joining the French Foreign Legion. So, once the Chinese china was cleared away, the doctor, Sangreal, Siege Perelous, and a plodding Bobby were footing it to the convent.

✳✳✳

In no time, the little masculine group had come out from under the apple blossoms and caught sight of the chapel's golden onion dome in the midmorning light. (Mother Deborah had about twenty peerless shots of the cupolas in their glory and cycled through them on the convent's website home page.) While doctor and dogs walked straight toward this lovely little bit of the Carpathians, Bobby scanned about for Zoe. All that was on offer to his love-hungry eyes, though, were a cluster of recumbent bicycles parked like a herd of restless broncos and a few of the mothers ambling across the scene. With a gloomy sigh, he shuffled off after the doctor to maybe make something of the day.

Dr. Fairfax was already standing on the stone steps before the chapel, with Sangreal and Siege Perelous, and pulling out his pocket watch, he gave it a glance. "I would say...now," just as a small tour bus swayed around the corner and cruised to a stop immediately in front of them.

The doors swung open and, as the doctor stood forward to meet the newcomers, out crept a band of nervous, shuffling matrons, each garbed in a stiff, new-from-the-bubble-wrap T-shirt that proclaimed:

Life's Better at Belleweather!

As they stared about in subdued fright, Dr. Fairfax greeted each lady with a welcoming reassurance. Once this optimists' club had gotten its collective bearings and formed up in a timorous huddle, the doctor leaned into the bus and chatted up the chauffeur, the very same elderly but hale German martinet who had been putting him and Evan through their paces in the pole barn the night before.

If Bobby were one to eavesdrop, or just had a sharper ear, he would have heard the driver's half-guttural warning: *"Du erinnerst dich an Edna. Sie sagt mir, dass Sheena dich sucht..."* But he let go of this rough nugget of knowledge, not only because Bobby spoke no German, but also because suddenly, inexplicably, maybe miraculously, a change came over his vision.

Like the leader of a one-man rebel uprising, without a question mark marring any of his words, Bobby called to the white-clad back in the door of the bus. "Dr. Fairfax!"

The ladies from Belleweather started, but the doctor simply turned about unperturbed. "Yes, Robert?"

"I'm gonna go find Zoe."

"A worthy quest," he said. And finishing with the driver, he went to his anxious guests and with a docentine hand invited them to consider the interesting architectural features on the chapel's facade.

***

What had happened within Bobby Lumbar? Perhaps he had remembered that happy afternoon with Zoe. Perhaps of the sight of those sad shuffling day-trippers from Belleweather (wherever that was) had moved him. Perhaps, when emotions flood to one pole they deluged back all the stronger. Perhaps he was feeling tired of playing understudy to Dr. Phineas Fairfax. Perhaps the myrrh-streaming icon of Blessed Symeona of Blainesville was so close. But whatever the cause, from deep within Bobby's out-of-shape gut, from his own inner darkness, *de profundis*, there arose a mysterious and hungering force, and in its atavistic, virile voice, it called him to turn away from his sluggish self-pity and to soar off into the lonely reaches of the unknown, to clearcut the fig groves, backhoe the pink blueberries into mulch, or chew off the padlock on the pump house door, to do any and all things to find his lady, his shining lodestar, Zoe Feldspar—and before she took any vows that she would not be able to get out of later.

***

Zoe, though, was not the only one who might never escape the gentle clutches of the Strange Sisters.

Bella's morning ticked by as she sat at the abacus, tallying up tubs of blueberries and bear-shaped plastic squeeze bottles of organic honey and the countryside junkies just kept coming. (After loading up on organic produce, these lifetime-givers to PBS went off to a nearby pavilion to listen spellbound to Mother Dragomira's "Canning and Cobbler" seminar, while in an adjacent tent, Mother Hyacintha with her concertina was leading the suburban children in a sing-along of "Botulism Ain't My Friend" and that rousing hand-clapper "Ptomaine, Ptomaine, No, Siree!") Martie, meanwhile, had managed to terrorize all of the bird life around the chicken coops as she took very inaccurate aim at anything nonhuman that came into view (and a few humans as well). And as for Baba, with her back wheels dangling over the muddy incline of the road and threatening to drag both truck and driver down into the swampy creek below, she passed her a.m. figuring out the winch, necessary before chaining her big rig around a cottonwood tree to inch-by-inch cinch it back onto the incline.

By late morning, though, these chores were winding down.

Having coaxed all of that maverick tonnage back onto the road, Baba had navigated the final twenty feet of springtime mud and dumped the paving stones into the foundation hole for the new hermitage. (This was the safest place she could find.) Following a ten-point turn that included knocking over a couple of trees and permanently denting the back bumper, she was rolling on down the drive again. Martie had ended up attracting emergency response teams from two neighboring sheriffs' jurisdictions, one setting up an enclosing perimeter and the second calling in the canine crew and a negotiator. Alerted by these lights and sirens, Mother Deborah put in a providential appearance and snagged the .22 from Mother Martina's pseudo-homicidal grasp, before accepting an offer to be a guest lecturer at an upcoming de-escalation workshop. (This was the trade-off so that the sheriff would just forget all of this silliness—no need for any distracting stories in the vein of "Crazed Nun Goes on Anti-Environmental Rampage" circulating online and soiling the reputation of an otherwise law-abiding member of the Merryweather-area community.) And while the Big Nun was busy nailing down the exact date for her guest spot, Martie shimmied off to discover Baba at the convent's commercial-grade diesel pump. (Her bionic nose had picked up the evaporation fumes since Baba was illegally topping off the tank. She also wanted to be sure that she did not light up pump-side.)

But when Baba and Martie showed up in front of her folding table of a counter, they found Mother Belladonna not at all ready to abandon ship. To the clicking away at the abacus beads, Bella's face had frozen in a rigid, toothy grin that repeated robotically, "Don't forget our special on by-the-pound white raspberries, the best that Mother Earth has to offer in these parts."

Before Martie could ask whether Mother Earth was one of the nuns, Baba waved a blistered but dehypnotizing hand in front of Bella's face. This legerdemain must have done the trick, since Bella blinked, her mouth drooped open, and her jittery digits dropped into her lap like overworked stewardesses jumping from the emergency exit at five thousand feet.

To ensure that her friend was fully present, Baba asked slowly, "Any word on the Happy Hags, Bella dear?"

But Bella merely muttered something and glanced down the line of fruit enthusiasts with their buckets.

"The Hags, sweetie," Baba gently pressed.

Then Bella gave her head a clarifying shake. "No. No sign, yet. What happens now?"

"Well, I can tell you that," came a cheerily booming voice, and the Big Nun herself manifested stage left with a wooden platter weighted down with sandwiches (slices of Abbey's Best Whole Grain™ slathered in herb-infused goat butter and stuffed with shredded red cabbage and day-old slices of quinoa loaf). Forgetting their chum, Martie and Baba fell on these rations like she-hyenas on the last carcass of an endangered rhinoceros, as a wild-eyed Bella crawled over her folding table and dove at the food like a lady wrestler in a grudge match. After giving an ain't-nothing-to-see-here smile to the folks waiting in line, the Big Nun said, "That's the spirit, girls," her helpers now in a graceless, chewing, gulping tangle of bodies, with one of them snarling something about hey, that's my pickle. "Fuel up," she went on, "'cause you know the fun never stops. Here comes your next project."

Then Bella, Baba, and Martie saw creeping toward the payment tent, inching nearer like an enormous and anxious blue caterpillar, a line of mature women in brand-new dark blue T-shirts reading something about Belleweather Bungalows and forgetting all about their ravenous gourmandizing. Our heroines, their jaws hanging half open, held very, very still.

✳✳✳

THE QUEST OF SIR ROBERT DE LUMBARE BORE HIM
FIRSTWISE UNTO THE PRECINCTS OF THE GREEN HERB GARTH
WHERE WITH MICKLE HOPE HE FAINED BEHOLD LADY ZOE SWATHED IN
    MOURNFUL HUES

Back in the land of Modern English, the Belleweatherians were still several feet from the U-pick checkout, when at the head of their line, Ronnie Johnson herself, defending her complexion from the sun by a broad hat and sunglasses, gave a meaningful grunt to the ladies behind her, and each began to move her head about in slow curiosity, sniffing the air.

Bella, Baba, and Martie, though, must have been downwind, since after another snort, the tour group was creeping toward the checkout again, now with the Big Nun leading on. "These ladies are old friends of Dr. Fairfax," she was saying to her undignified helpers on the ground. "He arranged this day trip for them, and the word is, ladies, you're loving it so far, aren't you?" A few of the Belleweatherians nodded. "The doctor was called back to the office, but these three mothers will take over and do the Strange Sisters proud." Ronnie Johnson tilted her head around the Big Nun to get a better look (or smell) of their new guides.

Keeping an eye out for the speediest escape route, Bella crawled upright. "But I thought I was spraying pigweed."

"You were, Belladonna, but—"

"But nothing," said Bella. "Pigweed's a scourge in these parts." The Belleweatherians had loped closer, with a few distracted by the organic seed display and old-time wasp traps, but just as many were swaying their muzzles back and forth, catching anew a curious musk upon the air. By now, Baba and Martie were also on their feet too, dusting off the Abbey's Best Whole Grain™ crumbs and straightening their wimples.

"Well, speaking of pigs," offered the Big Nun, "the curing shed's pretty bad. The brining trough needs a good scrub for all the heads and trotters we'll be putting up come September. Word is, there a bad infestation of wild hogs up in Segue and the sheriff asked if I'd like to come along for a shoot. I've never been in a helicopter, but I guess that's how you do it."

Bella was more than ready to pick off a few porkers for a good cause— or just spend the afternoon with a toothbrush and a jug of bleach. But as she and her companions stepped as one out of the shelter of the check-out tent to head for said curing shed (they hoped that it was in the opposite direction), they stepped into the quiet flow of the springtime breeze, which delivered their particular perfume to the noses of the uncertain Belleweatherians.

With grunts and snorts, in a rippling, seismic wave, the visitors lifted their faces, their nostrils flared, a demanding guttural growl of hunger rose among them, and our heroines once again heard, "Spare parts..."

At once, the tent became a swirling splattering maelstrom of pink blueberries, white raspberries, organic seeds, old-time wasp traps, hand-painted signs, cardboard tubs, and Heaven Scent™ handmade soaps as the Belleweatherians, bellowing, "Spare parts!" charged in fierce and hungry joy at the victims who would not escape this time.

Needless to say, their targets, forgetting all Gospel injunctions about giving to those who asked of you, chose to selfishly retain their body parts and fled the scene, while the suburbanites escaped in terror to their hybrid cars, leaving the Big Nun standing alone, hastily sending out a handy text. She did have the sheriff's private number, but after that business with Mother Martina, she knew to keep this one in the family...

✳✳✳

Bobby Lumbar followed the same grassy, daisy-strewn path that he and Zoe had made two days before to reach the summit of Smithville Dike. Drained of any residual chevalier gallantry and, yea verily, not caring whether *goeth hence* and *whither comest* meant the same thing, he squatted on the patch of grass where they had passed on that apple and looked about: the same views of the housing development and the same rainbow of Maytime blooms, but nowhere that girl to share them with.

But one thing did catch his attention. To the west, Bobby saw a continent of clouds creeping toward the dike, the convent, the berry fields, and Orphis with a suspicious, lowering menace, their scalloped underbellies flashing with lightning and growling like a Sky Father waking up with a hangover. Remembering those lessons from Mr. Peabody at the junior high science camp, he counted off the arrival of what the fellows on Level III liked to innocently call the "weather event." But even as he was ticking off the dramatic pause between lightning and thunder, a cold wind rushed up the slope, and a sudden and startling curtain of rain and hail in hard white pills was gushing down on top of him.

In no time, he was winding away down the dike, slipping through the wet grass and skidding down the mud, but happily calling out, "Zoe!" With his cold face, wet lab coat, ruined shoes, fogged glasses, and icy hair, this storm, like a chilling enchantment falling upon the land, reminded Bobby Lumbar that he was still on a quest. No longer as a noble knight, he was now the stoic hunter, and these curtains of water and ice were the pale, silvery, and cerulean tapestries woven and thrown up at him by a jealous and angry witch, to keep him from the silken and magical princess whom he sought.

✳✳✳

We now set aside both the *beaux gestes* of Sir Robert and the action stories of Rob Lumbar to reflect on the healing power of Orphis. Yes, Zoe Feldspar was still seething at the fact that Bobby had spoken to any other female *at all.* But rather than ride the typhoon of her emotions straight into the patient arms of Mother Deborah—who was so busy that she would have bypassed the velvet glove routine and gone straight for the iron fist of "It's time to grow up, honey"—Zoe had stomped off for the wasteland of wild weedy fields that spread beyond the bounds of the convent. There, armed only with a stick, she had spent the morning whacking a path through the grass, all while mentally venting her indignation at the male sex and planning precisely what she would tell that Bobby Lumbar and hoping that she would *never* see him *ever again.*

But as Zoe was preparing for posting online her list of irrefutable and viciously accurate insults that she was going to hurl at Bobby (these included *mean and stupid, stupid and mean, idiotic, nasty, two-faced, thoughtless, selfish, just-like-all-the-others,* and, the real zinger that was meant to sting, *bird-brained*), she felt fall onto her hand a lone droplet of rain, like a teardrop of the sky. Looking up, she saw that the sky was moodily shifting to a murky, gloomy black and moved to head back to Orphis, against the chilly wind that not only was bending the thistles and hogweed about her but also blew straight at her through the grass a gigantic white SUV.

CHAPTER XIX

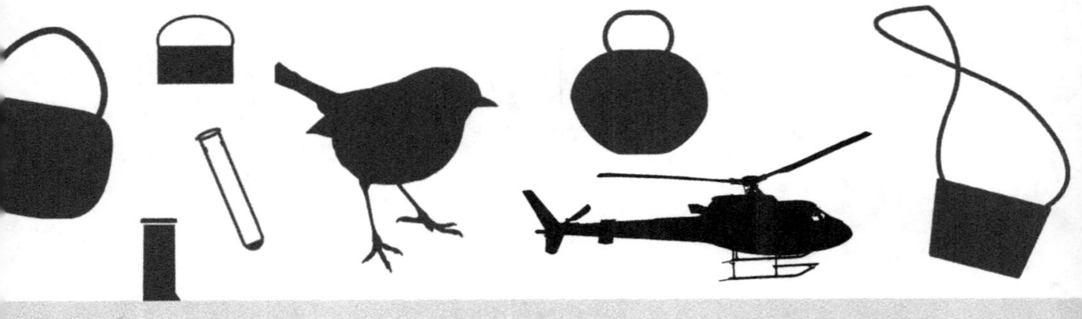

THE CABBAGE PATCH, OR KIDS THESE DAYS

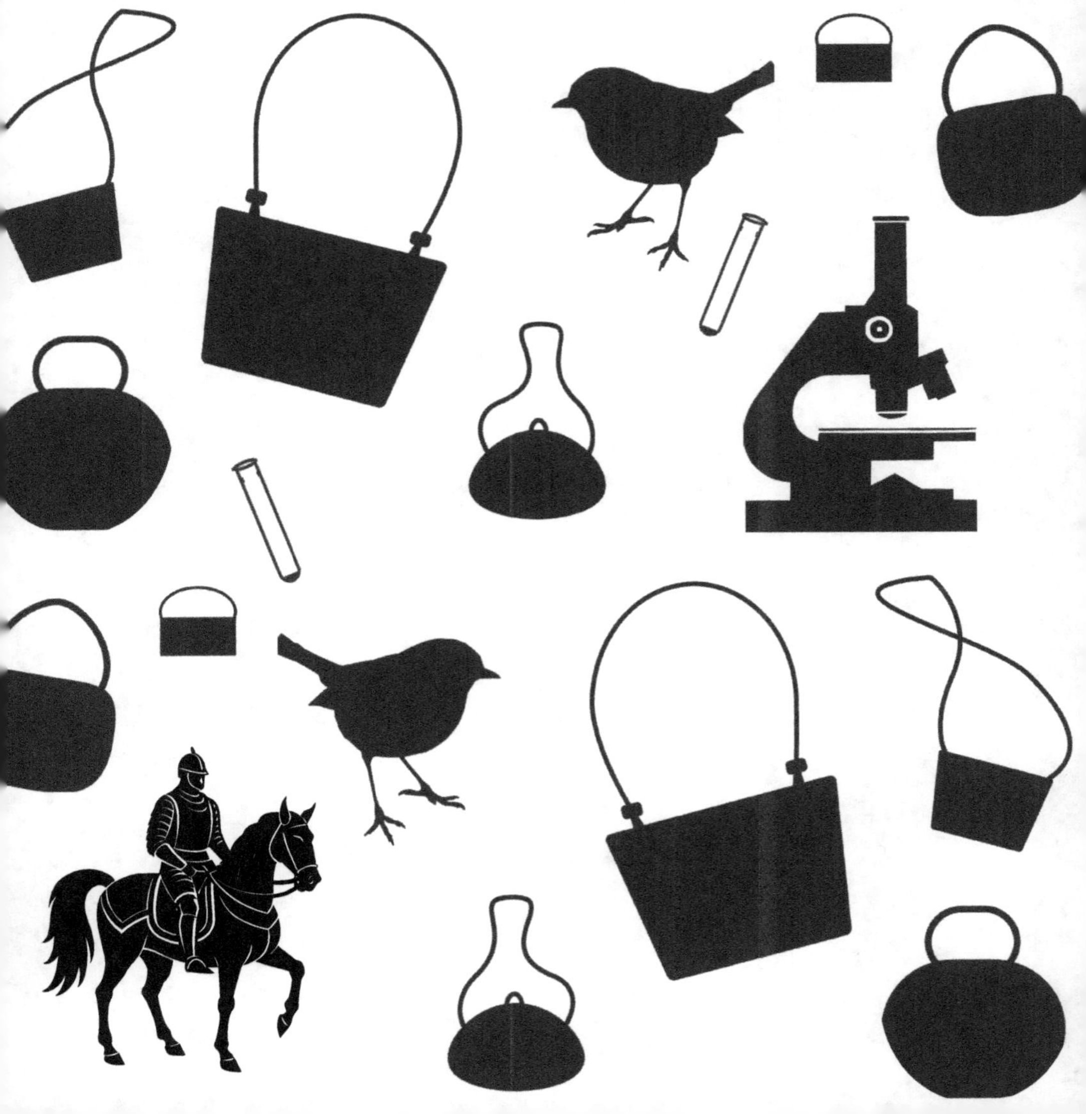

If Zoe was shuddering because charging her way came an SUV—being chased by a pack of recumbent bicycles and a horde of old ladies in matching blue tops, by the way—how would she have felt seeing to the midday horror matinee that led up to this?

Anyone imagining a convent as a place of serene contemplation would have chucked that fantasy into the curbside recycling bin upon seeing Bella, Baba, and Martie flee from the Belleweather Bungalovians, who, desperate to restore their dilapidating bodies with our heroines' gently used transponders, cardiac pace-drivers, and neuro-throbdobulators, chased after them with a single motive in mind, like a devouring river of siafu ants scenting a napping ecotourist just up the nature trail.

Bella, Baba, and Martie, though, had made good time. After leading their pursuers on the catch-us-if-you-can budget pilgrimage around all of the chapels, smoke sheds, cow barns, flatbed garages, and the echinacea-infusion barn (one of Mother Deborah's pet projects), they had shoved their way through the Japanese knotweed and climbed into Bella's SUV. As Bella frantically pressed the ignition button over and over (and so, starting and stopping the vehicle over and over), the Belleweatherians were clawing and gnawing at the doors, rearview mirrors, and headlights, blotting out all light for the terrified escapees cowering inside. (The security glass and tinted windows were not living up to their warranty.)

But just as one attacker wrenched off a door handle (and under the overpowering spell for "spare parts," accidentally ate it), the engine roared to life, Bella crammed her foot into the floor by way of the accelerator, and they were racing out of the hiding place, swerving through an obstacle course of laundry lines and losing enough of the attackers to see through the windshield.

After a blast of the horn to teach a flock of Buff Orpingtons some manners, Bella shouted, "Status report?"

Martie snapped back, "Just a second," and rolled down her window a few inches, only to have a geriatric arm curl down from the car roof and Ronnie Johnson pull herself down, shatter the shatter-proof glass, and force herself through.

Martie batted at her attacker with her dainty fists, until in a ballet of joint survival, Baba joined Bella in giving the steering wheel a sharp turn to the left, hurtling Ronnie Johnson rudely back through the broken window to splat into an unsuspecting compost bin. This sharp maneuver, however, also sent the SUV straight down a shadowy alley between a pair of those mysterious buildings that made up the convent, a lightless canyon that to Bella looked to be a mile or so deep.

Meanwhile, Martie—who had not learned to keep her head inside the cab—was looking backward out her window and shrieking, "They're still coming."

"I guess there's no pulling over for a smoke break, Bella dear?" asked Baba, as things darkened around them indeed, with only a rectangle of sky above them.

"Sorry," Bella grunted, keeping her own laser gaze on the track of impenetrable darkness in front of them and thinking that whatever architectural whatnots made up a good convent (all of those trapezas, scriptoria, infirmaries, cloisters, oratories, balnearies, and suchlike), they sure built 'em long and lean, since even gunning her rig to a soon-to-be-lethal velocity, they still had not reached the end of this particular alleyway. "You see anything out there, Babs?"

But before Baba could report anything, a disconnected fuse box suddenly wrenched away a side mirror, a rusting downspout gave the passenger side a very permanent scar, and the driver's side was mangled and scraped by an abandoned kinetic sculpture forgotten by Mother Nitriana—she had been trying to branch out from glassware—all while the hungry howls of the Belleweatherians reverberated just behind them.

Disregarding these ominous distractions, Baba lightly patted her hair through her wimple, no doubt wanting to look good for the mortician, and made ready to confess with a fatalistic last breath about the things you regret at the end, when she heard Martie give a small sniffle.

And in those milliseconds until this dark alleyway surely ran out and they became a kinetic sculpture themselves, Baba remembered herself and, grinding out the butt of her own oblivion, squeezed Martie's fingers. "Now, now," she told her. "It's time to be a big girl."

And as Martie mumbled, "Charlotte?" the darkness did end, for Bella's vehicle, like a futuristic tank, was charging up a beetling mountain of firewood that had blocked the end of the alley. With wheels spinning, car alarm blaring, and scrap wood hurtling into the faces of the Belleweatherians panting behind them, it catapulted up and out between the buildings in a magnificently symmetrical arc, sailing high above the parking lot next to the berry fields, its strafing shadow like a bird of prey over the hybrid vehicles below escaping the chaos of the checkout tent. Then landing on the new zinc-aluminum roof of the tractor garage, it ended its flight with a quiet and graceful drop down onto the bales of hay below. (Recent tours at Strange Sisters invite those visitors who doubt the truth of the Flying Ghost Car—called the Albino Elijah—to climb on up the ladder to the roof and behold the skid marks.)

After they had bounced off the hay bales and finished blinking in disbelief, Bella asked, "Where to now?"

"Maybe they know?" said Martie, pointing to a group of alert persons on recumbent bicycles several yards in front of them.

"No, Lily, they don't," Baba explained, guiding her hand downward to keep it from signaling the lynch mob. Unfortunately, the Happy Hags were already pumping their hand gears in unison and rotating toward our heroines like a school of hungry mama orcas aiming for a humpback whale with a bloody nose.

Hoping that one more sharp turn would not get them killed, Bella cranked her steering wheel hard to the right and bounced her pals into a just-watered quarter acre of little grayish-green sprouts—cabbages, kohlrabi, cauliflowers, collards, and broccoli plants destined for the convent's kitchen. The Happy Hags were right on her, switching to BMX mode, but just then, Bella gunned it up a line of baby cauliflowers and delivered smack into the faces a splattering spray of mud and slime, like a squid squirting a nebula of defensive ink.

This very rude attempt to flee only riled up their pursuers. Having crawled over the pile of firewood and caught up with the rest of the gang, the Belleweatherians, like carnivorous kangaroos, had leapt over the kohlrabi and landed on the roof of Bella's car, forcing our frantic driver to stop and spin, a move that did send the enemy centrifuging away in all directions as the scrape of their claws echoed metallically through the car's interior. Soon enough, they had regrouped and renewed the attack, as if Bella's car was a four-wheeled football bouncing up the wrong end of the pitch.

And so, the long day wore on.

✳✳✳

For Bobby Lumbar, trading his soggy duds for something dry back at Orphis was like taking a hearty draught in a woodsman's hut.

Once he was suitably attired, he headed for Zoe's room, prepared to corner her and unapologetically inform her just how things would work from now on. Once in position before her door, he gave the obligatory three knocks, endured a not unexpected silence, then made an end-run around any further quiet spells by trying the doorknob.

The door was locked.

He would have kicked it in, but to avoid scaring her into the arms of the owner of a chain of pet cemeteries, he headed for the kitchen, where Greta just might be playing wise woman to the lovelorn maiden. (Yes, Bobby was being naively optimistic, thinking that Greta was the sage voice of romantic reason, but this was Orphis.)

Walking in, Bobby found Greta wielding a hand mixer, with a dozen fresh eggshells littering the counter, as a portable DVD player played disc 2 of the Doing the Work trilogy. (This particular film was *Bake Away the Hate,* a feel-good tale about an artisanal ice-cream shop owner who comes to embrace "dessert equity." Greta was so entranced by the scene of Melinda gently sprinkling rainbow dragées on the vanilla supreme sundae that the meringue she was making for that night's baked Alaska started overflowing the bowl like pale, cool magma.)

But before she saw him and anxiously explained away this latest lapse into nostalgia, Bobby quietly tiptoed backward out the door. (Although "cured," Greta would probably need maintenance doses of equity and inclusion until her dying day.)

Thinking of one last outpost where Zoe might be nursing her romantic rage, moments later, Bobby was standing sprucely before the door into the lab. Reprising his performance as the alpha suitor, he gave it an energetic knock.

And as before, no answer.

Giving his role more depth and expression, Bobby tried this doorknob, and in a happy twist of fate—and of the knob—it turned in his hand. Taking this as nine-tenths of a green light, he opened the door, poked his head over the threshold, and with a swaggering smile on his lips, he said, "Zoe."

The lab was empty, but as he stepped away to carry on his hunt for Zoe—and he was sure that she was just waiting for him to find her—Bobby felt the sudden desire to peruse the laboratory of Phineas Fairfax. This was an opportunity not to miss, and giving Zoe a few more minutes to cool her jets, he stepped inside.

With the door shutting behind him, he took a minute to submerge in the smells and satisfyingly sterile symmetry of the place. Wandering down one of the counters, he took in its glass slides, its test tubes, its petri dishes, a pair of forceps, a microscope or two under plastic covers, probes like translucent peppermint sticks, tidy boxes of litmus paper, then scalpels, beakers, Bunsen burners—and a diaper pail...?

Just then, a subtle noise, like a smooth, rhythmic rocking, came to him. Turning cautiously about, Bobby saw at the other end of the room, beyond the work island and set above the floor on triangular supports, a wide, deep metal box, with a hydraulic arm gently pushing it back and forth in a quiet, metronomic motion. Above the box, from four fine chains, hung a lighting fixture like an upside-down box of opalescent eggs, each bulb, perfectly spherical and slightly prismatic, emitting a gently pearlescent glow, motherly and almost musical, as if light could hum a tune. But what was slumbering under this lullaby of light?

At this, his scientific curiosity asserted itself, becoming dangerously feline, and he crept closer, as if nearing the brim of a nuclear tower on one of its grumpy days.

Resting his hands on the edge of the box, he gave a gander at its contents—and would have run straight through the nearest wall if he had not been gripping the box in utter terror.

Within, in a pretty den painted with clouds and flowers, was rolling about a bizarre, squirming semi-oval entity like a living marshmallow. Pale and sweet, it was a fleshy blob swaddled in pink, bearing what might have been rudimentary organs of sense, like finger holes poked into bread dough, while here and there grew appendages like cones and buds of marzipan. As Bobby began to pant, one end of its glistening oblong body swelled and rose up toward him, apparently to sniff at the newcomer whose shadow had darkened the light that was its food. Pairs of eyelike holes widened to take him in, while several other small holes opened, and Bobby heard in a whisper, singsonging to the rocking of the box, "Da da da da..."

Knocking over a tray of staining dyes, a collection of flasks and beakers, and the plastic-protected microscopes, Bobby dashed to the nearest door. He pounded on it and clawed at its face until he found the knob... which turned in his hand. The door opened, and Dr. Phineas Fairfax, his lab coat as white as illumination, filled the doorway in a blinding silence.

Bobby gulped. "What is that?"

The doctor gave an easy glance around Bobby toward the box.

"It's Zoe's baby," he said. "It's sweet, isn't it?"

"And where's Zoe?" Bobby asked.

"You're just full of questions. I don't know. When her bad feelings have burned themselves out, she'll come home." And walking around his very dazed young guest, Phineas Fairfax picked up the microscopes from the floor, reverently set them back into their age-old places on the counter, and proposed, "Has the time come for the truth?"

Bobby nodded his head like a blacksmith's hammer on a suit of armor.

"Yes," decreed the doctor. "The truth."

Stepping peacefully to the rocking pen, Phineas Fairfax thrust his large hands into it, lifted up the thing in its rosy swaddlings, and bounced it a few times before his face, with the slightest smile, before whispering to it with undiluted soupiness, "Baby, who is your daddy? Hmm? Who is your daddy? Yes, what a sweet little thing you are. Yes, you are."

The entity reached out tiny bud-like projections, feeling the air and batting fruitlessly at the doctor's glasses, while its sense organs widened, one of them emitting bizarre and dulcet notes. (Bobby had to imagine that this hypnotic piping meant to lull its caregivers to sleep so that it might lap up their vital fluids.)

The doctor turned the little test-tubian toward Bobby, but it shrieked, shrank back, and tried to crawl into the doctor's lab coat. (Bobby wanted to shrink away as well but doubted that there was enough room in the doctor's coat for him too.) "All right, then, baby," said Phineas Fairfax, "back to nappyland." Laying the creature back into its futuristic bassinette, he eyed a console running along its edge. "A fractional adjustment toward the cyanic end of the spectrum, then a little etherized dextrose plasma..." After a press to a smooth button, the light box dimmed and a discreet hiss of carbohydrates misted forth, like fog over a mountain dell. "Daddy will be back soon," he said into the box, then told Bobby, "She'll be happy with that for now."

"But *what is that?*"

"It's Zoe's baby." When Bobby opened his mouth to point out a few key differences, the doctor said, "Not a 'baby' per se, but a BB."

Any reader skimming the dictionary for a definition of *querulous* would see a convenient image of Bobby's face.

"A basic body," said Phineas Fairfax. "One of MAXIFAX's greatest secrets. Among others. And, no, of course Zoe did not make it. I made it. Or, I designed it. Among others." Peering down through the strands of etherized dextrose plasma, he murmured, "My finest creation. But, for now, at least, this is Zoe's baby. As I said, Zoe is hypersensitive." He pronounced the last word with cautious and careful delicacy. "She will only heal by recognizing that there are beings weaker and more tender than she is. QED."

The doctor left the bassinette and walked through yet another door, into an unknown chamber beyond. Seeing himself trapped between the thing cooing in the box and the mad scientist, Bobby Lumbar rapidly ranked the second threat as the safer bet, and with the fleeting, phantom hope that he was leaving the realm of alien babies into one, well, without alien babies, he hustled after the doctor.

∗∗∗

It was maybe at about this time that Bella & Friends burst through the weeds and grass straight at Zoe. But since woes of the heart have a way of hogging the mental limelight, young Zoe probably thought that this homicidal SUV was just what happens when Bobby Lumbar was loose somewhere in the world.

But just then, the SUV zoomed to the left and, like a four-wheeled angel of death that was late for that plane crash, raced away down a rough old service road toward Smithville Dike. But as Zoe stood listening to the echo of its shifting into overdrive, like the last lugubrious note from an outdoor industrial music concert, she neglected to notice that a pack of recumbent bikes had begun to circle her or that a herd of blue-frocked ladies was staggering to a halt around her.

When she did see them, she noticed that the latter were humped over with hands on their knees and were panting for air, but the ladies in spandex were sitting straight of spine and were taking her in from behind their neon-reflective goggles with cool inscrutability.

But it was one of the blue-clad short-of-breath brigade, now showing some fortitude and straightening up, who caught Zoe's curious and concerned eyes with a fixed and fascinated gaze of her own. "You're so pretty..." She smiled at her.

Then one by one, her fellow deep-breathers creaked upright and gave each other a wily and conspiratorial glance, as one asked for all to hear, "Do you think she needs all of her internal organs?"

Through gaunt lips glutted on carbohydrates and ready for protein, one of the bicyclists muttered, "You know, who cares about fresh air? I think it is time for a little fresh meat."

∗∗∗

Bobby followed Phineas Fairfax into his inner sanctum, half-lit and mysterious. Through the gloom he saw the doctor go to a vintage stereo playing music of an antique mode, and suppressing a sigh, Fairfax lifted

the needle, silencing this melodious distraction. After an ominous quiet
flooded his dark little snuggery, he said, "*Addio, Signore Pergolesi.* So,
Robert, you seek knowledge?"

Bobby nodded violently but stopped before his head bounced off.

With an easy fatalism, Phineas Fairfax stepped to his bookshelves,
ran his fingers along the spines of volume after volume like the keys of a
great pianoforte, and pulled forth from the end of a shelf a binder black-
markered with *Wonderful World.*

Bobby lunged for it, but the doctor lifted it out of reach. "Or perhaps
ignorance is bliss?" said the doctor.

"No, it's not," said Bobby.

"But as men of science, it's a desperate tragedy, isn't it, to ever quest
for knowledge? But are we Promethean? Or Luciferian? We will find out.
Please, sit."

Bobby quickly found a pioneer knockoff wicker-seated chair and made
ready to listen.

The doctor, holding the binder, had begun pacing from point to point
through the ill-lit room like a solitary planetoid in a silent pirouette about
the quiet quadrant of very distant space.

At last, he asked, "Has MAXIFAX treated you well? I ask because if
you never return, they'll disavow all knowledge of your fate. Maybe they're
testing your mettle. We shall see. Or rather, you shall see. What did I tell
you before, the other night, during my biographical ramblings? I'm sure
I mentioned the universities and the sheepskins."

Bobby nodded.

"Well, in case I had neglected to dot every *i*: When I was young,
younger than you, I was considered very smart—very, very smart—and
after that vigorous run up the university fast track, the rising talent,
at eighteen, a prize catch, I crossed the threshold of MAXIFAX. I suppose there's still the same herd of overeducated yes-men wandering
Level III?"

The question forced Bobby to recall the livestreamed horrorscape of
Messrs. Noah, Ian, & Co. being put through their struggle session. After
a gulp of survivor's guilt, he nodded.

"*Sic semper.* I myself treaded that well-worn path for a couple of years as a nondescript histologist. I received my regular raises and tweaks to my title, a new box of business cards on the anniversary of my hire date, so maybe it was inevitable..." The doctor slid his fingertips over the cover of *Wonderful World,* as if feeling for a secret keyhole. "In the mediocrity which is MAXIFAX, my life had shrunk down to very quotidian dimensions, and one day—and here the tragedy begins to uncoil, the dragon awakes, you might say—I heard that primal song, that mating call from the eternal, that I needed to live for something bigger than myself. In school, I had been busy with Science and, as you know, Science is sometimes so big that it blots out all other lights. Suddenly, though, the physical universe became not high enough, no subatomic particle was masonried with mystery, nor could I find peace in Blake's grain of sand."

Bobby thought that Blake might be that lab tech in the oceanography division. But the doctor was still talking.

"I wished for more, for things higher and deeper, and I admitted to myself that if I died, if my metabolic processes ceased and my protons, neutrons, and electrons flowed back into the flux of physical universe... Well, there was no *if.* Death and oblivion wait like cutthroats around the bend for all of us, don't they?"

Given all that he had endured over the last few days, Bobby decided not to read too much into this bit of wisdom.

"Therefore, in my inane, bookish, overeducated, sheltered egoism, not to mention my despair and desperation, I began to think. I knew, which is to say, I imagined, that having a titanium brain, I *had to* do something grand and that with my titanium brain, I could discover what that should be. I saw at once that since I was not out in the cosmos amid the nebulae and event horizons, but here on this planet"—he tapped a finger assertively on a small Louis XVI table—"at MAXIFAX." He pointed the same finger toward what might have been the American Southwest. "Were I to leave my footprint for the future, I must work for this planet"—he jabbed at the fragile antique once more—"through MAXIFAX," and pointed into the (presumed) American Southwest once more. "It was at that crossroads in my soul that that invitation came from the unseen powers on Level IX

to give a presentation to a delegation from South Korea." He gazed past
Bobby into the shadows of the room, like an impresario peeking past
the proscenium curtain of memory. "The presentation to the gentlemen
from Seoul went well enough and I felt important. Let them do with me
what they wished. And that was what MAXIFAX thought as well. Phineas
Fairfax was young, morally and socially gelatinous, slippery clay ready for
the molding. They would make me their vessel. They were lucky to have
Phineas Fairfax. I thought so. They might have thought so. 'Twas then
that I put pen to paper to record my solutions for the woes of a world that
I knew nothing about." He held up the binder. "*Wonderful World.*"

"That sounds nice," said Bobby, unwittingly deploying his default
jargon.

"Doesn't it? But *Wonderful World* was not merely the reservoir for a
young scientist's fervid imaginings. No. *Wonderful World* was my vade
mecum for the entire planet, my plan for a perfect place for us all." He set
the binder on the ancien-régime table. "Note that I say 'a perfect place,'
not 'a better place.' I instinctively traded in that kind of terminology, since
I was one of the bubble people. You know the bubble people."

Bobby looked at one of the walls, expecting it to slide open to reveal
this parallel race in their hexagonal thought-pods, toiling wordlessly to
take over the world. This did not happen.

"You know them," the doctor went on. "The experts, the bureaucrats,
the academics, the middle managers at nonprofits, the polite people with
the soft hands and the quiet weekends. For the bubble people, the world
is axiomatically a pleasant place, a paved, level, and well-lit bike path to
utopia. As to perfection...Have you ever considered perfection?"

Never good at short answers, but a past master of true and false, Bobby
said, "No."

"Fair enough," said the doctor. "There exists a small problem with
perfection." He held up a finger at an easy angle. "Perfection is pure. It
can never tolerate or de facto exist with imperfection. Many a mind, we
know, hopes for a world without conflict and disease. They imagine society as a pretty little box and presume that everyone will fit into it. But
people are not perfect and will not fit in the pretty box, that nothing in

this world is pure, unsullied, and unalloyed, that no persons are perfect. Those same minds must recognize that. And most do. But a few do not. What do they do? What if"—he spread his hands as if honoring the rising sun—"we make perfection the 'new normal'? They must do as we say? They must believe what we tell you? It should work." Now he jabbed his finger at Bobby like the bill of a heron skewering a frog. "But it does not. Not all obey, and this is vexing. The irresistible force has encountered the immovable object, or as those Russian peasants said before being marched off to Siberia, the sickle has met the stone. So, if perfection is to be the 'new normal' and you are not perfect, then you are not normal and you cannot belong to society. Thus, rather than surrender their vision of perfection, they must get rid of those imperfect, ill-fitting people. And what does not conform, is"—he held back the word, like a leopard on a leash, then let it slip—"eliminated: killed, imprisoned, psychologically smashed, exiled. The guillotines, the gas chamber, the Gulag. You know, it really is appalling how very ignorant the very educated are."

Phineas Fairfax looked directly at Bobby.

"And I, sadly, was also too educated to follow these lines of logic, and almost as a game I naively submitted my *Wonderful World* to the powers on Level IX. After a perusal of my little All, they chuckled—and their chuckles resound like thunder, if you have ever heard them. They said that much was not new, which was humiliating to me, but they did say that at least one of my ideas had merit. At this point you are supposed to ask—"

"Oh, what idea was that?" asked Bobby.

"Since you asked: In one section of *Wonderful World*"—he held up again the corpus delicti—"I argued that, since it took so long to breed the consumers demanded in the global marketplace, to buy all of the plastic, pressboard junk that our factories disgorge, might we manufacture shoppers en masse?"

Again, the reader should open his dictionary to *querulous* to see a picture of Bobby's face. The doctor spurred his tale on.

"On hearing of this idea, some bright spark suggested—actually, it was Sheena Lypotrope, now that I think about it, who was already warming the corporate cockles on Level VII...In any event, Sheena suggested that these shoppers should all be women, since shopping is simply a postmodern variant on the archaic female instinct to gather and nest. And, as you know, all people begin physically as female in utero, so it all seemed meant to be. The powers on Level IX gave us the green light to this experiment, if you can call it that, and I became the ad hoc head of what I call the teratology division, breeding monstrosities to loose upon the world. Thus began the Age of the Feminoids."

✳✳✳

Sharing one meat-seeking mind, the gibbering cobalt-clad Bungalovians and the Happy Hags began to coil inward around a shuddering Zoe. But before this Maypole moment turned messy, a terrified Zoe suddenly asked, "What are they?"

Into view there came a-tramping a brigade of fresh females (though not as fresh as Zoe). Eschewing both spandex and matching T-shirts, this platoon was garbed in pink-patterned camouflage, their faces smeared in SPF-15 collagen-enhancing face paint, field glasses hung about their necks like insurrectionist folk jewelry, and the shoulder of each sported a high-end lady's handbag, no doubt weighted down with MREs and Noo-Life™ gummy chewables. (A girl needs to get her Botox somehow.)

The Hags and the Belleweatherians scowled at these interlopers, not only because they were putting off the tempo of their attack formation, but also because even more of them were breaking through the ragwort to outnumber them.

The Happy Hags gave a growl to warn them off, but one of these rose-colored soldiers of *fortuna* still stepped forward. Wrinkling her nose in contempt, like a feral poodle investigating a heap of very edible garbage in a non-biodegradable garbage bag, she smirked to a sidekick, "Looky, looky, Frannie. Johnson Series slag. Who told you you could go past the perimeter?"

A Belleweatherian raised a timid hand to give an answer, but now Frannie had figuratively taken the mic. "You said it, Angela. What's the point of jacking up the property taxes to build a bike trail system if the raisin ranch roller derby can hit the open road?"

A cyclist with the gaunt lips gave a snarl. "It's called freedom."

Frannie slipped a Noo-Life™ gummy bear to her beeswax-balmed lips and decapitated it, flicking its stevia-sweetened body into the weeds. "This one's got an awful big vocabulary. You know"—she grunted at the happy prospect—"maybe we should drain her brain a little so she doesn't talk so much."

At this, another Belleweatherian bravely posed a trenchant question. "And since when can you go past Smithville Loop without getting shot down by a death drone?"

"The Big Blond's turned off the sensors," said Angela. (Zoe noticed that at this name, the women around her quailed slightly with a shared dread.) Just then, Angela noticed Zoe and gave her the up-and-down. "But what's this one? You think she's got any moving parts she doesn't need?"

"We were just about to find out," said a Happy Hag.

"I bet you were," said Frannie, trying to gain the upper hand. "Don't worry, we'll share, if there's anything left."

And Zoe squealed out, "Bobby!"

"Now, you just stop interrupting, songbird," said Angela with a snide smirk. "I got an idea." Fishing her handheld from a camo pocket, she tapped the screen a few times and summoned another party on the other end. She said into the phone, "So, you didn't tell me about Johnson Rockettes being here. Yeah, well, I need to know what's happening on the ground. Uh-huh. Well, maybe if you were here...Uh-huh...Uh-huh. Whatever. I don't care. But take a look at what I found," and after another tap on the screen, she positioned her phone momentarily to take in Zoe's young, anxious, and apprehensive face, then brought it back to her ear. "What do you think? The wannabes are talking about a cookout, but I was thinking—"

And Zoe shrieked, "Bobby!"

"Yeah, 'Bobby,'" said Angela. "I don't know who that is."

"Bobby!" she shrieked yet again.

"We heard you the first time, sweetie," Angela snapped at Zoe. "Now, why don't you...What?" The voice on the other end must have been expressing a Strong Opinion, since Angela's face stiffened with attention.

"Uh-huh. If you say so. Well, that's what I said. And I get the commission on this one, remember that. What? Yeah, 'cause your memory hasn't been so hot lately."

Just then, from the murky skies came a crackling of lightning.

At this sign of approaching doom, Zoe stretched out a cry of "Bobby!" as if auditioning for a mixed-genre women-in-prison/slasher film. A few members of the raw-food fan club must have thought that Bobby was the local sky god, because the heavens gave out not only another brief grumble of thunder but suddenly sheet after sheet of rain and a generous bucket of hail, to boot.

As all and sundry hunched over at this assault from the atmosphere, Angela jabbed her phone back into her pocket, and Frannie, her SPF-15 collagen-camo face pack starting to run, straightened her spine and barked at her women-at-arms, "All right, ladies. I don't know how long this day's gonna be, but we're gonna handle it. So, chin up, as many as you got." (This kind of abuse incited strong devotion to the leader.)

Angela got into the act too and turned on the gloomy-faced Belleweatherians, who, with the change in the weather, truly had started looking like a fatalistic herd of cattle. She told them, "And I got a job for you too, you sad sacks." She took in Zoe with a scheming look laden with visions of the fun to come. "Her," she said. "Just don't bruise the fruit."

✳✳✳

At Faraday-Kage College, Bobby Lumbar had managed a pass/fail grade in the mandatory World History for Science Majors class but had never heard of the Age of the Feminoids. Hoping that it was like the Age of Ultron, he raised his hand, but Phineas Fairfax gave an understanding glance and continued.

"We began with the Johnson Series. Or, I should say, we began with the stages of preprotonic development to become the globella, the globulus, and the globus. But after the globus stage, we had the basic body, or BB." He indicated the door to the lab. "I humbly confess that after that point we all stood back in wonder, for after the BB gestated, she grew—quickly.

No one dared take any long weekends. Then followed the knowledge infusion because feminoids, as you know, do not learn."

Bobby Lumbar did not know this but said nothing to avoid slowing down the story.

"Skills and facts are simply injected, for want of a better word. They can speak any language we chose for them, play any instrument, operate any computer program, drive any vehicle, et cetera. Naturally, we were eager to see how they might fare, and after a splendid graduation ceremony, we the whitecoats sat back, ready to watch our girls make the world a better place."

Glad to be posing what might pass for an intelligent question, Bobby asked, "Did they make the world a better place?"

"Not really," said Phineas Fairfax. "The feminoids did well enough making purchases at the mall, but in the end, they cost money—their condominiums, their cars, their expensive coffee drinks. When I saw this happening and, knowing that large companies dislike unnecessary expenses, I sensed that my meteoric rise would turn into a very precipitous and painful fall. Very cagily, if I say so myself, I strategically braved a trip on the spiral escalator down to Level IX to preemptively express my concerns." He gazed into shadows again as if expecting to see their grim, unmoving faces. "All I remember is a voice from somewhere telling me, 'All is well, Fairfax. Carry on.' Imagining my position secure, I put my thinking cap back on and worked to keep this project going. And that was when I remembered that females, typically, rate high in what psychologists term agreeableness."

Bobby wanted to share his recent experiences with Zoe, but the doctor was slogging on.

"In a rare moment of using every part of the buffalo, I thought, what could we do with that agreeableness? Then came my brainstorm. You recall, my original notion had been to have extra people to help push the money around. But then, like Leto giving birth to divine twins, I thought: Everyone spends money, and the money does not care about who you are, your race, your nationhood, your worldview. What if we brought together, say, shopping and let's say, hypothetically, of course, the unity of all mankind? We'll all just love each other and spend money; love and money would flow the world over, and humanity would be as one big obedient family. I say 'obedient,' because in this mighty scheme, at the top would naturally hover a few handlers. Let's call them guardians, guardian angels, nature's aristocrats, all very Platonic. I descended to Level IX again and posed this idea, only to hear out of the darkness, 'World unity is not new, Fairfax. We hope that your well is not running dry.' When I heard this, I was certain that my star was collapsing into a black hole. But then a new voice said, 'Tell us, though, Fairfax, how would we bring about world unity?'

"I don't know how I conjured up my scheme all at once, but when you're under the ultraviolet eyes of Level IX, your brain becomes very, very productive. I said something inane about starting with people's emotions, since that's something that pertains to each of us, and I swear, I could hear their smiles in the dark. A year passed after that, and after plenty of MAXIFAX money had lubricated the tracks, my ladies—when they weren't haunting coffee shops and yoga classes—started appearing on school boards, in local political offices, at the head of nonprofits, as the directors of small-town libraries. Again: feminoids do not learn. But what you do not know is sometimes just as important. So, unbeknownst to me, Level IX had been instilling in the feminoids Machiavellianism, sociopathy, the ability to lie with a smile, and emotional manipulation. These new feminoids said the right things, voted for the right things, cried over the right causes, and sang the siren songs full of abstractions: inclusion, acceptance, diversity, change, transformation. But to include what? Accept what? Be diverse in what ways? And change into what? But I knew that I'd sown an evil seed when the bodies started to pile up. You see, again, unbeknownst to me, MAXIFAX had begun using the feminoids for paramilitary purposes, secret missions to lonely corners of the globe, to defray costs. But tell me, Robert"—the doctor sounded as if he were hypothesizing—"would you rather pass your professional life with people who are kind and mediocre or who are brilliant and cruel?"

Bobby thought of a few other combinations, but before he could rattle them off, the doctor said, "I spent fifteen years with that swarm, toiling in their smithies. I created the process for making the feminoids. *Facilis descensus Averno.* But in time, I saw what MAXIFAX was doing: they were fashioning a new world, advertised—note the word—as more 'united' and more 'progressive,' as if human society was a brand of floor wax. But in actuality, we were building a dismal hive of shopping, watching screens, and ignoring God, where people write short words that they can't spell, where the banks chain you into heavy debt starting in college, where peace will be ours, if only we surrender everything we are. If you wish to celebrate Christmas morning with your children or watch fireworks on the Fourth with your grandchildren, well, you're a retrograde bigot, aren't you? But, Robert, even when we cease to act human—in its best sense, of course— that yearning, that energy, does not cease. No, if we're no longer human, we must become something. So, what do we become? In the world that MAXIFAX—and I—fashioned, we become demons. We become animals. We become robots. A wide spectrum of choices."

Bobby felt the wicker-backed chair under him becoming like a stone chair in the kingdom of the dead.

"But why am I complaining?" asked the doctor. "The world had become wonderful, hadn't it. I'd gotten what I wanted."

He slammed his hands together. "Then and there, I escaped MAXIFAX. I took all of the data, all of my books, all the plans under my arms, all of the passwords, and MAXIFAX was left with a good number of globus-level BBs, I'll admit, but none of the complete instructions on making more. You see, to the overlords at MAXIFAX, I was their faithful lieutenant, and they left me to my own devices—a rare instance of the forces of darkness being naive and trustworthy. And at that point, I became the Edmund Campion of the biotech shadowverse. Whither might I go? Not to another company. Not to the government. Not back to our estate on the Conshohocken. Nowhere that would be dangerous for those around me. So, I chose Merryweather, the initial stomping grounds of the feminoids. Here I might hide in plain sight while keeping an eye on them."

With the plot throwing him two curve balls in succession, Bobby asked, "Keep an eye on who?"

"*Whom.* The feminoids, the first generation of them, at least."

"The Johnson Series," said Bobby.

"Excellent. Gold star. Yes. Merryweather, you know, is the great locus of the feminoids."

Bobby asked, "Merryweather? Like Lewis and Clark?"

"That was Mer*i*wether," explained the doctor, reversing the phonemes to disadumbrate the orthography. "No, Merryweather. Our town."

With this reminder that there was a town nearby, Bobby was about to miss the end of the lecture by darting out the door and doing everything in this power to find Zoe. However, a little voice squelched this impulsive call to romantic adventure, and he remained in his chair to find out What Was Going On.

And the doctor had more to say. "From the beginning, Merryweather was part of it: a nice little town for MAXIFAX to corrupt. Other loci of the feminoids do exist—well, go to any college town and see who runs the place. But, having created these fake women, I wanted to do my part and sustain them as best I could. The paternal instinct, you understand. But once I was settled, here, free of MAXIFAX, other voices began to speak to me..."

Bobby now thought that maybe he did not want to hear the rest.

"It was my pride," explained the doctor, diagnosing his own complaint. "Oh, yes, Fairfax, they said, now your hands are clean, but your labors will be taken over by hacks, stupid hacks. And to this I could only think, 'Out damned spot.'"

Bobby wondered whether this was a slogan for laundry spray, but Dr. Fairfax fleshed out his meaning.

"In my moral umbrage, I had abandoned science, but I had still dreamed the feminoids into being, I had been their Prometheus. Without me, an entirely new race of beings would not be wandering the world, the x-factor. But an x-factor that was not an x, but an I, and I thought that I was the unstable bond, the weak link in the chain of being. And to ensure that Phineas Fairfax would never inflict his mind on the world again, nor that there would be weakness again, I transformed. Bismarck wouldn't have approved, but I undertook a two-front war against myself, within and without, my body and my mind. First, this mortal coil." He spread his arms and opened his hands, as if making himself an anatomical dummy.

"First, I fashioned a conspectus of proscribed foods that would shame the Mosaic Code. Then I wore a back brace to drive my posture into a straight line found nowhere in nature."

Bobby sat up a little straighter than he had been and listened harder for a few self-improvement tips.

"I chained myself to an Ixion's Wheel of the most punishingly cruel workouts imaginable. My trainer said that I trained so hard, he was surprised that the dumbbells weren't broken."

Bobby thought he would put these at the bottom of his list.

"And then, my mind," said Phineas Fairfax. "I read all of *Larousse Gastronomique*—including the recipes. I read all of Shakespeare without footnotes. I read Proust and *Les Misérables,* Waugh, Wilde, Belloc and Chesterton, Dostoevsky and Solzhenitsyn..."

He mentioned a few more names, and Bobby wanted to ask whether any of them had a good podcast.

"Then I began Orphis and, we being neighbors, I met the mothers. Really, nothing happens without reason."

Bobby wanted to give a short list of things that had happened to him over the last two or three days that lacked rhyme or reason—except meeting Zoe, of course.

But just as Bobby remembered his lodestar, the doctor said, "Well, I can't think of anything further to bore you with. You should be about finding Zoe. Here, take this." He handed Bobby *Wonderful World,* like a signed and sealed peace treaty. "A souvenir from our respective misadventures. Sometimes we need those. As for me, I must answer the demands of fatherhood." And without a word, he went to the door into the laboratory and passed through it.

Bobby was ready to stand and pass through one of the other doors—they seemed to be everywhere here—until he heard, "Time's up, dink."

Familiar with the voice, Bobby looked up to see the talk ball sinuously floating through the dark, right up to his face, where it hovered mincingly, Sheena Lypotrope's face in a tiny hologram curving over its surface. "I have been exploring," she said, then asked rather testily, "What's that you're holding?"

"This?" he asked and held *Wonderful World* up to the sphere.

Its many tiny nodule eyes glowed with indignant contempt. "Speaking of graduate theses...Where're you at?"

"In his room."

"Jackpot. Come on, then. The data's right there on the shelf. Just grab it and I'll send you the coordinates to meet at."

Bobby gave a glance at the shelves, then told the ball, "No." Its many eyelets glowed anew. "I've got another project."

Before Bobby could snatch the ball and chuck it and into the nearby hippopotamus-foot wastebasket, however, it radiated a polar chill found only on the north end of Irkutsk in January.

Sheena now spoke in a dangerously moderate tone. "You know, I think that I can guess what your other project is." The ball now rotated about, and finding just the right angle, it projected upward a cone of mote-speckled light that, after a few flickers, showed him Zoe: quivering, bound but not gagged, encircled by recumbent bicyclists, the tourist ladies from the bus (no longer sad but anxious for something, maybe a snack), and a pack of other women in pink-patterned camo pants with flashy, overpriced purses at the ready. She was sobbing over and over, "Bobby! Bobby!"

Bobby reached for the image, but his hand merely passed through it, and the hologram shriveled into a silky prismatic wrinkle, like a night-blooming flower at the break of day.

Sheena cackled in gleeful spite. "My people are keeping hold of Princess Candyhearts until I can clear out one of my walk-in freezers. So, what was that lip you were giving me?"

"Give her back to me."

"The jokes just don't stop, do they? I'm guessing you never learned any serious negotiations skills, what with wasting your schizoid boyhood blogging about your ant farm." (It was a termite farm, Bobby wanted to say, but the squeezing of tender flesh was proceeding.) "But I'm generous, and I may even hand her back to you for your own biological research. First, though, you remember why you are there."

To any of her threats, though, Sheena Lypotrope heard no answer, only the stomp of Bobby's feet as he charged out of the room.

✳✳✳

Phineas Fairfax was tidying up the laboratory when the young human cyclone reappeared a second time, *Wonderful World* still in his hands.

"She has her," panted Bobby, leaning for support from one of the microscopes.

"Who has whom?" asked the doctor, gently extracting his fingers from the research equipment.

"Sheena. Has Zoe."

"Well, that's not good. I presume—"

But Bobby, dropping the binder and leaving one more mess for his host, had already dashed out the door.

Dr. Fairfax picked up his utopial thesis like so much more garbage, laid it on the counter, and breathing deeply to fuel his mind, opened the door that led outside. Standing on the threshold, he took a moment to smell, as if for the first time, the earth, the peony petals, and the gravel, now moist from the rain and hail, before giving out a sharp whistle. From under a pergola tangled with akebia and hardy kiwi came lumbering Sangreal and Siege Perelous.

Loping obediently to their master in the doorway, they squatted before him. With one hand, Dr. Fairfax supplied a desiccated liver square to each slobbering maw, then raised the other as if offering a benediction to crusaders. Loudly, clearly, and slowly, he told the beasts, "Zoe..." and at that name, the gentle giants turned away, snorting the air for her scent.

Now sliding his flip phone from a pocket, he murmured, "Time to summon all the clans," and dialed a certain number from memory. (Phineas Fairfax had long contended that contact lists rusted the mental machinery.)

On the other end of his phone, Mother Deborah told the not-so-mad scientist, "Another bus of pilgrims has just pulled up, but I am sure it's important, isn't it?"

"Yes," he said. "Time is of the essence," and with a mild thoroughness informed her what had transpired and that he would appreciate whatever help she and the mothers might provide, and naturally, Mother

Deborah agreed to rally the troops in any way she could. (Mother Deborah was no fool. Having heard more or less all of Dr. Fairfax's tortuous path to redemption over mulled organic pear cider on autumn evenings, she privately guessed that a mighty flock was finally coming home to roost.)

Thanking her, he closed his phone and went to look at Zoe's "baby." Between its coos and gurgles, it seemed to be adequately metabolizing from the cloud of simple carbohydrates. Satisfied on that front, he went back into his sanctum.

Alone in his room, he stood unmoving, his head momentarily unpopulated by the strains of Pergolesi, furtive and murine schemes, or fleeting, chiropteran plans. But with nothing coming to his senses, his ear easily caught a small, crafty scratching from the floor.

Looking down, he saw a small sphere of many eyes moving of its own accord, snaking away in an ophidian track toward a dark corner, escaping perhaps.

With a peaceful certainty, he chuckled. "No, no, little one, you might get hurt there," and bending down, he deftly pinched two fingers about the truant. Before dropping it into his pocket for later dissection, he gazed deeply upon it, his glasses almost aglow in fascination before mellowing with esteem. "No demerits in regard to workmanship," he whispered, his breath briefly clouding its jewel-like eyes. "Like a marble from Fabergé, or the finial on a seneschal's staff of office. Oh, or the fossilized carapace of a *Megarachne servinei.* Or the pommel of Lohengrin's sword. No, I think *Megarachne servinei.*" Humming the wedding march, he scanned its silvery skin for any seams and securements, then brought the ball close to his lips, and as if coaching a suckling cobra from its egg, he whispered into it, "Sheena...? I'm right here, Sheena."

Then another sound, now from the door into the laboratory, spoiled his contemplations, for the door had burst open, as if from an avalanche, and his chamber chilled, its walls whitening with hoarfrost, and he heard a glacial voice intone, "And I'm right here, Phin."

CHAPTER XX

RAINY DAY PEOPLE, OR HAIL, HAIL, THE GANG'S ALL HERE

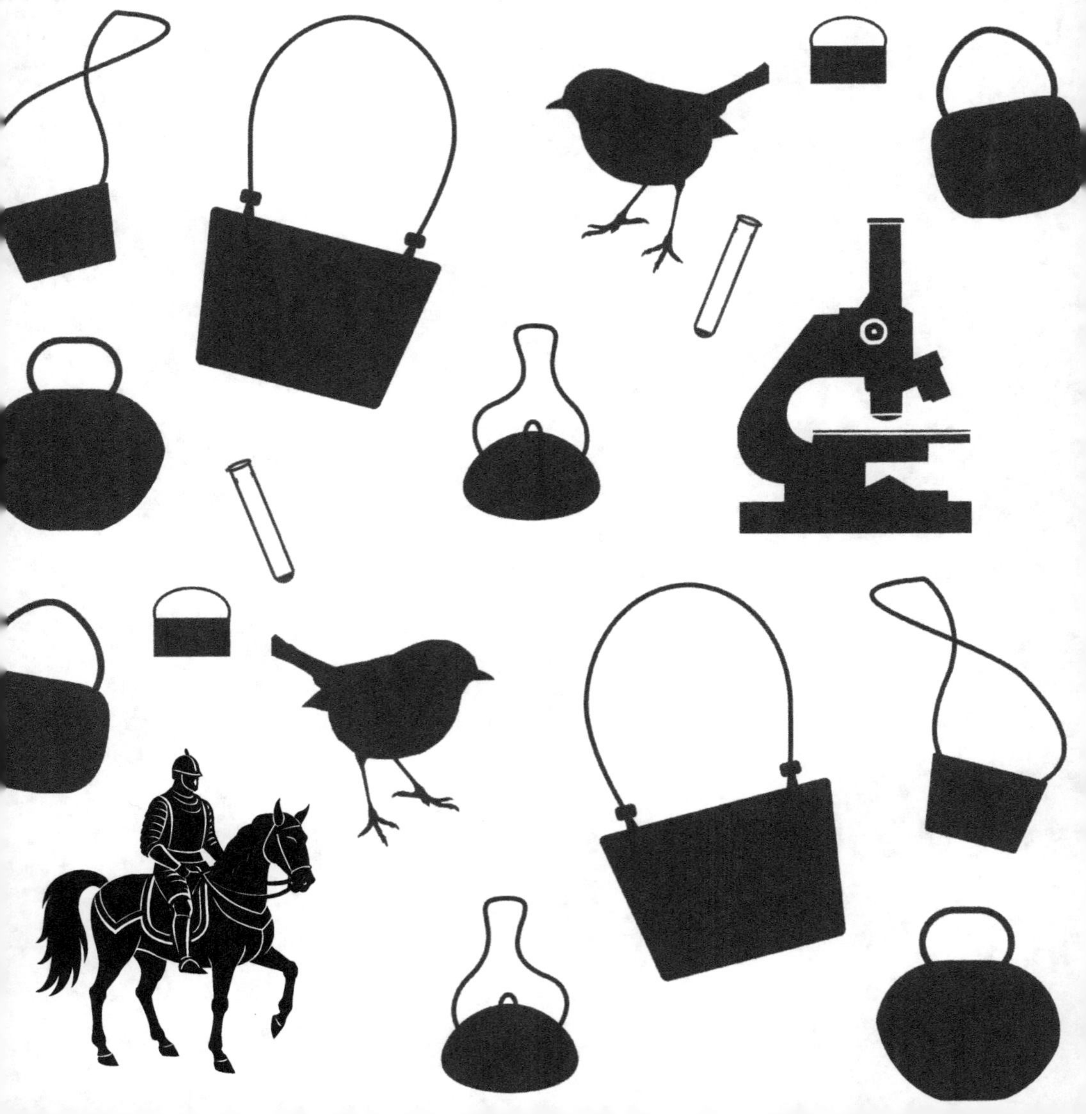

If Phineas Fairfax had not found himself with a novel (if familiar) challenge of Sheena Lypotrope, he might have enjoyed the scene playing out for the energetic if desperate Bobby Lumbar.

Since the human male lacks the same high number of neuronal connections as a female between the hemispheres of his brain, he risks acting with either cool detachment ("Kill 'em all and let God sort 'em out") or fiery emotional involvement ("Kill 'em all and let God sort 'em out"). If Bobby had been thinking with even a pharmaceutical rep's free sample of logic, he could have reasoned that Zoe was not just wandering around like a snowy doe at the animal park. But Bobby's protective passion had poured quick-setting concrete over any logic, and as the underbellies of the rain clouds flashed with lightning, he was on the run, in search of his lady.

Thinking that she might be at the water tower, trapped like Rapunzel at its heights, he dashed there first but only saw Mother Johanna's forbidding mycological silhouette bending down, staring at him. Whatever dread he felt toward Mother Johanna, Bobby doubted that she was in league with Sheena Lypotrope, and hurried on to the orchard. But thinking better of getting lost in there (he was finally using the logical part of his brain), he wasted another three or four seconds staring at his immediate surroundings for a clue as to What to Do Next when he saw an ATV sitting right there in front of him.

✳✳✳

A few acres away, with the wind rising and threatening another drippy assault on the day-trippers, Mother Deborah and Mother Ariadne were herding pilgrims out of their bus and into the chapel when one of the convent's ATVs came charging across the parking lot and screeched to a providential halt mere inches from their inky hemlines.

After a bounce to regain his equilibrium, Bobby pushed up his glasses and told Mother Deborah, "These aren't too hard to figure out after all. Where's Zoe?"

But no sooner did Mother Ariadne say, "The last time I saw her..." than Bobby barked, "Thanks!" gunned his engine, and in his speedy departure, sprayed wet shards of gravel at the pilgrims' bus (and at a few pilgrims, who were forced to cultivate a forgiving heart after Mother Deborah reminded them that they weren't any better than St. Stephen).

But as Mother Ariadne was ushering the ailing devotees with their aching joints on through the oaken doors of the chapel and the *ooh*s and *aah*s commenced, Mother Deborah, bringing up the rear in the spotty rain, felt soft nudges from both left and right. A bit put out at this interruption (she was practicing in her head her thrilling, vivid, and soul-stirring retelling of the life of Blessed Symeona of Blainesville), still she looked down to find Sangreal and Siege Perelous sitting back on their massive haunches and obviously awaiting further instructions.

Hearing from afar the roar of an ATV going full throttle, she looked at the beasts and asked, "Zoe?" The dogs scooped deep barks from their bellies like calls from a cavern, and she repeated, "Zoe. Zoe's not here. Find Zoe." And with that, the two dogs loped off, their wet, twitching noses sniffing the rainy air, to trace after a trail that they alone could ken.

But before turning into the chapel, Mother Deborah gave a glance to the ubiquitous bulk of Smithville Dike. (If ever the reader ever receives a postcard from the convent gift shop, they will notice it looming in the background behind the chapel.) With the sharp hearing that is the sine qua non for anyone in a supervisory position—that, and the inability to be unmoved by tears or excuses—she caught again the rumble of Bobby's ATV zooming away; then she heard the dogs baying as they disappeared behind the scriptorium. "Well, Lord," she said as the plicks of rain became a shower, "time to see whether one heart is better than two noses."

And as she hustled inside the chapel to begin her performance, the turbulent sky gave out a benevolent growl of thunder.

✳✳✳

Feeling an almost spiritual bond with his ATV (his grandmother could have squeezed out of this adventure an online seminar for her website), Bobby heaved and bounced through the soppy grass back up Smithville Dike. Up top, he jumped from his charger, leaving it putt-putting in the grass to add a little carbon monoxide to the wet and bracing air, then waded through the grass to a venerable old stone jutting from the ground (actually a chunk of concrete used as "fill" in the old days), claimed it as his aerie, and scanned the land about him.

But he saw nothing and no one.

The gray, lightning-lit sky, though, told another, weirder story. While not beholding Zoe gliding by on angel's wings—which would have been a bad sign—Bobby did see shoot by in speedy succession a trio of bizarre sights: first, flying toward the convent, a swarm of perfectly round, dark spheres, like strings of black pearls trying to roll along in the air; second, making for the same destination, an aerial drone, black and bat-like, not unlike a certain model tinkered together by Noah in the privacy of his mother's basement (and featured in the opening credits of more than one guy's night video); and finally, circling the air above Orphis, like a sky-beast seeking prey, a dun-metal helicopter, its wasp-like tail erect.

Bobby Lumbar let out a "Hee-ya!" as he hopped back onto his ATV, startling a juniper hickwall from its knobby perch, and then set off down the dike, gamboling through the wet grass, while calling out, "Zoe!" over the roar of his engine. The threatening sky answered him with a gust of wet wind, a flash of cloudbelly lightning, a grumblesome grunt of thunder, and an icy downpour of rain and hail, making him wish that his glasses came with windshield wipers.

With his lenses blobbed with hailstones, the ground steep and uneven, and the grass slick with rain, it is understandable that for a few seconds Bobby lost command of his vehicle and, in his battle to regain control of it, made a sharp jerk to one side, headed straight through a rogue stand of that ubiquitous Japanese knotweed, and coming through these tall Nipponese stalks crashed smack into the back bumper of an enormous white SUV.

✳✳✳

Like an embassy from the Ethereans (or even the Astralites), Dr. Sheena Lypotrope, cozy in a lab coat lined with yeti fur, spilled through the doorway into Phineas Fairfax's lair on a stormfront of chill white vapor, its tentacles of frigid mist snaking forth in a crackling web and frosting the floorboards, then seated herself on the largest seat she could find (an authentic travel trunk from the 1940s, complete with stickers from Singapore and the Malay Peninsula).

At this show of bad manners—and Sheena had even matriculated from Stifflehurst—Dr. Phineas Fairfax remained unmoved and unmoving, offering only an indulgent smile. At last, having dropped into his pocket the talk ball like a silvery gumball down a candy-machine chute, he walked with apparent absentness to the cellaret of many bottles and favrile glasses, drew forth a pair of tumblers and a cut-crystal flacon of whiskey, and arrayed them on a nearby small, octagonal Turkish table. Having poured his preferred beverage into one tumbler, he lifted it to his unbidden guest. "A little nip, Sheena?"

"Not while I'm on the clock, Phin."

He took his own an initial sip. "*Morituri te salutant*, then?"

As she petted the cryptid fur collar of her lab coat and ran her fingers through her Rheingold hair, Sheena asked, as if discussing a prized tissue sample from a prehistoric burial, "So, tell me, Phin, how does perfection strike you?"

Phineas Fairfax sampled the tumbler a second time. "So, you're finally perfect?"

"Not yet."

"In that case, I am unstricken. And, logically speaking, you are not perfect, since *yet* and *perfect* cannot share semantic space. But I'll not ask in what kind of hellish hamster wheel you keep poor Helsingfors chained to maintain this"—he moved the tumbler about like a crude searchlight seeking out the best encapsulation—"this monument to science."

"To better living," Sheena said.

He placed his tumbler onto the octagon of Ottoman tiles. "So, to what am I indebted, after all these centuries?"

Sheena indicated the chair that Bobby Lumbar had so recently warmed, and Phineas Fairfax, understanding, stepped over a puddle of icy water and took a seat.

"Oh, and that's MAXIFAX property," she said, as the talk ball that he had secreted into his pocket rolled out into the air and floated back to its mistress, where it sat in one of her palms. "So," she said, "the program."

"Ah, the program," he said. "Let me see...You're running out of my babies-in-a-bottle? Is that the case? I had estimated another generation or two was slumbering in the freezers."

"They're already out and about," said Sheena.

"So, we are at the end of an era."

Sheena nodded, her hair like molten gold poised to pour onto unsuspecting foundry workers. "And the girls we have out there are getting old, Phin."

"We're all getting old. Present company excepted, naturally."

"Naturally."

"Or maybe 'naturally' isn't the best way to say it."

Sheena Lypotrope's expression might have smiled, but the nipping and tucking had done their work. "No, Phin, I don't get older. I just get..."

"Newer," suggested Phineas.

"Let's focus. As you're maybe aware, Phin, some things—say, wines, cheese, antiques—make money as they get old."

"Yes, I have a bottle of Côte-Rôtie 1947 to sell in case things get bad."

"But living things, after too many birthdays, they cost money."

"But I had always understood," said the doctor, "that due to fermentation, wine and cheese are essentially living things."

"Not after I swallow them whole. So, Phin, your wind-up dolls, the old ones? They're not making us any money, and we can't make more to replace them because we don't know exactly how."

"That's where I'm supposed to come in."

"With a brain like that, you could have gone places, Phin."

"Like Hell."

"Phin, I'm serious."

"But, if my ladies are costing you so much, why does Level IX want to make any more?"

"The new ones won't. It's been worked out. It's a question of limiting their lifestyle."

"Minimalism? Bug sandwiches? Fifteen-minute cities."

"Trust us," said Sheena.

"And by 'us,' we mean MAXIFAX."

Sheena went on. "When we greenlighted your vision of tomorrow, we can admit that we didn't plan for a way to put on the brakes."

"Always work backward," he advised. "There's less rush at the last minute."

"The Phineas Fairfax I knew..."

"Who no longer exists," he assured her.

"That's troubling, because that Phineas Fairfax broke his signed contractual agreement with his employer—the one with all the fine print?—by disappearing one day with all of his data, the legal property of MAXIFAX Laboratories. But: We're ready to forgive."

"Don't hold your breath for an ardent mea culpa."

"But MAXIFAX can reconcile with you, because MAXIFAX has a new vision. The next level," she said like a mantra, as if selling time-shares to survival bunkers. "The folks up top..."

"I would place folks 'up top' somewhat lower." Her unwilling host smiled. "Tell me, doesn't MAXIFAX really just levitate uneasily over a pit of molten rock? But, I'm sorry, the vision."

"Not a hundred grannies on school councils, Phin. No, no, millions and millions, *billions* obediently shopping, playing along with whatever the fellows on Level IX think up next." Her tone leveled out to the dangerously reasonable. "Is that so bad?"

"Yes. Yes, it is, because it will mean the end of civilization, which I happen to enjoy. It will be the end of human life as well, which I can take or leave, depending on the day, but nonetheless..."

Sheena said, "Exactly, Phin. So, how did you do it? The fine points."

"It's like Roman mortar or Greek fire, isn't it? How did they do it? The secret's lost. But that's why you sent Robert here, wasn't it?"

"Do not get me started on that boob."

"Forgive the non sequitur, but do you mind if I retrieve my bubbly?"

"Yes, Phin, I do."

"Sad. It would have been a nice prop."

"So, Phin, how'd you make our ladies?"

"No. I will not help your latest nightmarish fantasy come to pass."

"Phin, we can try to make new units ourselves..."

"I'm sure that you already have."

"But what if we make a mistake?"

"And you already have."

For a moment, Sheena Lypotrope almost sighed. "Do you want to risk your work just dying or something?"

"It's the 'or something' that MAXIFAX excels at, isn't it? Sheena, I do not care. Detachment. Stoicism in the raw. *Apatheia*, as the hermits in the desert said. But I do know that MAXIFAX will never gamble much money on you playing at Prometheus. So, with that, Dr. Lypotrope..." He stood and turned toward his cellaret to retrieve his oaken beverage.

At this act of autonomy, Sheena raised her hand, and the talk ball released a laser blast that struck a dark corner of the room, sending something jangling to the floor with a brittle clang. (This had been a Trapezuntine icon lamp from the late fourteenth century, a Christmas present cum votive offering for the mothers, after the inexplicable disappearance of the doctor's carpal tunnel syndrome, acquired from writing all of those bogus prescriptions for placebos and multivitamins.)

"Do not even think of moving toward the exits," she said, "because this show is not over. Sit."

✳✳✳

With things clipping along at such a dramatic pace, we really cannot, like a daytime talk show hostess, sit Bella, Baba, and Martie down and ask how they were feeling. Having just escaped one brush with death, they found another one coming right at them from behind in the form of an ATV slamming into their bumper. (Bella, though, was glad that she had splurged on the spring-loaded back-bumper package.)

To Martie, that dull thud was the knock of a battering ram. "They're back!" She gulped and gripped at the door handle to make an escape and flee like a frantic Dorothy Gale across a nearby field of deliriously waving pink and pale purple opium poppies. (These were for bread-seed, thank you very much, although in the back of her head, Mother Deborah thought that once society had collapsed, the Strange Sisters would corner the market on artisanal morphine—Mother Mawseed's™, she would call it.)

As ever, Baba offered the (literal) restraining hand. "It's safer in here, sweetheart," she said, elegantly removing Martie's frantic paw from the door handle. "I'm sure that was just a freak meteorite. They have them in these parts."

"Or it could have been that!" Martie gasped, pointing to the driver's-side window.

Following her friend's fearful finger, now Bella turned to the window and—as much as they could in an enclosed space—jerked back in surprise. An ominous and amorphous silhouette was bending in on them and calling out at them through the glass, which they hoped was not, "Do you taste good?"

As Bella told Baba, "Get out your assegai," she tried to imitate her friend's easy savoir faire and gave an unaffected, almost accidental press on her window button. But when the glass had lowered, Bella uncomfortably recognized young Mr. MAXIFAX with his glasses and lab coat, albeit Appaloosa-ed with springtime mud. He was leaning in and asking with anxious determination, "Hey, have you seen Zoe?"

Martie came to the inadvertent rescue. "Oh, it's you," she said. "Oh, Baba, let me go. Hello again," she said with a wave.

The young fellow returned a fast wave. "So, where's Zoe?"

"Well," said Martie, "maybe we don't want to tell you. I mean, what did you do to her? No, no, don't tell me. I don't think I want to know."

"Ignore her, please," Baba asked of him, then reminded Martie, "It takes two to tango, dear, doesn't it? And as I recall your last fling, you needed a few dancing lessons."

Bobby was about to be scandalized at the loose morals of the nuns in these parts, until behind his golden glasses, his eyes widened with masochistic nostalgia and/or a blaze of pyromaniacal revenge. "I knew it!" he shot at Bella. "It is you!"

Bella looked first at her companions and then around the young sci-entist's shoulder as if Bigfoot were wandering by at just the right time, before pointing at herself to confirm that she was the focus of his ire, but his hands were already plunging through the window.

But before Baba could show her close-quarters skills with that assegai, the cruel howling of ravenous she-beasts broke around them, and every-one's blood dropped 66.6 degrees Fahrenheit (i.e., it froze).

"They're back!" Martie shrieked, recoiling at the shrieking, slobber-ing old gals she was seeing through the windshield, the sunroof, and the passenger-side window.

Baba hinted strongly, "Bella dear, I don't see any speed limit signs."

Gleefully taking the suggestion, Bella hit the gas, only to soon find that while she had put plenty of space between themselves and the ladies from Belleweather Bungalows, she had not left the junior booby behind. At the first spray of weeds and mud from her spinning tires, he had leapt onto her sideboard (an add-on that she now regretted) and was coming along for the ride, his sullied lab coat billowing behind him like the war banner of an avenging angel.

✳✳✳

Meanwhile, Zoe Feldspar had no idea where she was being dragged off to. But then, neither did her kidnappers.

After she had been ringed about by the kombucha commandoes, re-cumbent bicyclists, and a cadre the blue-shirted war cattle (those who had not gone after that immense white SUV), they were on a forced march to points unknown. But this was no heroic anabasis, since in no time, Commanders Frannie and Angela were in crass and open competition. (The kickoff time came right as they were marching past the old render-ing shed, even then spewing the fragrant fumes of semi-solidified Heaven-Scent™ soap.) It seemed that both knew exactly where to find not only shelter but also a phone-charging station, a strong defensive position for the upcoming assault, and a parks-and-rec-funded multilingual trail sign. Making things none the easier for these lady landsknechts during this internecine struggle was yet another unwelcome wall of rain and hail. Each and every trooper in the battalion was moaning as she wiped pink rivulets of face paint from her eyes, and more than one sent a message up the chain of command that she was missing her favorite One Love Channel premiere livestream and couldn't they stop for rations? (Overhearing this, Zoe feared that this meant herself.) Not making the mood any cheerier were the reverberating growls of thunder rippling sporadically out of the clouds, like the voice of a disapproving parent threatening to come on down there if you girls did not straighten up.

As soon as Frannie sighted another structure (they had circled around to the other side of the rendering shed), she loudly told Angela that this would be as good a henroost as any and issued the general order to "Halt!"

Hearing this, the platoon gratefully shuffled for shelter under the slate-roofed eaves of the old whitewashed soapery. A few even poked their heads through the door to enjoy the smell of the rose-bergamot essential oil, only to retreat with coughs and weepy eyes from all of the lye. In no time, most were squatting on the wet ground, chewing on plant-based protein bars with bitter churlishness, furtively checking their Facebook feeds, and occasionally sniffing in Zoe's direction and dreaming of the dinner bell.

But while her captors were looking at their little screens, Zoe saw emerge out of the clouds something like the species of a giant and bizarre plastic insect. Branded on its undersurface with a prominent Greek (or maybe Cyrillic) Γ, it circled their makeshift camp a few times as if demarcating its target, then whirred directly toward Frannie and Angela and hovered to a stop immediately in front of them.

Thinking that these two were about to be carried off to an egg chamber, Zoe tried to catch what snatches she could from their powwow. Angela was setting the record straight for her little hovering friend about "the Big Blond," and at this name, the drone sent up many a high-pitched squeak and beep. "Yeah, you tell her that," said Angela, and the drone sent up a flurry of squeaks and chirps. "Well, that's really nice for her," said Angela, "and, no, I don't care." (Squeaks and chirps.) "Well, you tell her, finders keepers." (A whine that swelled into a blare.) "Yeah, that's what I said, 'cause everything I needed to know I learned in her kindergarten." But then, with a cruel and startling quickness, like a barracuda taking out a clownfish, Frannie sent an assegai-armed hand up in an arc and down like a guillotine blade, to cleave right through the drone's lateral rotor. The hoverer squealed with the pain that only an AI device can feel and teetered toward the ground, almost crashing into a rain puddle before righting its flight and limping on its one propeller off around the rendering shed and maybe away to safety.

"Little punk," sneered Frannie.

Trying to reclaim some authority after this show of force, Angela shouted at the troops, "Things have changed, ladies." Said ladies looked at her with wet, sullen faces. "We're on our own now. We won't get any help from the Big Blond."

One Belleweatherian shouted back at her, "That's not why're we here!" (This rebel had been furtively streaming the One Love Channel and was a bit miffed at having her rom-com interrupted like this.)

"We are here—" began Frannie with as much volume as she could muster, trying to smother out her rival.

"We are here," countered Angela, "to show the Big Blond how it's done. We don't need her." The faces before her changed from sullen to disturbed. "You think that the Big Blond cares about you? No, and she never has."

This rallying cry should have flowed more or less seamlessly into a speech á la Henry V or William Wallace, but the Indians were smarter than the chiefs.

The rebel Belleweatherian deprived of her rom-com stood up and demanded, "Just cut to the chase. What do we do with this one?" She meant Zoe.

"Finders keepers," said Angela. "We found her—"

The Belleweatherians, Happy Hags, and a few of the camo-feminoids shared a warm, cynical chuckle. The chief of the Hags rolled forward to within two inches of Angela's alpine-grade hiking boots. "We found her. We keep her. You can watch if you want." And the cynical chuckle became a hearty chorus of satisfied grunts.

A bilious-faced Belleweatherian stepped up to Zoe like the royal taster. Her hair was a weird combination of inch-long white roots running into bunched-up bun of dyed cherry red.

"I used to be a real redhead," she said. "I keep eating carrots to make it come back, but it hasn't worked," and with purrs and snorts, she burrowed her nose into Zoe's dripping, coppery tresses, as a wincing Zoe tried to shrivel into nothing.

After a last invidious sniff, the Belleweatherian fell back, leaving Zoe to nervously confess, "But I think your hair looks pretty." (She did not like to lie.)

"And I think yours looks pretty too," said the cherry-haired crone. "Very pretty," and opening her dentured mouth, she lolled out her beef slab of a tongue, eager to taste.

Just then, around the rendering shed charged a pair of enormous dogs. As more than one Belleweatherian gasped, "Oh, look, it's the doctor's doggies!" these bestial cavaliers charged directly into the hungering horde and broke their ranks in two. Forward through this gap Zoe ran, fleeing with her rescuers.

The pack of wet and disorganized feminoids that they had left behind was for only a moment stupefied that they had lost their prize. But they did not want to lose her, and in just as short a time, the Happy Hags, the kombucha commandoes, and the ladies from Belleweather Bungalows became supremely rageful. They would not be denied their pretty prize.

✳✳✳

Back at the other end of this fruit-farm/puzzle-factory plexus, the battle of minds and wills between Drs. Fairfax and Lypotrope was at a stalemate. Phineas Fairfax's serene fearlessness was stymying Sheena's simple plans of terrorizing him into submission with the threat of incineration, and she disliked any protracted intellectual duel. (Such combat made her brain throb, and since her brain was the only part of her person, other than her heart, now shriveled into a four-chambered, unfeeling prune, that had never been surgically tinkered with, it might fall prey to the effects of stress.) In fact, had either of our rhetorical pugilists heard cassette recordings of exorcisms, they would have noted a disquieting similarity to their own protracted, give-not-one-inch-of-ground donnybrook. (Father Maximilian would know for sure.)

It was Sheena Lypotrope's turn.

She had been promenading in an infinity loop between their seats, the talk ball following her in midair like a cub reporter hungry for a good line. But having gotten her fill of exercise, she sat down again, the talk ball now hovering at her shoulder like a familiar spirit. She said, "Phin, I think you want to be on the winning side."

Sitting back almost kingly in his wicker chair, his arms folded before him, he said, "I am already. This is what victory looks like. I would, though, like to hear more about your Napoleonic strategy to go ahead with another generation of units."

"And another and another," said Sheena Lypotrope. "With your eager cooperation."

"Tell me, Sheena, when you say 'cooperation,' do you imagine that the second *o* has that umlaut or what's it called over it? You know, coöperation, like an Edwardian emoticon? I do. Such images fresco my mentation with new and vivid hues."

"All those books have contaminated your mind. Try getting out more."

"Said the Queen of the Nether Regions. So, whom do you worship at the shrine in your cubicle, Hecate, Kali Ma, or Lilith?"

"I have my own office suite, thank you. And she's the Aztec one, with all the heads around her neck."

"And human hearts," said the doctor. "Coatlicue."

"Is that how you say it? I still say you should get out more."

"I have my experiences. I have my friends."

"The neighbor ladies? The Goth chicks?"

"Yes," said Phineas, "they dress in black. And having renounced motherhood, they become mothers, *mirabile dictu.* At least they live in reality."

"That's what you call it?"

"I argue that monastics and artists are the most valuable members of our society."

"Remind us to change that."

"People will always live and die for something beautiful, something true, and something good."

"Phin, I'm not here for a philosophical debate."

"Good, because you're losing. I will always concern myself with good and evil. And you seek to do evil."

"No, no, no," she countered quickly. "I seek to do business."

"No," he said plainly. "Evil. The genus *Maleficarus*, or wrongdoing, presents three species."

"Please, Phin, this isn't life sciences class."

"*Maleficarus stultus*, *M. inhumanus*, and *M. desidiosis*. Stupid, mean, or lazy. As for your unwitting man on the ground, Robert, I can say that even given our very brief acquaintance, he is neither mean nor lazy."

"Which leaves stupid," Sheena said.

"Uninformed. You, however..."

"Are evil," Sheena said with theatrical finality. "Yes, Phin, whatever moves this along."

"Tell me, though, in your grand plan: What about the units out there wandering the plains right now?"

"Your poor Johnson Series and all the rest? We have plans for them, Phin. Don't worry."

Dr. Fairfax's face took on a concerned cast.

"Are you envisioning a snag, Phin?"

"No, not a snag. But, you see, I've not forgotten how to speak MAXIFAXian. You said, 'plans.'"

"Yes, I did."

"But they're still human beings, Sheena."

"I don't know what a human being is, Phin, but those ladies are not human."

Phineas Fairfax chuckled.

"I don't see the joke, Phin."

"I still stare in wonder at the resemblance between you and a reptile." Then, like molecules in liquid flux cooling into sharp, many-faceted crystal, his tone hardened and his next words were like blinding blades of color. "If you lay one finger on any of my girls..."

"They're not your 'girls,' Phin. And don't play the sensitive New Age guy and call them 'women' either. 'Fully formed units,' you called them, when they came out of their pods. I remember it distinctly. They're not girls, they're not women, they're not even animals. They're science projects. Your science projects. Very effective science projects, yes, and yes, I am a little jealous—"

"You mean 'envious.'"

"You just don't want to kiss your one and only success goodbye."

Dr. Fairfax might have been forcing another chuckle but gave out only a sigh. "They never had a chance, did they?"

She shook her head in satisfaction. "No, not with me around."

"I could destroy them all, you know, if I so chose."

"Oh, this'll be good," said Sheena. "Do tell."

"In your"—he seemed to grope for another perfect encapsulation of her state—"suprawomanhood, if that's a word..."

"It is now," said Sheena.

"Very well. In your suprawomanhood, you fail to recognize that a true and complete man possesses power, though he may never use it."

"Remind me to find one of these true men in the wild, and I'll add him to the menagerie on Level VI."

"They're everywhere, but their silence conceals them. The true man has a sword he never draws, a gun he never fires."

"Well, I don't have a sword, Phin, so this will have to do," and with a raise of her hand, the talk ball delivered a blast alongside the doctor's head at the wall where hung his vintage neon sign proclaiming, "Give 'Em What They Want." It fell just shy of the Oriental rug with a clamorous metallic rattle.

Phineas Fairfax merely looked over his shoulder as if catching sight of an old chum at a supper club, but Sheena said, "We've reached that magic milestone where you eagerly cooperate. Please, stand up..."

"But you wanted me to sit," he said with fake guilelessness and did not stand.

"Phin, don't try me. I don't want to hit anything valuable."

"I do have all sorts of nice things, don't I?" he said, glancing about once more. "One of the side effects of civilization. I know you expect instantaneous compliance, but other than threats to reduce me to a heap of ashes..."

"Which may not be off the table."

"...what else do you have to offer?"

To avoid any wrinkling, she stifled a chuckle of contempt. "This is not a negotiation."

"Well, then, you're at an impasse," said Phineas Fairfax. "Are you imagining that Robert J. Lumbar will still come to your aid? Or has he served his purpose?"

"That dink and I have an understanding. He does as I say, otherwise he'll become what Agents Bush and Cheney spoke of as 'collateral damage.'"

"Oh, do tell, Dr. Lypotrope," said the doctor. "I yearn for the details."

Sheena shook her head gravely, as if sawing through neck bones.

Phineas Fairfax, though, nodded as if nailing in an iron spike. "Well, you need not tell me anything, of course, for thy plans will come to naught. You see, I saw Robert run into that rainstorm to find and save Zoe from you."

"Zoe?" asked Sheena, aghast. "What a name. When everyone's turned into just a number, it'll be a simpler world."

"I don't know how he'll save her, but I for one revel in witnessing that young man find his inner resources."

"You know," mused Sheena, "while I think about it, never name your meat. It just makes it harder come dinnertime."

"I imagine that Zoe has a long life before her."

"I will take care of little Miss Zoe."

"Crude, Sheena, very crude. That kind of threat lacks the clean, hands-free efficiency of our modern—"

"Postmodern."

"—high-tech society. No." He smiled. "Robert will not be available to help your nefarious ends along, and your crass use of Zoe as a pawn has backfired."

"Phin, I will deal with them later, trust me."

"Must I?"

"But if Booby isn't available, then it devolves on you to be my little helper."

"And we return to the beginning."

"But, Phin, unless you help me"—she gave a fake simper—"the world will be a lonelier, less-populated place."

"The world will not miss me."

"And how about your little girlfriends in black?"

"I have known those women for almost ten years. I don't know how, but a life-giving power fuels everything that they do. Whether from the heavens or from the earth..."

Sheena sighed. "Here comes the poetry."

"...it's an invisible fire from an invisible hearth. If you approach them, Sheena, you will either be converted and offered to the heavens or—"

"Or what, get composted and offered to the earth? I get the gist of it. But I do understand"—she slowed her delivery as their eyes met—"that you also have a couple of dogs."

Now the doctor blinked. "What do you mean?"

"I mean you have a couple of dogs."

"Yes?" his voice fissured in confusion as he saw clearly what was coming.

"And, Phin, it won't be clean or efficient, or postmodern." Sheena saw behind his glasses eyes that had glazed with an unnamable emotion. "I bet you named them and everything."

The doctor only swallowed slightly.

"Come on, Phin," she said, "draw that real man's sword. Save the day."

In a shrunken, cracking voice, held complete by will and dignity, he said, "But they're innocent."

"Not anymore. Not anymore. Collateral damage. Dr. Phineas Fairfax, formerly of MAXIFAX Laboratories, has put them on my bad side. So, come on, Phin. The game's up."

Now the doctor stood.

"I really should revel in this," said Sheena. "I wonder whether there's a Nobel Prize for discovering an old friend's soft underbelly."

The doctor quickly turned toward a door, but the talk ball gave out a slender warning shot.

"No, no, no," Sheena said. "Not that way. I think you know where to look." She nodded at the banks of bookshelves behind him.

He looked over his shoulder, then back at her. "I think you might be on the wrong track, Sheena."

But Dr. Lypotrope only shook her head.

With eyes now lambent and clear, he straightened his back and went to the bookshelves and began a desultory, aimless scan of the varied and manifold titles he had collected over the decades.

"That way, Phin," she said, nodding toward the binders.

"You're acting as if I don't know my own library."

"And you're acting like you do. I know it's down there."

Now he was inspecting spine after spine of coffee table books, about the Masai, the Royal Ballet, and the barns of New England. "It's not as if I've accessed it in a while," he said. "It might be scattered all over the place. Floppy disks, VHS tapes...You know the sound quality is better on those?" He was looking in a box of old Polaroid film. "Not here, and those cuneiform tablets in the bunker." He creaked open a lacquer box painted with Chinese unicorns.

"You know, Phin, we haven't talked about your sister."

He closed the little box. "Phoebe was just nominated to the Portuguese Academy for a poem about autumn light on a wooden fence. Are you going to send her to a firing squad too?"

"And how's your mother?"

He was peering behind a framed print of Pepin the Short on his throne. "As unapproachable as ever."

"That explains a lot. And the Ambassador?"

He drew out a long-untouched tome, blew off a film of dust, and read the spine. "Hmm," he said. "I need to read this one again. Papa acted as consultant on that peace deal between the Parsi separatist group and the junta that's running Baluchistan right now." He slid the book back and journeyed down the shelves.

"All our hard work down the drain, I guess. And your brother?"

"Hmm, nothing here either. Oh, he might've been martyred by some animists last month in Upper Ghana. We're waiting for word from the consulate."

"Then you should hope that a violent death is a recessive gene in the family. To the right now. A little more. Uh-huh. Keep moving."

He had come to the shelf containing his manifold three-ring binders. Taking up one of them, he distractedly flipped a few of its colored plastic tabs. "Let's see...Hmm...Fascinating. I still have to know, Sheena, if you knew already where to look, why've we been wasting time with our little verbal tarantella? Why not just grab it and make off back to the underworld?"

"Ritual humiliation, of course. And maybe I enjoy talking with you. And because it's fun. It feels good to make you squirm and pull your chain."

"*O tempora, O mores...*"

"My beta-endorphins are through the roof right now."

"I am sure," he said, flipping a few more tabs. "Just watch out for the crash. You know, if everyone believed the same—"

"Believe me," said Sheena, "they will when we're done with them. Set that one on the bed. Now let's get on with it."

He gave a cursory perusal to the bright plastic tabs in another binder. "This one too?"

"On the bed. And those ones too."

"Those are just—"

"Now."

"Give 'em what they want," he said and negligently piled binder after binder of data, one after another, on top of one another on the patchwork quilt. In little time, the notebooks towered tottering and unsteady as high as his head, and he held open an inviting hand at them. "Behold, ziggurats arise. Or an Aztec temple, maybe to Coatlicue. Come. Worship at the shrine."

"It better all be there," Sheena said, then turned the talk ball. "Fire at will."

The ball's many eyes glowed to life and it whirred about to barrage the doctor with volley after volley of laser blasts. Suddenly, though, it squealed, flew to a point immediately in front of Sheena Lypotrope, dropped low, and projected upward a translucent cone of light that held the face of a woman in pink camouflage face paint.

"Lumbar?" the woman was calling. "Lumbar? You hear me? This is Birkin Bag."

Sheena Lypotrope leaned into the hologram, and the face of Frannie turned to her. "Birkin Bag, this is Big Blond. What about Lumbar?"

Through the hologram rippled noises of ATVs revving to life and a woman's voice calling, "Mothers, nets at the ready!"

"Birkin Bag," shouted Sheena, "what's going on?"

"Everything," wailed Frannie to the rev of ATVs in full charge and a choir of women's voices delivering up the war cry, "Blessed Symeona, defend us in battle!"

At that, the transmission sputtered out, and the cone of light broke apart like a thousand electronic butterflies dissolving into the void.

"Birkin Bag?" shouted Sheena. "Birkin Bag?"

Dr. Phineas Fairfax calmly offered a diagnosis. "Your plans are going awry."

Sheena barked at the talk ball, "The chopper, now!"

Obediently, talk ball shot toward a window, broke through the glass, and took to the stormy air.

But when the doctor turned about to ask Sheena Lypotrope about her own next steps, he saw that he was alone and the door through which she had so chillingly entered stood gaping open, with the frame, the floor, and the ceiling all about it encased in a thick glassy glaze of ice and a prickly, hoary frost.

CHAPTER XXI

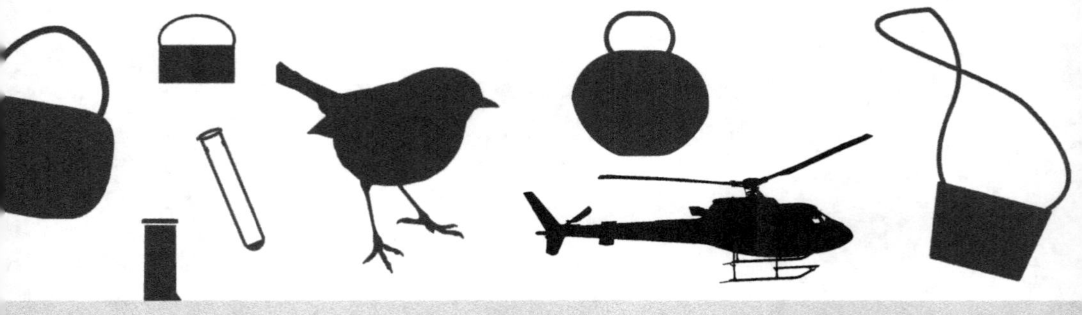

THE BATTLE OF ORPHIS, OR NUNTHELESS

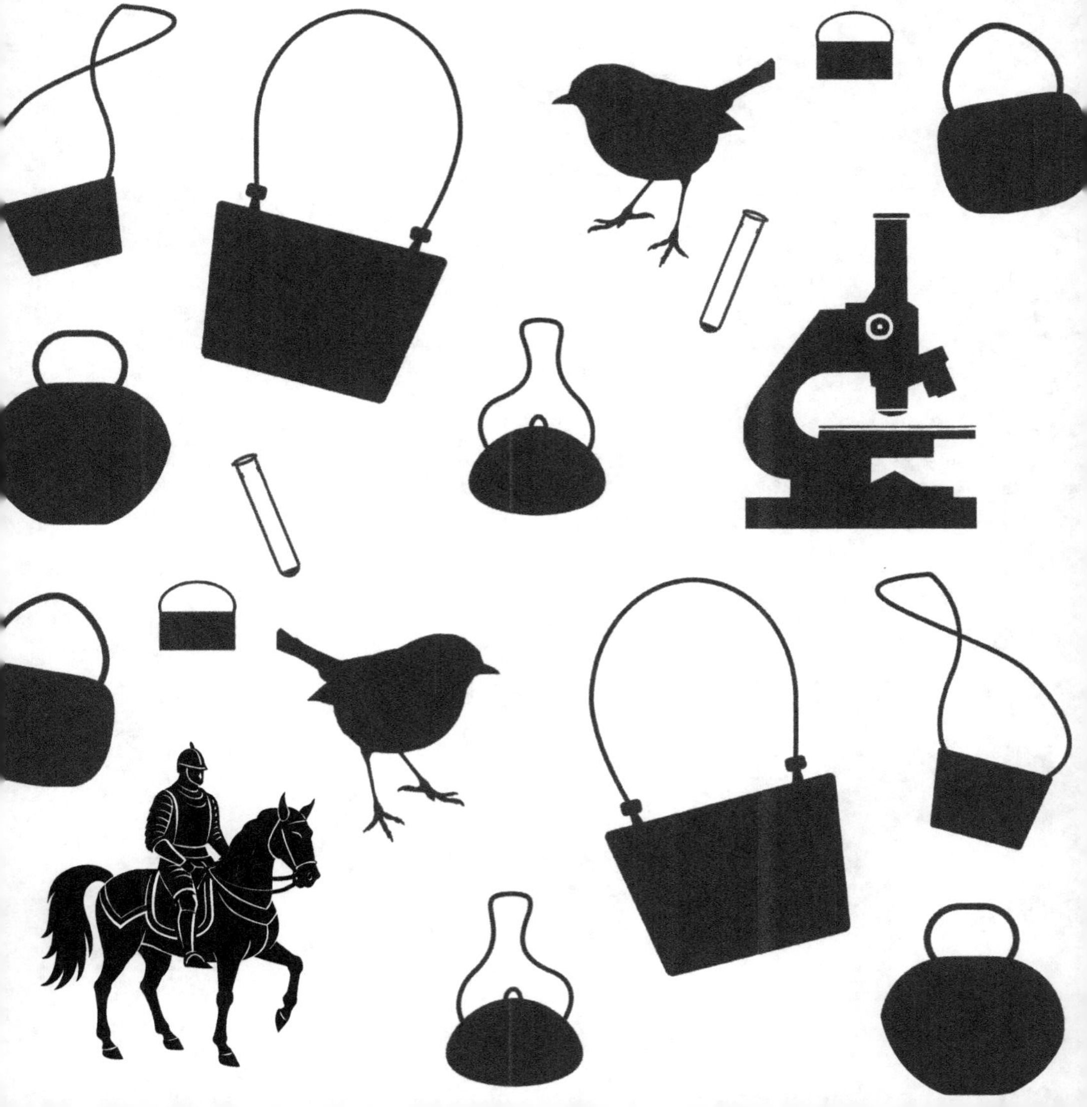

As Bobby held on for dear life to the gigantic SUV, slippery with mud and icy-cold rain, swerving and bouncing through an obstacle course of ruts, potholes, and old cattle guards, the (supposed) nun at the wheel was trying to chuck him off, all while escaping from a mad pack of howling old ladies chasing after her like post-nuclear baboons.

At the same time, Zoe had her own problems. With Sangreal and Siege Perelous running alongside like four-legged motorcycle cops, she was fleeing back to the convent as a motley pack of recumbent bicycles and desperadas on sore wet feet was charging to catch her.

✳✳✳

In very little time, Zoe and her escort reached the yard before the chapel, its gilded domes like lighthouses welcoming her home after the tempest—only to see that the dogs, forgetting all canine gallantry, had veered off and were making a beeline for the end-of-the-pilgrimage barbecue, a long plaza of open-air grills smoking away, perfuming the drippy, chilly air with the gritty perfume of marinade, spicy rub, and splattering animal fat. In the face of these savory smokey fumes, the most devoted of pooches might waver.

Hunching over in the drizzling dregs of the latest downpour, Zoe herself made briskly for the festivities, hoping for safety in numbers and—after the day she had had—a teriyaki pulled-pork gyro.

The pilgrims were already lined up, looking eager for both food and shelter, though more than one face hinted that this weather was making their joints acts up. Distracted by their lumbago, these pious travelers did not notice the soggy Molly with the streaming red hair wending her way alongside the corn on the cob, until she called out, "Mother Deborah! Help me!"

But everyone noticed when she cried out, "They're here!" and smack through the coleslaw tables broke a contingent of recumbent bicycles. The next wave was rosy-cheeked camo queens in their sopping garden-palette tactical ensembles and pistachio-green berets, and puffing along in third place came a cadre of Belleweatherians. (In all charity, they were unused to prolonged exertion, preferring the rapid stampede at any female signature-gatherer who got through the Bungalows' iron fencing.)

"Hungry!" hissed the newcomers. "Hungry! We're hungry!"

But before Mother Deborah could aim the invaders toward the corn-bread buffet and tell Mother Euphemia to load up the grill with a few more roadkill kabers marinated in fennel root, the blaring honk of a once-white SUV, spattered with mire and its wipers thrashing back and forth in a frantic rubbery fandango, zoomed through the crowd. Scattering the pilgrims (who could move when they had to), this rogue chariot wove through the other invaders, splashing them with a venge-ful wake of mud and scattering them in all directions. Then sounding the horn again, it skidded along the undefended flank of a tour bus, slammed on the brakes, and spun about in an auto-show pirouette before crashing into a long-disused power pole and sending the young man who had been gripping the driver's side hurtling off into a vat of organic potato salad.

In no time, Bobby Lumbar had freed himself from the side-dish pit, and with his lab coat soiled to the microfibers with soy mayonnaise and his glasses splattered with chives and Dijon mustard, he made straight for Zoe, dropping dollops of Yukon Gold potatoes with every anxious step.

The young people careened into one another, becoming one, a scene of joyful reunion that should have started the end credits rolling. But Bobby, while smothering Zoe's cold, wet face with a flood of warm, wet kisses, canceled out any romantic bank with, "Sheena told me she's after you. She said—"

Hearing her rival's name *again*, Zoe drew back, and—in spirit at least—her face took on the gorgonian aspect of an entity from the land of the dead: the goggling bloodshot eyes, pinpoint pupils shooting forth bolts of lightning, hideous wiry incarnadine hair fanning out in all directions, boar tusks dripping scarlet gore, eleven fingers on each ruddy hand, claws like shards of steel, etc.

Seeing her face now practically steaming with figurative rage and rancor, Bobby stepped back. But instead of making for the nearest bomb shelter, he unwisely tried to reason with her. "Zoe, look—" he said.

And through the annihilating blast of fury that followed, Bobby Lumbar heard nothing, was temporarily blinded, and missed seeing Zoe flounce off in indignant disgust.

But just as his senses were coming back to him and he was checking his glasses to see that the lenses had not shattered, Bobby heard a voice screeching, "Don't let her get away, girls!"

Slipping his glasses back on, Bobby now saw a wall of active granny types charging in a phalanx directly at him, tripping and stumbling unathletically around him, heading straight for Zoe.

Just then, someone—some kind of glue-gun-for-hire in pink and desert tan—barked, "Halt!" and the lot of them tramped to a stop.

This bossy commando granny brushed against Bobby, then took her place at the head of the pack. Pulling out her glue gun, a relic from her Martha Stewart phase, she pointed it toward the beaten, battered, and befouled SUV that had given Bobby that unwilling lift. As everyone craned their necks in that direction, she called out, "What do we see there, girls?"

The one-time luxury sport utility vehicle was now a finalist for the Lifeless Heap of Wreckage of the Year award. Steaming and smoking with toxic vapors, its cracked headlights now stared into the distance, its technically shatterproof windscreen was webbed with billions of tiny fissures like a desert lake in August, its front bumper hung by a single bolt like a botched dismemberment, three of its tires had sunk to the ground, while the fourth, mortally wounded, hissed like an expiring snake, and all as the claxon call of its car alarm throbbed out two or three times, dwindled to a snuffed-out whine, and perished into painful silence. Then came a kind of automotive death rattle, and the chassis seemed to unsqueeze like a metallic accordion, playing forth one ultimate, pathetic grating note, like polar bear claws down a chalkboard. With that, those inside forced open the doors, and a trio of disheveled nuns crept their way out with squinting eyes and black habits dusted with white air bag talcum powder.

These three stars of the dash-cam bloopers reel shook themselves back to life and blinked at the glowering gray skies in the hopes of finding a little sunshine coming their way. This, though, would not be in the forecast, when Nun № 3, with the resilient quickness of an infant, kitten, or any other soft-skulled creature, gave an excited wave to the commando grannies. "Oh, Bella, Baba, look, it's Angela! Angela, sweetie, over here!"

Baba (Nun № 2), who had been trying to light a little something she had scrounged from a pocket (it may have been a roll of antacids), broke in, "Lily, honey, I think Angela's cosplaying. Let's not interrupt her fun."

"And look how you're dressed. Oh, Bella, and there's Frannie."

Bella had already verified that their immediate surroundings had too many familiar faces, or at least one too many, when Angela told the troops, "There's fresh meat on their menu, girls!"

But this did not move the masses. In fact, one of the exercise fanatics on her bicycle even said, "We'd rather have lamb, not mutton, Angie girl. Or an old red hen."

This was meant for Baba, but before we find out whether Baba gave a cool riposte, Zoe stomped back onto the scene.

Splitting through the troops like a virgin plow breaking old sod, she pulled her parking brake smack in front of Bobby Lumbar and set about a tongue-lashing that included something about Madison being right all along. Still, Bobby was ready to throw her over his shoulder, like a Roman on a day trip to the Sabines and was about to do just that when the hags and harpies round about him sent up the news flash, "Look, girls, she's come back!"

Frannie—hoping to ingratiate herself with the high-protein faction of the army and maybe even land Angela on the vivisection table—now called out, "Grab her and let's go, girls!" and obedient to any voice of command that gave them what they wanted, the ladies' auxiliary of the Huns and Visigoths fell on Zoe, held her aloft like discount booty, and charged away with her chanting, "Spare parts! Spare parts! Fresh meat! Fresh meat!" leaving Bobby standing alone, hearing Zoe's frightened, fleeting voice sinking away with the cry, "Bobby! Bobby!"

All of this was interrupted when Angela called out, "Let's take her in there!" and the Happy Hags, Belleweatherians, and camo Bag Ladies came to a sudden, disorganized stop in front of the convent's chapel. Confronted by this edifice, narrow and towering, with its stone porch, carved wood, wainscoting of colored tile, and three golden onion domes lifting ornate and fanciful lowercase *t*'s, now flashing in a fleeting beam of sunlight, they stood staring in a curious confusion as their hive mind echoed out, "Does not compute, does not compute."[2]

But before their collective confusion caused them to overheat and fall down in a heap, a besplattered Bobby came running up, with Siege Perelous and Sangreal at his side. (They had gotten their bit of barbecue and were now eager to get the baddies by the throat.)

But as Zoe cried out, "Bobby!" and the dogs sent up howls of attack, Angela gave a bark out, "Defensive line! Defensive line!" only to hear the creaking of oaken doors, the tramp of wet feet, and the creak of muddy wheels into the depths of this bizarre little building. Unwilling to make a last stand, Angela joined the mob and darted inside, grabbing the cast-iron doorknob and pulling it after her, even as Bobby leapt onto the stone porch and the dogs violently tried to claw their way through the weighty wood.

✳✳✳

Just as a delivery driver might relax at the end of a day by watching dash-cam videos and a homicide detective might unwind by taking in an episode of *Axe-Killers Are People Too,* so Mother Deborah, when she could not drop off in slumber, was wont with a cup of skullcap tea in hand to peruse the bank of grainy screens of the convent's many, many security cameras. Had she not had her hands full with busloads of pilgrims, bouts of rain and hail, a smoky bank of barbecue grills, and a rapid string of text messages from Dr. Fairfax, our abbess would have gotten quite the eyeful from the screen labeled "Chapel/Interior."

---

2   When the feminoids were being prepared for life outside the laboratory, an apoplectically vocal minority at MAXIFAX had sent up refrain after screeching refrain at the assumption that they should be infused with *any* knowledge *at all* concerning religion, art, architecture, philosophy, or history, since the future (as envisioned by MAXIFAX) had no need of such quaint, nostalgic trivialities. All that any feminoid need know was that existence began in the coffee shop and continued at the mall (this was in the days before online shopping), and need never end at all, as long as the conveyor belt of newish body parts kept rolling along—and the pit mines in Africa kept on disgorging the cobalt for their hepatic transponders. The reader by now should not be surprised to discover that this uncultured and godless cabal was made up of ambitious toadies who spent their weekends soaking in Sheena Lypotrope's hot tub and drinking her cabernet sauvignon blanc.

The lady barbarians were making an unholy mess of the place. To the righteous shudder of thunder and the sharp crack of lightning outside, one contingent had shoved the pamphlet rack against the great doors to keep anyone from pushing their way in, a few more had taken down the brass banner poles and were crisscrossing them against the same (in case of a battering ram), the Belleweatherians were protectively pressing around Zoe like a herd of carnivorous auntie elephants and looked to be sniffing her hair, and the riders on recumbent bicycles, between the occasional wheelie, took turns circling about the room, scrawling a black ring of skid marks like a sorcerer's circle on the mosaic floor. (This occult relic Mother Deborah would have a hard time explaining to future tour groups).

As desecrations went, this was not quite Napoleon stabling his horses in the Kremlin's cathedrals, but about now Mother Deborah would have stopped watching (a) to call the sheriff, with a reminder to keep these shenanigans out of the papers, before (b) hauling down the shotgun for a postmodern reenactment of a scene or two from the Old Testament.

She also would have missed a plot twist as Angela, sniffing around at the far end of the chapel, yelled out, "And who do we have here, ladies?"

The rampagers set aside their destructive tendencies to look up and see Angela scrounging behind a sort of august, antiquey workbench draped with cloth of gold and set with a couple of candles (i.e., the altar) and lifting into view something shaped like a nun. In a tone not requiring an answer, Angela asked Bella, "We met at the kombucha place, didn't we?"

One of the camo queens put in, "Oh, I know that place," and a sizable collection bobbed their heads, with one enthusiast adding a quick review of this other place that had the *best* marionberry scones. But before any other Merryweather lifestyle influencer could pull out her phone and share the camera roll of her brunch date at the bubble tea place, Angela took Bella by her dye job, hauled her into the open, and dropped her to the floor. She hissed, "Hold still," before sinking both hands up to the moisturized elbows behind the altar again, musing aloud, "And *who* do we have *here*..." and heaving Baba up for inspection.

Martie, though, ruined Angela's big finale. Popping up all on her own, with a fiery and ecstatic blaze in her eyes and a hand raised like a prophetess's, she declared, "I invoke the laws of sanctuary!" giving an unwittingly fine impersonation of Stewart Granger. (She had no idea what she was saying, but this was the most colorful choice from her intracranial "In case of emergency" drop-down menu.)[3]

Unimpressed, Angela whipped out her glue gun. "What are you doing here, you crones?"

Before her discoveries could say anything, Ronnie Johnson, of all people, shouted, "Who cares? We got the little girl here."

Zoe, naturally, started waving across the chapel at them. "I'm sorry, mothers," she said, a bit more timidly than the situation demanded, "but could you maybe...?"

Right then, Frannie charged forward and, planting herself between all parties concerned, gave Bella and her pals a cynical if apologetic dog-eat-dog smile. Pirouetting around on one combat boot, she faced the feminoids, now cramming the little church beyond legal capacity, and like a voodoo priestess starting off the show, wailed out the sacred words, "Spare parts!"

In no time, the gilt, cedarwood, and red-candle shrine that had known only the delicate dawn-glow tones of Matins and the slow Slavic melodies of vespers seemed to shake and sway, throbbing and tottering to the rhythmic, ravenous, contrapuntal, craving, slavering, anthropophagic chant of "Spare parts! Spare parts!"

"Spare parts!" Zoe's handlers called out and tossed her over and over up into the air, as if she had made the winning touchdown.

But in the midst of this homicidal, homecoming merriment, Bella suddenly yelled, "You don't want her!"

Frannie seemed too enraptured in her own performance to notice this unsolicited altruism, but Baba asked over the noise, "Bella dear, I thought that in your book, *help* had always been a four-letter word?"

"I know, I know," Bella said, before belting out a second time, "You don't want her!"

---

3   All thanks to Dr. Guagamal, from the days when he was still young, supple, and marginally human. This same feature supplied an array of useful expressions in Tagalog, Swahili, Maghreb Arabic, Ladino, Yakut, and Ebonics, should the need ever arise.

This call for moderation, though, looked to be landing like an ice cube in a volcano. The crowd was now well into the swing of things, peppering Zoe's repeated flights up to the ceiling with the cheer, "Spare parts!"

Suddenly, they heard, louder than any cultic cacophony, the slobbering howls of at least two gigantic hounds (and in a church, of all places...) followed by a young man's voice calling for, "Zoe!"

The ladies were none too happy that this Y chromosome and his mutts had, during the full-frenzied throes of their maenad ecstasy, broken into their "women-only space," and except for Ronnie Johnson, of course, they wrinkled their faces in horrified disapproval.

It was left to Zoe to be the voice of inclusion and in an all-in-one mating call, Mayday, and general introduction, she called out, "Bobby!"

After a quick wave about the room to cover his end of the hellos, the man of the moment smashed with warhead force first through a jaunty and defiant pair of recumbent bikers and then a palisade of Belleweatherians. Reaching Zoe, he seized her about the waist like a tree nymph and tossed her over his shoulder, leaving her to protest this rough treatment at some future date.

As a quick flash of lightning traced the frame of the open back door of the chapel and a grunt of thunder warned anyone even thinking of pursuit to just stay put, Bobby, Zoe, and the dogs escaped outside into the wide, wet, but much safer world.

As the chapel's back door slowly and inevitably shut, the feminoids, Belleweatherians, and Happy Hags, who had been circling about Zoe like the strangling clouds of a cyclone, now sullenly, silently, and sinuously stilled to a stop. That frightened and succulent girl, the not-so-serene center of their storm, but who, to their dizzy and hungry eyes, had been a sheet cake in human shape festooned with frosting roses, had been snatched from them. They fell into a frightening and static vacuous noiselessness, devoid of any words, breath, or even thought. This did not last long, though, and converting from quietism back to the religion of youth and beauty, they sent up a mushroom cloud of rage, a sonic explosion of fury that cracked the windows, shook the brass chandeliers, toppled the banner poles, and snuffed out the tiny flames of the votive candles in their little red glass holders.

With the chandeliers still creaking and swaying like elaborate pendulums looking for a heretic to slice clean through, the mass of the feminoids, Belleweatherians, and Happy Hags turned about like aged Busby Berkeley dancers to face Frannie, Angela, and Angela's three nunly prisoners.

Taking the latest thunderclap sounding high above the onion domes as a curtain call, Ronnie Johnson stepped forward, pushing aside a couple of Happy Hags, and strode with certainty and intent right up to Angela. Fixing her eye, she said, "We're still hungry."

Before Angela could put her in her place, though, Ronnie Johnson pivoted her gaze to the three "nuns," and her eyes opened wide on recognizing Bella. "Sheena..."

Reaching forward, she clutched Bella's habit and yanked it away, revealing a head of metallic blond hair. She hissed, "Sheena...," the word like the call of doom from a dank and Stygian cave. Then, in a sleight-of-hand quicker than any unsuspecting bystander would have believed, she snapped the habits from Baba and Martie.

Guessing where this was going (and seeing a chance to checkmate Angela), Frannie inserted herself, purse and person, between all concerned and stared hard at Ronnie Johnson. "No," she said, in a tone that was supposed to resound with unassailable authority but ended up as flat as a scolding.

Ronnie Johnson's eyes narrowed into unblinking arrow slits. "Don't worry." She smirked at Angela. "We want a real blond." And after a speedy toe-to-top-knot glance over Baba, she added, "And we don't want to get poisoned by any of that Peruvian red rinse."

Baba raised a nonexistent cigarette to her lips and blew a bit of imaginary smoke in her direction. "It's Venezuelan, sunshine."

"Hey, what about me?" asked Martie, thinking that she deserved her own helping of abuse and scorn.

Ronnie Johnson said, "Just a second, little girl, while I take a step back. There. I want to be able to see all of you. Hmm...No, don't change a thing. You'd only get better."

Ronnie Johnson now waddled back into her herd, where she and it fell into conference. After some rumbling that came off like the echoes of malfunctioning plumbing, she lumbered back to Angela and Frannie and told them, "We've got a date with a sweet little redhead."

And with that, the Belleweatherians broke off from the mixed and motley mob that had been using up the oxygen and, like a herd of soggy bison, shuffled to the back door of the chapel. There they yanked the door off its hinges, and with much bellowing and snorting, they forced their way through en masse and set off on the hunt.

This left the field to the Happy Hags, all the happier to see their less-athletic neighbors making for more nutritious pastures, and the original expeditionary force, the Bag Ladies with their survivalist-series clutch purses, glue guns, oat-based protein bars, and collagen gummy snacks: a slimmed-down, mean-if-not-too-lean core corps that should have been just what the holistic healing center ordered—but for what exactly, Bella, Baba, and Martie were blissfully unaware, until they saw them turn at them as one and give them a greedy stare.

"Charlotte?" asked Martie.

Maintaining her trademark mask of apathy, Baba whispered, "Lily, remember, big-girl time."

Now Frannie showed that she had taken graduate courses in backstabbing. Opening an arm to the three "nuns," she told the troops, "Well, ladies, we lost the sweet and tender one. But any port in a storm, right?"

"And we never liked you anyway!" one of them shouted from the crowd.

"You mean me or her?" Martie pointed at Baba.

"Or her!" shouted another.

While Baba was wishing that she had her narwhal ivory cigarette holder on hand so that she could strike a dismissive pose—and take a last drag—while delivering a withering riposte, Bella said, "I'm glad they don't know me."

Frannie told her, "They don't like you either," before yelling out at the crowd, "What are you waiting for? Let's get this party started!"

With an ominous click, the Happy Hags secured their helmet straps under their chins, and with a grind of their gears, they turned their steeds toward our heroines and began advancing in their direction.

Just then, a wild-eyed Bella, like a bargain-hunter during the last five minutes of a tag sale, fell on the ornate tree-stump stand upholding the miraculous icon of Blessed Symeona of Blainesville, seized the image with both hands, and lifted high her prize.

"Looky here!" Bella told the feminoids. "This thing's worth ten of us."

Out of the crowd someone yelled, "The only thing that's worth anything is a new hepatic transponder!"

Martie said, "She's got you there, Bella."

Frannie then unhelpfully stirred the pot. "And what about the apical pseudothelium?"

Several members of the lynch mob shouted back, "Yeah!" and "You got that right!" and "Totally!" and "Where's mine?" and similar halloos. In this rah-rah-rah over apical pseudothelia, the pot was at a gory froth, almost boiling over.

But then, just perhaps, Blessed Symeona of Blainesville must had decided to answer an unspoken prayer, as Bella heard the deposed Angela telling someone on her phone: "Doogle? Doogle? Yeah, it's Angela. Yeah, Angela. Hey, what's the resale value on miraculous icons? Well, duh, if I had enough coverage out here, I'd look it up myself. Uh-huh? Uh-huh? Great."

And like an eagle swooping down on a dainty kestrel, Angela snatched Blessed Symeona of Blainesville from Bella's grasp. "Mine," she frostily informed her victim. "You know how many periorbital neurosynthopodes I can buy with this thing?" Ignoring the enraged Frannie, Angela turned to the feminoids, now within striking distance, and shouted, "Looky here, girls! We're all gonna be rich!"

✳✳✳

Outside, the pilgrimage barbecue was scattered about in a debris field of soggy paper plates, inert blobs of potato salad, and tumbled-over lunch tables. In the midst of it, like a wet and windblown traffic cop trying to manage a drag race, a semi transporting a nuclear warhead, or a delivery truck with open bay doors strewing packages in its wake, stood Mother Deborah. Never one to go with the flow, she was taking the events of the last half hour as a very aggravating opportunity to build character,

as if Providence had served her up a helping of corn on the cob doused
with jalapeño. But as she was triaging these many crises (crazed invaders
taking over their most sacred piece of real estate, pilgrims asking in twos
and threes what was next on the agenda, and the fact that they had run
out of briquettes), one of the mothers, still armored in oven mitts, came
running up, pointed her greasy tongs at the chapel, and yelled, "Mother
Deborah, look!"

The chapel doors had opened and the *legionneuses* who had been
rudely holding it down as their impromptu fort stomped and/or bicycled
out onto porch. One of them, very much the techno-Boadicea, jutted out
in front of the others and looked ready to present some demands.

This spokeswoman (we know her as Angela) shouted, "Who's in charge
here?"

The pilgrims and nuns began to cower behind Mother Deborah, as
if she were a blast shield, until she herself, like the dorsal fin of a massive mother orca heading for a cocky kayaker, swept forward and halted
just out of range of the other woman's glue gun. She informed the other
woman, "I answer for the management here."

Angela had her doubts. "I hope so, 'cause I don't talk to any little
people."

"Do I look little?" asked the altitudinous abbess.

"I get it, tower of power, you're not wearing your flats. But gimme the
higher-ups. I need to talk business."

"If you saw my higher-ups," said Mother Deborah coolly, "you'd probably burst into flames."

"Whatever," said Angela. "I'll just keep it simple." She whistled over
her shoulder. A flunky hurried into view and handed her a squarish object.
Just then, the choppy gray and white clouds overhead again parted ever so
slightly, and the sun shone a ribbonlike ray of light onto the golden, oily,
and glassy face of the icon of Blessed Symeona.

Salaciously drawing the tip of her glue gun up and down the gilded
frame of the icon—and the eyes of Blessed Symeona might have widened
slightly in dread—the hostage-taker said, "One false move and I paste up
your baby doll with glitter and elbow macaroni!"

The pilgrims and nuns behind Mother Deborah sent heavenward their cries of "Blessed Symeona of Blainseville, pray for us!" before realizing that it was Blessed Symeona who needed the prayers.

Mother Deborah hooked her thumbs in her broad black belt. "We don't cotton to those kinds of tactics here."

"You do now, sheriff," said Angela. "All righty, stretch, you throw a few numbers out and I'll decide—"

But before Angela could hum along to any numbers, integers, or even Roman numerals, the air filled with a syncopated symphony of clicks, beeps, and electronic shrieks. A swarm of tiny electronic monsters, war drones and talk balls, like black-and-silver locusts descending to devour the harvest, were coming in, squadron after squadron, down out of the sky.

Whirring through the mothers and pilgrims like aerial Mongols, they dragged a mother or two along over the gravel by her prayer beads, tried to temporarily blind a few with the pinkish rays of their scanners, and churlishly chased the frail pilgrims, clutching their Canadian canes or seeking to flee in their ergonomic four-wheel-drive walkers, straight into mud puddles before pulling up, only to swoop down for another round of fun.

But while the pilgrims with flailing limbs and frightened faces were fleeing to the fringes of the fray and disappearing into barns, garages, sheds, and the gift shop, Mother Deborah moved not a micron. Just as she was thinking that the Strange Sisters should plant an acre of citronella and corner the market on home-style bug repellent, she saw through a fresh line of talk balls shooting across her field of vision what looked like an insurrection on the porch of the chapel. Up from behind, the chief negotiator had dashed another of her camo-smeared sisters, who rudely snatched away the miraculous icon. With a vindictive "Ha, ha, ha!" audible over the whine of talk balls, this robber ran back inside the chapel, clutching her prize almost as devotedly as her Birkin bag. With her retreat, the other women-of-war—including the bossy one who had lost her throne—all turned tail and followed her back into the shrine, no doubt to avoid ending up as collateral damage.

Mother Deborah knew that this did not bode well, but at this crucial juncture when she had to make an executive decision, the wet air behind her shook, first with the resounding rev of ATV engines and then the zealous crusader cry, "Blessed Symeona of Blainesville, we have come to save you!"

Mothers Deborah turned about and beheld both a terror and a wonder.

Forth from the orchard, from around the corner from the gift shop, and out of the muddy lanes winding in from the U-pick fields chugged a rumbling cavalcade of every ATV possessed by the Strange Sisters Fruit Farm. With the single headlight of each set on high-beam, like a four-wheeled cyclopean pack of she-wolves coming forth to find its prey, the nun in the seat of each was a shadow-clad chariotrix, her bone-pale butterfly net raised like an oriflamme, her robes fluttering behind her in the eventide wind like the semi-substance of a bodiless specter. But this alone made the spectacle, for following this FFA phalanx, out of the twilight and into view loomed up, like a mechanical mountain chain, a wall of monstrous war-making metal shadows: every tree shaker, bed former, weed spray boom, pruner, and forklift of the Strange Sisters, each captained by a nun, like an amazon upon a dragon. As lightning wove the clouds in wires of energy and flooded the heavens with rippling rivers of electricity, the arms of these machineries reached up into the grim crackling air like the appendages of alien entities, latter-day mangonels, trebuchets, catapults, and battering rams, hydraulic horrors with carburetor growls and the diesel voice of doom. As one, mothers and machinery broke forth, creeping and rolling inexorably toward the chapel, to save both it and the holy image of the woman who taught that those who hate must love.

Mother Deborah certainly appreciated this enthusiasm but did not want things going too far. Before she could sort out the goats from the sheep and lock the hotheaded ringleaders in the old smokehouse with a breviary for a few weeks to nudge them back onto the straight and narrow, however, one of the ATVs broke ranks, zoomed straight at her, and after a satisfying swirl through a mud puddle, chugged to a stop in front of her.

After batting away a talk ball like an electronic mosquito, the abbess said in a tone demanding only the essentials, "Mother Euphemia, did you throw this together?"

After a healthy dose of cool, wet evening air, the nun smilingly admitted, "Yes, Mother."

Mother Deborah sought to charitably, if firmly, redirect this ewe lamb. "Mother Euphemia, I know you've always wanted to do more, but—"

A second ATV zoomed up, this one bearing Mother Sulpicia, the one who had zazen-ned her way through that Zen monastery. As invigorated as Mother Euphemia, she mused aloud, "This reminds me of Krishna and Arjuna in the *Bhagavad Gita*..."

Seeing that she was not going to make headway without an army of her own, Mother Deborah tried another tack. "Mother Sulpicia, we've been dragging you to vespers for years. Couldn't you think of something a little more...Abrahamic, maybe?"

This call to orthodoxy must have soared in the nun's ears like an angel returning to the sixth heaven, for over Mother Sulpicia's face there gleamed suddenly a weird light, and she spluttered, "Oh, I'm prophesying! I'm prophesying!"

Mother Deborah suspected that this might just be carbon monoxide poisoning, but Mother Sulpicia was already asking, "Oh, oh, do we have a megaphone?"

"Dr. Fairfax has a megaphone," said Mother Euphemia.

"Well, Dr. Fairfax isn't here."

"Oh, wait a second..." Mother Euphemia called back to the line, "Mother Paraskeva!"

In no time a third ATV rumbled up and Mother Euphemia told the driver, "Paraskeva, look in your toolbox, quick."

The rider stretched uncomfortably about, flipped open the plastic lid of a plastic tote bungee-corded to the back end, and produced—because you never know when you might need one while trimming the suckers from the saskatoon bushes—a megaphone.

Mother Sulpicia breathlessly demanded, "Oh, give it to me," and once it was in hand, she straightened up in the seat and told Mother Deborah, "How about this?"

And clearing her throat as if it were the barrel of a musket, the reject from the lamasery placed the megaphone to her lips and called up to the skies scattered with talk balls and drones, *"Remember, O Lord, the children of Edom, in the day of Jerusalem."*

The nuns with her quieted, and those arrayed for battle fell silent as the words of the Psalmist wove through the gloaming.

"Who say: Rase it, rase it, even to the foundation thereof." Sitting even straighter, if that was possible, Mother Sulpicia delivered the very sharp end of the stick. *"O daughter of Babylon, miserable: blessed shall he be..."* Then up and down the line of ATVs, other mothers chanted out the verses as one, until there gushed forth like a wave from a lethal nocturnal sea the single, unified, politically corrected verse, *"O daughter of Babylon, miserable: blessed shall* she *be who shall repay thee thy payment which thou hast paid us."*

Now the other nuns on their ATVs and tree shakers were shouting, *"Rase it, rase it...!"* with a spotty *"even to the foundation thereof"* coming through.

For once in her life, Mother Deborah sighed.

The tigress had slipped from her leash, and she would have no way to explain all this to the insurance investigator. (Their policy did not cover military operations.) On top of it all, because of this very noxious blot on an otherwise admirable professional record, she thought that the earth should just open up then and there and swallow her whole.

As Mothers Euphemia and Paraskeva careered back to join the line, Sulpicia told Mother Deborah, "You know, Hell ain't full yet, is it?"

But before Mother Deborah could remind her that, no, it was not, but might be soon, Mother Sulpicia had the megaphone to her mouth again and yelled at the warriors, "Mothers, the nets!" Then she, too, bounced away over the mud puddles and rejoined the line.

Hoping that the ground would not devour her just yet, Mother Deborah looked at the chapel: its leaded windows were aglow with some light from within. Refusing to speculate what might be going on inside, she distracted herself with the army to her rear. Taking in their double ranks massed in righteous anger, she threw up her arms and opened her bosslady mouth to try to hold back the flood with one final, forlorn fear-of-God warning. But an anonymous mother on her ATV was crying out in a voice that shook the green apples onto the muddy ground, "Blessed Symeona of Blainesville, we have come to save you!"

And as another flock of wicked drones swept down from the gloomy air like a hive of electronic hornets, the revving of a dozen ATV engines shook out in a battle roar, and the Strange Sisters, spraying gravel and coiling up clouds of diesel exhaust, charged forth to meet their foe.

The Battle of Orphis had begun.[4]

✳✳✳

The Battle of Orphis unfolded like a four-dimensional origami. Under a shroud of brooding, repellent, and chilly rain clouds smothering the sun, which minutes before had glinted on the onion domes, and with the air smelling of their exhaust, the mothers in their ATVs rumbled forward in a vanguard line, their headlights like will-o-the-wisps escaped from a drainage ditch. To their rear, the tractors and tree shakers, their lamps flashing like the eyes of giants, lumbered on toward the chapel, now in the grips of the invaders.

This steady-as-she-goes strategy ceased in an instant. To the buzz of drones, the squeal of talk balls, the hiss of wet and expiring briquettes, the rattle of yet more hail on the trapeza roof, and the litanies of pilgrims cowering in the fruit-drying shed, the battle broke out in a four-wheeled wave. The ATVs rolled ferociously up onto the steps to the chapel porch, while the heavy equipment charged the shrine on two sides. In no time, this direct approach dispossessed the icon poachers and kombucha junkies inside, and the Bag Ladies, tripping over the pamphlet rack and the processional banner poles, streamed out from the front portals in a chorus of hissing, howling, and baying like the howls of cacodemons. (Their bicycling allies took the more circuitous route,

---

4   Nitpickers at the Merryweather Historical Society regularly point out that this melee was more accurately the Battle of the Sorbo-Ruthenian Women's Monastery of Blessed Charles of Austria and the Servant of God Zita of the Exarchy of Blainesville. But those pettifogging purists need to remember that sometimes packaging matters as much as the product. On another note, in the massive triptych icon painted to commemorate the event (as if it were the Battle of Kosovo or the Fall of Constantinople), the anonymous artist includes two mighty mastiffs, their sagging necks bound in spiked collars and their heads ringed in halos.

exiting via the back door and wheeling around the building to meet in martial choreography.)[5]

But just as one of the bell towers toppled earthward (someone had been a little too enthusiastic with her tree shaker), its cross smashing onto a recumbent bike and hurtling its rider hundreds of feet through the air and back down into a hay bale somewhere offstage, from around the corner of the convent complex charged one of the pilgrim tour buses at full speed, its driver slamming on the brakes and sending the thirty-seat chariot round and round in a doughnut in the middle of the action. The combatants scattered as the bus wobbled and bounced to a stop. The driver's-side window slid open, and old Roger, with his Vietnam Veteran ball cap, popped out his head with the war cry "Blessed Symeona of Blainesville...!" To this, the nuns called out, "Pray for us!" and revved their engines, then gunned their way back into the fray.

With the crusader spirit on the uptick, the battle entered what ardent amateur strategists called the Just-Sit-Back-and-See-What-Happens Phase. This was a kaleidoscopic vortex of every imaginable permutation of physical combat, mechanized assault, trickery, bravery, warrior élan, skull-duggery, surprise offenses, spraying of mud, synchronized butterfly networking, and outright hair-pulling and shin-kicking, all amid a buckshot of shrieks, sobs, name-calling, pleadings to the Almighty, and scratchy communiqués to someone called Big Blond.

One of these did the trick. Probably someone back on Level VI at MAXIFAX was watching the livestream and decided on a hasty, half-dignified withdrawal of all aerial forces, because as Roger was flashing his high beams to his worn-almost-to-nothing Creedence Clearwater Revival cassette on the tour bus stereo (all the better to chase the Happy Hags around the parking lot), out of the deepening dark of the wrung-out rain clouds with a wicked sound descended a swarm of drones, like an air show out of Dante. Save for throbbing red lights carbuncling their sides, these gadgety gnats were as black as deep space. One contingent

---

5 Once news of the battle had hit the internet, but before it had ossified into urban legend, the Merryweather Chamber of Commerce, under the tab "Recent Goings On" on its website, was quick to euphemistically paint the townie combatants as "long-time fixtures of Merryweather's vibrant downtown scene" and/or "members of our city's enviably active senior exercise community."

smothered the windshield of Roger's bus, while the rest swept with despair-inducing precision over the battlefield, slicing and skewering the air with razor-thin fans of red light, scouring through the combatants for their predetermined prey, which they quickly discovered. Swooping low and projecting pterodactyline claws, the drones snatched up one by one the feminoids and the Happy Hags, only to splutter. Unable to attain altitude, they dragged their loads back and forth, whining angrily, until a signal, taking form as a crackling wire of ruby light, shot through them all, and giving their loads a unified and vigorous shake, things lightened considerably as back down to earth, not quite like manna, but just as handy in a pinch, came a rain of recumbent bicycles and more than one Hermes Chaine'd Ancre Bag, Cleopatra Clutch, and Niloticus Crocodile Himalaya Birkin.[6] So, the drones toted away their foes, kicking and screaming, into the gloomy, roiling sky, while the mothers, their butterfly nets limp in the mud and their diesel tanks nearing empty, gaped heavenward in astonishment.

The Battle of Orphis had come to an end.[7] The clouds that had been weighty with hail now hung sagging and somber, like the heavy-weather gear of angels, and here and there, slits of random sunlight slipped earthward to illuminate the dregs of combat. Across the background was galumphing Hesychia, the water buffalo that Mother Martina had acted as doula/midwife/cheerleader for the day before, along with little Hugo; a nebula of very chilly bees was skidding about the air looking for a crack in a tree to colonize, since its hive had been used as biological weapons by one side or the other and now littered the parking lot in a waxy wreck like a mobile home after a tornado; and darting back and forth flew a stray flock of drones like raiders looking for the village granary to pillage, while another knew not where to go and spangled the air like wind-up fireflies. Despite the excessive enthusiasm of those few mothers, the chapel still stood, and the light of the perishing day gleamed over the surviving onion

---

6 This was indeed like manna, since Mother Deborah gave them a good cleaning and sold them under the "Gently Used" tab on merryweathergalore.com.

7 This was fortunate for the convent's insurance adjuster, who had to call in help from five neighboring counties to tally up the damage. To cover the premiums, the prices of white raspberries and handblown wasp traps would be higher than market rate for decades to come.

dome,[8] teetering to one side, as its grateful bell, hanging exposed to the wind, ding-donged a victory song out over the battleplace. In threes and fours (there was safety in numbers), the pilgrims made for the tour bus captained by Roger. A smaller one, chauffeured by Dr. Fairfax's gymnastics coach, had returned after all the fun was over to pick up the ladies for Belleweather Bungalows, only to drive away with more passengers than it had brought, since the hardier of the pilgrims were willing to hang off of the sides just to get out of this place. (This particular configuration of passengers reminded Herr Stackenwalter of that providential lorry ride in the summer of 1945 that brought him as a little lad from Brandenburg to Bratislava.) As for the other tour buses, one had been gutted by fire and a second dropped from the sky in the strawberry fields by a division of elite drones deploying new MAXI-Lift™ antigravity rays. Nonetheless, the events of the day had strangely invigorated some of the pilgrims, and as Roger gunned it down the road for town (any town), they decided by straw poll that as long as they brought extra nitroglycerine tablets, they would return next year, while more than one pious traveler thought that even if they had not received a miracle of healing from Blessed Symeona, it was at least a miracle that they were still in one piece.

---

8 An overenthusiastic Mother Eustasiana was finally pegged as the spark of this conflagration and was sent to Blessed Symeona's nunnery way up in the Northwest Territories, to live on rainwater and uncooked lentils for the rest of her born days. (In an act of charity, her new abbess did allow her lentils to be cooked—before being served cold—on Christmas, Easter, and Pentecost.)

CHAPTER XXII

CHOPPER GODDESS, OR IN-FLIGHT APOCALYPSE

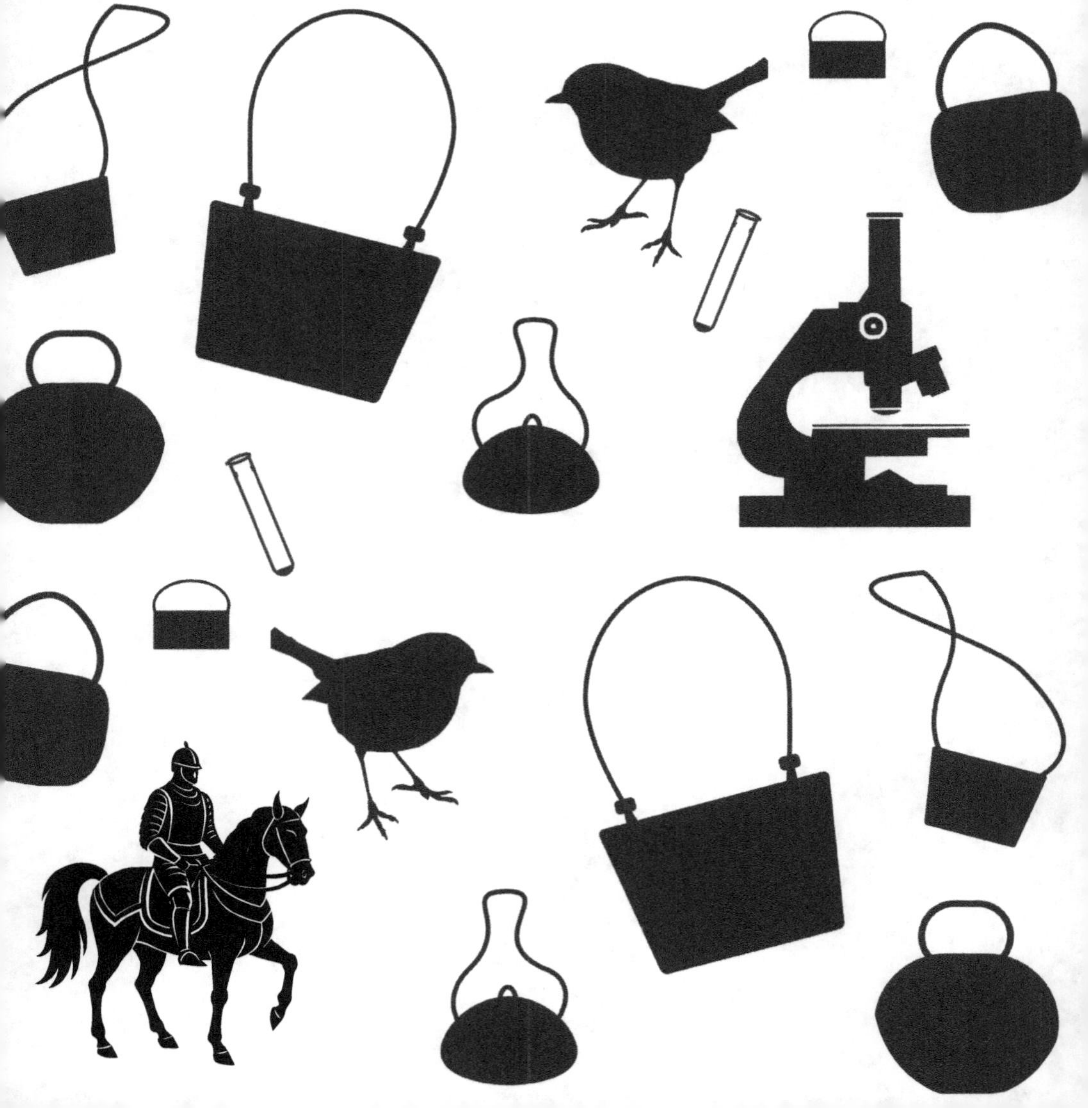

Having celebrated their latest reunion with a round of burning kisses, Bobby and Zoe were now ambling hand in hand under the shadows of evening back to Orphis in the orchards near the convent.

But this quiet reprieve ended when they heard, like the call of a night bird, the plangent, pleading cries of "Spare parts! Spare parts!"

Bobby looked behind them down the lane of trees, then reached out to draw Zoe close—but Zoe had already climbed up a kindly old knobby apple tree. Glad for another incident to share with their grandchildren, Bobby followed her lead; but once they were crouching in the branches like a couple of early hominids on a first date, Zoe put one finger to her mouth and pointed another at the ground.

Like a herd of Belgian blues suffering from the staggers, into view came a band of Belleweatherians, zigzagging and unsteady from the chilly rain and no doubt disconsolate from being deprived of their sweet and tender Zoe. Now and again, one mewed, "Spare parts!" and then another, as if unsure whether everybody had heard right, lowed, "Spare parts!" Between hunting calls, they would raise their noses in a disquieting synchronicity and inhale deeply, their proboscises twitching in a prehensile sway, like rats pinpointing the nearest sewer grate.

Bobby whispered, "What're they doing?" and Zoe silently pointed to herself with (just maybe) a tear in her eye. Bobby drew her close, the fringes of his filthy lab coat draping over her like the soiled wings of a guardian angel.

Suddenly, with a gasp she pointed to the ground again. One particularly large and hale specimen (Poppy Mecanopsis, for those interested in the fine points) had halted directly below and was leaning against the tree, sniffing curiously at the bark. Turning to her companions, she gave out a low grunt, bobbed her head at the tree, and then stared up the trunk with a knowing intensity.

At once, the other Bungalovians surrounded the tree and peered up the trunk for a little ripe fruit. Without a word, one cupped her hands and a second filled the impromptu stirrup with her muddy foot; at two more points around the trunk, other pairs copied this buddy-buddy move, and in no time, Poppy Mecanopsis was counting off, "And a one..."

But they stopped, and as their nostrils glowed and their eyes blazed, they turned their heads in unison. Those offering their hands broke away, and those standing on said mitts took a tumble but, bouncing up, still joined their sisters to escape into the shades of dusk.

Watching them retreat, Zoe guessed, "They're headed straight for Smithville Road."

Bobby said, "Then let's get you back to Orphis."

But once they were on level ground again, our plucky pair were clinging to each other once more when they saw what must have frightened off the ladies from Belleweather.

Staggering toward them up the lane between the knobby trees came three swaying shapes. Like dark ghosts hardly touching the ground, they were three nuns, staring ahead and stumbling along with a traumatized gait, like charred trees that had uprooted themselves to get out of town during wildfire season.

Zoe ran toward them. "Mothers, are you all right?"

Bobby might have been moved too, but recognizing one of them and remembering that recent combination speed test and monster SUV/mud rally, he shouted, "You!"

Martie gave a cheery, "Oh, Bella, look, it's your old boyfriend."

"No, no, no, *no*," Bella spluttered. "I told you. I have way better taste than—"

But Zoe had heard, "your old boyfriend," and turning on a dime, she exploded at Bobby like an IED disguised as a box of Valentine's Day chocolates. "You sick, *disgusting*"—she stalled before revving up again—"faithless, cowardly, inhuman, *disgusting...*"

Baba waved an imaginary hookah pipe. "You said that already, dear."

"...spineless, *two-faced*, untrusting—"

Baba went on. "I think you mean 'untrustworthy,' dear."

Zoe hissed at her like natural gas straight out of an Arctic wildlife refuge. "Whatever, red." Baba tucked a few strands of Simone's repair work back under her disheveled habit, and Zoe returned to the vivisection. "First, you're seeing that *Sheena* and you *lie about it.* And now you're hitting on nuns!"

"Oh, but boys are like that," said Martie, batting away a stray talk ball that was trying to scan her face. "And who wouldn't lie about Sheena?"

"Yes, boys do lie," said Baba. "Or that's what I remember." (Had Mother Deborah been present, she might have added, "If I had a plenary indulgence for every vocation that started out as 'just a little misunderstanding'...")

But Bobby was keeping to the facts, and he pointed at Mother Belladonna. "She threw me in the back of her car."

And now Zoe, with eyes glowing like carnelians, aimed her guns at Bella. "You did that to my boyfriend?"

"Just a second, sunshine," said Bella, waggling a slow finger at this romantic greenhorn. "I just said, I have way better taste than—"

"Oh, and you're saying there's something wrong with my taste in men?"

"No, I wasn't criticizing your taste in *men*. I was criticizing your taste in overgrown vice presidents of the junior high science club."

Whether Zoe took this as an insult to Bobby or a snide critique of her own taste, it mattered not, because she was making ready to leap like a she-leopard at her (perceived) competition, whether or not she had been consecrated to the Second Person of the Trinity.

But before she could get all Shaka-Zoe on her opponent, things became very blustery, just as an unwelcome voice descended from the half-starry sky above them. It ordered them, "Look up, you dinks."

Zoe, Bobby, Bella, Baba, and Martie looked up.

Just above them, Sheena's personal helicopter, *Willendorf I*, was lowering into dangerously close range, until it was hovering like an immense locust just above the treetops and conjuring up a storm that weltered the branches in wave after rhythmic wave of annoying, noisy turbulence. From its dark dun-metal underbelly shone a trio of searchlights that swiped about, found the little band, then dimmed, at which point the lateral doors of the sky beast creaked open with a rumbling, metallic shudder.

Out of the side of the craft emerged, floating free and taking to the air like a newborn star, a great pale sphere of platinum light. Within its shining, translucent shell, streaked in pastel prisms of protective energy and crackling with fine static, levitated Sheena Lypotrope, a goddess in a lab coat, inflexible, indifferent, and bewildering, a chryselephantine archon descended into the subpleromic realms.

But before anyone fell on her face with primitive awe and started chanting, "Shee-NA! Shee-NA!" the lady of the hour cut to the chase.

"Freestone!" she called down to the material plane.

Hoping that she maybe meant someone else, Bella, with a questioning look, pointed at her nearest neighbor (which was Baba). Sheena dispelled any confusion. "No, but she'll be next. It looks like you're getting dressed for a funeral. I wonder whose it'll be? I have a pretty good idea. So, what did you have to do with that mess back there?"

"Back there?" Bella guessed that Sheena meant Frannie's ill-executed hostage-taking and general mayhem-making. "Oh, back *there*."

"Yes, *there*. That mess damaged several serviceable units, whose parts we will need replacement. And as I informed you several days ago, I know exactly where to find those parts."

During this visit to the principal's office, Bobby had slipped next to Zoe and whispered, "Let's get—"

But Zoe whispered back, "But who is that?"

"That's Sheena. She's not important. Come on."

"*That's* Sheena?"

"Yeah," he said, pulling her away. "Come on, let's just—"

But Zoe marched forward, shoved Bella out of the limelight, and snarled up at her perceived competition, "Hey, grandma!"

Within her lofty bubble, Sheena widened her eyes in confusion, and in a moment that seemed to disintegrate into timelessness, Bella, Martie, and Bobby all froze, expecting the collapse of all matter into a black hole. Baba even stepped up and rested a fatalistic hand on Zoe's shoulder. "Sweetheart, how about we just keep *Apocalypse Now* the name of a movie, hmm?"

But Zoe was as hot as an engine block at the Grand Prix and told Sheena, "Just who do you think you are?"

Crude and uncooked insubordination never went down well with Sheena Lypotrope, and she showed her displeasure in a super-duper-nova of rays of wrath that sliced down through the trees, lopping off a few rotten limbs and scattering all the coyotes in a quarter-mile radius.

But as the half-charred branches snapped off and fell to the ground, Zoe remained unfazed. "I mean, really? I mean, why don't you just keep your girdle on and go sit in the corner?"

From of her nimbus of power, Sheena spoke in syllables that trembled and shivered in the air like bats flown from an ice cave. "Who do you think you *are,* little tiny girl, to *assume* that I wear any kind of *foundation garment* to maintain this magnificent...magnificent...Oh, one of you, give me a word!"

Martie offered, "Fake?"

Sheena glared down at her and mentally marked her for slow annihilation, but she had already dug up a gem and resumed her delivery with "...this magnificent *Aphroditean* curvature?" And casting wide her arms, she would have revealed a sample of the aforementioned hubba-hubba, but her billowing lab coat got in the way.

Bobby hurried to Zoe's side to hustle her away from the complaints department, but she gave him a dainty rhetorical snort. "I mean, look at her. You think she doesn't binge-drink silicone while she's watching the Great American Family network?" (At this, Bella whispered to Baba, "And I thought it was the Home Surgery Network.")

The sphere constraining the might and power of Sheena Lypotrope stilled for a mere eternal moment of terror. Then the mother of all dragons within opened wide her eyes upon her prey. "No, little girl," she said. "I will refresh myself with something...sweeter." Like a celestial Glockenspiel doll, she rotated to Bella, Baba, and Martie. "For the next couple of minutes, you're safe." Then, at Bobby, "Since you're not doing anything with her, I shall. Off we go."

Immediately, Sheena's hand shot up like a machete, and from the star-speckled sky, an elite flock of black drones swooped down like aerial Praetorians. Weaving amid those on the ground, they darted from person to person, from face to face, clicking and whirring. But this performance must not have been what Sheena had originally envisioned, and she barked, "The redhead, you gnats!" With this clue, they ganged up on

Baba (her habit had been blown askew by the helicopter's bluster), but as she was halfway up into the air, Sheena Lypotrope shouted, "No! The pretty one!"

The drones dropped Baba on top of Bella and Martie, then turned their pincers on Zoe, and in no time, she was understudying Mother Babulia in this off-off-Broadway production of *The Flying Nun.*

But the drones found things a bit heavy, as another body was added to the passenger manifest, with Bobby making a terrific leap and seizing tight Zoe's lower half. Still, the drones rose squealing into the air until Sheena Lypotrope's antigravity sphere indulgently floated aside, and they hauled both Bobby and Zoe into the chopper, its doors then creaking and clanging shut behind them.

$$* * *$$

Sometime earlier, in the quiet mellowness of the rainy evening, Greta had been sitting safe on a stool in a corner of the lemon-scented kitchen and flipping through the glossy, steak-filled pages of *Paleo 4 Two,* with occasional glances at the tiny TV/DVD player combo on the counter playing *Snickerpoodle,* disc 3 from the Doing the Work trilogy. (Unlucky-in-love Lindsey is tasked with staging a stand-up comedy festival to provide disabled rescue dogs with their own service animals and meets handsome veterinarian Glenn, who provides free surgeries for puppies with cleft palates.)

A quiet thunk interrupted this dreamy virtue-fest, and Greta looked up from a recipe for a beaver tail and bear paw confit to see Dr. Fairfax at the kitchen door.

He apparently noticed the movie playing on the counter. "Ah. One of Amy's offerings." (The director of *Bake Away the Hate, Chocolate Frosting,* and *Snickerpoodle* was one Ambrosia "Amy" Megara-Milano, a "hyphenoid," a boutique species of feminoid that was just being hatched from their pods when Phineas Fairfax was planning his escape from MAXIFAX.) He smiled to himself, then told Greta, "I wanted to say that the common rooms and garden look very nice."

Hearing this, Greta suppressed her own smile, remembering that, after all, "attention to detail" was a diagnostic sign of white supremacy, and she silently committed herself to schedule obvious mistakes throughout her workday in reparation for any deaths from smallpox among First Nations peoples.

The doctor moved to another topic. "Tell me, Greta, would you be able to hold down the fort, I mean for a long time, if I weren't here?"

Greta nervously closed *Paleo 4 Two* and even muted Lindsey and Glenn on their first date (a trip to the organic hemp farm for tree-free puppy pads), then asked, "But why?"

The doctor reached into the unlit hallway behind him and brought into the homey light of the kitchen a yard-long weapon projecting a small, oblong, sharp-nosed rocket. With one swoop, he heaved it onto his shoulder and gave it a pat. "Because I do need to go shoot down a helicopter."

∗∗∗

With all of the excitement up in the air, Bella, Baba, and Martie had been slipping between the untrimmed pear, quince, and hardy loquat trees to make their getaway, until a contingent of drones with rosy searchlights blazing came whirring down among the trees after them. With jabs and mild electric shocks, Sheena's pesky little helpers herded them back to the clearing under the helicopter, before buzzing up to rejoin their mistress in midair and fly clumsily about her like moths worshipping the full moon.

Her unwelcome gaze like a slowly incinerating death ray, Sheena asked, "Who do I see here?"

Baba suggested, "It's 'whom,' Sheena dear." (Unlike most of her graduating class, Baba had actually completed her "Declining relative pronouns" infusion session, while everyone else had been watching *Steel Magnolias*.)

Not to be derailed, Sheena Lypotrope counted off, "Goldilocks, Little Red Riding Hood, and"—she waggled a frustrated finger at Martie—"the other one."

"But I want to be Cinderella," huffed Martie.

"If you want cinders..." A drone shot a blast at one of the hardy loquats and rendered a smoking twig. Sheena returned to the task at hand. "You, the peon," she told Bella. "What follows will not be pleasant."

"It never is," said Bella, glad to have thought up a quick one before the guillotine drones swept out of the sky.

Sheena stuck to bullet points before breaking out actual bullets. "Units. Damaged. Replacement parts needed. Oh, look, replacement parts," she said, and to close the meeting, she raised her hand in that trademark gesture that foretold pain and suffering to come.

But with Zoe immured in the helicopter, Martie now took on the role of plucky ingenue and suicidally said, "I told you before, you don't have *any right* to do anything to us."

"Turkscap," she said, with eyes narrowing in disappointed impatience. "We've talked about this."

"No," snarled Martie. "You never talk *with* anybody. You talk *at* people."

Bella and Baba drew back in unprofessed awe that their pal could navigate the subtleties of prepositions, even as she carried forward the attack. "You just think that we're just supposed to obey you like"—she looked to Baba and Bella when the word kicked in—"like *robots...*"

"Close," said Sheena.

"...or *androids...*"

"Feminoids."

"...or *cyborgs...*"

"You're getting warmer."

"...or *something weird.*"

"And the crowd goes wild."

"But we're not weird."

Bella felt compelled to comment, "Not all of us."

But Martie, her eyes shining like newborn stars, would not be stayed. "We're *people* too. We're *human beings.* With *rights* and stuff."

"And 'stuff'?" said Baba. "It had a nice flow up to then, sweetie."

"But that's what Dr. Guagamal said."

Sheena Lypotrope mentally penciled herself a reminder to have her colleague mysteriously disappear, never to be seen again. "Turkscap," she said, "it's not that you don't have 'human rights.' You do not have rights, period. Because you are not human. And while we're at it, those human beings you see milling around at the coffee shop and the EV dealership? They don't have rights either, unless we tell them they do."

Still, Martie persisted, "No. No. We matter."

"No. No. You don't."

The glow on Martie's face neither faltered nor did it fade. "Oh, I remember, I remember—what Mother Maybellina was reading when Bella was eating that extra soy burger." (For the record, there is no Mother Maybellina, but the reader during dinner that evening had been Mother Ethelburga-of-Wessex, who somehow did retain her maidenly peaches-and-cream complexion despite the rigors of fasting.) Drawing back her shoulders, Martie said, "We're made in the image and likeness of God."

"Of who?"

Martie carried on tossing pearls before majestic blond swine. "The Creator." (Martie was now recalling something about being "endowed by our Creator with certain inalienable rights," from her infusion entitled "Civics for the Politically Unengaged.")

"Creator? It's fun to pretend, isn't it? But no," said Sheena, and the static about her antigravity sphere blazed into a blinding fright wig of hungering astral energy. "I am your creator."

Suddenly, a wave of throaty, threatening barks disrupted this nightmarish display of interdimensional puissance, and through the dark trees burst Sangreal and Siege Perelous like a pair of grand Palladian monsters, and up they leapt at Sheena Lypotrope in her sphere.

Sheena only hissed, and her protective shell floated upward like a postapocalyptic soap bubble.

As indefatigable as ever (remember the note in her file), Bella grabbed both Baba and Martie, telling them, "Never let any crisis go to waste, girls," and forcibly escorted them into in the darkness of the opposite direction.

Within seconds, though, that darkness was filled with the beams of MAXIFAX moonlight as *Willendorf I* swept her searchlights wildly back and forth, seeking out the escapees. After a low pass over their heads, she executed a very agile pivot, then zoomed back, her searchlights like luminous lances straight at Bella, Baba, and Martie—though their habits should have made a handy camouflage. Felipe and Darshan, as much as the wage slaves of the next mega-multinational corporation, were apparently enjoying the thrill of the chase, but before they could spit out a few drones to snatch the ladies up on a one-way trip to bye-bye land, said ladies found themselves once more alone in the evening gloom. The searchlights had left off of them and were now slicing through the tree cover some distance in front of them.

If they had been as agile as the helicopter, Bella, Baba, and Martie could have scurried off. But Martie just had to ask, "Who's that?"

Not far from her original position, *Willendorf I* had slammed on her brakes mid-air, to cast her searchlights down onto an ATV, a lone and magnificent figure straddling its seat like a Crusader upon his armored warhorse.

It was Dr. Phineas Fairfax.

CHAPTER XXIII

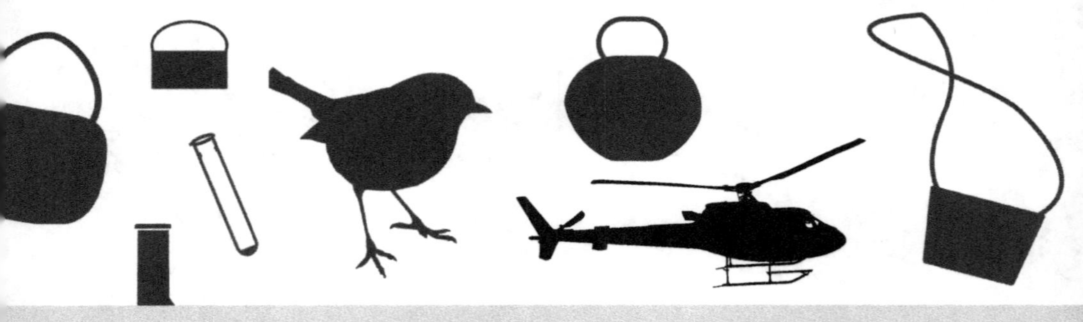

SECOND CHILDHOOD, OR DADDY'S HOME

With the folds and fringes of his lab coat billowing and curling like the crests of tempest waves bearing his barks to Outremer, Dr. Phineas Fairfax seemed to hover in terrifying beneficence, like a mountain cold and white, the sweat on his brow like chill silver rivers cleaving icy stone, and his eyes like platinum-haloed stars between hoary crags. He was, in a word, Daddy.

Bringing the rocket launcher up to his shoulder, he called over to Bella, Baba, and Martie, "Are you all right, Mothers?"

Bella said, "You know we're not really nuns, right?"

He gave a knowing nod. "But are you safe?"

"No, they're not," came a reverberating reply, and down between Phineas Fairfax and his potential rescuees floated the bubble of Dr. Sheena Lypotrope, the woman within like an enormous Lovecraftian tadpole ready to hatch out and contaminate the stream of existence.

With the rocket launcher in motionless readiness, Dr. Fairfax told her, "You will do no harm to my children."

Her mouth slithered into a smile. "They're a little old to be your children, Phin. And they're not yours. Those units belong to MAXIFAX, which means—"

This bout of family court unexpectedly recessed when, overhead, *Willendorf I* began to rock and shudder in aeronautic conniptions that second by second became more intense and threatened to involve those on the ground.

But above the rev and roar of the helicopter, Phineas Fairfax shouted, "You will not harm my children!" and bending his launcher upward, shot a rocket directly at it.

✳✳✳

After Bobby and Zoe had heard the side doors of the *Willendorf I* slam ominously shut behind them and they had been unceremoniously plunked onto the chopper's grated metal floor, the drones that had captured them had fluttered up to the ceiling, to hang themselves up like electronic bats and await another summons to terrorize the world of flesh and blood.

Bobby pulled Zoe to her feet with the mandatory, "You all right?" and while she nodded, Bobby looked about, hoping to recognize something. (This was Bobby's second visit to *Willendorf I*, but on his maiden voyage he had been bound, gagged, and groggy from whatever had been in that energy drink.)

Playing it suave, he said, "This way," and grabbed the nearest door handle. Giving it a quiet turn and finding it unbolted, he whispered, "Come on," leaving Zoe to whisper, "Can you fly a helicopter?"

"Let's find out," he said, and they stepped into the cockpit beyond.

Felipe and Darshan, thus far in our saga mere names, were now sitting in the flesh at the controls and scanning the gauges, buttons, and knobs around them, until one of them (Darshan) noticed the new arrivals and grunted, "Hey, dude," before Felipe offered a "Welcome back."

Bobby thought on his feet. "'Sup," he said and gave Zoe a quick, significant look. "So, like, Sheena said that I'm supposed to, like, help you guys?"

Darshan said, "Just a second," then turned around for a better look at the new grunt, only to say, "You're not Sheena."

Zoe waved a few fingers hello. "No, I'm not. And I mean, who'd wanna be, right?"

Darshan gulped. "Totally."

Felipe asked, "What's going on, bro?" and turning, got himself caught up in the same, sudden red-haired turbulence.

With that feigned innocence that just begged for a big smart man to show her what was what, Zoe said, "Oh, so how do you fly this thing?"

Felipe and Darshan each unbelted as quickly as he could to give the young lady a one-on-one tour, leaving idiotically both their seats unmanned, just before a fearsome explosion rocked the craft and sent them all hurtling about.

✳✳✳

While Dr. Fairfax coolly drew forth a second projectile from a lab coat pocket, a dismembered piece of landing gear from *Willendorf I* dropped like space junk straight into the earth directly beside him, and like an unedited scene in the director's cut of *Brush Hogs Gone Wild,* the chopper was now twirling, twisting, tipping, tilting, tearing off the tops of the trees, and sending down a rain of unripened fruit, branches, and leaves.

It also sent down Bobby and Zoe.

These two baby lovebirds would have had a hard landing had they not plummeted straight down onto Sheena's antigravity sphere, their quiet bounce followed by a gentle and feathery landing on to the ground.

Sheena Lypotrope's landing was not so downy soft. Not really used to rough handling, and what with bodies and shoes and getting bumped into untrimmed tree limbs, her antigravity sphere, which looked like something from a futuristic beach blanket B-grade bijou reel, burst apart with a loud, gooey pop, splattering Bella, Baba, and Martie with a viscous, if harmless, ectoplasm.

Up out of the quivering pool of prismatic slag that had been Sheena's protective pellucidum, Sheena arose, to stand unmoving, glowering, and glutinous, not at all an agreeable and beckoning Venus on a half shell. After noting out of the corner of her steely eye that *Willendorf I* had righted herself but was veering away out of sight, she turned on Phineas Fairfax.

He was still fully armed and directing his rocket in her direction. Neither flinching nor smiling, she said, "You've damaged MAXIFAX property, Phin."

"Which is no concern of mine," he said. "Only they are."

Sheena considered Bella, Baba, and Martie wiping the goo from their faces, and chuckled knowingly. "Ah, souvenirs from your glory days. But do you have as much concern for these?" And she barked out, "Ladies?"

Down from the sinuous black tangle of fruit tree branches all about them swung feminoid after feminoid, like a tribe of over-evolved chimpanzees. (During the lull before storming the metaphoric beach, they had voted to call themselves the Grrrrillas, if that helps.) They had shed their daytime drag of pink camo for a slimming black and their parfait shades of face paint for MAXIFAX's own Shady Lady™ nocturnal covertising "masquing spread."

At this latest iteration of the goon squad, Baba theorized, "I guess Frannie and Angela started up an Al Jolson tribute band," but Bella had once more opted for "flight" instead of "fight" and was tugging her and Martie off into the pawpaw trees.

But this latest attempt at escape was x-nayed with yet another corps of the Grrrrillas dropping down in front of them. With their night-vision goggles glowing into action, these Sally Stormtroopers were making straight for them.

Just then, a harsh voice filled the trees. "You will not not harm them!" and the ground before Bella, Baba, and Martie blew up in an explosion of dirt, muck, old fruit, and several yards of long-abandoned drip lines as Dr. Phineas Fairfax on his ATV rode into the breach.

Shoving his rocket launcher into the cubby behind his seat, he told Bella, Baba, and Martie, "Come aboard."

Once they had quickly, if uncomfortably, scampered onto this last train for anywhere, Dr. Fairfax turned the Grrrillas. "And as for you ladies"—he revved the engine—"the chase is on!" Gunning his steed, he raced with his not-so-maidenly maidens off into the night.

✳✳✳

Nearby, and without the help of artillery or a small-engine vehicle, Bobby Lumbar was trying to affect his own escape. For about the hundredth time that night, he was telling Zoe, "Come on," but just as he reached out to grab her, a glaring searchlight, waggling back and forth from the night sky just above him, put a new light on events.

Holding a sweaty palm to his eyes, Bobby made out a wounded *Willendorf I* returning to action, only to see the searchlight pivot away from him and on down the lane—where by its light Bobby saw, for one fleeting second, Dr. Sheena Lypotrope chasing Zoe into the darkness.

In such moments, stupidity comes to the rescue, for Bobby heard from above, "Hey, bro!"

Bobby cocked his neck up. Through an unseen speaker on the chopper's underside, a young male voice was calling down. "Bro, hey, what's going on?"

The Bobby Lumbar that lurked about earlier in this saga would have just stared gulping and nonplussed at Zoe disappearing into the shades. But the Rob Lumbar of the present paragraph needed a military-grade surge protector to contain the heaving solar dragon of glittering electrons of virility and action that charged golden and incandescent through his battleman brain and brawnifying biceps. He yelled back over the din of the chopper blades, "Give me a lift. I'll show you."

Either Felipe or Darshan answered down, "You're the man, man. Stand back," and as Bobby scooted away, the helicopter came nearer the ground and uncoiled a strap ladder for Bobby's on-boarding convenience.

Once Bobby had been hauled into the hold and the doors had hissed shut behind him, Felipe asked, "So, where's she going?"

Bobby spoke like he knew what he was talking about. "That way," he said with a nod of the head. "Sheena's caught one of those crazies to sacrifice to the boys on Level IX. We just got to meet up with her."

And on cue, they heard a loud, harsh crackle come through Felipe's headpiece. "Big Blond to Oaxaca Dawn."

A suddenly nervous Felipe responded through his mouthpiece, "Oaxaca Dawn."

Bobby heard Sheena snarl, "I'm looking up at a water tower."

Bobby nodded vigorously at Felipe and mouthed, "Water tower. I know where that's at."

Felipe nodded back at him, then told his mouthpiece, "Big Blond, we know location. Arrival within one minute." He silenced his device and asked Bobby, "You wanna take the wheel? It's a lot of fun."

✳✳✳

With Sangreal and Siege Perelous loping alongside his ATV, Dr. Phineas Fairfax chugged to a stop beside one of the many doors of Orphis. Leaping off in a single bound, he told his three refugees from Sheenastan, "At this point, you have three choices."

"Oh," brightened Martie. "Strawberry. I want strawberry."

Baba elevated an elegant finger to indicate her selection. "Santiago."

Through what might have been a suppressed sigh, Dr. Fairfax asked Bella, "Are you the responsible one?"

"I'd call it desperate, but what d'you need?" she said.

"Umm," Martie hummed, waving a hand. "Strawberry?"

"And I can take La Paz," said Baba, "if I have to."

"As I was saying," he went on, now focusing with calm eyes into the gloom behind them, "either fight..."

Bella shook her head, and Baba nodded in agreement.

"...flight..."

"La Paz will still work," Baba said.

"...or..."

But our weary Wendies never heard this option, since Dr. Fairfax said, "'Flight' is now the optimal choice," for the Grrrillas were charging at them out of the dark.

✳✳✳

When vital chunks of *Willendorf I*—and then Bobby and Zoe—had been dropping from the heavens, a good deal of chaos had ensued, with drones whizzing about like wind-up gadflies, Sheena Lypotrope had sunk her ice-blue press-ons into Zoe's red hair like a snow leopard with the unwelcome promise, "I think I can get plenty of stem cell lines out of you," and started off with her into the darkness.

But they had not gotten far into the nasty, gnarled fruit trees when Sheena asked Zoe, "All right, guinea piglet, just get us out of here and maybe I'll use some anesthetic. Which way?"

Zoe was twisted to one side, but waved her arm toward the wide, dimly lit terrain in front of them, only to suddenly shriek, "What's that?"

"What's what?" said Sheena, letting go of her luscious little sparrow to find her bear spray.

And Zoe was off, like an innocent fawn leaving the cougar behind.

✳✳✳

Phineas Fairfax quickly opened the nearest door into Orphis and the three "nuns" passed within. (Steely-eyed and cynical, Bella gratefully accepted the doctor's open-door policy, since too many of her generation had taken "equality" seriously and scared off all of the gallant and kind-hearted men by calling them pigs; Martie was just glad not to risk another injury to her precious mannies by using her hands at all; and Baba took this as cosmic compensation for having to open her own door back at Lovelies Salon.)

Phineas Fairfax twisted a few deadbolts to put a little more protection between them and imminent annihilation, and finding a nearby two-shelf bookcase weighted down by a long-untouched set of *Encyclopedia Americana*, he pulled it in front of the door.

"That won't hold them long, but I hope as long as it takes to ready the boiling oil. Wait here," he said. "I'm sending someone else to bring you on," and with his dogs at his unsullied heels, he wended away down the hallway and around a corner.

As soon as he was gone, though, from behind the locked and buttressed door, Bella heard a sniffing, the searching inhalations of many noses, but then a scratching, a testing of the wood by sharp, manicured nails or vampire-grade incisors seeking to gnaw through. Bella lowered her finger to the doorknob: It was turning a few degrees to the left, then to upright, only to roll to the right, where it halted.

Baba whispered, "Bella dear?" as she gently laid a hand over Martie's quivering lips.

Bella looked up at her.

"He did lock the door," she said, while Martie, still in her grasp, pointed to the battery of deadbolts, raised an affirming thumb, and nodded strongly.

Bella whispered, "We just have to stay quiet."

Which was met from the other direction by a raucous, "Mothers, here I am!"

Whirling about like spinnakers in this latest storm of life, Bella, Baba, and Martie saw coming at them a pretty, youngish blond (i.e., Greta), in one hand a wire whisk dripping blobs of meringue and in the other a utility blowtorch at full, pale blue blast (for that restaurant-quality sepia singe on the baked Alaska—which she had started to put together for no one in particular).

"Dr. Fairfax said bring you to his office," she said, freely waving the blowtorch about.

As the short bluish flame brushed dangerously near, Bella drew back with startled, widening eyes and asked with a gulp, "And who are you, sweetheart?"

"Oh, sorry about that." Greta chucked her wire whisk over her shoulder and, with a now-free hand, turned down the flame. "There we go. The doctor wants me to help you."

"The-Doctor-Wants-Me-to-Help-You sounds like an Indian name," said Martie. "What do you think, Charlotte?"

But with one amber-tipped finger to her lips, Baba was pointing out that the door was now cracking open. Around its edge crept mud-stained digits, then wrinkling hands, and finally forearms in tight-to-bursting black spandex nightwear.

Then Greta yelled out, "Dr. Fairfax said to take any and all necessary measures!" and cranking the flame on her blowtorch past any legally allowed setting, she sent straight out at the invaders a horizontal pillar of atmosphere-warping azure flame, only for a second pullulating wave of feminoids to flood in.

And with that, the three "nuns," with Greta, their living ball of string, abandoned the outer defenses and made for the castle keep—a.k.a. the doctor's office.[9]

✳✳✳

What with all of those moonlit romps to scout new sites for small-bird cemeteries, Zoe knew the local terrain by both day and night and in

---

9 This seemingly shifting kaleidoscopic mandala of corridors was quite intentional, Phineas Fairfax having mapped out Orphis in a Minoan mouse maze. Supposedly, this was to maintain the inmates' "residential integrity" (i.e., to prevent escape). Any ex-orphs who inadvertently encountered one another in the outside world, at a big-box store, say, after forcing themselves to say hello, were known to nervously repeat the legend that somewhere in the complex there still wandered an early patient who had forever lost his way and survived only by eating the flaking discount wall paint.

no time had broken out into the clearing that ringed Mother Johanna's water tower. But as she was darting on straight for Orphis—where for some reason all of the security lights were suddenly spluttering on like electronic fireflies—out from over the tangled trees of the orchard arose a fearsome rectangle of shadow, lights, and noise, and *Willendorf I* hovered to a midair stop right above her. But a familiar voice, now hearty, direct, and no-nonsensical, now sounded down at her.

"Zoe," Bobby called through the speaker, "I'll come get you. Here, you take over." He was talking with some invisible pal on the chopper. "Yeah, it's cool. What? They're saying there's not enough room to land here. Climb up the tower. What? Well, Sheena can walk home."

∗∗∗

But Zoe was only halfway up the water tower's colossal legs when she heard from ground level a harsh, put-out, and displeased voice; and looking down, she saw Dr. Sheena Lypotrope circling beneath her like a white she-wolf. "Oaxaca Dawn!" she was shrieking into her phone. "Oaxaca Dawn!"

Zoe very sensibly kept climbing upward.

Soon she had crawled over the railing that ringed the platform and, straightening herself up, looked around for the helicopter.

But it was nowhere to be seen.

Instead of scanning into the distance, however, Zoe noticed the beauty of the night sky and fell back into that sensitive romanticism that had landed her in Orphis in the first place: The rain clouds that had been so generous all day had moved on, leaving the firmament as clean as a polished black agate, its lightlessness touched only a pearlescent moon rising over the east. Very pretty.

And then she felt two vicious hands sink into her red hair.

"Okay, toots," said Sheena, applying generous pressure and pushing her down. *"Sit."* Keeping one tigress hand on Zoe's head, she snarled into her device, "Oaxaca Dawn, for the fiftieth time, this is Big Blond. Oaxaca Dawn, come in. Over."

As a sheepish answer crackled back from *Willendorf I* ("This is Oaxaca Dawn, Big Blond"–gulp–"Over."), Zoe noticed down the catwalk something disturbing the darkness where the water tank curved into the night: a shape, shadowy, gaunt, and grim, first peering around the water tank and then stepping out onto the platform.

Wraithlike it came creeping toward them until it stilled, to almost levitate on the platform like a pylon of shadow—or a silhouette of oblivion. A nameless, never-known wind arose and blew about the robes covering this eerie, ominous figure, billowing and threading them into the night like cosmic vapors or the sails of the ship of the dead swelling away from the shores of life.

Zoe cried out, "Mother Johanna!" and after a selfish survivalist dash, was sheltering behind her.

"What do you think you're doing?" snarled Sheena Lypotrope. "I don't like my organ donors shirking their duties. You come back here right now."

It was precisely then that the moon rose above the railing of the tower. Seeming to float behind Mother Johanna's cowled head, it ringed about in a silvery halo, and whether or not the leathery nun knew what was transpiring to her rear, she spread wide her arms and at the towering blond invader robed in white sent out a stream of murmurs from the cave of her cowl. "The love of money...God and Mammon..."

This did not impress Sheena Lypotrope. "What are you," she said, "one of Phin's experiments?"

While keeping intelligently out of range, Zoe put her in her place. "You don't talk to her that way. She's trying to become a saint."

Sheena Lypotrope could only sneer, "And I'm on my way to becoming a goddess."

What looked like the night wind blowing Mother Johanna about was actually her leaning into Zoe and giving her a guttural command. The girl stepped away, and the old hermit turned back to her unwelcome guest.

With ancient eyes accustomed to the light of moon and stars, Mother Johanna saw more than Sheena Lypotrope could guess and sent up a rasping, bronchial laugh that shook her hidden frame.

"What's so funny?" Sheena felt forced to ask.

"I didn't know," wheezed Mother Johanna, "that a goddess was subject to so much gravity."

In shock, Sheena Lypotrope's mouth opened like the bay doors of a bomber ready to dump its payload. The fight was on.

✳✳✳

"Hey," snorted Bobby, as *Willendorf I* had veered away from the water tower and toward the complex of Orphis. "What's going on?"

Darshan played it cool. "New orders. I guess Big Blond wants a visual on the team insertion." The chopper flew in a leisurely circuit above the sheds, dormitories, and reeducation cells visible below them through the cockpit windows.

Even in a fly-by in the dark, Bobby made out a dramatically seething and frantic scene. The chopper's searchlights, strafing negligently back and forth, showed in pass after pass a score of doughy women in too-tight black combat gear swarming around the central buildings, hammering on the doors, and swinging expensive handbags onto the windows.

"All right," said Bobby with a little heat. "We're done here. We gotta get back to the water tower."

Darshan was sheepish. "Big Blond doesn't—"

"Then too bad for Big Blond," barked Bobby, and jumping over Darshan in a move straight out of *X-treme Twister*, Bobby seized the controls, and *Willendorf I* lurched sideways through the night air.

✳✳✳

Down below in Orphis, in his office, Phineas Fairfax was standing, as if before a forbidden shrine, at an antique Chinese bureau. Faced in numerous discreet and inscrutable brass-fitted drawers containing yet more secretive little compartments, it would open for him once he had found the right key. And so, readying himself for an apocalypse—or maybe a mass extinction event—he stood flipping through a ring of keys peering at each as if it were a coin from a sunken trove.

"Flux and change...," he murmured, then flipped to the next key. *"Plus ça change*...No, Phineas. No. Or maybe so. What are we doing?" He slid one key into the bureau, but the drawer did not open. "Eternal return... Perpetual motion machine." Another key, into the same keyhole. *"La machine ronde..."* He tested another. "Man and machine. Or woman and machine." The lock clicked submissively open, and pulling the drawer toward him, he breathed, *"Deus ex machina."*

He felt inside the wide, rectangular space within, knowing what he sought, and soon drew out a small, dignified box lacquered in cinnabar and set with mother-of-pearl patterns of Oriental unicorns.

He carried the box to his desk and, in the lamplight of the faux Tiffany lamp, took in the box's inlay, blazing white and prismatic. "A backup for your backup," he reminded himself. "Is this what you had in mind, Sheldrake?" (Sheldrake Lypotrope, of the Club of Rome, the Bilderberg Group, the Bohemian Grove, and the local Moose Lodge, had been Sheena's father, the scion of an old if not venerable mid-Atlantic clan— think H. P. Lovecraft rather than Nathaniel Hawthorne. He had advised a much younger Phineas, when his coppery beard was a few mere unbridled wisps of orange, that he should always maintain a diverse portfolio, always have a backup for your backup, and know where the back door was, just in case. Eerily, Sheldrake failed to follow his own advice, and on an expedition of Mayan ruins in the Yucatan went missing, being last seen entering unaccompanied into a vine-choked shrine to Kuchuma kik' the Blood Gatherer and never stepping out ever again. Once his disappearance was seen as an accomplished fact, everyone in their mansions along the Conshohocken for a long while afterward sipped their martinis in a quiet, pious, and knowing fear, figuring that old Sheldrake's debtors had finally cleared their books. As for Sheena's mother, Siobhan née Ó Cléirigh, she remained respectably unmolested by the dark lords of Xibalba and was oft seen in the village having a discreet luncheon with Phaedra Fairfax.)

From somewhere in the complex, cries, shrieks, and sundry other uncivilized sounds suddenly noised their way into his attention, and he immediately tugged at the silken ribbon trapping the waxen seals along the box's lid. So began the end of all his works.

Lifting back the lid, Dr. Phineas Fairfax saw first a note written to himself with the command:

Go back for them.

Slipping the note into his lab coat pocket, he came next to another box, something like a cigarette case salvaged from a UFO crash site, cold, amoral, and metallic, of an alloy known only to MAXIFAX. Lifting it out, he stared on it as if it were a gnomish suitcase bomb, until he heard again the cries outside, now coalescing into, "Daddy!" and "Doctor!"

Going to the door into the hallway, he opened it and heard the chaos overtaking Orphis coming closer, jigging and kinking its way through the corridors. "It was not supposed to happen yet, Fairfax," he said, but without leaving the threshold, he cracked open the unfeeling outworldish metal tinderbox.

Within, he saw what seemed to be thousands of tiny, tiny amphibian's eggs, almost slumbering. But now exposed to the air, they squirmed and moved.

So, like an angel holding a bowl of plagues, Dr. Phineas Fairfax held the box before him, turned his hand, and sent out a fine, dark, granular cascade, like a black bridal veil. But this somber tulle did not spread down to the floor; instead, it rose like a murmuration of birds or a sinister semi-sentient cirrus cloud, then broke gently apart into single miniscule spheres like microscopic black pearls. "Fly away, little midwives," he said, and away they skimmed to the left and right as the doctor stepped back. "*Alea iacta est.*"

✳✳✳

As a sensitive soul, Zoe was never one for blood sports, but the combat between Mother Johanna and Dr. Sheena Lypotrope was disturbingly enthralling, as if she were witnessing the clash of primaeval nebulae, an icy, crackling battle between noble gases and dark matter—that was, before the dirty tricks kicked in (kicking, biting, and eye-poking) and Zoe heard herself rooting loud and proud for the home team favorite.

The most dramatic turn came, though, when the combatants twirled about, with Sheena about to chuck Mother Johanna over the railing for a one-way trip to the ground below, but Mother Johanna acrobatically rotated about and landed on Sheena's back like a limber she-bear pouncing onto a bucking Palomino. Just as she was ringing her bony arms around her neck and digging the dried-branch fingers of one hand into Sheena's platinum tresses, though, out the dark sky arched *Willendorf I*, her pilot apparently unable to find the brakes, and the chopper careened straight into the water tower.

The water tower shook, its metallic supports like the legs of Talos teetering and groaning, until the same forces serpentined back upward through the metal mass and popped the rivets securing both the tank and the deck under the feet of Zoe, Mother Johanna, and Dr. Sheena Lypotrope, tilting it, warping it, and sending it and its three lady occupants hurtling earthward, just as *Willendorf I* was zooming upward in a sharp corrective move. (Bobby Lumbar was not steering it at this point.)

Missing by inches the whirring, Charybdis blades of the chopper's tail, Sheena Lypotrope—seeing a chance to show the hag that this goddess was *not* subject to gravity—reached out both hands in mid-freefall, grabbed at *Willendorf I* as if hitching a ride on a pterodactyl, and yelled, "Got it!"

But as the chopper rose higher and cleared the now-tankless legs of the water tower, it made another correction, spinning about and sending Sheena Lypotrope twirling like a top into the wild midnight-blue yonder, over the treetops of the orchard, until she was swallowed up in the fruity forest below.

As for Zoe and Mother Johanna, they and the water tank landed a bit closer in, but not without an explosion of leaves, snapping branches, and half-ripened fruit.

✳✳✳

Ignoring the fact that his glasses were smashed, because Felipe had socked him one to get his hands off of the controls, Bobby Lumbar was peering down as best he could at the water tank, now at the gaping crater at the edge of orchard. "Drop me down there," he said.

"But, dude," said a fuming Felipe, "why not just throw you out in midair right here?" and as Darshan reestablished firm control of *Willendorf I*, Felipe, with nary a word of thanks for not getting them killed any sooner, did exactly that.

✳✳✳

Bobby's arrival on terra firma was not as messy and lethal as the bookies would have hoped. After a relatively short drop, he made a not quite cushiony, but comfortable-enough landing on a pile of plastic-wrapped hay bales, like a slumbering heap of gigantic wild marshmallows. Following this came the slide down, down, down, and then the roll onto the weedy gravel, which in the dark was, yes, a nasty surprise. (The mothers stored the hay there for feeding the water buffalo. If Bobby had rolled down the other side, he would have been facing a service road leading straight to the convent. How else did the mothers come and go to Orphis so quickly? No getting lost in the woods for them.)

Just as he finished shaking himself off, he heard out of the night, "Bobby!" like the call of a bird seeking her nest.

Squinted with his good eye into the gloom, he saw grayish-black criss-crossing, upright blobs and four outsized sticks (the orchard and what was left of the water tower) and above these an endless void of deep, vacuous blue (the sky) besmirched by a glowing white blob (the moon).

Hearing "Bobby!" again, he told himself, "All righty, Robert J., you're the man, and man is the tool-using animal," and patting himself through this lab coat, as if he were cop and convict at the same time, he felt in one of his pockets...his smartphone.

And he remembered. In the cockpit, in the cubby of *Willendorf I*, Bobby had found—and pocketed—not only this ultimate necessity for modern life but also his wallet and his keys, filched from him on his first ride. By rights, as long as his debit card showed a positive balance, he could have headed off into the horizon.

But he had a maiden to rescue.

So, he called out, "Zoe!" a lion's roar, informing any and all boogeymen, ne'er-do-wells, rogues, and highwaymen to stand down, lest their lives and fortunes be made forfeit. Then, with a firm squeeze to the On button, a rapid but deft tapping of his password, and a touché swipe up the screen, the world—and the phone's flashlight feature—was his again.

He heard her call again from near the line of the trees, and he answered, "I'm coming," and charged into the now well-lit, if fuzzy, nocturnal terrain.

The voice of Zoe came back. "Is that you?"

"It's me," he said, almost falling onto a tetanus-infested pile of salvage wood from a broken-down shed. (In true rustic form, Mother Deborah knew that unscrewing the old fittings and then sawing up the boards for kindling was not only good farm economy but would also make a convenient, hands-on penance for some erring novice.)

"But where are you?"

"Right here!" Bobby shouted, now nearly tripping over a coil of dripline tubing.

"But where is that?"

"I'm coming, I'm coming," Bobby said, squinting to make out the way ahead of him.

"I can see your light. This way. I'm waving at you. Over here! Can you see me?"

And (accidentally) stumbling right up to her, he hurriedly rallied the charm as if slipping in a bachelor-button boutonnière. "Why, yes, I can," he said. "And a lovely sight it is."

Bobby expected her to swoon, but she said, "Mother Johanna's this way," and tugged him through weeds, grass, and a spinney of small trees to the "inclusion site," as AM late-night might phrase it.

The water tank squatted half embedded in the ground, like an immense and looming alien egg in its nest, aglow in the moonlight. Up from its base jabbed a recently deceased plum tree or two at queer angles, with a netting of telephone and/or cable lines hanging around its girth, and loose limbs and branches from neighboring trees making an impromptu victory crown about the apex.

Zoe picked her way closer. "Mother Johanna? Oh, there you are."

The light from Bobby's phone showed the old hermit lurking about the muddy edge of the crater, like a specimen of rare wildlife caught on camera. She was tapping the water tank with a snapped-off plum tree branch, cocking her head for an echo or an answer, like telegraphy into the void, before giving the tank a jab or two. Very soon, though, she rested the stick against the tank, seized something on its metal face, and with a yank, pulled up a small porthole door.

And muttering a few lines from a Bronze Age religious text (Bobby heard, "In peace in the selfsame I will sleep, and I will rest..."), Mother Johanna crawled inside the metal egg and let the door fall shut with a clang behind her.

"All right, she's fine," said Zoe. "She's just going back to bed. Now where to?"

"I'm gonna find Dr. Fairfax," he said. "But you need to stay here."

Zoe balked. "Just a second. If we're going to spend the rest of our lives together—"

"I'll let you know if that's gonna happen," he said.

"—then we'll face danger together."

"Then do you mind, strong and empowered female, if I go in front and take a bullet for you?"

"That's all right. But then I'm not that strong and empowered."

"Funny how that works."

"Just no prenup, okay?"

Bobby leaned close into her, and his stubbly mouth smirked. "You'll sign whatever I tell you to sign," and with a wink he told her, "Come on, let's go find those bullets."

✳✳✳

Coming up to Orphis, Bobby and Zoe saw that every security light had been triggered, half of the windows had been spider-webbed with blows from, say, a heavily weighted woman's purse, and the rest were smashed in with the good-sized decorative rocks that the doctor scattered in the garden beds. (Their size and shape suggested the decapitated heads of stubborn patients.) Meanwhile, as if goblins had opened up the cages at the exotic bird farm, weird noises, calls, cries, pleas, and exclamations sounding something like Lesson II from that Berlitz download Bobby had practiced with before that sophomore trip to Canada were flying out of from the same broken windows. At the same time, reminiscent of a college library after anarchists had declared it their autonomous zone, doorways to the outside had been crammed with whatever moveables the invaders could drag into play—furniture, whiteboards, coat racks, retired airliner drink carts, boot driers, two-drawer filing cabinets, and shag rugs from the kinetic play cells.

"How can we get inside?" Zoe asked.

Bobby snapped his fingers. "Hey, I know!"

Pulling her around the next corner, they came to the doctor's semitropical Malaysian knockoff of a patio. "Right through here," he said and led her up that path through that stand of whispering banana trees and up to the door into the doctor's bedroom. It was undamaged and unlocked.

Within, the doctor's private sanctum was dim and somnolent, lit solely by a small Deco lamp on a bureau. From across the room, though, through a half-visible door came cries of "No, Daddy! No!"

Staring at the door, Zoe asked, "Are there bullets in there?"

"Maybe," said Bobby.

Zoe held a hand toward the mysterious portal, but through his mangled glasses, he gave her what couples know as "a look." Then drawing himself up and straightening what was left of his glasses, he said, "Making a blind man do your fighting for you. Your dad better have a whole herd of goats for your dowry." (In his myopia, Bobby did not see Zoe gasp in surprise, because according to current records at the State Department of Agriculture, her father actually did hold the largest herd of milking goats in the greater Merryweather large-animal agricultural zone, right there at Feldspar Farms, right outside Smithburg.)

But while Zoe was catching her breath at this serendipity, Bobby marched forth to the other door, brazenly swung it open, and guessed he should be glad that his glasses were broken, since he did not think that he wanted to see what he thought he was seeing.

✳✳✳

Sheena Lypotrope came to in the darkness of the orchard, on her back in the muck, but never down for the count. Rapidly bringing herself into an upright position, she immediately sought communication with *Willendorf I.*

"Oaxaca Dawn," she relayed, "I'm back in this stupid orchard. Oaxaca Dawn, I'm in the orchard. If you can hear me—"

"Big Blond, this is Oaxaca Dawn," came Felipe's voice.

"Oaxaca Dawn, I don't feel like playing hide-and-seek, so tell me as soon as you find an open patch."

"Big Blond, we've pinged your position and are now starting on a visual of the adjacent area."

"Just make it fast," she said, then took a moment to scan the starry spaces above her for a sign of her whirlybird. "Oaxaca Dawn?" she told her device. "Oaxaca Dawn, come in. I'm not seeing you. Hey, what's that?"

Sheena Lypotrope was no longer looking up at the sky but had seen something in the trees around her. Indeed, between the trees all about her, she saw numberless pairs of glowing eyes, like constellations of stark and staring stars, all turned at her.

If the mannish matrons who moulded the maidens at Stifflehurst had taken their charges on more summer campouts, Sheena Lypotrope might have guessed that she was facing a pack of wild hunters and maybe climbed a tree or broken out that bear spray. (It would no doubt work on things other than bears.) But only after a fleeting wash of light from the curious moon did she see that these were not coyotes, feral pigs, or even those megapossums that had escaped from the labs at the nuclear waste depot in Fulcrum up the interstate, but a contingent of units from the Johnson Series, all clad in a camouflage of dark blue.

Then *Willendorf I* lost her signal. For many minutes, Felipe and Darshan flew the chopper back and forth, around and around, scratching vain lines and circles in the air above the orchard, as Felipe continued to signal through both his radio and out through the speaker on the chopper's underside, calling, "Big Blond...Big Blond...," but no reply eked up out of the trees. Then at last, deciding that something had transpired on the ground and that alone they could do no more, Felipe and Darshan radioed MAXIFAX, then steered the chopper to the south and west, to return *Willendorf I* to her faraway lair.

✳✳✳

"Robert," Bobby heard Dr. Phineas Fairfax say, "I see your spectacles have not survived the struggle. Please take these." Coming up to him, he gave Bobby another pair of glasses from the interdimensional depths of his lab coat pocket. (No guarantees about the prescription). But as Bobby slid them onto his face, he was truly sorry that he saw what he was seeing.

The doctor had stepped back to stand with a pleased and serene expression, like a benevolent shepherd, amid a happy collection of bouncing, bubbling, bulbous BBs in baby pink, true-love pink, first-rose-of-summer pink, and—a sign of hope in deepest night—rosy dawn pink. All of these proto-humanoids were gleefully bouncing against an unbounded vista of unscrewed heads, arms and legs in black spandex, smart accessory bags and night-on-the-town clutch purses, and odd eyeballs staring up at the very tall man in the white coat.

The doctor beckoned young Mr. Lumbar to brave this new world, but like any cagey traveler, Bobby had reservations. "What did you do?"

"What I had to do," said Dr. Fairfax, half in admission, half with pride.

Unsure whether he should be impressed or stricken with dread, Bobby said, "You killed them."

"Of course not." The doctor smiled with genial tolerance. "That would be neither ethical nor moral. I merely set them free. And what does Zoe think?"

Zoe was coming through the door right behind Bobby, who put out a hand to protect her from accidental dismemberment. The events of the preceding several hours, though, must have hardened her, because after picking up a loose Swarovski bag (and an Yves Saint Laurent Sac De Jour as a backup), she said, "Well, that's too bad," without asking for an explanation.

Just then, at the open door into the office, Greta appeared, pushing about a made-to-last AV department movie projector cart (sans the projector, of course).

"Ah," said the doctor. "Put them three or four in each of the empty beds, and I suppose push dressers against the sides to keep them from rolling all over the place."

"That's probably what our pioneer ancestors did," said Zoe.

But before Greta blurted out something about "settler colonialism," Phineas Fairfax intoned, "Every couple of generations we're tested like this. When you're done, come back for the rest. I'm sure that Zoe will help you. Robert and I will address the extremities."

Hearing her assignment, Zoe happily joined Greta in gathering up the baby blobules as if they were GMO-free cantaloupes on close-out sale at the farmer's market, all the while prattling on about ASMR lullaby streaming channels, dextrose misting systems, and ceiling mobiles of the planetary system around Rigel VI. (Bobby might have misheard the last one.)

Very soon, the kinderwagen was laden to the gills with the first wave of cooing, squirming BBs, and Zoe and Greta rolled it away on down the hallway. The fun did not stop, though, as Phineas Fairfax told Bobby, "A jailbreak appears in progress."

Because Greta and Zoe had cleared a path through the welter of limbs and torsos, one of the remaining BBs, squealing and cooing, was now nudging, rolling, and squeaking her way in a slow horizontal avalanche for the door to make her vagrant escape. (This may have been either Frannie or Angela—time alone would tell.) But stepping through the others as if they were a living cake walk, the doctor picked her up and passed her to Bobby, then closed the door.

Bobby nervously accepted the rosy little BB and even stared at its squinting "face," complete with little dimples, tiny feelers, and a cluster of indentations that were no doubt extremely important. Beguiled into thinking that it was a sweet, endearing, creature, Bobby brought up a finger to tickle what he hoped was a safe patch of flesh, when it shrieked in horror at this threatening monstrosity and snapped at his finger.

"Ow!" he snarled.

"Be careful," said the doctor. "A few may have rudimentary teeth."

While Bobby sucked his punctured digit, his assailant jiggled with glee and snapped its primitive mouth at him again, all in fun, no doubt. Phineas Fairfax took the budding cannibal and quietly scolded her. "Now, that's not nice." At once, the squirmer stilled and even sweetened the air with a placid purring. After a paternal chuckle, the doctor gave a tickle to what must have been her chubby belly, before saying, "To return to your recent concern, Robert: No, I didn't kill them. I am not the stern paterfamilias. Come, a seat," and he held his free hand to the purple plush chair while he himself leaned back against his mid-1950s chief scientist desk.

While giving his little recalcitrant a toss in the air, Phineas Fairfax said, "Orphoplasmodystrophase."

"And in English?" asked Bobby, watching the BB gasp with joy at each toss.

"Orphoplasmodystrophase. You've had your organic chemistry. A little something that Helsingfors and I came up with over drinks one night. As Sheena's father told me once, 'Always have a backup for your backup.'"

"Sheena had a father?"

"She did," he said, with a precipitous drop on the *did*. "So, orphano-plas*mene* is the multichain polymer we concocted to glue the various parts of the feminoids together as they formed. Orphoplasmo*dystrophase* breaks those bonds, and you are left with"—he turned the specimen squirming overexcitedly in his hands at Bobby—"the BB within. But what was to be the delivery system?"

"Delivering...?" asked Bobby.

The doctor said, "The enzyme, of course," and holding the BB with one arm, with his free hand he plucked from a cleanly detached head a sapphire-blue balaclava spangled with press-on stars and moons. Rubbing his fingertips over the cloth, he showed them to Bobby: Embedding his fingerprints was a layer of fine dark granularity. "Nanobots. I've seen them under the microscope. They're almost seamless. And they have one sole mission in this life: to seek out the ambient presence of organic waste products that only orphanoplasmene produces, find the source, bind to any organic receptor site on the target, and release its quantum of orphoplasmodystrophase, at which point the feminoid disassembles. Isn't that so?" he cooed at the BB in his arms.

Bobby did not feel so scientifically detached. "That sounds gross."

"We think that, because the human body is to us a cohesive unit, death seems the ultimate evil. But a feminoid body contains a core, the BB, and everything else is window dressing. I can take these little ones and make whatever sort of person I wish from her. I could make them into mermaids or centaurs, frankly, though I never would. Because when life hands you humanoids"—again he tossed up the living dough ball and it shrieked with emotion—"make little humans." Catching the bubble of potential, he said to himself something that to Bobby that sounded like, "Try, try again, Phineas."

Through the closed door to the hallway came the sounds, closer and closer, of a rapid, frantic creak-creaking, like a windmill in a rising cyclone, and Greta burst in, with Zoe behind her with the empty AV cart. She faltered out, "Doctor, Zoe told me what happened to Lola."

The doctor's tone became sharp. "To whom?"

Greta caught herself. "I mean—you know. Oh, I'm sorry, I'm sorry, I'm sorry."

Recognizing Greta's instinct for perfection through destruction rearing its ugly, basiliscene head, Phineas Fairfax said in a voice like a desert wind at the setting of the sun, "We all make mistakes, Greta."

"No paint sprayers, Greta," she told herself, "no paint sprayers..." and closing her eyes, she breathed in the warm wisdom on this balsam breeze.

"Excellent, Greta," said the doctor with an almost ceremonial care, as if enclosing a queen into her tomb. "No paint sprayers." Then he quietly asked Zoe, "What happened?"

While Greta chanted to herself, "I was *not* manifesting internalized white supremacy, only racists seek perfection...," Zoe told the doctor about her kidnapping, the helicopter's aerial hijinks, and the colossal tumbling of the water tower. The older man slipped his flip phone from his pocket. "Mother Deborah will need to know that," he said, quickly tapping out a coded text. Sliding the phone back into his pocket, he sank into unabashed if brief cogitation, before rising to the surface. "The National

Registry of Historic Places doesn't need to know all of the details, do they. It would just confuse them. Greta?"

Greta's mantras had begun to versify into an exorcism prayer against Aunt Jemima and Land O'Lakes butter, but hearing her name, she shook herself out of her own trance. The doctor said, "You and Zoe, please carry on gathering up the rest of the specimens? They're cold, and they also might dehydrate. Then, please dig out every spray bottle in the place and start making up a dextrose solution. I'll get you the recipe. As for the rest of this"—he meant the handbags, spandex, heads, legs, and arms, a brave band of the latter now crawling with their last bits of energy toward the door—"Robert and I will address it soon enough."

After Greta and Zoe had left with another crop of bumotious babyoids, Dr. Fairfax considered the array of limbs and extremities yet remaining. "I think that Mother Deborah will let us use the flatbed."

Bobby said, "For the Viking funeral?" imagining that they would drive it to a lost lake and roll it into the depths.

He shook his head. "For the drive to Cullaby Junction Road. The 'No Dumping' sign's in for replacement, so they won't have much of a legal leg to stand on. It can be a good out-of-doors project for us before we rescue Ian."

"Ian?" said Bobby.

"And Jeremy, and the other fellow."

"Noah? Or Kevin Chang?"

"Such a vast social web you weave. No, Noah. I forgot that Kevin was part of your cabal. Tell me, Robert, are you familiar with the history of the can opener?"

This non sequitur interrupted Bobby's budding plans for a quick dart out the door and brisk hunt for Zoe Feldspar to start life anew. He shook his head. "No."

"It seems the sealed metal can was invented first and Civil War soldiers were stuck trying to open them with bayonets. Then some clever engineer devised the can opener. Symbiosis prevails. Well, the same quandary arose for me over orphoplasmodystrophase and orphanoplasmene. I had created an 'off switch' for my creations, but there was no way to efficiently deploy it—until Ian, with assistance from Noah and Jeremy, created those nanobots you saw."

"How do you know them?" Bobby asked with authentic stupefaction.

"I escaped MAXIFAX, but I did never abandoned it. I have a whole constellation of sub-rosa contacts in the labs and cubicles throughout that great underground empire, other shining souls who know that they are trapped in the void and that their masters work evil." From his lab coat pocket, he produced the now-empty lacquered cinnabar box and from it in turn the note. He handed it to Bobby. "*Tolle lege.* Take and read."

Reminding himself to break out that Berlitz CD again, Bobby took the note and read it aloud:

Go back for them.

"Ian and Noah and Jeremy. And when I do so, I will need someone brave, trustworthy, and, frankly, young at my side when I go rescue them. But first"—he retrieved the note from Bobby and solemnly laid it back in its blood-and-poppy red sarcophagus—"I understand that there's a sick water tower that needs a doctor. Come, help me dig out my meteorite."

The doctor was just stepping across this office for the door to his sanctum when he cocked his head quickly, almost haphazardly, at one sizable pile of rapidly desiccating limbs,[10] and he stopped. "Robert, behold," he said. "It appears as if the Cordilleran orogeny of the Late Cretaceous is reenacting itself in the middle of the floor."

He was bandying about this obscure geologic reference because, up out of the detached arms and lower legs now tumbling down to the floor around them, there arose, like junior varsity volcanoes in competition to be the first to erupt, three very weary nuns in black habits.

"Well, that wasn't supposed to happen," he said. "Tell me, Mothers—and I use the title loosely—"

Bella pointed at Baba. "She's the mother figure."

———

10 For the curious, feminoid parts do not decay but do dry out, and on Level VII copious vats, like lidless canopic jars brimming with generic moisturizer, stand full of arms, legs, screw-off heads, and similar curiosities, occupying chamber after chamber.

"No," said Martie, "she's the crazy aunt."

This genealogy lesson was cut short when Bobby Lumbar made a leaping lunge right at Bella, only to have the doctor catch him by his lab coat collar and haul him back from the kill.

He laid his hand firmly down on his shoulder. "Sit, Robert."

"But she tried to kidnap me."

Stepping over a pile of arms and legs to defend her reputation, Bella said, "Just a second, Troy, or whatever your name is—"

"I think his name's Robby," said Martie.

"—I was just the bag lady."

"Bag *man,* Bella dear," said Baba. "And we understand the grammatical double bind."

"When do I get to have a whack at her?" Bobby fumed.

The doctor still acted as referee. "A true man seeks justice, Robert, not revenge." Angry that the wheels of justice needed a lube job, Bobby sat with clenching fists and steaming ears, while the doctor addressed the party of the second part. "Mothers, ladies...I'm glad that you're still with us, but my scientific mind is in a state of confusion. You should be...not like this. Tell me, have you been in contact with large amounts of Na_2CO_3 of late?"

Their three faces stared at him before their three heads shook.

"Have you visited the Dolomite region of Italy or rolled about in a limestone quarry?"

More tripartite headshaking.

"Ah...the dawnstar rises." The doctor looked to Bobby knowingly, but Bobby was still waiting for a chance to hop up and have a vengeful go at Bella. He asked the ladies, "Have you been using any homemade laundry soap of late?"

Raising her hand, Martie gleefully squealed, "Borax!"

"Close," said the doctor with a tutorial flair. "But that is a good guess."

Baba whispered to Martie, "Washing soda," then told the class, "Borax is $Na_2B_4O_7 \cdot 10H_2O$."

"Or...?" asked the doctor.

Since Martie and Baba said nothing, Bella huffed, "So, it's my turn? Whatever," and she rattled off, "$Na_2B_4O_5(OH)_4 \cdot 8H_2O$."

"Yes," said the doctor. (He should have pulled out a gnarled old tobacco pipe to perfect the image.) "Tell me, while hiding under the debris of your sisters, did you hear me speak of the enzyme I used to...disrupt their bodily integrity?"

"Can we just take it outside?" asked Bobby, getting his own ideas about disrupting her bodily integrity.

"No, you may not. I'll start by saying that you should be very glad that Mother Deborah is so frugal, because the mothers wash their habits in a mix of borax and sodium chloride, and that saved your lives, because the enzyme—"

"Orphoplasmodystrophase," said Martie.

"Sometimes the lights are on," said Bella.

The doctor continued. "Excellent. Because orphoplasmodystrophase, normally lethal to members of your sisterhood, binds to sodium chloride, plain old washing soda, which stops it from completing its function. And with its short lifespan, orphoplasmodystrophase expires before the sodium chloride degrades. As we speak, your habits are probably sprinkled with poor dead nanobots."

Martie made a face and started slapping her sleeves. "Cooties! Cooties!" she sniffed, until Baba intervened with, "Stardust, Lily, it's just stardust."

Bella shook an arm, and a veil of dead nanobots floated almost glamorously to the floor. "Where's that leave us?"

"If you stay right there...," said Bobby.

The doctor told her, "You should be out of the woods. Unless you wish to shift off this mortal coil, in which case—"

But right then, Bobby leapt up from the plush purple chair straight at Bella like a gryphon.

Now, Bella Freestone had not survived to this point in our narrative out of sheer luck, and just as Bobby sprang from the floor, she sent up a trembling finger and, with a horrified look, gasped, "Look! It's Sheena Lypotrope!"

Sports scientists are still investigating exactly how a body can rotate in midair, but Bobby demonstrated it for the class, making a bizarre corkscrew motion, and actually cast his gaze backward, creating a precious crack of time for Bella, Baba, and Martie to trip over Frannie and Angela's leftovers and flee into the hallway.

Bobby, meanwhile, flopped hard onto the one patch of floor without an Oriental rug, knocked his own wind out, cut his lip, greenstick-fractured a rib, deviated his septum, and broke his glasses again.

And, adding insult to several injuries, when he finally caught his breath, Bobby saw that, no, Dr. Sheena Lypotrope was nowhere in sight, only Dr. Phineas Fairfax, offering a hand to pull him up.

"Come, Robert. Let's find that meteorite."

✳✳✳

A short time later, Dr. Fairfax and Bobby Lumbar, with his taped-up glasses, made for the remains of water tower. In his hands, Bobby bore the doctor's meteorite wrapped in chamois cloth, like an offering to the forces of light, fittingly, as the eastern horizon was becoming elegantly edged in glowingly electric hues of gold, yellow, bronze, peach, and chemical-spill orange, as if a distant power substation was being devoured by a silent river of lava and sending out its last surge of electricity to the Greater Merryweather Utility District.

With this radiance rendering their lab coats almost golden, like the caftans of ambassadors journeying from Prester John to Cathay, Bobby and Dr. Fairfax walked up to the tankless water tower, no longer a nostalgic reminder of bygone heritage days, but a relic of a lost and doomed civilization, armored in rust and government-issue exterior paint, but defiant of death, its gigantic legs against the sunrise frightening silhouettes seeming ready to trample any who trespassed its realm.

As for Mother Johanna's hermitage, the glimmer of newborn daylight on its flaking shell was like a welcoming caress to a survivor of the storm. Phineas Fairfax quietly laid his hand on its bulk, as if feeling for a throbbing, metallic pulse, then gestured for Bobby to lay his head on the metal and listen. Bobby played along and did hear subtle sounds, almost bouncing about the inside of the water tank, like blind cave fish bumping about the edges of an underground pool.

As the doctor listened, he had shut his eyes and begun playing the air with his fingers. Stepping back, he said quietly, "Lauds, I think. Let's let her finish, then we'll say hello." Drawing Bobby back, he asked, "So, where did the helicopter hit the tank?"

Bobby pointed up the tower's legs at an obscure point.

"Then, the visitor, please," requested the doctor, and Bobby handed him the interplanetary object. Considering the water tank on the ground, he murmured something about angles, unfolded the chamois cloth from about the outworldly object, and after a suppressed sigh at the sacrifice, chucked the meteorite smack into the disturbed earth alongside the water tank, like a baby Ankylosaurus next to its mother.

"Excellent," the doctor decided. "The water tower itself slowed its descending force, and the impact of the water tank onto the ground almost immediately afterward destabilized the superficial layer of soil, and so it rolled toward the tank. Voilá. We barely missed falling victim to another Chicxulub event," he concluded, invoking the frightening cataclysm that wiped out the T. rexes and allowed those small, scurrying, ratlike creatures to become lords of the earth. "Now let's see whether the lady of the house is receiving. Where's the door?"

Bobby led him to a section of soldered metal where hinges and a crude handle suggested a point of entry.

Having quietly taken a slow, meditative breath, the doctor tapped on the metal.

Neither word nor sound came forth.

He tapped again. "It's Dr. Fairfax."

Bobby asked, "Can she breathe in there?"

Phineas Fairfax nodded rhetorically, then tapped again. "Lola? It's still Dr. Fairfax."

Her door cracked half open with a creak, and Mother Johanna showed her cowled head.

In the short time that Bobby had known Mother Johanna, she had not changed much, going from terrifying to hideous to best-be-avoided-at-all-costs. Filling her doorway to capacity (it was a tiny door), she was hiding herself from human eyes with ragged draperies of petroleum-black cloth;

but her cracked fingertips—and a stray, talon-like finger—gave away that someone more or less human lived inside of that inky cocoon. Phineas Fairfax began making quiet, unobtrusive conversation with her as if she were Madison's clone, while Mother Johanna barely hissed a pleasantry or two in return.

But the hushed mood of the early-morning moment came to a noisy end as Mother Deborah and an assistant nun (Mother Apolinaria, the convent's accountant and legal eagle) bumped up on ATVs.

While Mother Apolinaria snapped images of the one-time water tower and its toppled tank with the convent's smartphone, Mother Deborah's concern was chiefly for her charge, and she was not shy about asking Mother Johanna directly, "Were demonic forces at work?"

Mother Johanna only hissed, "Bad drivers…," and sank an inch or two back inside her metal hovel, her signal to let her return to her rusty grotto.

After an understanding smile and a gestured blessing from Mother Deborah, Mother Johanna gratefully clanged her door shut behind her.

The doctor was quick to say, "She is a living saint. Just a saint. And have you seen the meteorite?" He held a disinterested hand to the space object nestled in the weeds nearby. "Maybe this was what precipitated the calamity."

Mother Deborah gave Dr. Fairfax a knowing look, just short of an unflinching stare. "I see a meteorite," she said and eyeballed roughly the space rock's apparent trajectory. (A WNBA hopeful in her teen years, Mother Deborah had set aside athletic fame to study astrophysics—until Someone Else interrupted those plans. Still, she knew her classical mechanics, Newtonian, Lagrangian, *and* Hamiltonian.) Giving a sigh, she said, "I bet the insurance company will buy that, especially with 'a meterorite' right there."

"It is a real meteorite."

"No doubt. Maybe we can leave it there for a while, for the homeschoolers to see?"

"I am sure. So, with that out of the way, Mother…"

"Yes?"

"Could I make use of the flatbed this morning? Robert can come with Zoe and get the keys."

⁂

Later that morning, a tired Bobby Lumbar and a weary Zoe did stroll to the convent and fetch the flatbed; and while coincidence is not always causation, the visible change in his mood after this errand did give Phineas Fairfax a chance to theorize that Something Might Have Happened Between Them.

Both while they had been loading the by-now drying-out pieces of the Bag Ladies onto the flatbed military tarps behind plywood side walls and while the doctor had been giving him the directions to Cullaby Junction Road, Bobby Lumbar's answers had been monosyllabic. On the winding, dusty drive to the drop-off, Bobby's eyes were fixed on the driving task, and his hands were almost embedded into the steering wheel. For his part, Dr. Fairfax enjoyed the excursion from the cracked leather passenger seat and avoided generating any conversation.

Driving them away from the discount landfill in the woods, Bobby continued his impersonation of a deaf-mute, but Phineas Fairfax now knew that some fruitful conversation was in order. After the flatbed was finally moving up a relatively level stretch without ruts or potholes, the doctor said, "It was a necessary evil. It's what the men of the tribe have to do. Like policework, or war, or hanging a man at dawn. And if we can, turn left there."

Bobby grunted and turned the flatbed with a fine swoop through a crossroads.

The doctor's flip phone beeped with a notification, and he looked at the screen. After a moment, he said slowly as he typed out, "Santiago." Replacing his phone, he nodded toward a neighboring field, where a brazen-horned and bewhiskered herd held sway as lairds of the meadowland. "Highland cattle," he said.

"Moo," said Bobby.

The doctor moved to lance the boil. "And how was your walk with Zoe this morning?"

Bobby's next grunt sounded like a sinking battleship swallowed in its own wake.

"With the BBs to keep her busy, you're not as exciting as you were," said Phineas Fairfax. The depths that had swallowed the battleship roiled for a moment, then were cold and flat once more. "Let's go right where those llamas are," said the doctor, and to avoid thinking and speaking, Bobby steered as he was told.

"Do forgive me, but I'm just glad that her energy's turned to little living humanoids instead of small dead birds."

"How about big living humanoids?" asked Bobby, delivering his longest sentence of the afternoon.

"It's a bitter pill right now, but the thrill for her will pass. I doubt she's going anywhere. And you yourself have work to do."

"What do you mean?" asked Bobby.

"I mean, every man needs a few adventures under his belt. Ah, and so, they begin. What do we see here?"

Slowing the flatbed, Bobby saw, immobile and forlorn among a disinterested home-freezer herd of grazing Angus beef cattle, a military-grade helicopter and a pair of familiar young men in regulation MAXIFAX flight uniforms running through the green field straight toward them and waving vigorously.

✳✳✳

Back at Orphis, the community room looked like it had been commandeered by a baby-shower marketing firm. In the midst of any number of BBs bouncing about in cardboard boxes and dog crates, Zoe was chatting it up with Greta, sudden mass motherhood being the hot topic as they stirred pots of dextrose mixture and secured their jerry-rigged cribs and holding pens. Again and again, though, Zoe, like a coloratura singer on a bel canto binge, unfurled her plans for Bobby Lumbar in his unsuspected role as lifelong protector and provider.[11]

---

11 Translator's note: To save paper, this tête-à-tête has been redacted by removing several thousand variations on "like," "totally," "whatever," "Oh, I know," and "I'm sure," as well as those nuggets of therapeutic pyrite such as "manifesting," "healing journey," "centering phase," "mindset," "abundance," "No one's gonna be there as much for you as yourself," and the perennial "Be sure to invest in your own self-care."

So, with all of their honeybee buzz, Zoe and Greta barely noticed Mother Deborah walk into the room, accompanied by a pair of young postulants carrying as many spray bottles as the Strange Sisters could spare. (These two young ladies were a couple of backbenchers on the convent roster, and Mother Deborah thought that by exposing them to child-rearing, she could pull off a Maria von Trapp on them.)

At the sight of so many BBs jumping for joy all over the floor like so many wind-up Easter eggs, these nameless maidens gasped and recoiled, holding the boxes of bottles in front of them for protection. Mother Deborah guessed that this would happen, but nudged them into the fray, then told Greta, "Can you show the girls where you need the supplies put?" Understanding that this was not a request, Greta left with both the two postulants and a BB in each arm. (In all fairness to the anonymous young ladies, Mother Deborah had only learned about this new life-form a few days before but knew that she had to play the part of the steely-eyed veteran.)

Mother Deborah sat herself on the arm of an L-shaped couch stained with years of dog slobber—Sangreal and Siege Perelous themselves lay snoozing in a corner, having scarcely cracked an eye at her arrival—and immediately Zoe, toting two BBs in her arms and without introductions, set to delivering salvo after salvo of romantic, excited prattling about motherhood-by-proxy and How Things Would Be with Bobby.

Mother Deborah only raised a hand. "Sweetheart, I need to find the cheapest flights to Santiago, so this needs to be fast." Zoe looked at her, expecting a lead on discount bridesmaids' dresses, but the abbess said, "Just forget about that young man." (She did not get into a management position without the ability to be blunt.)

At this rank heresy, Zoe almost dropped her BBs. "But—"

"No, sweetheart. You've known him for two days."

"I think it's been three."

"Maybe. But this isn't love—"

"But you don't even know him."

"Neither do you."

Not realizing that her attack had been deflected by logic, Zoe tried another tack. "But what do you know about love? You...you don't..."

Those in management positions also must have the ability to keep skeletons firmly entombed in their closets. Mother Deborah deflected the accusation. "Love is sacrifice, sweetheart, not—"

"So? He can sacrifice all he wants for me."

"I know you're bubbling over, sweetheart..."

"Yeah, 'cause I'm the prize."

"...but if you try to force him to do anything, or to love you, or to marry you, or to be your prince consort—"

"Prince Charming," said Zoe.

"—or what have you, he may agree, but in time he will hold it against you. He has to choose you. A man's a funny animal. You take away his toy, and he'll spend the rest of his days trying to find it again. I think before you become anyone's wife, you need to be a mother for a while."

With a blush that almost matched her hair, a mortified Zoe plunked her BBs into an empty dog-food shipping box and started for the door, but Mother Deborah simply grabbed her by a belt loop, pulled her back to the drool-stained couch, and handed her a fresh BB. Then, with the straight-on delivery of a pikeman at the Siege of Vienna, she asked, "Do you know what you should do in your life?"

Zoe nervously bounced the humanoid, then tried for the "right answer." "Well, my passion is—"

"No," said Mother Deborah. "Your *vocation*. Your calling."

"Is it Bobby?" Mother Deborah shook her head, and with tears bursting through, Zoe gulped. "But what about me, what I want?"

"What about you?" This was a new question, and Zoe's face took on the look of an Irish setter asked to do long division. In this limbo, Mother Deborah reminded her, "It's never about any of us alone, dear, because we're not alone in this world. There's me. There're the mothers. There're your new babies."

"BBs," said Zoe quietly.

"Very well, BBs," said Mother Deborah. "And there's Dr. Fairfax."

"But Dr. Fairfax scares me."

"Dr. Fairfax scares everyone."

"Except you," said Zoe, wanting at least one of her touchstones to still be solid.

"If you say so. He just keeps me on my toes. But, you know, I bet you he's scaring someone right now."

∗∗∗

With the breeze of May blowing his lab coat behind him like the wings of a mighty white eagle, Phineas Fairfax exited the flatbed and strode toward the pair of pilots. Bobby debated renewing his acquaintanceship with Felipe and Darshan, but for some reason, decided to risk it—if only to have a chance to bop Felipe in the eye—and catching up with the doctor, he stood at his side.

Phineas Fairfax had taken a dated clip-on MAXIFAX photo ID from his bottomless coat pocket and clipped it to his breast pocket just as Felipe and Darshan reached the fence. He told them directly, "I'm Dr. Fairfax, from Level VII. We understand that there was an incident." Felipe and Darshan stood dumbfounded, and the doctor went on. "We know. We always know. But"—his tone mellowed—"these things do occur. So, what's the situation right now?"

Before either of them could confess what the doctor already surmised (they had simply run out of fuel and had landed in the most convenient open space available), Darshan pointed at Bobby. "It's you. You were—"

"Yeah, it's me," said Bobby, getting into the swing of things, drawing his shoulders back, and taking off his broken glasses to show his glossy shiner and assorted other wounds in the midday sun.

Felipe said, "Bro, look at you."

"When you survive a fall," said Bobby, technically telling the truth, "this is what you get."

"Ah," said Phineas Fairfax. "So, that was you. I see a report going to Level V."

"It was him," said Darshan, happily chucking Felipe to the wolves.

"I don't care," said the doctor. "That was Master's Candidate Lumbar you decided to pummel. Didn't his lab coat signify anything to you?"

Felipe gulped. "It was dirty."

"I still don't care. On any mission for MAXIFAX, you work as a unit. Success for one is success for all, and the wrongdoing of one is the wrongdoing of all. At the same time, though, we do recognize that you demonstrated a willingness to use physical methods, which can be useful, so we will overlook this insubordination. This time."

Before Bobby could say that he was not willing to overlook anything, Darshan nervously asked, "What're you gonna tell Big Blond?"

"Nothing, right now. So, the chopper's out of fuel."

Felipe and Darshan's journey through the emotions had gone from hope to dread to wonderment.

"Does it need JP-8 or straight diesel?"

"Straight diesel," said Felipe.

Bobby slipped his glasses back on and joined in the fun. "Everybody uses diesel out here. We'll just get a requisition."

"Remember, Lumbar—and all of you—that Karl Marx and Friedrich Nietzsche had a baby and its name is MAXIFAX. MAXIFAX doesn't *ask* for anything. It takes. We understand there is a community of nuns near here with a big fruit operation. We'll make them remember what that vow of poverty's all about. As for you two, get in the back of this rig and we'll drop you at one of our satellite camps until it is time to return here."

"What is it?" asked Darshan of the flatbed.

"No wonder you guys ran out of fuel," said Bobby. (He was enjoying this and was willing to forgo bopping Felipe in his kisser.) "It's a truck. We used it for a little errand while you guys were making your friendship bracelets."

"Errand?" asked Felipe.

"You're just full of questions," said the doctor. "We were just taking out the trash. Would you care to see what MAXIFAX does to those who have served their purpose?"

Felipe mumbled, "I don't think we're done serving our purpose?"

"Say it like you mean it, son," said Phineas Fairfax.

Darshan shouted like a new recruit, "We're not done serving our purpose, SIR!"

"That is correct, pilot. You haven't, because after we get that diesel, you're going to fly us back to MAXIFAX, no questions asked."

FLY AWAY HOME, OR BIRDS OF A FEATHER

By January, things had quieted down at the Strange Sisters Fruit Farm.

Autumn was over, and there were no more hybrid-driving suburbanites and electric-car condo-dwellers braving the mist, the golden leaves, and the overhead honking of migrating geese to gather up the pears and persimmons for their cobblers, ciders, and stevia-sprinkled fruit rings (always a nutritious and earth-friendly after-school snack). Along with the strings of blinking bulbs from their annual Oh, Noel! Lightfest, the sales tents had been folded up and stored in the pole barn, the unsold heirlooms wasp traps were hung up to hibernate until next year, and the extra apples and pears dried for fruit rings had been pureed for applesauce or brined in spirits and syrup for liqueur. The orchards had been pruned, the ground was muddy, the air was wet and cool, and the sky was gray. On such a day, Mother Deborah, warmed by her Strange Sisters fleece jacket, took a well-deserved break, firing up the flatbed and tooling alone down Beaumont Road into Merryweather to the post office to loot the convent's PO box.

Having secured the government-issue white plastic tub of bundled correspondence safely in the passenger seat, Mother Deborah drove to her secret sunny spot just past the recycling place and, sipping an iced caramel latte (she needed something to repent of), went through the bundles to the music of the passing semitrucks.

Most of that week's haul was solicitations for any number of worthy causes; then the utility bills (to be paid in the smallest possible increments, since the mothers made their own candles, occasionally hauled water from the creek, and passed the hours in psalmody rather than watching cat videos on the internet, so they should get a letter of commendation instead of this hat-in-hand routine); then letters from the nuns' family members (which Mother Deborah steamed open to peruse, since her girls had left the world behind and she had to answer for their souls before the Almighty); then letters to Mother Johanna pleading for spiritual counsel and insight; one letter for Zoe; and lastly, a whopping two letters for herself.

The first missive to her bore a line of foreign stamps sloppily glued on, with a postmark reading, around the top, "SANTI" followed by some illegible letters and, around the bottom, CHILE. Slitting it open with her utility knife, she drew out three pages stapled together.

The first was a mock-up of a brochure in Spanish, not unlike that for Orphis, for La Mission de Beata Gertrude la Premonstratenseña de Aldenberg. Its cover showed three confused-looking ladies in street clothes and sunglasses, their heads shrouded in habits, and native-weave bags full of vegetables at their sensibly shod feet. Immediately behind them stood a dingy if dolled-up storefront currently suggesting a chapel, day care, or small-engine repair shop. (If her dreams came true, Mother Deborah hoped to see said dingy storefront blossom into a towering Spanish Baroque alcazar, bubbling within with countless plaster cherubs, seething august frescoes, all of the gold of the Incas, and several prominently placed gold-and-crystal reliquaries containing the incorrupt bodies of a few of her best girls.) The caption under the three women read *"Nuestras primeras postulantes Babulia, Belladonna, y Martina."* On the opposite side of this mock-up, in breviary-black ink, was scrawled, *Best I could do. Now let me go train some guerrilla fighters. Belladonna.*

Mother Deborah chuckled and flipped to the stapled second page.

This was from Mother Babulia and read *Mission Accomplished* above a roll call of South American fruits: the maqui berry, the uñi, the egg fruit, the uvilla, and the calafate berry, all the usual suspects. These were all possible candidates for planting at Strange Sisters. Mother Babulia's notes beside each read like a reworking of the Seven Dwarfs: *mealy, squishy, thorny, bruisy, pithy,* and so forth, along with, *One lady's opinion: Just tack a Spanish name on anything and they'll think it's exotic.* Mother Deborah appreciated the leads—anything to keep the hipsters oohing and aahing and the integrated pest management/silvoculture/pollinator zealots mollified. (Mother Deborah knew perfectly well that the Strange Sisters' back-to-the-land lifestyle was sympatico with these earth worshippers; but any misguided camaraderie with the ugly chicks who ran the co-op and there would be a shrine to Gaia set up in the gift shop in no time.)

She read on. *Have tracked down some old lineages of heirloom tobacco. Just had to sample them. Remember, you did say that would sell.* The abbess sighed at the possibility, but again, this was not the freewheeling Middle Ages, when any old convent could brew beer and breed racing dogs and no one would blink an eye.

The last note was written in the bubbly script popular with girls who have just graduated from ponies to horses.

Thank you for saving our lives. How long do we have to stay here? I talked the police here into letting me drive, so we can head north to the border, which I guess is wide open. Give Hugo a HUGE-OH hug for me! ♡ ♡ ♡ ♡ ♡ ♡ ♡ and a line of hearts.

"Ah, girls." Mother Deborah sighed, returning the papers to their envelope. "I hope the food there tastes good."

The second envelope to her was bursting at the corners and taped along the seam and bore no return address but was postmarked from a town along an interstate in Iowa. This cocoon might have been sent from the Hawkeye State, but Mother Deborah guessed that the pupae within had been sent to the sender, with orders to be mailed off to her anonymously.

Now putting her knife's serrated blade to good use, she sawed through the tape, exposing the contents to fresh air. In separate, unaddressed, and unpostmarked envelopes, a letter to a lawyer, one to the title company, one to Zoe, and one to herself.

She gave a glance to her chatelaine watch. The fun was over, and it was time to head home. Once back at the convent, sometime that evening, by the flickering light of the security footage screens and with a steaming cup of apple mint and lemon balm tea to keep her company, she would pass the evening reading the one letter; but the other should go to its intended addressee.

✳✳✳

When Mother Deborah took Belmont Road Lane for the back end of the convent property, she veered to the right at the hand-painted sign that read **NONE WILL EMERGE UNCHANGED** and took the road less traveled through half a mile of paranormally gloomy, gaunt, and leafless trees, all gray and brown in the early winter, until she rolled the flatbed around a curve and stopped before what had been Orphis. Quite a change had come over the old place.

Those who had survived their time there no doubt recalled the complex of Orphis as a collection of low, discreet, and cojoined practical architectural boxes, which in the old days of studio TV could have filled the bill as a military installation, drilling operation headquarters, or clandestine government research facility. Now, it had been invaded, overtaken, and colonized by the home-and-garden outlet on Beaumont Boulevard. Most of the earth, dirt, space, or what have you around the buildings had been commandeered for gardening and was now thickly mulched with layers of maple and hazel leaves, like patchwork quilts for those chilly winter nights, and awaiting spring planting. Some was already built over with raised beds in the shapes of squares, hexagons, pentagons, parallelograms, and an isosceles triangle, where grew shivering winter crops of kale, mustard, beet tops, spinach, and green onions. Filling the upright plane loomed a menagerie of scrap metal farm beasts, a rooster, a family of pigs, and a Stegosaurus, then an aluminum windmill and kinetic yard art that jangled, twirled, and bobbed with the brush of a briefest breeze. Finally, the bird feeders, one hanging before a brand-new replacement window, were doing a whopping business.

Pulling the parking brake, Mother Deborah stepped down and headed up a zigzagging walkway of concrete pavers for what was the new front door. While Phineas Fairfax, with his in-house labyrinths, narrow and windowless hallways, and manifold portals, had been one for mystery, discretion, and premeditated obfuscation, the current management had crowned one door as queen, and over it hung a wood-framed sign, hand-painted with flowers and set with fanciful tile. It read:

LITTLE LOVELY LADYLAND

Mother Deborah gave a knock, and when the door opened, she saw that it was living up to its name.

Whatever the room had been in Dr. Fairfax's day, now it might as well have been one of those undersea chambers in the palace of a Greek god of the sea, one of those fishtailed denizens with three thousand giggling nymph daughters that embodied breaking waves, foam on the sand, cuttlefish, tide pools, whirlpools, seaweed, eddying currents, and recipes for clam chowder. Painted in blues and greens and decorated with lines of glitter-and-elbow-macaroni art projects, it was teeming with uncountable BBs, who, after that last six months, had grown into screaming, giggling grade-school-sized girls, all hurrying back and forth in busy streams. Whichever one had opened the door had darted off, but in no time, another was gleefully shrieking, "Mama Deborah! Mama Deborah!" As one, they swirled about her, their arms reaching up like the tenacles of sea anemones, while one yelled to someone to get Mama Zoe *now!*

While waiting for Mama Zoe, Mother Deborah chatted with a few of the more eager girls (the rest had ebbed off to terrorize other parts of the complex) while giving an approving glance at the crucifix on one wall and an icon on another. Before Phineas Fairfax had disappeared to pursue his unspecified mission of mercy, he laid down a few conditions for Orphis Nova (his own private name for the place, which, the reader should note, did not stick). It would be a seedbed for a better, more righteous future: Not only were images of the sacred hang (just out of reach) in every room, but in a move rivaling anything that St. Vladimir pulled off, he also ordered the mass baptism of all of the BBs—once "discernible human features" had replaced their buds and indentations, of course. Mother Deborah had considered cleaning out the silage sprayer and filling it with holy water, but thought the better of it. Instead, in a shindig that just might have done penance for the Battle of Orphis, on a brilliantly sunny day with a sky like polished turquoise and its cirrus clouds like spun sugar about to ignite, in the chapel of Blessed Charles of Austria and the Servant of God Zita, with the nuns of Strange Sisters acting as godmothers and each holding her new goddaughter, Father Maximillian poured the saving waters in quicksilver rivulets over each blob-like head, and the bronze bells in the chapel's last upright belltower clanged forth.

In no time Zoe appeared, wearing her own Strange Sisters fleece, with a hefty Strange Sisters shoulder bag (laden with homemade snack bars) weighing her down to one side. She almost looked like she had just given birth to three thousand mermaids. The overly anxious naive waif who not so long ago had overseen the last rites for the American robin and the common rock pigeon, after an endless round of diapers, pacifiers, fights over dolls, mob screaming (little girls in groups can do horrible things), and the infamous November Sniffles Pandemic, was now the monosyllabic house mother, her small, formerly sweet mouth deflated into a thin pinkish line from continual yelling, her bonfire hair bound up in a rag scarf like a cork on a caldera, and her eyes peering and scanning for infractions and nonsense.

Careful not to call her "sweetheart" or "young lady" in front of her charges, Mother Deborah gave the mistress of Ladyland the letter addressed to her. "Personal delivery," she said.

Zoe sighed as much as she dared, then slipped it into her jacket pocket.

"If you want to mail him back," said Mother Deborah, surmising the identity of the sender, "send it over with one of the girls."

But Zoe was yelling, "Febronia!" at one of the girls who was transgressing some rule of civilized society. (Faced with so many unnamed BBs, Phineas Fairfax had just gone through the calendar of saints and, if the names sounded reasonably feminine, handed them out like bowls of soup to the needy, as each little BB was brought to the font; this accounts for the high prevalence of Glycerias, Pelagias, Mauras, Malinas, Macrinas, Julittas, and Agrippinas. He did, though, wisely pass over saddling one little BB with the name Third-Finding-of-the-Head-of-John-the-Baptist.)

The latest swell of chaos reminded Mother Deborah that, in a tightly contested debate as to the new name for the place, "Little Lovely Ladyland" almost lost out to "Daughters of Babylon Girls' Reformatory." From what she was seeing, Mother Deborah was willing to bet a few cans of soup that a new sign might get hung up any day now.

Zoe was yelling out over the tempest, "Come on. Time to go see Mama Johanna and then—"

"But it's raining," wailed the girls as one.

"No, it's not," Zoe told them, playing the weather bunny. "It's *sprinkling*, and you're not made of sugar, so you won't melt. Unless you want to help Mama Greta stir the meringue by hand and then your arm'll fall off."

Mother Deborah could only smile inside that this degree of managerial and mob-control instinct, undiluted by notions like "compassion," "empathy," or "personal growth," still thrived in these decadent days. The future was in good hands.

✳✳✳

That night, apple mint and lemon balm tea was the soothing beverage of choice, both at Little Lovely Ladyland and at the convent. Once the girls had been put to bed—whether former BBs on the fast track to adulthood or young ladies consecrated to the Almighty—both Zoe Feldspar and Mother Deborah had a steaming cup on hand as they read the mail.

Having discovered early on that sweaters cut down on the heating bill, Zoe was bundled in two layers to keep warm while comfily sprawled over a chaise longue in the doctor's old quarters. With the letter from Bobby in hand, in a homespun romantic ritual, she drew the envelope under her nose as if it were the craft of Lady Elaine drifting by Camelot and smelled for that men's cologne that reminded her of her father.

Then, using her pinkie finger—she had never heard of a letter opener and could not write out a check either—she opened the envelope.

The letter was short, and his grammar was bad.

Zoe, Dr. Fairfax said write something fast because were going on another mission somewhere probly without postal service. Maybe he means no internet. I get in a little bird watching. I keep an eye out for B. lumbarensis whenever I can. But no bird is as beautiful as you.

(There followed some intimate points that the reader need not know about, unless she wants to hand over her own love letters over for public consumption.)

At the bottom of the page, he wrote, Do you like the picture?

It took a second look in the envelope, but Zoe found the photo in question, the first she had seen of him since he had left that night in late May with Dr. Fairfax. It showed Bobby, but he had undergone a change. He was sporting a bandage about the head, his scraggly blond beard hung from his jaw like seams of gold from a cliffside, and his eyes (behind his latest pair of glasses) seemed to be contemplating mountain heights yet to be conquered. His previously unimpressive torso had thickened noticeably, and with the sleeves of his lab coat rolled up, Evan-like veins showed on his forearms and hands, signifying hard and vigorous use. All in all, a young chieftain striding into the uplands of maturity.

A knock sounded and Zoe said, "Come in."

Out of the shades of the far end of the room appeared one of the little lovely ladies, in a long pale pink flannel night dress, a modest number, but playfully printed with teddy bears in pastel blue, green, and yellow. She came up to the chaise longue.

"Yes, Pasha?" (The girl's full name was Parasceva, a mouthful for anyone.)

"Mama Zoe," she said, "Thecla's hogging all the blankets."

"Well, tell Thecla that someone will need to help Mama Greta cut carrots tomorrow."

"Justice has spoken?" asked Pasha.

"Justice has spoken."

"Can you tell her?"

"I guess I'll have to," said Zoe. She stood with a sigh, only have the picture drop to the floor.

Pasha retrieved it and, still learning to mind her own business, gave it a look.

She asked, "Is that a boy?"

"No," said Zoe, seeing that isolation in the country and accelerated growth was depriving her girls of a few bits of essential knowledge. But they could cross that bridge in a week or two. For now, she simply took back the picture and slid it back in the envelope. "No," she said, "that's not a boy. That's a man. And he's mine. Now let's get you back to bed."

✳✳✳

In the office of the convent, Mother Deborah sat at her desk, and with the multi-feed screens of the security cameras blinking and blipping nearby and that herbal tea within reach, she caught up on her mail.

The fat, tape-bound envelope lived up to its girth, mostly because of legal documents on their latest junket to Phineas's lawyer (a close personal friend of his old German gymnastics trainer). But within them, almost like a stowaway, she found a letter from Phineas Fairfax himself.

It ran:

Prophetess, if I ever come back, I will plant you a palm tree, for all you're doing for me.

Keep me posted on the latest wave of sea change coming over Orphis. Is my little bit of Malaya still there at all? I am picturing it a vale of smoking stumps, as if the Japanese Army had just marched through. BBs have a poor aesthetic sense, but that is why they were created — <u>why I created them</u> — in the first place. Make the world plastic, make the world ugly, make the world safe and the same, shop and obey and live in your box, ad infinitum, ad nauseum. Maybe they'd benefit from a short musical evening every now and then? An evening of motets?

How are Sangreal and S. Perelous? They're good boys, a bit august, but solid as a rock. Let me know if there're any bills from the vet + I'll transfer some money. When you can lay down the twin crosses of leadership and farmsteading for a minute, could you please visit Goth and Magothy in the garden? and at least make sure that the stone is wiped clean? I don't want the <u>lares et penates</u> to rise in anger and curse the <u>domus</u>.

I don't know about the youngsters. Robert says not a word about her except at letter time and I make no inquiries, discomfiting, polite, or artificially sympathetic. He's a better man after all we've done together and I can only hope that he'll surpass me, which truth be told is not much of a feat. I promise to bring him back someday in one piece, then they can do the rest of their growing up together. But don't say anything to Zoe. She doesn't need to daydream more than is necessary.

Thank you, thank you, thank you, Prophetess.

Yours,

Ph. F., PhD

Postscript: Has there been any sign of Sheena Lypotrope? If you hear or learn anything, let me know. At all costs, I cannot have her reappearing and sullying your holy place. In that light, I can only frame this self-exile of mine as my bribe to the Almighty, to keep all of you safe. (I am no better than the Evil Smiths, I suppose.) You mothers don't try to make a perfect world, because you don't have to. You live as if you're already in paradise. Still, I can only wonder where Sheena is, and since MAXIFAX has long, long tentacles, I'll stay away for now. But let me be the bait. Let the lioness come find me instead.

I sail on, on to Outremer.

A knock brought this literary evening to an end.

"Come in," said Mother Deborah in her best midrange managerial tone as she slipped the letter back into its envelope.

Mother Margaret-of-Cortona stood framed in the door like an aquarelle print from a thrift store. "The sheriff's here," she said. "He's caught someone tangled in the fence around the orchard by Smithville Road."

Glad that she had read the letter when she did, since it looked like a long night ahead, Mother Deborah took her Strange Sisters fleece from its cow-head by the door and, with the other nun, slipped outside into the nocturnal January gloom.

* * *

Mothers Deborah and Margaret-of-Cortona came billowing up to the Merryweather sheriff's patrol car idling near the chapel. Considering the fright showing on the face of the young man hunched over in the back seat, they might they as well have been a pair of phantoms. He gulped and gasped, taking them in with a wild confusion, as if trying to make his eyes bigger and to shut them at the same time. But after a moment, he settled down and looked away, his face and untrimmed curling hair and beard glistening with sweat under the back cab's glaring ceiling light, before staring forward and anxiously jigging one leg up and down.

Mother Deborah nodded at Mother Margaret-of-Cortona, and she sank back into the night. The abbess and the sheriff were alone with the suspect.

"So, Bob," she asked, "what do we have here?"

The alleged trespasser only blurted out, "No, no, please, no!" and looked ready to make a run for it when Sheriff Bob closed the patrol car door on him and left him with just a grilled window between him and the night.

The sheriff said, "I guess he jumped the fence into the orchard 'long Smithville Road and was messing around, then tried to get out and got stuck in the barbed wire. I was just driving up to Cullaby when I saw him. You want me to just bring him in?"

"Anywhere but out there," gibbered the frantic young man through the grille.

Sheriff Bob leaned into the window. "And what's out there?"

The young man turned to the grille, and eyes showed so strongly that the rest of his face seemed to disappear. "I heard them," he whispered.

The ability to say nothing, like an industrial clamp for the mouth, is another implement in the toolkit of an effective manager, and on hearing this, not a word now escaped Mother Deborah's lips.

But Sheriff Bob asked, "And who's 'them'?"

The young man turned from the metal slats as if the truth were in some other direction. "Maybe I didn't hear anything."

Sheriff Bob looked to Mother Deborah. 'This could go on a while," he said, then told the suspect, "Start talking so this lady can go to bed."

Mother Deborah offered, "I'll tell you what. Warm and dry's always better than cold and wet. Let's go into the trapeza."

"What's that?" said the young man.

"The mess hall. This way." Sheriff Bob walked him to the convent.

✳✳✳

Mother Deborah let her guests into the trapeza, brought up the lights with a heavy clunk of the wall switch, and gathered them at the end of a lengthy wooden table.

"What's your name?" Mother Deborah asked the shaggy young man, who had only marginally calmed down.

"Elijah."

"Good name," she said and glanced to Sheriff Bob to assume the role of bad cop.

"So, what's going on?" he said.

"I have this podcast," said Elijah.

"Which one's that?" asked the sheriff.

"Can I have a water?"

"Yes, you can have a water," said Mother Deborah. "Don't squeeze him too hard, Bob," and she fetched a coffee cup of nature's best from the nearby kitchen.

Elijah took a cautious drink. *"Backwoods."*

"Backwoods?" said Sheriff Bob.

"Backwoods: Terror in the Trees. True horror. I'd heard about what's been going on here and I wanted to see."

"See what?"

Elijah said, "The Moo Run."

Sheriff Bob looked at Mother Deborah about what was going on, but she looked as though she already knew.

In the months since Dr. Phineas Fairfax had slipped off with Bobby Lumbar, the Strange Sisters had not been lazy. Like their medieval foremothers, they had carried on redeeming the land, putting in its place Bobby's old nemesis, the abandoned orchard with its wild, suckering, and twisted trees. But as the mothers were going from tree to tree, doing their clip-clip-here, clip-clip-there, they had come upon a strange sight: a bizarre track of bleak soil streaked in stains, like ragged strips torn from a lab coat, a track that ran off toward the fence line that bordered Smithville Road.

But despite all of their toil and patience, the mothers had not been able to coach any living thing, no sapling or even a patch of pennyroyal, from this pale-stained toxic tilth. Even the odd thistle or weed that sprang up drooped and shriveled. They found, too, that no animal would cross this track and the earth along both of its edges was spotted with the nervous paw marks of raccoons, skunks, possum, and deer that picked along the path to risk death on Smithville Road instead. Weirder still, rocks dug up during the planting of a new tree nearby and placed on the path just to sit out of the way were found the next morning to have rolled away in the night, and some were found set in the trees. After this, one mother, more curious than wise, snuck into the orchard at night and went to the track; under the light of both the moon and the Milky Way in bright concert, she saw on the poisonous path itself not only a desperate pattern of human tracks, made by stylish but sensible shoes, but also all around them a mob of cloven prints like the stamping feet of spectral cattle. So, the mothers began to call this infernal nature trail the Moo Run.

Mother Deborah did not know that the word had gotten out.

But even as she began imagining herself giving tours to the Merryweather Folk Society, busloads of not-easily-frightened homeschoolers, and the wide-eyed girls from St. Anastasia's, Elijah began to tell his story.

"I jumped the fence from Smithville Road, right where the track starts—or ends, I don't know. I just wanted to get some thermal imaging shots, you know, to say I was there? So, I fired up my goggles and was filming around. I didn't see anything, just the trees and, um"—he dosed himself with some more water—"an owl, I guess, flew overhead. But then, I didn't see anything, I swear *I didn't film anything.* Hey, where's my camera? Where's my goggles?"

Sheriff Bob leaned into him. "In the car," he said. Elijah calmed down.

Now Mother Deborah said, "You didn't see anything."

Elijah shook his head a few more times than he needed to. "No, but out of the corners, the corners of the trees around me, I heard these voices..."

"Voices," said Sheriff Bob, his own very flat.

Elijah nodded. "Voices of, like, women."

"This is a convent, son, maybe..."

Mother Deborah said, "I doubt it. I did a room check before I went to my office. Besides"—she pulled out a mighty ring of keys and jangled it—"nobody's getting a raincoat and flashlight without me knowing it."

"That's a good system," said Sheriff Bob. "So, Elijah, what were these voices?"

Elijah glared at him, like the zealot of a new religion facing a heretic. "You don't believe me."

"You heard something," said Mother Deborah. "Go on."

"It was like a lot of women, angry women, like women at...at a riot. There weren't any words, but, you know, you knew it was voices. Then they changed. They weren't voices anymore, but like animals, like a river of animals, like hungry cows, like moaning, hungry cows."

Sheriff Bob looked to the abbess, and she shrugged. "No cattle 'round here," she said. "Did you see anything with your goggles?"

"Tracks. Human tracks, cow tracks. They shouldn't be giving off heat, but they were." Elijah suddenly demanded, "Let me go, let me go," then he begged, "Please. Anywhere but here."

"Talk," said the sheriff.

"Just get it out," said Mother Deborah.

"Then came the scream," said Elijah. "Like a scream. A woman screaming. But it wasn't a scream. It was like an echo. It was coming from somewhere else. But it was coming again and again, like a radio signal, a distress signal, just over and over. And the cow sounds didn't stop, so it was like this wave and that wave, and they were smashing into each other right on the path where I was standing, and I couldn't move. It was like a flood coming in from both directions, but it was worse, 'cause whoever was screaming, you could tell, was just trying to escape, 'cause the cows were trying to catch her and...and get her, and..."

Elijah put his hands on his face, then put them down. "Then the screams went away. It was quieter, and I thought I was a little safer. I mean, I could still hear the cow sounds, and I started to run, but that's when they changed again. I said they were like women's voices, you know, angry, angry women?" Elijah looked into a dark corner of the dining hall, then up at the sheriff. "But I don't think any more now that they were angry. They were hungry. 'Cause when they changed, to human voices, to real women's voices, their sounds made words..." He sniffled and wiped his wet eyes, then with hammer blows of his voice, he said, "And I won't ever, ever forget what they were saying."

Mother Deborah stepped up to him and, with two fingers, lifted his bearded face up to her. "What were they saying, Elijah?"

And in low and trembling voice, he said, "Spare parts...Spare parts..."

The End

APPENDIX

MERRYWEATHERANA, OR
A PATCHWORK OF ANCIENT HISTORY

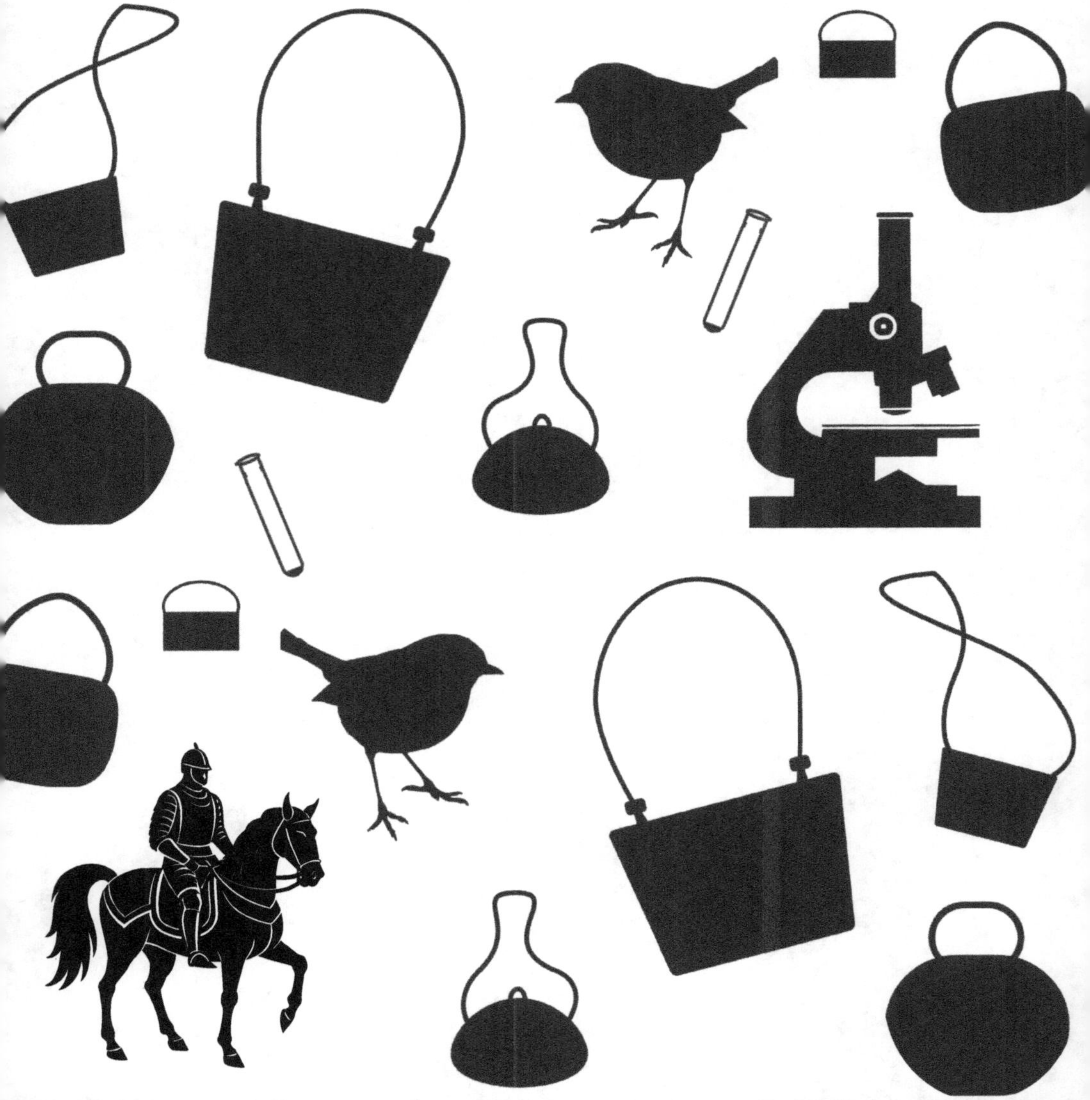

Our little piece of paradise was originally the spacious land claim of Eleazar Meriwether, one of those small-eyed fellows with the huge beard, floppy felt hat, and a resistance to malaria, who sprang out of the ground in days gone by, a star-spangled daguerreotype who took advantage of the absence of any lawful authority to make himself the chieftain-in-chief of all that he surveyed.

In the next generation, one of his semi-legitimate children managed to lure the railroad to send the choo-choo through town. (The moldy records in the Merryweather Historical Society basement suggest that this was either Vercingetorix or Scipio Africanus Merriwether, their mothers being the occasional "wives" of Eleazar, one Rebecca-Evangeline Littlesmall and her competition, Sophia Heddlerod.) But the boom for Merryweather started in real earnest when Vercingetorix Merriwether (or maybe it was Scipio Africanus) looked the other way as the Freemasonic hazelnut and prune planters muscled out the good, strong Methodist farming folk while giving a giddy-up to the local political machine (which has been in motion ever since).

We do not know what the heir to Eleazar Meriwether thought as he contemplated the dark hills round about and the rows and rows of hazelnut and prune saplings running into the horizon. But we know for certain what ended up in the laps of his children (Priscilla, Hiram, George, Isaac, Henry, Bertha, and Augusta Merrywhether) and his forty-one grandchildren: They ruled over a watercolor lithograph of Populist-Era prosperity and respectability, complete with blocks and blocks of books-in-the-black businesses, an agricultural college, an immense bronze fountain with the symbolic figures of the Prune Harvest and the lovers Corylus and Avellena, ultramodern architecture in the form of Arts and Crafts cottages, bubblers to stave off rampant drunkenness, and a boulevard lined with Queen Anne mansions and elm saplings. (Saplings abounded in those days.)

That Silver Age took on a bit of tarnish, however, when the railroad, that descending aortic artery of any thriving local economy at that time, took a beating from the automobile and the motorway. (The city fathers of Merryweather—specifically, Edgar Edwin Merryweather—told out-of-state investors that Route 4 bordering the old Pringle prune ranch was a "significant highway," but no one quite bought it.) Finally came the 1950s and the interstate that never veered quite close enough to town, and so Merryweather fell into small-town sleepiness, its slumber to be broken only by a kiss that smelled suspiciously like Pinot Grigio.

GLOSSARY

Archaeopteryx: The first bird, the proto-bird, the Orville and Wilbur Wright of the lizard world.

Baxwbakwalanuxwsiwe': And, yes, the apostrophe matters. In the Kwakiutl mythos, a markedly unpleasant entity covered in gaping, blood-stained mouths, inhabiting the farthest north of the sky world, and keeping company with his wife, Copper Woman, and nastily enormous birds, such as Qoaxqoaxualanuxsiwae.

Bibi Besch: If you were alive in the 1980s, then you know Bibi Besch.

Blessed Charles of Austria and the Servant of God Zita: Famed husband-and-wife team noted for ruling the Austro-Hungarian Empire and keeping the right flames alive.

Corylus and Avellena: To the classically educated of Merryweather's Progressive forefathers, the personifications of the hazelnut tree, whence came so much of their lucre. To the Marxist-educated Progressives lurking in modern Merryweather, a very odd statue that they were not sure whether to haul into the river.

"Delenda est Carthago": Cato the Elder's slogan to gin up the venerable senators of Rome to take out Carthage in the Third Punic War.

Delta Burke: If you were alive in the 1980s, you know Delta Burke.

Edmund Campion: Elizabeth Regina thought that he was the best and brightest that sixteenth-century Oxford had to offer, until it came time to draw and quarter him.

"*Facilis descensus Averno*": More Latin. Falling down is easier than getting back up. More or less.

ghost chilis: Known to anglophonophobes as bhut jolokia, this shriveled red crossbreed of *Capsicum chinense* and *Capsicum frutescens* brings chutneys to the edge of incandescence. They also put in an appearance as elephant repellent.

Gondwanaland: About 550 million years ago, an immense island floated innocently around the South Pole. It was covered in giant horsetails, conifers, and ferns and assorted insects, the compacted remains of which now stoke the debate on fossil fuels, quite literally.

Heisenberg's uncertainty principle: Difficult to explain, but that probably says it best.

honeybush: *Melianthus major,* one of Africa's contributions to the Western gardenscape.

hyoid bone: As bones go, a bit of a rebel, sitting under the chin and not attached to any other bone or much else.

juniper hickwall: No, this is not a real species of bird.

Kafka trap: Darned if you do, darned if you don't.

Kuchuma kik': Lord Number Four in Xibalba, the Mayan Hell, where he plays host at meals where human blood is served.

landsknechts: Hop into your time machine and fiddle with the dial until you end up in the sixteenth century. They were everywhere, causing havoc in their lace-and-breastplate ensembles. "Lady landsknechts" might be something like lansquenettes, *oui?*

Linda Evans: If you were alive in the 1980s, then you know Linda Evans. (This game of tormenting the younger readership should stop soon.)

macros: For those not obsessive about their diets, "macronutrients": carbohydrates, proteins, and fats.

Manichaeism: Black and white, flesh and spirit, this or that, either/or.

Megarachne servinei: It was this big, prehistoric spider, see? Twenty-one inches long. Tell your husband to fish that out of the bathtub and see what he says.

"Morituri te salutant": The second half of a longer phrase delivered by gladiators up to the man who paid to watch them kill each other.

Outremer: "Beyond the Sea." It is a very pretty name.

plenary indulgence: A kind of get-out-of-jail-free card, except jail is Hell.

Potala Palace: The Vatican City of the Himalayan plateau.

Precambrian: Occurring before the Cambrian period, a prehistoric period occurring before written history. See *Gondwanaland.*

Qoaxqoaxualanuxsiwae: Not something found at the pet store, this Cannibal Raven clacks it beak in the company of Baxwbakwalanuxwsiwe'.

St. Stephen: He could claim the title of the First Martyr.

Sun Tzu: Know your enemy.

trapeza: In eastern monasticism, the mess hall.

Trapezuntine: Of or relating to Trebizond, nowadays going by the name Trabzon, in the neighborhood of Pontus, Bithynia, and Colchis.

Waschbär: The "wash bear," or raccoon. Those Germans are so clever.

Xibalba: The "bad place" in Mayan mythology. It contains such inviting dwellings as Razor House and rulers named One Death and Seven Death.

zenana: In ancient India, the ladies' quarters.

ABOUT THE AUTHOR

Andrew Shaffer, who gave the artistically discerning, the truly literate, and the reading public in general that treasure, which is *Mad, Mad Marjorie*, lives in Portland, Oregon.